REKINDLING CONNECTIONS

NICKY ABELL-FRANCIS

A Bittersweet Journey of Love,
Lust & Desire

Published in 2014 by FeedARead.com Publishing

A CIP catalogue record for this title is available from the British Library.

Acknowledgments

Thanks to all for being patient in my never ending writing of this novel. A special thank you to Gabrielle of www.labelleauboisdormant.co.uk for my brilliant cover. To Oliver Taylor for allowing use of my first original cover. A great photo shot and inspiration for the storyline. For the fun and ideas from my travels with Jackie, my lifelong mate and husband Ron. To my gorgeous daughter Jade for the many hours I have focused on my laptop instead of being a fun mum. Sincere regards to Suzanne for advising on my dire grammatical errors and to Susan Miller of www.allwordsmatter.co.uk for her professional proof reading and support along the way. To all the many friends who gave me material for some of my characters and storylines, indebted to you all. It has been a fun journey. Your desires can come true. See me on the red carpet some time.

.

.

Chapters

Chapter 1

FINAL MOMENTS OF THE BIG CITY

A muffled groaning sound came from the far end of the hotel suite. Busy street life outside seeped through into the dimly lit interior. Across the queen sized bed lay two figures forming soft undulating mounds beneath the bed sheets. A shrill siren broke the quietness of the bedroom.

'Gee, what did I do last night?' murmured the fragile voice of Zara, the sound causing the body beside her to stir. Leaning back on the feather pillows her brain tried hard to recollect the last twenty four hours. For one awful moment she froze registering that she wasn't alone. Hesitatingly, she glanced sideways at the slumbering form. Deep and heavy breathing could be heard from beneath the covers. Turning, rather cautiously Zara peeked over the top of the white bed linen.

'Oh, my god,' there she was naked and in bed with a complete stranger. No tiny recollection of how they'd met, or what the hell she'd done with him for that matter. What would the girls think of her? It wasn't worth imagining what Bruce would think if he found out. Zara noticed her strewn clothing on the floor nearby. How to retrieve them was going to be some feat in itself without disturbing her unknown visitor.

The bedtime occupant grunted and turned. Stretching out a limb, he slammed a heavy thigh across Zara's body. Gritting her teeth and sucking air through them she now laid pinned to the bed. How was she supposed to move now? First disentanglement without waking the stranger and; second allow herself to get suitably clothed before he came round.

Surveying the room, her head throbbed with the effort. A vague recognition flashed through her brain cells of some heavy alcohol consumption the previous night. Zara detected the faint sound of running water from the en-suite. Her throat was now feeling parched. The joys of a large glass of cold liquid were enticing her to attempt moving pretty quickly.

Looking back over the young male who lay sprawled across her bed, she viewed his athletic body. He lay perfectly still and quiet in the hazy light of the hotel room, chest moving rhythmically, the gentle arch of his back just visible above the covers. He appeared young, mid-twenties maybe. A shadow of morning stubble enhanced his dishevelled appearance. Trying hard to recharge her memory of where they'd met, Zara rubbed her temples gently in the hope this would miraculously help. No, it wasn't there. What in hell had she drunk last night?

Glancing around the dimly lit room Zara noticed discarded items randomly littering the floor, accompanied by two half-drunk bottles of Champagne. Hawaiian garlands decorated the table lamps either side of the bed.

From the bedside table she picked up a tumbler containing what looked like a cocktail. She sniffed gingerly. The strong smell of mixed spirits confirmed her opinion and a nauseating wave came over her. Once it passed, she noticed there were four tumblers, not just two.

Uneasiness crept over her as the possibility she may have got up close and personal with more than one member of the opposite sex flashed in front of her. No, Gina wouldn't have allowed her to stoop that low. She had more decorum than that, even if this was possibly her last major weekend of freedom. She gently tried to manoeuvre her body round and slide free from under the comatose individual. The movement started to arouse the stranger once again as the gentle touch of his hand brushed past her shoulder. Turning back to look, she met the glazed eyes of her finally semi-awake neighbour. Bleary eyed, he ran a hand through his dishevelled hair.

'Urrg, what time is it? That was one great party last night; you girls know how to have a wild time. Thanks for letting me crash. I certainly won't forget you two in a hurry.' Zara flushed and gulped.

'Err!' Slightly stunned and unable to say much, she felt even more anxious. Blinking hard, she tried to obtain a little distance. By shifting furtively towards the edge of the bed, now that his weight was no longer pinning her down.

The cascading sound of water stopped and shortly after, the en-suite door opened. Swivelling round like an electric bolt had hit her, Zara stared at the emerging figure in the half light, unsure of who to expect. It was Crystal!

'Hello gorgeous, glad you're awake.' Zara looked indignantly at her, trying hard to indicate discreetly her concern without letting the dozy Prince Charming next to her notice what she was doing. Raising her eyebrows and gesturing towards him, she mouthed to Crystal silently.

'Who is he?'

Crystal giggled coyly as she sat down on the bed, her towel barely covering her vital statistics.

'This is Christian.'

Zara noticed that Christian suddenly looked rather perkier when he saw Crystal's body perched rather provocatively at his feet.

'We had rather a wild night and all of us ended up back here.'

'All of us! But I was sharing with Gina. You were with Amber and Bella. What happened to them? How many more party goers were there?'

Crystal smiled, 'Just Christian and Lance. Our group couldn't take the pace. You, me and Christian carried on till later, hence the pounding headache you're probably enduring? Lance escorted the others back to their room. Gina must have decided to join them. Not sure what happened to him, but we had a hell of a time back here.'

Zara shot a very worrying look at Crystal. Whispering as quietly as she could she felt the urge to ask the dreaded question?

'Tell me we didn't? Tell me I didn't at least?' Crystal leant forward her towel revealing more than just a cleavage. Distracting the worse for wear bed fellow from listening too closely, she whispered in Zara's ear.

'No honey, you didn't. Christian had the desire in him and tried his best to seduce you, but the poor sweetie had drunk way too much rum punch. Besides you weren't having any of it. He didn't stand a chance.'

Zara fell back against the pillows unsure whether to be relieved or concerned. 'Oh great, thanks Crystal.'

Christian now had sufficiently woken enough and after viewing the delights of Crystal at such a close up range, he now had experienced a shot of adrenaline to allow him to carry on where apparently they'd left off the night before.

'Ladies, what do you say, recuperation is always better with the hair of the dog. Fancy joining me for one more bevy?' He lusted longingly in Crystal's direction. Christian was now recuperating from the punch a tad too quickly for Zara's preference.

'No! You can count me out. Fresh air and a strong shot of New York caffeine is in order now I fear. Don't let me stop you two,' replied Zara sharply. Sliding swiftly from beneath the covers she backed out of harm's way. Grabbing a garment from the floor, she walked as discreetly as she could towards the en-suite door.

'I'll just freshen up and be out of your way.' This parting shot was directed at Christian his face looking a little disappointed at her retreating exit.

In the warm shower Zara managed to awaken her senses as the razor-like spray stimulated her body back to reality. They must have had a hefty night. She decided her best option was to rustle up the rest of her party and enjoy some frivolities in the world of retail therapy. This weekend was for enjoying and she didn't want to waste a moment more. This was her hen party after all. With Gina, Amber and Bella having travelled from the UK to join her and Crystal....well there were expectations to show the girls the delights of LA. Apparently that included too many cocktails and frolicking in hotel rooms with strange men.

Grabbing the hairdryer, she winced at the memory of the night before and attempted to tame her now soaked auburn hair. The machine had more jet stream than a tornado plane even on its lowest setting. Her usual glossy sheen was lacking this morning, probably from the excesses of lack of sleep and alcohol consumption. A slick of lip gloss and bronzer to highlight the faint smattering of freckles that thronged her nose finished the final effect. Well, that would have to do. No time for a beauty overhaul. Deciding to leave Crystal to the delights of her beau, Zara flung on any top and skirt she had to hand. She was pretty certain the privacy would be appreciated. Sharing rooms wasn't ideal if one was spoken for and the other fancy free. Sliding out of the en-suite she noticed Crystal and Christian were clearly preoccupied beneath the covers. Grabbing her bag and jacket, she quietly opened the hotel suite door and exited as silently as possible heading to the hotel foyer. Here she could ask reception if they could rouse the others with a polite call. It was time to find out what the rest of the girls got up to last night.

~ ~ ~

Once the girls had been rounded up they headed off to Madison Avenue. Zara, the British ex-pat was glad of the company of her long-time friends from home Amber, Gina and Bella. They were all experienced on how to tackle a city, especially when the mission was to shop till they dropped. A fixed route had been planned. Zara was unsure if she could keep up the pace though with her excessive partying the night before. Bloomingdales was first on the agenda, huge and completely mind boggling.

'Does anyone need anything? Or are we just browsing? As the departments in this place are well confusing, we could spend all day in here. It's your hen weekend Zara so you call the shots.' said Bella, a chorus of mixed replies clamoured above each other.

Zara decided to take some control, 'Well if we all want different departments we should maybe pair off and meet later, say in an hour at the main doors. What do you think?'

'Yep, good idea,' said Gina, 'Come on then, let's get going.' She impatiently fiddled with her handbag, eyeing her exit and the stairs to the next level.

Amber heading directly to the accessory department accompanied by Bella, where she examined a rather fine and expertly crafted handbag the size of half a cowhide.

'You'll need a mortgage to buy that, cheaper to buy the cow and make the bag yourself than pay the going price,' smirked Bella. 'It's more expensive than my car back home.'

'I see your point,' laughed Amber. 'Does it look better than the car though?' Bella looked at Amber

13

rather weirdly and shuffled off to look at some more reasonable merchandise. Not before the sales assistant had looked rather loftily in their direction. When Bloomingdales had been trail blazed on every floor, the girls emerged to explore more of the city. Due to the vast amount of streets, the girls' route march became a little haphazard. Approaching 5th Avenue they decided to window shop. As they sauntered along, Bella commented on the absence of Crystal.

'She's being entertained at this moment in time. Shopping was way down her list. I just hope the guy lives up to her expectations otherwise it might cost him.' Zara's eyes rolled. The curl of her lip said it all.

'I can imagine,' retorted Bella. 'Even I wouldn't fancy upsetting Crystal, she seems to get what she wants, when she wants.'

The late morning sunshine beat down, gradually heating up the city streets. The temperature rising steeply as the skyscrapers and human traffic that thronged the pavements, suppressed any cool air that was left. Zigzagging their way from street to street, attracted by anything that caught their eye, it wasn't long before they started to get a little lost.

'Where are we heading? I've got no direction sense now, particularly as my head is on the verge of spinning with retail therapy,' declared Zara who by now was feeling a little worse for wear. The warm sunshine and excesses of the night before were taking their toll.

'We've got to head across 5th Avenue towards 53rd Street, let me attract Bella's attention,' replied Amber as she looked over her shoulder towards Bella. She had drifted over to peer avidly in the Tiffany shop window, where tray upon tray of gleaming gemstones attracted the eye. Amber's shrill shout achieved the distraction needed.

Once Bella's all round attention to follow them had been acknowledged, the girls waded through the thronging masses of New York patrons. The crowds jostled for room on the pavements. A siren echoed loudly in the distance, the noise getting louder and closer by the second. Traffic shunted from lane to lane, all trying hard to avoid being in the wrong position as the NYPD approached.

A car swerved rather suddenly when the driver panicked at the speed of the police vehicle homing in on him, the car clipping the edge of the kerb. In a flash of a second the driver was unable to rectify the situation. The front right tyre mounted the pavement and ploughed forward. With a loud screeching noise grating the atmosphere as the driver braked sharply coming to a shuddering halt, the front fender smashing into a water hydrant. Slightly shaken by the suddenness of the crash they decided to move away from the busy thoroughfare, wandering aimlessly down a couple of side streets that appeared quieter and a whole lot less crowded.

'Is it safe to wander down here?' Bella asked, looking a little uneasily over her shoulder, her eyes scanning every alleyway as they passed. She furtively looked for anything out of the norm.

'You've been watching too many late night cop programmes; not all of New York is shady,' giggled Gina.

'No I haven't. But even in London you have to be a bit careful. We look easy targets. I certainly don't look like a typical New Yorker.'

'What the hell does a typical New Yorker look like?'

'I don't know, just not touristy like us.'

Zara decided to nip the argument in the bud early. The two girls always rubbed each other up the wrong way. Not adverse to a healthy but prolonged debate, both had feisty opinions on most subjects normally opposite sides of the spectrum.

'Oi, you two stop bickering we're here to enjoy, not be catty with each other! Bella, don't worry I'm sure we're in a pretty decent area. I've checked out the more unsavoury areas and they're a long way from the main shopping locations. Besides we'll be hitting the meatpacking district in a moment. It'll be easier to move around there and we can stop off for a bite to eat.'

'Ok, ok I'll stop panicking,' Bella moved up closer though, towards Amber. Feeling she might have a little quicker reaction than Gina if there were any dodgy citizens around. Knowing full well Amber did taekwondo regularly, certain a kick from Amber would ward off any assailant.

The traffic was calming down and a steady trickle of cars passed by. Falling into a sense of false security they casually ambled along unaware of the motorbike that appeared to be tailing them. It weaved in and out of the small number of vehicles at a very slow moving pace. The bike rider monitored their every move and the traffic flow in front. As the traffic thinned out the bike suddenly picked up speed and lurched sideways. Arcing in a gentle curve it travelled precariously close

16

to Zara who was now positioned on the outside of the pavement, adjacent to the kerb. Distracted by her friends' chatter, she stepped off the kerb to skirt a lamppost. In that split second the front wheel of the bike jarred Zara's leg, forcing her violently sideways, and her hip crashing into the concrete post. With the momentum of force her upper body followed, violently banging her skull against the hard surface. Feeling the impact for several seconds, oblivion descended, her mind plummeting into closing darkness.

~ ~ ~

The steady beep of the heart monitor repeated itself. The only sound emitted in the tiny private hospital room. Zara lay still and motionless. Her leg heavily encased in plaster along the upper thigh. Her head wrapped cocoon-like in bandages.

Bruce sat silently holding her pale, limp hand, stroking her face delicately with a fingertip. His shoulders stooped, eyes staring vacantly at his fiancée.

'Please wake up darling!' He lowered his head to rest, feeling her heart beat against his face. What the hell was he going to do if Zara didn't regain consciousness? It had been twenty four hours now. The wedding would have to be delayed. He wanted it perfect for her, just as she looked now, peaceful and serene. His heart was at bursting point; the shock of the last day had been too much. Stress at work, the nuptial arrangements and accommodating the families' rules of who should or shouldn't be at the event of the year, had crushed his spirit. What should be a happy occasion was turning into a mammoth trial.

He'd kept a lot hidden from Zara, lest she became alarmed at the protocol he'd had to adhere to. Connections were everything here in New York and the Hamptons; his business depended on it. Bruce had never divulged the true depth of his real work to Zara. He wanted her to enjoy the preparations and not to fret where the huge amounts of money might have to be found for the big day. He'd reassured her family a lot had been taken care of through his vast business contacts. Calling in some favours had helped the bank balance a little, though the business was running short of funds.

Setting up an auxiliary branch here in the city of New York had come at a huge price. Movers and shakers in the loan market all wanted a slice of the cake. Just securing the office space had entailed a lot of capital up front, and protection money was now being requested.

The underground element was always ready to welcome a new player if and only if, they invested a little into their own business. They would then allow a steady stream of clients to the door.

Zara would never have understood. The English just didn't operate like this, indeed his ancestors never had, but life in the big U.S.A was different. His parents had led a rather sheltered life, living off his mother's inheritance, never having to get to grips with the business world. He began to feel the welling up of a panic attack overtaking his body, beads of perspiration trickled down his forehead and the uncomfortable sensation of tightness in his throat had begun. Gripping tighter to Zara's hand, he raised his head to kiss her delicately on the lips.

'Zara, can you hear me? Please just move a finger or flicker a lid for me. Please darling.' His anxiety was interrupted as the door opened gently and Gina slipped silently into the room.

'Hi Bruce, how's she doing?'

'Not good, she hasn't come round yet. The knock on the head must have been a big one. Luckily, only the right thigh was broken not her hip, from the fall and impact of the bike. It's unbearable seeing her like this, she just doesn't respond.' Bruce appeared totally exhausted, his face grey from lack of sleep. A faint redness was starting to outline his brown eyes.

'It'll be ok, it just takes time. Rest is the answer at the moment for her and for you. We can sort out any arrangements…., you just say the word. I've extended my leave from work so I can stay over here longer before returning to Scotland. Amber will have to return tomorrow as arranged, she has Chloe to think of, but we can all rally round.'

Bruce looked away trying to hide the turmoil inside. If only she knew the strain he was under. Zara's accident was a major distraction on top of everything he was dealing with. The heart monitor flickered and the numbers increased slightly. Bruce's eyes shot to the monitor as if it was some evil device.

'What's it doing? Do we need to get a nurse?'

'Relax; it's just Zara's pulse quickening. She can probably hear us, even though she isn't fully conscious. It's a good sign.'

Bruce sat back further in his chair relaxing a little. He carried on watching every part of Zara, flicking his sight from her face to her hands. He noticed a slight quiver of Zara's bottom lip, her breathing deepened and just slightly a faint movement could be detected of her fingertip.

'Did you see that?' Bruce's adrenaline was pumping now.

'See what?'

'Zara, her fingertip quivered slightly.'

Gina looked intently at her friend. She still lay motionless. Stroking his shoulder Gina tried to steady Bruce's emotions. Certain nothing had happened, tiredness probably unsettling Bruce's mind and eyesight.

'Just be patient.' Doubting very much if anything had altered, she settled down to unload the provisions she'd bought for them. Not that they were required at this present moment in time. Food, drink and magazines were the last thing on her friend's mind.

Bruce lent in closer, holding Zara's hand and talking softly into her ear. She seemed to stir again. Unbeknown to Bruce, Zara was aware of his faint voice and the shadowy image of someone standing over her. She tried hard to move her tongue and produce some sound from her dry throat. The process was hampered by her brain feeling heavy as lead. The bright lights of the room seemed to spin in ever decreasing circles. Struggling, she managed to utter softly,

'Where am I?' Her voice felt detached as if someone else was speaking for her.

Bruce immediately held her hand tighter, 'It's ok, darling, don't fret. You've been in a small accident and unconscious for a few hours. Just stay still and avoid moving too much, your thigh was hurt in the crash.'

Zara tried to shift but the heavy weight of her leg in plaster hindered her considerably. Bruce looked at Zara who appeared confused and unfocused. Her eyes locked onto his face. A fine sheen of sweat glazed the surface of her skin. Clutching his hand even tighter she uttered, 'Brett, what's happening to me?' Bruce looked alarmed immediately.

'Why on earth does she call me Brett?'

Gina glanced away from Bruce to observe Zara. She wasn't sure what her friend had divulged of her past history. She was certain they weren't in contact any more. Hesitating she replied, 'It's probably the knock, she's getting her words mixed up a little. Don't take it to mean anything.' Trying hard to avoid eye contact with him, she wandered over to Zara.

'Hello gorgeous, you gave me quite a fright, how you feeling?'

Zara smiled a look of relief on her face. 'Gina, I don't remember much, boy do I feel groggy. Can you and Brett help me sit up more?' Gina leant in closer.

'You mean Bruce, your fiancé…., our mind is a little muddled at the moment.'

Zara looked really confused now. Trying hard to unravel her memory cells bit by bit, she started to get vague flash-backs and was trying hard to piece them slowly together but in rather a jumbled format. When Bruce left to find a nurse, Gina spoke quietly to her.

'Zara your memory is recalling distant facts. It will take a while probably to remember everything up to date, but it'll come I'm sure.'

Zara attempted to remain calm. Her head was pounding now. Lying still and trying hard to clear her mind, Gina gently caressed her forehead gently. 'We'll sort you out; don't worry, just rest for now.'

Zara found herself wrestling thoughts backwards and forwards. A host of worries started to rear their ugly heads, as memories of her impending wedding and how long the extent of her injuries could take to heal. Slowly Bruce's name emerged but she still only recalled Brett in her mind's eye. She hadn't thought of Brett for so long and now at the least appropriate time he was larger than life. The jolt on her head must have juggled her brain cells. Her eyes became watery. Trying hard not to show how upset she was feeling, she closed them allowing her body to relax, eventually dropping into an unsettled and fitful sleep.

On his return, Bruce released Gina and sat patiently by Zara's side, until he was too shattered to keep awake any more. He decided to inform the nurse to contact him immediately if she woke and he'd return at once. But now he needed sleep. Hailing a cab outside the hospital, Bruce collapsed in the back seat exhausted from the day's proceedings. As the car sped through the now fairly sparse traffic, his eyes slowly shut with the soft motion of the vehicle.

~ ~ ~

Zara's health gradually improved with each day passing. The mind settled and recollection of several memories returned, jumbled but at least in situ. Bruce was now keen to take his fiancée home as soon as possible pestering the consultant in charge for a date on a daily basis.

'Well Mr Loxley, I feel Zara will be ready for release shortly if everything continues to heal nicely. It will take a while to repair fully but if Zara promise's to rest sufficiently, I think she'll be fine for the wedding and off the crutches. Otherwise, hobbling or a wheelchair down the aisle will be the options. The head injury will need a little longer to assess so we won't confirm a date just yet.' The doctor checked for reassurance and acknowledgement his words were heeded.

Bruce just felt relieved his fiancée was in one piece, the wedding being the last of his worries. Zara smiled sweetly at the doctor when informed of her options after his examination.

'No worries, I will definitely take your advice: No Manhattan shopping for me for a while. On no account do I want to be hobbling on my big day.'

Thoughts of bad karma doing its best to destroy everything sprung to mind. Maybe she wasn't meant to be doing this. Shaking herself quietly she pushed the thought to the back of her mind. This was probably one of the many after effects of the knock on the head. Her memory now working normally she knew Bruce was the perfect partner. Nothing was going to stop her dream wedding now. The joining of the elite was not far off. She had to be recovered and well enough;

cancelling at this late hour would be too awful to bear. Focusing on gaining her health back was of utmost importance. She couldn't let everybody down, not now. This was the final stage.

Chapter 2

DIRTY MONEY

Two figures approached the front entrance of Loxley Holdings. The smart office stood dramatically in the old part of Lower Manhattan. Its frontage newly gleaming from marble cladding to its exterior, a smart glass door led the clientele into a wide auditorium, where sat a very prim and smart receptionist. Mature and world weary lines etched her now aging face, her telephone manner impeccable from many years of experience. The receptionist viewed the guests with some caution. Sitting up a little in her seat she hesitated in her phone call as the two male visitors approached her desk.

Placing the receiver down on its cradle, she looked up to greet the gentlemen cordially. The first was tall, with dark tapered hair; a scar grazed his features staring jaggedly out of his smooth tanned cheek. Stubble protruded from his jaw line. He stepped forward to introduce himself; dressed in fine Italian cloth he appeared like any other smart business gentleman who happened to grace the office, though Rose, the receptionist, still felt intimidated even before he had uttered a syllable.

'We've come to see Mr Loxley. Haven't had the pleasure of meeting you before, it must have been your day off when we were last here.'

Rose looking hesitatingly over her horn rimmed spectacles at him, followed protocol.

'Have you got an appointment with Mr Loxley? May I have your name please sir?'

'We don't need to have an appointment to see your boss, he prefers us to just pop by if he's in town.'

The man stared, penetrating his gaze into Rose's heart. A frown spread across her face like a shifting shadow. The client's persona made her uneasy. Reaching for the intercom she pressed the connection button to Bruce's office suite.

'I'll try to see if he has some time available but he is a very busy man, only in town for a couple of weeks.'

'Yes, we are aware of his tight schedule.'

'Heard his fiancée had a slight accident, bit stressful for Mr Loxley but we will pass on our regards to him. Business has to come first I'm afraid.'

Rose stalled for a moment. The receptionist was unaware anybody knew of Zara's accident, it being so recent and Zara still in hospital. Concentrating hard on the second man who was shiftily nosing around the room she connected the phone line, wanting to remove the strangers as quickly as possible.

'Hello Mr Loxley, sorry to interrupt you. I have two gentlemen to see you. They haven't got an appointment, but urgently need to talk business while you're in town. Is it possible?' Rose was praying it was, otherwise she would be in the firing line. They didn't look like they would take no as an answer.

~ ~ ~

Bruce sat back in his chair, tired and desperately wanting to complete his workload. The dregs of two espresso coffees lay side by side. His jacket cast aside on one chair piled high with a multitude of papers. Having been up at the hospital for so long he'd got extremely behind. Work was money and he needed it badly. It looked as if the answer would have to be a yes. Sighing deeply he pressed the intercom button, 'Yes, ok send them up Rose, and thank you.'

'I will, let me know if you need anything, Sir?'

Bruce paused in reflection as he looked out of the small window overlooking the striped awnings of the local deli and coffee shops. The side streets were littered with them. From here he could see the goings on of Lower Manhattan. Not the most favourable of spots but a good hard working community. The blank empty windows of the opposing building stared back at him. He sat puzzled at Rose's comment. She never enquired if he needed help. Before he could put much thought to it, heavy footsteps approached the door and he leapt to his feet to greet his impromptu visitors.

The door swung open rather abruptly and Bruce took a step back. He seemed stunned and lost his composure for just a fraction of a second, trying hard to steady his nerve. He invited the two men in immediately, offering them a drink. The weightier guy sat down, grinning broadly at Bruce. Leaning back in his chair he bridged his hands together resting the top of

27

his fingers against his lips. Pausing, he lowered them and spoke.

'Hello Brucie boy! Thought we better catch up and sort out our few problems we've been having. By the way, sorry to hear about your fiancée's mishap, terrible that should happen on her hen weekend. Never mind, she's young, bones mend.'

Bruce sat down feeling rather sick to the core; he'd been putting this off for a long time. Payment was going to have to be completed. Reaching for the cheque book, the tall guy soundly flattened his hand. 'Come, come, cheques can bounce as you know from experience with your lovely clients, cash is the only option. Maybe you can send your little assistant out to do some work for a change?'

Bruce withdrew his hand and pressed the reception button trying hard not to appear shaken by what he'd said.

'Rose dear, would you pop to the bank for me? I need to make a withdrawal.'

'Yes sir, how much would you like?'

'I'll ring the bank direct myself and request the figure, just need you to pick it up and pop back. Thank-you that will be all.'

Rose grabbed her coat, unsure what to make of Mr Loxley's request. Placing up the notice 'Gone to lunch,' she locked the main doors behind her and stepped out into the warm New York sunshine.

Bruce sat listening to the two business men's propositions, looking at the figures presented and loathe to accept them. He knew he had little choice.

'Just sign here and our work will be done. Best regards on your nuptials. We do hope all goes well. Certainly don't want any more mishaps occurring. You need to keep that girl under surveillance a bit more.' With the departing comment, the stocky and rather unfriendly guy laughed smugly.

On Rose's return the envelope was placed on Bruce's desk. Discreetly exiting the room, Rose left the three men to complete the transaction. Bruce's hand slid the money towards his business associates reluctantly.

'It's been a pleasure doing business with you; things can run smoothly if everybody abides by the rules. See you in say three months, just after the wedding if I'm correct. Hopefully you'll be rested and keen to check up on business this side of the country again.' He swiftly shoved the paperwork into his jacket and both men left Bruce to mull over the final remark. He reached for the phone dialling immediately the number to his LA branch.

'Steve, we need to talk figures urgently.' Bruce sat back twirling his pen frantically in his hand. Leaning forward he pressed his temples, closing his eyes to the outside world in an attempt to block the problems slowly rising around him. He was glad Zara couldn't see him now. This dilemma would have to be kept quiet no matter what.

~ ~ ~

Later that day Bruce returned to the hospital, eager to see his fiancée and leave the day's dramas behind.

The morning's meeting preyed on his mind and set an uneasy overtone to the imminent wedding arrangements. He couldn't imagine Zara's accident was not just that, a chance in a million of being in the wrong place at the wrong time, but it made Bruce think twice about messing with the establishment. How naive could he have been thinking he could get away from being targeted?

The New York branch was beginning to be a burden. It wasn't the exciting proposition he had entertained a year previous. Sure he had heard the rumours that any new business in certain parts of the city, normally had to fit in with the customs of the neighbourhood. But having to be intricately involved with the committees and paying good hard earned cash just to be able to open up, was another. The ongoing payment to allow his business to continue was just one issue he hadn't faced up to.

The financial commitment had been huge. It was a gamble but he was prepared to take that risk, still was, if he could pull through this slight downturn in operations. Bruce's viewpoint was that the small fry business man was of no interest to the big guns. Now, once trading awhile and building up a reputation, he could see why they might want a cut of the action.

Looking from the other angle he could also see why a lot of small fish keep the bigger fish contented. A small deposit here and there would add up to quite a lot over the year. Who wouldn't target the weaker guy? No, he would just have to juggle the two offices somehow.

A loan from his parents was out of the question. He was determined not to be the leech his brother had become. At least he'd earned the respect of the family. Marrying someone like Zara was something he'd always dreamed of. Now the pressure was off and he was proud that she would shortly be his wife.

The thought of Zara being affected by his predicament tore him in half. At least she loved him and would probably understand... he hoped, or run for the hills? Never being one for the girls, he'd laid in the shadow of Frederick for so long that for once he felt he had the upper hand in meeting Zara. This situation had to be kept under control and secret. He couldn't jeopardise anything in the run up to the most important day of his life.

Taking a deep breath he entered the corridor leading to Zara's private room. He prayed she was improving more and her memory was clearing. Not remembering his name had been a big concern. It was as Gina said, the knock on the head. He was sure of it. Putting on a cheerful front, he entered her room brandishing in front of the biggest bunch of blooms he could find.

Zara looked up as Bruce came in and smiled, clearly taken aback by the floristry that was coming towards her.

'Crikey, you want me to get hay fever?' Bruce's face instantly fell but lifted a little when Zara playfully poked him in the ribs in jest.

'No, I just wanted to make the room seem a little more summery for you, as you're confined to barracks for the moment.' Glancing hesitantly to check Zara's response he stepped forward to kiss her. Still unsure of how her reactions were from day to day.

'Come here, they're lovely. I've never had such a massive display before, I don't think anyway?' She seemed to try and force her memory to work, scratching her hairline as if it would miraculously encourage the brain cells to go into overdrive.

'How do you feel today? Have the headaches got less? You seem much brighter.' Bruce was relieved she seemed more alert and able to chat.

'Yes they've relented, thank goodness. Not sure if it's the drugs they feed into you or they've gone naturally. I'm sure I could be sold on the street for a lot of money with what I've been given. I'm pumped up to the eyeballs.'

Bruce laughed. Zara's weird British humour had returned. He had kind of forgotten a lot of the quirky ways his homeland had compared with the Americans. One day he had a feeling he would like to live back there. He could regain a little of his roots and experience it first-hand.

'How's work at the office, everything ok?' Zara asked intuitively, her memory obviously returning extremely well as this was recent recall not the past. Bruce remembered his own conversation with Gina when Zara had first recovered consciousness.

'Fine, not much to concern you, just clerical work, shifting money around, usual story,' he replied somewhat nervously.

'I hope you aren't money laundering? I've heard many a story of financial companies using normal punters' money in untoward dealings.' Bruce's face went pale for a moment and he decided to change the subject rapidly. Not before Zara had detected the visible change of expression on his face at her words.

'I've been talking to the consultant in charge of you; he seems to think it won't be long before we can get you up on crutches and moving. Then the final date of the wedding can be assessed once we know how the leg might be healing. But it looks like you can come home shortly.'

'Great, I'm feeling really stressed not being able to move. Even though I feel a little groggy, the thought of moving and being more upright I'm sure will help my head. But we can't change the date of the wedding. What of all the pre-booked arrangements? It'll be a nightmare.' Zara's voice quavered and she looked now close to tears, visibly stressed at this option. Bruce leant in closer and gave her a cuddle to reassure.

'That's the least of your worries; we can do anything we want. Nothing is set in stone. The venue in the Hamptons can easily be moved I'm sure.'

Although Bruce knew in fact it was unlikely being the most popular destination there. Keeping that hidden for the time being might prevent Zara fretting. Her immediate reaction would be to push herself too far, too quick. Then where would that lead to?

~ ~ ~

A week had passed painfully slowly. The hot sultry sunshine shone relentlessly through the hospital window where Zara lay, waiting for Bruce to arrive. The final day of release from what she considered her prison cell. It was a room with a view indeed, but lack of freedom to waltz around and seeing the fantastic weather outside had made Zara particularly uncomfortable and getting pretty frustrated.

'Some bloody hen weekend this has been,' thought Zara as she arranged her belongings for the umpteenth time. A sharp rap on the door of her private room and in marched the consultant who had been assigned her welfare.

'Well young lady, we have the release papers today and no doubt you are itching to leave our department, so I won't delay. I do hope you have had a pleasant stay even though under difficult circumstances.' He winked and with a flourish of his pen handed Zara her paperwork. Smiling back and humouring him as best she could, she replied,

'Yes, your hospitality knows no bounds, but possibly could you get some more cable channels for next time, there is only so much sitcom a girl can bear in a day.'

'I'll put it on the priority list.' Grinning at her he bade farewell, leaving Zara once again twiddling her thumbs.

Glancing over towards the daily news sheets her eye caught one of the headlines. The small article was hidden well amongst the many advertisements. The feature clearly showed someone had a grudge to bear. Intrigued she leant forward to read more. The situation of the small business holder in the city was being hounded out by corruption and organised gangs. Zara sat back and then one word made her sit up and take a lot more notice. It was the area most targeted. Precisely where Bruce's current office was based. Reading further, Zara noticed the main contributor to the article had not been named for fear of reprisals and went into more detail of what the consequences of non-negotiation with the gangs had led to.

Zara began to suddenly see more than she wanted to. The nervousness in Bruce's voice, the odd twitch when work was mentioned or his mobile rang. Was Bruce being affected by this? Why wouldn't he be? They were hardly going to miss one business out over the rest.

Looking down at the plaster gripping her thigh, she regressed back to the time of the accident. Try as she might, no recollection surfaced of what had happened seconds prior to being hit. A strong sensation of fear settled in her bones and she shivered despite the warmth of her surroundings. Her close association to the article via her fiancé's business was a little too close for comfort. The subject would have to be broached. The door opened suddenly and Zara's nerves shot into action, she was relieved to see it was only Bruce.

'Hi gorgeous, cavalry has arrived to escort you home,' he leant forward and smacked the biggest kiss on Zara's rather surprised face. Sitting down on the edge of the bed he sensed the tension in Zara. She seemed flustered all of a sudden, her hands fumbled to retrieve her last belongings from the side cabinet.

'You ok? No setbacks, they happy for you to be released?' He looked quizzically at her.

'Yes, all seems to be fine. Can't wait to get out of here.' Zara tried hard to cover her emotions. Now was not the time to start bringing up the subject, she wanted to get out of here and preferably away from Manhattan as soon as she could. Bruce swept up the papers and magazines lying strewn across the bed. A moment of recognition at the article headlines that glared up at him was clearly indicative on his facial expression. Hastily he closed the paper and turning away from Zara shoved them neatly into the nearest waste bin.

'Why did you chuck them away? You might want to read them later.'

'No, it's just more to carry. Besides don't want to waste a day like this reading the tabloids. I want to treat you to something nice after all you've had to put up with.'

Zara was now even more certain Bruce was covering up something as he fussed with her luggage. Yes, it was blindingly obvious he wanted her not to see the article. Discuss it they would. No way would she be going into marriage if he couldn't be honest with her. What other skeletons were in the cupboard to be uncovered? More to the point, if she was going to be targeted for money issues she would like to be aware and vigilant of her predicament. Wouldn't anybody? Money was the bloody bane of her life. Living in a tent on the side of a mountain seemed rather attractive at this moment in time, minus the broken thigh bone of course. Zara glanced round one more time at the room that had been home for so long; keen not to return too quickly. Slowly she lowered herself into the wheelchair and entered out into freedom and some long needed fresh air.

Chapter 3

THE WEDDING

Mayhem erupted as a flurry of activity ensured each and every woman looked her divine best for this prestigious event. The room lay scattered with various contraptions to primp and gloss every appendage. A layer of heavy perfume and flowers mingled in harmony together with the warmth of the morning sunshine. It shone sharply through the gothic window like a laser. Commotion was erupting, due to lost items in the frenzy that was now meant to be the bridal suite.

Zara sat patiently looking into the oval mirror before her. A huge feeling of apprehension was beginning to take over deep in the recesses of her mind. Her stomach lurched backwards and forwards. Second thoughts at the lavish event before her started to resurface.

Bella was trying hard to tong Zara's hair into what resembled a toilet brush. Noticing her look of concern she thought the best line of defence was to explain her intended aim.

'Don't look so worried, it's got to be tweaked yet so they hang down into a river of ringlets.'

'Okay, it's just at this precise moment they look as if they're going upstream,' muttered Zara under her breath. Try as she might, she was feeling tetchy. The slightest of things were clearly agitating her. Shifting uncomfortably, she tried to remain seated with the tugging and shoving Bella was inflicting on her.

Amber glided over, looking serene and calm amidst the mayhem. Intuitive as always, and looking gorgeous even half clothed, she sensed something was wrong.

'You ok? I get a feeling you're not as calm as usual.'

'My stomach is doing bloody somersaults.'

'That's butterflies, we all get them. Nerves take over. Once you see Bruce they will dissipate I promise. You're doing the right thing. He's perfect for you.' Amber looked deeply into Zara's eyes, holding her shoulders for support.

'I know, but at the moment these butterflies are bouncing around like space hoppers.' Amber's gentle touch had the influencing calm she needed, but a residue of anxiety remained.

'Right, enough of all this, the headdresses need to be put on now,' declared Bella, clearly trying to distract Zara from the situation and the distressing problem of hair. Bella's hairdressing skills were under pressure this morning. Maybe a little too much gel was the start of it, and with luck the hair would drop a little she prayed silently.

As the boxes that lay on the floor were opened, Bella rather gingerly lifted out the first of the delicate headdresses for each bridesmaid. The bright orange blossoms shot through with dark evergreen foliage were a perfect complement to Zara's hair and dress.

Zara glanced at Gina as she caught sight of it and her reaction was immediate.

'Oh! No way. Have I really got to wear one of those? Nobody said I had to resemble a flower fairy, that wasn't part of the bargain.'

Zara tried hard to suppress a giggle at Gina's flare up.

'I know, I'm sorry, but if I had told you, would you not have declined my offer? I so needed you here.'

Gina's face expressed total disgust at the creation Bella was placing on her head. Past history had made Gina rather reluctant to be of the fairest sex; slightly tomboyish, her past escapades with the male population had normally ended in a disaster. Gina finally admitted defeat, calling time on men at large. For now that is. With Gina's attention span, it could be altered at any moment.

The news although startling, came as some relief to Zara after one past episode of mutual attraction for a certain unsuspecting male. Fireworks could well have erupted. A few things in life are better left discreetly hidden from view. Particularly where Gina was concerned, her tendency to change her mind was done on a frequent basis. Better to let some ghosts rest in peace.

'As it's you, I'll relent, but it's coming off as soon as we hit the reception.'

Bella tutted, 'Don't fuss, it's only some flaming flowers.'

'It's alright for you, you're addicted to weddings and dressing up like a fairy. Must be the wedding cake you like so much?' replied Gina.

Bella looked in disgust at Gina retorting, 'At least I get to taste some.' Twice married, Bella was unfazed by the proceedings and everything they entailed.

Detecting a row brewing. Zara decided to step in. The last thing she wanted was an all-out war amongst the bridesmaids on the big day. Distraction was required immediately. They'd been bad enough on her hen weekend so on no accounts did she want it at her wedding.

'Right now, dress next. I'll need some help to get in the creation. Looking like a flower fairy is the least of your worries when you see what I've got to wear.'

It hung from the hanger looking exquisite. Zara and Crystal had spent hours trying every dress on earth, finally choosing the first one she had set eyes on.

After being poured into the gown, Zara viewed her reflection in the full length mirror. The dress encapsulated every curve of her body. Breathing was slightly hindered under the tight restricting fabric. It appeared stunning in the bridal shop. Now, in the late summer of the Hamptons, it felt like she had been wrapped in cling film and was slowly being compressed by a boa constrictor.

'Push your breasts up a bit, might give a bit more room around the ribcage,' Bella suggested half-heartedly.

With much shoving and hilarity, Zara stood encased in her bridal gown. Amber whispered in her ear. 'You look gorgeous, he will be so proud of you.'

Zara wasn't thinking of Bruce, but of his mother. Would she be proud? This was a big event and she wanted it to run like clockwork. Some of her mother-in-law's friends were no ordinary guests. They could be very particular and scathing for that matter if something was not up to scratch. Oh well, her own family would give them a run for their money if anything was to be said. Maybe it was all the background stress of relatives that might be the real reason for her concern.

Peering at her reflection in the oval mirror, she relaxed a little. Yes the gown did look rather stunning - until she moved. Her heart missed a beat again with the fluttering of uneasiness edging up from deep inside. Swallowing hard she glanced around at her bridal helpers, each one had experienced far more than she ever had. Children, marriages, divorce, and even worse death. She felt quite naive in comparison to what her close knit friends had been through. No, she would have to pull herself together. Taking a deep breath as best she could, she summoned her entourage to depart.

'Girls this is it, let's go and meet our audience.'

Amber led the party out stopping off on the way to collect her daughter. As she emerged from the bedroom tears sprang from Zara's eyes. The little girl was dressed so prettily, her eyes twinkling with excitement. Innocent to what life would bring her. Zara brushed a tear away that started to trickle down her cheek and ruin all the hard work Bella had put in to perfecting her complexion. She followed the party downstairs to assemble at the side entrance of the country house.

Stepping out into the luscious gardens, a cream Cadillac rolled gently forward to meet them, crunching the smooth gravel beneath its pristine tyres. Zara's father was duly extracted from the bar before the party was finally ready to leave.

'What are you like? I thought it was the bride that needed a stiff drink, not her father.'

'I was just toasting the event with your father-in-law, a man after my own heart. Likes to get away from the women and put the world to rights. Zara, you may have chosen well.' Zara was slightly put out by this remark.

'Dad, I'm not marrying the family, it's Bruce I chose.'

'Yes, I know but it always helps to get in with the opposition.'

Zara decided to keep quiet; she dreaded to think who dad would have chosen for her bridegroom if he had the choice to make the final selection. The requirements wouldn't have been for her benefit that was for sure. Her work was going to be cut out trying to keep both the fathers' out of untold mischief.

Once the entire ensemble was seated, the trio of cars pulled away slowly. Circling around the drive at the forefront of the mansion they proceeded to enter the main avenue, which led out to the far side of the extensive grounds, towards the main location of the wedding nuptials. The avenue of trees closed in overhead, allowing a peaceful coolness to envelop the cars. Each tree was encircled by purple irises, creating a misty hue at their base. The view stretching as far as the eye could visualise.

The procession drove slowly through the tunnel to emerge once again into the brilliant warmth of the sunshine. Turning left, they glided to a halt at the entrance to a secluded cottage. Immediately on alighting Bella fussed over Zara, aligning her dress,

42

checking the hair had eventually dropped a little. Gina by now was trying hard not to scowl, as the blossoms started to set off her allergy.

Crystal on the other hand was becoming clearly excitable by the proceedings. Prancing around insisting the group stood in the right position for the photographer, whom she decided to outrageously flirt with. Adjusting her low lying gown to reveal more than should be on display at an official function, Crystal clearly loved every minute of the schmooze and glitz of a Hamptons' wedding. Bella grimaced discreetly trying to encourage Crystal to contain her enthusiasm.

'Crystal, rein it in. It's meant to be a wedding not a Pirelli calendar shoot. The poor photographer won't have his mind on the job by the time you finish.' Crystal narrowed her eyes at her. Pouting and clearly wounded by her remark.

Bella guided the group through the main gate of the cottage, leading them into a tiny circular courtyard shrouded by a tight privet hedge. Zara had fallen in love with the venue as soon as she'd set foot in the grounds. Crystal had done her proud in sourcing such a place. Nothing else compared.

'Here we go Dad, this is it.'

Her father squeezed her hand. 'Just enjoy, it will be over in a flash.'

Zara smiled; secretly glad her father was here. With his strong grounding affect and ability to make anyone see the funny side of a predicament, his presence was reassuring to her.

The garden whispered softly with the sound of the wind running through the tall reeds that stood proudly each side of the steps. Slowly Zara walked across to the far corner of the open space where an evergreen walkway beckoned.

Hesitating, she took in the soft breeze that ruffled the vivid orange blossoms adorning her headdress, scents of the summer flowers invigorating her senses. The coolness here was welcoming.

Taking a few deep breaths and smiling at her father, they proceeded to enter the archway as the wedding march played. Ahead of them lay a path of orange, speckled gold with a central geometric stone. The design led the eye beyond and down to the awaiting guests. Each side was framed by small trees heavy with red blossom and soft mossy turf covering their roots. Their scent drifted delicately on the breeze.

Behind Zara the path sloped gently from a higher platform like a shimmering, rolling carpet. Here sat majestically a huge Chinese urn. The orange metallic sheen framed Zara perfectly as she strode confidently forward to her awaiting audience. Nearing the end of the path Zara could see through to the inner courtyard strategically framed by hanging blossoms of wisteria; their purple hue in stark contrast to the energetic buzz of orange that lay behind her.

The pathway appeared to melt away into the space to a soft buttermilk shade. The same geometric stones guiding her towards the large water feature of dancing nymphs where her future husband awaited. He stood proudly gazing at her. Clasping her hand, a look of relief reflected out from his eyes. Her stomach leaped higher than ever now. This was the final countdown.

The inner courtyard was crammed with guests. All eager to see the couple take their vows. When the main legalities had completed, Bruce leant towards his bride. The scent of Zara's bridal headpiece was exquisite, her lips were sweet to his taste buds. He savoured the flavour ignoring the stares and cheers as he kissed her softly. Smiling, he met her gaze. Finally he had achieved his dream. Zara was now his official wife.

Now the most important part had been completed, Zara finally had a chance to scan their guests, her nerves having distracted her from acknowledging who was actually attending. A sea of faces uttering best wishes met her gaze. Turning, the bride and groom retraced their steps as a married couple, sprinkles of confetti showering down upon them.

Gina sidled up discreetly whispering, 'It's time to party. By the way you look fabulous, but you still owe me one. I won't forget.'

Zara grinned, 'I knew you'd come round.'

'Yeah,' Gina raised an eyebrow, 'Don't think it will be staying on all evening.'

'As if I would,' murmured Zara. Clasping tightly to her new husband's hand, they slowly retreated back to the cool interior of the cottage garden's entrance.

Chatter and hilarity ensued as the entourage, now relieved of their duties made a return to the mansion house accompanied by the privileged guests for the main festivities. The Hamptons clientele knew exactly how to party in style. Within minutes, Freddie, Bruce's younger brother, had sidled up to Amber like a praying mantis. His campaign of sheer persistence over the past year had been second to none. All hot chicks from the racing circuit had been left by the wayside, as he tried every trick in the book to woo and seduce his chosen target.

Long distance had been his greatest hurdle and lack of personal funds to keep jetting backwards and forwards to the UK. Bruce had been the golden goose in allowing him too conveniently to pop over on pretence of business for his brother, this placing some strain on Zara's relationship with Bruce behind the scenes.

Amber, as polite as ever, greeted his attention with gratitude, but was no easy pull and was in no way prepared to drop her gauntlet as quickly as Freddie would have liked. He was now becoming ever more desperate in his quest... Amber was the desired target and nothing was going to stop him tonight.

Out on the dance floor Bella was starting to let her hair down. Bruce's father was the unwilling victim, swinging the poor guy from the rafters. Zara noticed his bewildered face as he twirled past, Bella hanging onto him for dear life. He had no chance to escape now that Bella was in full jiving mode. Champagne and the warm sultry weather was a potent combination for his constitution. Loosening up and getting accustomed to Bella's style of dance, he lost all principles by one stage. The music cranked up with a beat that got faster and more provocative by the minute. Bella dirty danced with him so close to the mark; her poor husband felt the need to rescue the fella in case he suffered a heart attack.

'It comes to something when your top bridesmaid practically seduces the father of the groom leading him to risk accident and emergency!' piped up Gina, trying hard to make her voice heard above the music. Both girls looked on in astonishment.

'He kind of deserves it a little. Thinks he's the perfect gigolo. Bella's just testing him out, might slow him down for a while. Been a fair few times I've had to bat him off with a sharp instrument. You can see my concern about Amber and Freddie. What if he turns out like his father? God help us.'

'Amber's cool. I'm sure she can put any guy in his place. People can change. If she's keen, she won't give up wearing the trousers.'

'Suppose not. As it's my big day, let's go for it. I can't have everyone enjoying themselves more than me.' With a twirl of her flamboyant frock, she led Gina onto the floor to shimmy with the best of them.

Backstage the party proceedings continued to include the usual banter, disagreements, raucous behaviour and sheer exhibitionism that most weddings tended to sink to. Even the gentry of the Hamptons could demean themselves with copious amounts of alcohol on offer.

As the evening drew in, the wedding took on a more chilled atmosphere. Feeling now overheated in the glamorous figure hugging frock thanks to an energetic set on the dance floor, Zara slipped quietly outside to gather her thoughts plus a well-deserved breath of fresh air. The dress was still causing her some discomfort. It might be coming off shortly, whether it was tradition or not. She didn't care if the senior Mrs Loxley was unimpressed or not.

Walking delicately towards one of the terrace stone walls she had to lift the heavy dress from grazing the floor. Zara sat down looking over the mansion gardens that lay like a carpet, stretching out towards the edge of the lake. She could just glimpse the blue expanse in the far distance.

The sun had started to ebb creating a huge glowing orb over the horizon. Any sounds became distant as she focused on the view. Yes now she was an honest woman and maybe, just maybe, this was the right direction. The turmoil of knotted nerves earlier was just that, nerves. Anyone would have experienced them marrying into the Loxley clan. They were no average Jones' she had realised, especially after Zara had been formally introduced to some of Bruce's close family and friends. Though what opinions they had of her small private bunch she'd rather not contemplate. They didn't have to live in each other's shoes. There was at least thirteen hours of air miles between them. Any clashes could be dealt with in some way. Bruce had mentioned the Scottish side may have to be met at some time. That was a little closer to home; she could combine a jaunt to see Gina, multi-task with one airfare that would work out fine.

Zara just prayed the Scottish line were a little less pretentious than their American relatives. A slight sense of apprehension kicked in again. Shaking a little she hugged her knees to her chest, not an easy feat with the long tight gown she was wearing. Deciding to prolong the moment as long as she could, she sat silently absorbing the atmosphere before she would be noticed as missing and would have to return to the throng again.

48

Soft jazz notes drifted out to the terrace, fading and then becoming stronger as each melody followed. All she wanted was just a few more minutes to focus, a few more moments to take stock of this huge change. Just a few more seconds of freedom.Before her new life began.

Chapter 4

THE JOURNEY NORTH

Ten years previous

Zara sat on the Express to Scotland, excited at meeting her old buddy Gina, remembering far back when they had first encountered each other at school. Standing there daunted by the class in front of her, a friendly hand clasped hers and Gina cheerfully announced that she could be her friend; a smile and a hug completed the union. Zara was now fully integrated into the new playground.

Both sported the latest pigtails and complained ferociously that they didn't like boys at all. How times had changed. Their friendship had evolved and developed via aims and desires, changing but always remaining close. An unspoken connection between the two of them, both practically joined at the hip. No one could break their inner circle; they laughed at the most absurd jokes, intuitive to the other's feelings. They could have been twin sisters, with the great advantage of a few less rows that siblings so often experienced.

The scenery raced by in a blur, voices chattered in the background merging with the clanking of the express wheels. Zara found it somewhat strange as she travelled around the country, whether destined for north, south, east or west, the voices always echoed from the destination ahead. Strong local accents danced around, ebbing in and out of conversations.

Excitement always set in; she really loved the variety that her homeland gave in such a small country. Now the Scottish lilts were weaving their charm. Some so broad she was unable to distinguish the words at all. Most were a delight to the ear. Soft and rolling like whisky on the tongue. She melted inwardly; there was something very sexy and comforting about it.

Visiting Gina was like a complete escapism from reality. She could let her hair down, be carefree and forget the anti-social hours she kept at work. Rid of responsibility, student roots were beckoning her now....

Her thoughts were rudely interrupted by an irritating ringtone. The immediate rush and frenzy of activity enveloped the compartment. Several passengers started to delve in their bags, searching for the dreaded invention that controlled the human race. Each and every one put on red alert with their automatic reaction, led by this tiny piece of electronic wizardry.

The woman in front retrieved her mobile first. Zara sat quietly observing her closely, finding it rather a novel way to amuse when travelling long distance. Boredom was never her strong point. Though Bella, one long-time friend, had a major obsession with this particular past time.

An incident sprung to mind and Zara couldn't help but grin. Same situation, train bound and bored to the back teeth, Bella had become entranced with a fellow passenger. Never discreet and sometimes appearing a little vacant, she had forgotten that she was in a public arena and not observing from the side lines at a polite distance.

Throughout the entire journey Bella had fixated her gaze on one travelling companion. The unwavering attention had caused the woman to assume Bella had lost her marbles and was about to accost her. She duly reported poor Bella to the guard, leading and culminating in a very embarrassing incident, involving full interrogation and expulsion off the train at the next station.

Mind you Bella hadn't given up. Dusting herself down, she invested in a fabulous and rather glam pair of dark shades, in an attempt to disguise her unusual habit. In hindsight this did tend to exaggerate her unusual looks, accentuating her into the realm of possibly a complete nutcase to the fellow traveller. Good old Bella, if you needed a laugh to lift your spirits she was the girl to do it.

The scenery now started to change dramatically to a more rugged and windswept landscape, indicating it wouldn't be long before the Express would be pulling into her favourite city of Edinburgh. Zara felt great passion for this place, as if she had finally returned home, to her roots. Possibly in a past life she had been a wild woman living on the Scottish moor, windswept and waiting for her Braveheart of the north to whisk her off her feet; very Emily Bronte thought Zara, although she was sure Wuthering Heights was set in Yorkshire, never one to read avidly let alone remember the details. Whatever its magic, she adored coming north for a fix of the fresh air and wildness.

The train clanked and rattled slowly into the station. Zara waited patiently as the Express stopped. The fight to the door was always a challenge. The amount of possessions travellers brought on a train was unbelievable; saying that, Zara had not come light, she liked an outfit for all occasions - not exactly a fashion victim but keen to look the part for any pursuit. Gina though, was more her own trendsetter, being a student, the sheer lack of money led to a sense of eccentricity in her street style. Attention was not unbeknown when Gina hit the town.

The electric doors parted and swarms of impatient travellers melted onto the platform, in a dire rush to get to the ticket collector first. Zara trundled her rather flash luggage to the gate, looking forward to seeing her friend as she scanned the throngs of people waiting to greet fellow travellers at the barrier.

Spotting Gina instantly amongst the smiling faces, she waved frantically to catch her attention, and swiftly side-stepped the few doddery old timers to beat them and get to Gina. Hugging her like a long lost soul, she was ecstatic at seeing her friend after so long.

'You look great, how are you? Was the trip ok? Not too boring I hope?' Gina was clearly breathless as her sentences tumbled out in a mad rush.

'Steady, one question at a time. Yes I did a 'Bella', eavesdropping and studying a few fellow passengers and then read a good book. What's the itinerary for the weekend, I can't wait?' Gina pulled a wry face at the mention of Bella.

'Bet she's been up to her old tricks and now she's got you addicted; nightmare. Now the plan of action I feel is a quick introduction to my friends from university, I know you miss being part of it now you're a fully-fledged worker, so a little revisit is in order. Then there's a fab wild, and I mean wild, party at Greg's house. Finally we can finish off at one of the clubs, as it's a special weekend jaunt.'

'Fine, but I'm going to treat you to the Spa. We've got to do it in style, especially as it's your birthday.'

'Why not? That would be perfect, de-chill and catch up on all the gossip: a perfect combination. Can't ask for more, bar a tiny little hot number I've seen in Pankira, but I might have to wait for that till payday.'

They battled their way out of the station on to Princes Street. The mass of tourists and commuters facing them was like a constant tidal wave. Once onto the main street Zara could see the splendour of the city. She stood transfixed for a few seconds scanning back over to the old and traditional part of Edinburgh. Then looking up towards the battlements of the castle, she absorbed the history and greyness of the city that lay out in front of her.

'You ok?' enquired Gina, concerned why she was hesitating.

'Yeah of course, I just love taking it all in, the atmosphere and everything. You're so lucky to live here.' Gina looked a little weirdly at her friend.

'I don't think Edinburgh is a patch on Brighton. They're all old codgers up here; at least Brighton has a massive student community. Ours are a bit more uptight than your lot.'

'Nonsense, you've got it all up here. I'd have loved to swap places.'

54

'Well one day we might,' laughed Gina giving her a squeeze and boot up the bottom to move on.

Zara grinned. Other friends had come to visit Edinburgh with her in the past, declaring that the whole place was dirty and grim. Zara dismissed this, shocked that they thought this way. The drama and mystique was testimony to the ravages it had endured. The whole place seemed to exude a certain charm. They normally got shifted off her Christmas list rapidly.

Weaving in and out of the shoppers, the girls finally reached a little side street and peace descended, away from the hub of the main centre. It was here Gina shared a small apartment. As normal, the rents seemed to be cheaper the higher up the rooms. Zara knew this would mean a hard slog up the stairs with her suitcase and she braced herself for it. Gina laughed as she attempted to lift Zara's case, needing two hands to even get some slight leverage up one stair.

'What the hell have you brought this weekend? I can hardly lift the bloody thing.'

'Just the usual,' her face grimaced severely as she grabbed the other handle and tried to hurl it up the next stairwell with her friend's help.

'What are you achieving? You'll never learn. Downsize is the word now and that means your wardrobe as well,' smirked Gina. After heaving for the next five minutes around the four flights of stairs, they finally stood at the door to Gina's flat.

The accommodation had wonderful views over the city, if you didn't mind standing on the bed to appreciate it, or looking round the odd chimney pot or two. The two girls collapsed onto the sofa, giggling at the exertion of getting there. It was peaceful. Sunlight drifted in across the rather tatty rug, IKEA of course. Obviously the cheapest a student could provide to have a cutting edge apartment. Zara thought back to her home, it was so different to this, but it was comfortable.

Everyone at Gina's seemed friendly and always available for a shoulder to cry on, as she had only been too aware when her friend had a few personal traumas. It was a fair few miles from Brighton and popping up to offer assistance wasn't easy with her new job and the uncertainty of her vehicle actually making the journey. Once recovered, the kitchen became their port of call. Refreshments were now the order of the day.

'What coffee are you into? Is it some dung beetle new tea or some other weird combination you're drinking?' Zara laughed as she raided the kitchen cupboards. Gina was semi-vegetarian and seemed to eat and drink the most bizarre stuff.

'No, just good old caffeine addicted black stuff I'm afraid; haven't had much time to shop.'

Zara could plainly see this was the case. It was a good thing she was treating Gina to dinner as eating out was the only choice for tonight.

Refreshed and unpacked they headed off to visit Gina's close friends on campus. Then the thrill of a big chill at the Spa beckoned. On frequent occasions the girls had met at various locations to enjoy a Spa facility. Any physical side was never entertained of course. It mostly involved extensive lolling in the hot tub putting the world to rights, or covering more gossip than the local rags could report in a month.

Today was nothing different. Grabbing their skimpy bikinis, both girls struggled to undo tangles of straps quickly so no time was wasted. They shot out to invade the Jacuzzi before the teatime rush of members stormed the Spa.

'This is total and utter bliss, we should do this more often.' Zara seemed to drift into a trance-like state which sadly didn't last long. The tranquillity stopped rather abruptly as Gina nudged her in the ribs.

'Look at that, not bad abs.'

Zara opened one eye to see what her friend was getting excited about. Eyeing the god-like apparition approaching them she tried to be discreet, 'Gina, you are so masculine in your appreciation of the male form.'

'No I'm not, but you've got to agree it's definitely not a six pack, more like a ten. I wonder where he trains regularly? I might have to see if my grant might stretch to a membership if it's here.'

'He's probably just on business; you'll never see him again.'

'Hmmm, maybe,' murmured Gina clearly mesmerised by the gleaming torso heading in her direction. A girl can dream.'

As Mr Abman approached them he smiled, prompting Gina to start her full on fluttering eyelash routine, in a vain attempt to leave a lasting impression. Zara tried hard to suppress a laugh when she caught sight of her. Clearly aware of the effect he was having on the two girls, he stayed under the shower for more than was necessary. Sliding into the pool, he started to swim towards them, gliding through the water with ease. At the end of each lap Gina maintained eye

57

contact, which seemed to be working in gaining some attention from the athlete. Sadly, a dedicated sports athlete he definitely was. Lap after lap he swam. Maintaining count was proving hard work. The girls had given up ages ago.

Zara always admired her friend; she would take a situation and pursue her goal with no fear. Zara on the other hand was slightly shy; yes she could hold a good conversation with anyone, but if she had the slightest twitch of admiration her demeanour became a shadow of its former self. Being unable to string a sentence together, combined with turning an unflattering shade of puce at the same time, was a bit of a hindrance in the chatting up stakes.

'I'm going for a sauna, Gina; join me if you like, if you haven't already overheated enough?'

'Ok, but I've got to sit near the door to admire the view.' Zara, at this remark, rolled her eyes. 'You're getting worse.'

Once they had melted every sign of tension within their bodies, the friends decided to glam up for the evening meal. Mr Abs was still ploughing effortlessly through the water.

'At least you know what he does for that rippling torso and that's only part of it. If you're interested, the swimsuit may have to be frequently used and not just in the hot tub.'

'I'll have to think of another way to attract his attention, as I'm not keen on becoming the next Channel swimmer.' Regular exercise was not Gina's thing.

By eight o'clock dinner beckoned. The inactivity hadn't increased the appetite but the constant gossiping had. Once slipped into something more formal, the girls headed towards the lift. Zara glanced across at Gina; she was carrying a bizarre carpet bag so cumbersome it very nearly stopped people accessing the lift full stop.

'There's me taking you to the hippest restaurant in town and you're carrying something that looks as if you're moving house.'

'I know, but I didn't want to leave it in the locker as they shut the Spa by eleven and I've got to get it to Sarah's tonight, she has a client for tomorrow. Besides I might set up a new trend, half the people who eat here probably won't know one Vuitton from another.'

'I didn't see you bring it in, I'm surprised you ever got it in the locker in the first place. You would need a crowbar to jam that in.'

'Funny ha, ha, it was dropped off by one of my consultants. I pass it on you see amongst the group of girls I work with.'

'I did wonder. Thought you had the crown jewels in there. Slightly extravagant for the skimpy bikini you had on earlier.'

With her passing comment, the lift doors parted leading straight into the hotel restaurant. Zara stepped out elegantly, loving everything about the place from its grand ceilings to the ornate crystal chandeliers. The interior oozed tradition but with a slight modern twist. Dusky silk lampshades in midnight black shed a soft diffused light throughout the restaurant.

Centre stage a huge display of fruit and flowers towered upwards, woven intricately into a flowing sea of colour. Curved dark wood chairs complemented the stiff white linens covering each table.

Zara appreciated food served correctly. It always seemed tastier the more time and effort that had been taken. This was one place she definitely loved to come to again and again.

'Your decision to where we sit being the birthday girl: centre stage or window seat?'

There was no reply, Zara turned just in time to see the lift doors closing behind her. Where the hell had she gone to now? Zara prayed no one had heard her mutterings as a few diners looked up. Smiling sweetly at the head waiter she wandered back towards the lift.

It seemed like eternity, but in a few moments the glass fronted lift doors parted with Gina at the rear declaring rather loudly, 'Excuse me madam, you could clearly see I was trying to get through last time. Will you kindly shift your suitcase so I can at least get by?'

The woman huffily lugged the rather smart case out of Gina's way. The spectacle was obviously more interesting than their fellow diners' conversation. Now a fair few eyes were transfixed on the departing lift. Zara cringed inwardly, raising her eyebrows at the head waiter as she went forward to help her friend.

'Bloody cheek, the old battle axe deliberately stopped me from getting out. She could see I had a lot to manoeuvre through and who the hell wears a hat in a lift? We're not in Buckingham Palace,' muttered Gina in rather too loud a voice.

'Every time she spoke to the guy she was with, the ruddy feathers kept smacking me in the face. I nearly de-plucked her, she was annoying me so much.'

Zara tried not to laugh and make the situation worse than it already was. Embarrassment was setting in.

'Do you want to leave the bag at reception? It's rather big to take in the restaurant? I've got a vision of the waiters flying over it with hot soup or something. Anyway you never did tell me what you've got in there?'

'I'll tell you later. You don't want to know really.' Rather reluctantly Gina passed the dreaded tapestry bag over to the concierge, who was summoned abruptly to whisk the said item away, allowing harmony to ensue the restaurant once again.

'Good evening ladies. Table for two or are you joining anyone tonight?' Zara replied swiftly lest Gina came out with another embarrassing remark.

'No just the two of us.'

'Lovely. Would a window seat or central area seat be suitable?'

The head waiter analysed the two of them rather too closely, perhaps wondering what other mayhem they may cause at his exclusive establishment.

'Window seat please,' piped up Gina. Zara breathed a sigh of relief, only too aware of the other diners gawping at them. She was now anxious to sit down and blend in. The window would be nice and discreet.

The head waiter snapped his fingers to beckon one of the more junior waiters to show the girls to their table.

'Marcus will be your waiter tonight, anything you may need, he will provide for you.'

'Yeah, I bet he will,' Gina smirked.

'Shhh! He'll hear you.'

Zara had to agree, trendy establishments normally employed trendy waiters. A typical stereotype: tall, dark with the cutest derriere to be found. Vital statistics were to fit and look impeccable in dark trousers, creased to perfection, slightly tanned to offset the snow white shirts provided as uniform, and without doubt look good in a pinny. Quite a tricky achievement but Marcus fitted the bill perfectly.

Weaving in and out of the tables with a fling of his hips, Marcus led the girls towards their window seat; the perfect position with captivating views out over Edinburgh city. Once seated he gently laid the stiffly starched napkins upon Zara's and Gina's laps.

'If you require anything ladies just beckon me to you. I will return for your order shortly. Will you be drinking tonight? I can highly recommend the Australian white if you desire a light vintage with your dinner.'

'Yes that would be nice thank you.' Zara tried hard to pull her gaze away. Not to seem too obvious she was gawping. Both girls watched the retreating Marcus until he disappeared out of sight.

'Not bad, two in one day. Things are looking up, I think we could be requesting a few things tonight,' Gina chuckled. 'No wonder there's never any decent looking men around on a Friday or Saturday night, they're all working as waiters, only released into the wild after midnight. Why all the gorgeous ones have to do a job like this to make money, I'll never understand. They could be models or gigolos and earn bucket loads more.'

Both girls creased up with mirth before Zara composed herself and kicked Gina under the table to conform, after noticing a few stares aimed in their direction again from fellow diners.

'By the way, you were going to tell me what was in the bag for Sarah. What sort of job have you both got then?'

'You may laugh, but she's just taken on a part-time business held at people's homes. Party plan type of thing. I got talked into helping her and now have a few consultants as well, that I have to deliver stock to. It's easy, brings in some cash and I can fit it in after college or weekends if I need to.'

'Sounds ok, what exactly are you all selling?'

'Ummm! It's kind of difficult to explain. Sarah has to keep it discreet, particularly as she can't let her parents know. They're quiet, respectable and old fashioned type of folk. I collect the stock. All deliveries go to my flat. I then sort out the orders for her and get a slight cut of the profit. Sarah does most of the parties as she has more time than I do, easy really.'

Intrigued Zara leaned in closer. 'What exactly is she selling then?'

'Sex toys, you know whips, willies that sort of stuff.'

Zara nearly choked on her bread roll just as Marcus appeared with their wine.

'Are you ok madam? He asked pouring a glass of water for her. If she wasn't mistaken a slight smirk had appeared at the corner of his mouth. She prayed he hadn't heard Gina's last comment.

Once she had composed herself they ordered with the help of Marcus. Although fully coherent in basic French, some of the unusual dishes hadn't been covered with GCSE examinations. Steak and chips was the highest standard of food Zara could recall.

As the retreating derriere of Marcus sashayed into the kitchens, Zara hissed as quietly as she could.

'You're telling me you've been carrying a bag of dildos around? What if anyone had opened it? They would think we were hookers trading our wares at the hotel.'

'High class hookers, it is five star.'

'Not even high class hookers have chocolate willies in their attire,' coughed Zara, 'Say there was a security alert and bags were to be searched? I think I'd die of embarrassment.'

'Calm down, that won't happen. Anyway you've got to laugh! Think of poor Sarah's job with demonstrating half the contents, that's what I call embarrassing.'

'True, I hadn't thought of that. She's pretty brazen that's all I can say.'

Zara calmed down with a few copious servings of wine that Gina plied her with, along with a little wicked eye contact they both gave Marcus. By the end of their meal the issue of the bag had been forgotten and the girls left for home, slightly worse for wear by now as the drink started to take effect.

Outside the air was misty and cool, bringing the girls slowly back to their senses after the heady wine they had consumed.

'Taxi madam,' piped the doorman.

'Yes please, I'm not lugging this one bit further tonight. The lift incident was enough. No way am I trudging up Princes Street with it.'

'Good, as on a Saturday night carrying that merchandise I would be way too uncomfortable,' volunteered Zara.

As they waited patiently for their cab to be summoned the girls made small talk with the concierge. Having visited a few times before they were now on first name terms.

'Don't you ever get bored doing this job? It must be hell in the winter,' enquired Gina shivering a little in the light breeze.

'No, it's great for meeting some really interesting characters. Never a dull moment I can tell you. Besides when could I chat to two gorgeous girls on a Saturday night without even trying? I've had a fair few telephone numbers pressed in my hand.'

'Yeah, I bet you have,' replied Gina.

As they chatted, both girls were not concentrating fully. Suddenly out of nowhere Zara was pushed aside by a young man, barging straight into Gina, grabbing her arm and bag with one defiant movement. The suddenness and speed nearly pulled her with him halfway along the pavement. Her foot twisted badly as she stumbled sideways, the stiletto heel piercing the copper grating at the foot of the hotel stairs. Losing her balance she fell awkwardly backwards losing her grasp on the heavy cumbersome bag.

'Oww! My foot,' Gina shouted out indignantly, strong by any young girls' standards, but no match for the speed of the assault. Slightly winded, a sharp pain was searing through her ankle from having her foot at such a precarious angle.

'You ok? Did you have much in your handbag?' Then reality hit home as she saw beneath Gina's arm her neat imitation Gucci bag.

'Oh crickey, he didn't take your handbag, he took the ruddy big one didn't he? I said it looked as if you had some serious stuff in it.'

Gina looked stunned for a few moments not comprehending what had happened. 'Damn; I'll have to report it stolen for Sarah's sake. I'm pretty certain she isn't insured for any loss of stock. It will cost a fortune for her and me. I'd run after the sod if I could, but my ankle is killing.'

The concierge summoned the police immediately; alarmed he hadn't had his eye on the job fully. The intimate details of the contents had to be declared in the statement, much to Gina's disgust at having to divulge this information to the two officers on duty. The girls squirmed in their seats back at the private room they had been ushered into.

'I can't believe we get into such situations. I've never been so mortified in my life. There I am thinking it couldn't get much worse,' whispered Zara discreetly behind her hand.

'Don't rub it in. I'm worried about what Sarah's going to say,' Gina looked somewhat perturbed at this stage.

Once all statements were finished, with much banter from the two constables, whereby the girls had excelled in making Friday night a whole lot more interesting than the usual bar brawl they were normally called out to, they finally allowed the girls to return home with one departing statement. 'Just to reassure you girls, we will endeavour to look out for any unsavoury selling of the said items at local markets. But you might like to look on the bright side ladies; you've probably put a smile on the face of half the women in Edinburgh by morning.'

'They do have a point,' grinned Gina perking up a little, 'There was some wicked stuff in that bag, fancied trying some of it myself.'

'Gina, pack it in!' squealed Zara as she escorted her briskly into the taxi sent for them before any other incidents could take place.

Chapter 5

CHANCE ENCOUNTERS

Dappled shadows danced across the ceiling, twirling and shimmering gently in the early morning sunlight. The gentle hum of the city's traffic drifted in and out of Zara's ears. Rolling over she glanced at the clock, pretty certain it was sadly time to emerge from her comfortable bed. She scanned Gina's bed to see if she was still asleep. Gina had very generously offered Zara her own divan while she slept on what resembled a rather rickety camp bed.

The space was bare. All that resembled Gina was an empty cocoon of a sleeping bag. A faint whiff of coffee permeated Zara's nostrils as she leapt out of bed, leading her to emerge groggily from the bedroom.

'Hi sleepyhead, it's about eleven. I think we might have to go out for brunch. I haven't got much here,' sighed Gina.

'Sounds fine to me, couldn't you sleep? I thought it would be me having to drag you out of slumber.'

'No, I had to speak to Sarah and tell her the bad news. It was on my mind most of the night. It's done now, can't change the situation.'

Slowly Zara's brain chugged into gear as the streaming coffee brought her back to reality and the past twenty four hours sprang into mind.

'I forgot the nightmarish escapades of last night; it's a new day it can only get better. I'll take a shower and we can hit the streets.'

'Ok, deal, but I need this coffee first to steady my nerves.' Gina sank down amongst the scattered garments strewn across her settee, resembling a tiny pixie that was ready to be engulfed.

The petite cafe Gina had brought Zara to was already bustling with early shoppers and a few extremely frustrated kiddies. The harassed mothers were clearly attempting to provide a quick fix for their offspring, before they were dragged into the melee of the Saturday High Street again.

Sitting in a tiny alcove, they decided to watch the world go by and avoid the turmoil of the kiddie brigade. They ordered the biggest fry up on the list. Conversation became stilted until the meal had been devoured. Leaning back in her chair a look of contentment crept across Zara's face.

'It seems strange, you stuff yourself with a massive meal prior to bedtime and still wake up ravenous. You'd think you could last until midday at least.'

'You may not have noticed, but it's gone midday already,' laughed Gina.

'Clearly I need this more than I thought.'

'By the way, we haven't had time to catch up on your old private life, how's the relationship front going with you know who?' enquired a very inquisitive Gina.

'Not exactly sure, it's kind of awkward. I hardly see him really. I think it's more a physical thing on his part. I'm seeking a whole lot more though. Being laid back and not caring isn't exactly working either.' Zara wasn't keen to talk in-depth about the subject and swiftly changed topics. But Gina remained undeterred.

'When you do meet, does it go well? Is there any spark? Or does it just not feel right? Reason I'm asking is how do you know he's the one, your soul mate? There are so many people you meet in a lifetime. When do you know who is the right one to welcome with open arms?'

'Bit deep for you Gina. I thought you were of the type anybody should be given a chance and your life path is up to you. Make your own mistakes and you've got to take the responsibility for the idiot you've chosen.'

'Yes, I can vaguely remember my profound thoughts at the time. People can change their opinion of course. The girls I share with were having one of those diverse conversations last night. The subject of how things just flow in some relationships, but not in others. Some become a bloody battle even if you appear compatible. Others you gel with and feel you've known them all your life, but you might be different as chalk to cheese. Understand what I'm saying?'

'You are funny, never known you to get drawn into a conversation like that. But yes that could be the case with me. Whenever I attempt to see Tyler I always have a hell of a time arranging it. If I'm going to get a delay, problem or cancellation it's always with him. Being in limbo before the date has become pretty frustrating. By the time we do get there I'm so exhausted with the stress of imminent disappointment, I can't relax and enjoy the moment. Let alone be the highly sexed female he desires. Does make you wonder why I was given the chance to meet him in the first place. Maybe it's a test, a learning curve or something. Why else would people come careering into your life?'

'Look at it this way, what is Tyler teaching you about yourself?'

'Not to fall for drop dead gorgeous guys who love themselves more than me, and can't see further than their own satisfaction,' Zara replied rather sarcastically.

'Could be a tricky one, this? I'm noticing a slight despondency here. If it isn't working maybe it's not the right time. Why flog a dead horse as they say. More fish in the sea.'

'Very enlightening, I'll think on your words of wisdom when I'm crying into my Cornflakes when he dumps me. Let's not dwell on him and set a plan of action as far as this weekend goes. It's time I had some fun.'

'Ok, after this I've got to show you Underbelly. They're the latest talent to come out of this city and playing in the park later; it's just a promo gig for them to get known more. I know the drummer, he's in my year, so have to show some support; you'll adore them.'

'Who thought up a name like that? Zara scoffed.

'I have no idea, but definitely hot material; you wait until you hear them. I can guarantee they'll be a major distraction.'

The park below the battlements was vast. Spring sunshine permeated through the trees that were now in

71

full blossom, an explosion of pinks and whites spread out mimicking candy floss from afar. All set against the dark craggy rock wall leading up to the fortress above.

Set in the centre was a large stage surrounded by permanent seating. Already a small group of girls were milling around the front of the stage, anxious to get a prime position. At the rear sat a few elderly couples, uncertain what might be going on but happy to grab a free sit down.

'Crikey if we were home my way, you wouldn't get that on Brighton Pavilion,' Zara declared, 'normally get charged if you lean against a lamppost to do your shoelace up. Let alone sit down and enjoy a free concert in the open.'

'Bit mean spirited your local council. They may say the Scots are tight arsed but I haven't found them miserly since I've been up here. Come on let's grab a seat before the old dears take them all. They're going to be on in a minute.' Gina sprung into an Olympic sprint.

Within seconds of getting seated the band started to emerge on stage. A scruffy looking lad tested the microphone creating an ear piercing screech attracting a few more to take their seat rapidly.

'I hope they sound better than that.' Zara yelled covering her ears tightly.

'Be patient, you'll enjoy them, got to get warmed up yet.' Gina started clapping, nudging Zara to do the same. The acoustics improved as the style of music softened and became easier on the ear. A few haunting melodies were neatly sandwiched between the heavy Indie Rock the band seemed to prefer.

'I take it all back, not bad. I might be tempted to grab a CD at the end,' declared Zara.

'You old groupie,' Gina shouted as they joined the giggling mass of young students to get a closer position to the stage.

After the dying notes wavered on the air the girls left to wander back through the old part of the city, enjoying the spring sunshine, dropping in and out of a few quirky shops that Edinburgh had to offer. Haggis, whisky and every tartan under the sun, it had become a tourist's Mecca. Impeccable taste could be found if you had a local to guide you. Gina knew exactly where to go to avoid the souvenir tack sold in the main commercial streets. After a leisurely amble the girls approached the more upmarket part of town.

'Come on; let's see if we can grab a spring bargain in Harvey Nicks?'

'I doubt it, but what the heck we can have a look. My grant might not stretch that far but I can dream,' said Gina looking wistfully at the displays as they entered the main hall. Within minutes Zara had grabbed an armful of clothes, dragging poor Gina towards the changing rooms literally unable to see ahead as she grabbed more and more items as she staggered past the rails.

In the next hour the girls trawled the store for the most ludicrous of styles, costing an entire mortgage payment, to some sexy, hot numbers that left little to the imagination. Both beyond the girls' reach, even on Zara's wages.

'Come on, there has to be a bargain basement section; we can't leave with no items. I'll be wistfully daydreaming all week about what I can't have.' Gina looked dreamily at one of the sheer numbers clinging to the mannequin. 'That would look hot but flippin seventy quid for some lace is extortionate.'

'Yes, and you might need some hot underwear under that, you're no Kate Middleton you know.'

'Ha, ha thanks for the compliment.'

'Ok, let's be practical, next floor down, maybe, just maybe a cheaper range might exist. They do fusion ranges now for the poor amongst us,' scoffed Zara clearly trying to be positive.

Finally with some success they clasped their very rare budget purchases and headed to the tills. The haughty sales assistant stared at the items, clearly restraining a look of disdain at the clothing chosen. Zara distracted Gina, knowing full well if she'd noticed the woman's look; a full blown sarcastic comment would have left her lips.

'At least we've got something new to dazzle the Edinburgh crowd,' Zara squealed delighted with their purchases, however frugal.

'Yeah, but it won't wash with the Uni crowd. They're into pretty casual attire. But later we'll be partying high end style.'

~ ~ ~

Greg's party was an eye opener for Zara. Any soiree she was privy to be invited usually consisted of a couple's house gathering, boring most of the time, improving the more alcohol consumed. This party was going like no other and the time was barely seven.

Music was pumping from the rafters. Greg's pad was a little rough round the edges but he sure knew how to accommodate his guests.

Stone steps led up to a rather imposing black door with a brass knocker. The huge bay window adorned with a scantily clad young girl, who happened to have no fear of leaning out in a precarious fashion. At the precise moment they arrived she let out her own loud rendition of Queen's 'We will rock you,' finally deciding to yell obscenities at two passers-by as an afterthought.

Remembering what Gina had said previously that dressing up was not on the Uni crowd's first thoughts when partying, she could see why now. As they tried shuffling down the corridor Greg came bounding through, elbowing any stray party animal out of the way. Tall and lanky he stood towering above them, a broad smile across his features.

'Hi Ginny, and whose the lovely friend? I heard you were up visiting from the south, what gorgeous part of the region might that be? I'll put it on my list to visit,' Greg's eyes darted over Zara quickly, clearly taking in every detail of her in a split second.

'You can forget Zara; she's not interested in poor sexual beings like you. So don't think you can get your filthy mitts on her,' retorted Gina.

'Oh, come on now. Anyone who's a friend of yours cannot possibly be unaffected by my charming and I have to admit it myself, devastating good looks.' At this point in the conversation Zara winked with approval. Obviously a player by nature but charming, he looked

75

fun. His openness was endearing, no hidden agendas. It was refreshing.

Grinning, she took his hand to be led into the hub of the party. Tequila slammers were already being devoured at a fast pace. Zara was introduced to all and sundry by Greg. A fair few females hung on to him every step of the way, throughout their tour of his house.

'You seem a little god-like to all these fancy free females. How come you're so popular? You have these parties often?' Greg glanced sideways at her.

'Why of course, easiest way to get laid. Provide a few freebie drinks get the freshman students tipsy and they're all over you.'

'Surely the older students don't get so easily led second year round?'

'Sure they do, like to compete with the new ones, prove they've got it in them to party still. Normally get drunk quicker and then it's rich pickings.'

'Now you're sounding sad, I'm not impressed. I've obviously got you all wrong.' Zara gave him a disappointed look, pouting her bottom lip out.

'You think, but you know I'd have seduced you too. Look you're hanging on my every word.'

'No I'm not!' Zara whacked him in defence.

'You are and you know it.'

Extracting herself from Greg's company before she gave him more kudos for pulling her, Zara felt the need to wander and explore a little. The students she surveyed seemed to vary in personality. She was feeling a little envious that they had the whole world in front of them. New careers, businesses; she wondered who might be the next big talent. Though, some had a little way to journey by the looks of it. Maybe all that essay writing and revision might be a bit of a drag to return to.

By nine the real party animals had come out to play. A few worse for wear individuals were now dancing on the kitchen table. Luckily no stilettos were being worn. Zara had to refrain from joining them, just her luck to wear the wrong choice of foot attire, a major prevention in going wild. If she took them off the constant throbbing pain of replacing them would render her feet helpless for the rest of the night. They had to stay suctioned to her feet at all times. Probably a good thing, as shaming herself in unknown company may not be an ideal scenario.

Leaving the dancing companions behind, Zara wandered into the lounge to be taken by surprise by Greg who appeared from nowhere by her side.

'We meet again. Knew you couldn't stay away. Having a good time? It's nice to see a new face as I've got to know most intimately by now. Tell me a bit about yourself. I'm not going to get much from Gina - bit too over protective of you. What's your line of work? You are no way a student, not fresh faced enough,' asked Greg with a glint of mischief in his eyes.

'Thanks, you're saying I look past my sell by date to be here?' She wasn't sure if he was serious or just teasing.

'No, not at all, in fact you're pretty gorgeous. Quite intriguing, look as if you've seen a bit of the world, unlike some of these creatures I hang out with.'

'Well I probably have. Shame my world weary face is showing so much. I'm a sports physio. At the moment I work freelance at a clinic. Fingers crossed I should be working with some semi-professional sports clubs. Can't say it isn't hard work to prove your worth. It's a competition even if you get recommended, but I love the job so I'm prepared to give it a go.'

'Wow, I thought you had your head screwed on. Can't say I'm in the same league yet, got to obtain some vital bits of paper first.' Greg led her to the centre of the lounge, guiding her into the fray to dance. Greg's style of dancing was way too wild for Zara. Soon she was regretting the high heels and contemplating going freestyle and flatfooted whether she could walk again later or not. By ten o'clock the party was heaving and Gina, having extracted Zara from the praying mantis of Greg, suggested they head off to their main destination the Missouri Club.

~ ~ ~

The evening air cooled their warm, clammy skin as they tottered down the street to hail a taxi.

'Did you like the Uni crowd? They're great fun. End of term parties can be mega wild. You've got to come up summer season.'

'I'll put it in the diary straight away. Greg was nice, I liked him.' Zara looked sideways at Gina to check her response. It was very quick and very derogatory.

'No way, don't you be led up the garden path by him. He's terrible with the opposite sex. Fun I grant you, but don't even go there for getting attached.'

'I knew you would say that. I'm only winding you up,' chuckled Zara. Gina screwed her face up with disdain again as she hailed the nearest taxi they could see.

'Just take it from me, stay well clear.'

The Missouri Club lay at the top of the city. No garish entrance but just a discreet wall plaque situated above the main ornate door frame. The street lay off the main thoroughfare and would have been unnoticed unless the person was aware to investigate the side road. Missouri was a venue for indiscretions for many a select client. Elite and private, this members' only club was for a few in the know or who happened to be from privileged circumstances.

Standing guard like a stone statue was a very imposing gentleman. Dressed immaculately he clutched the usual clipboard, alongside a fair haired younger woman; she too was impeccably dressed, greeting and chatting to each client as they entered through the main entrance.

Zara pulled Gina back after stepping from the taxi, unsure if they would be allowed in looking at the ominous list of names.

'I didn't know it might be guest list only. How the hell are we to get in here?'

'Relax; I know how to pull a few strings. I may just be a student for now, but I do know a few people who actually work for a living in the real world.'

'Well I hardly think that Sarah's job of sex toy retailing will give us kudos to get in a select branch like this.'

'No, I didn't use Sarah as a recommendation. I used my brother; he's got some good connections via his legal work so I gave him my little sister pout to pull a few strings, works every time.'

'Gina, you devil.'

A mention of names and they were in. The club filled up fast as the girls weaved their way in and out of the throng of dancing clubbers. The air was hot and smoky from the dry ice that seemed to drift like wisps of lace. It twirled above the dancers mimicking their every movement.

Corridors led into small intimate lounges, eventually opening out to the main dance arena. As they entered one of the bar areas the scene was quieter and cooler. Seats set back in tiny alcoves decorated with delicately carved dividers. Dragons and serpents graced the many surfaces carved into the walls, adorning chairs and table legs, reminiscent of a Japanese temple.

Upon the low lying tables, small dishes could be ordered as you sat upon oversized silk cushions. Background lighting was produced from ornate bronze lanterns. Their candlelight glowed through a fine meshwork, softly enhancing the ambiance of the bar, producing shadows to twist and dance across the walls. The effect was if the serpents were alive, weaving and twisting in some kind of oriental fire dance. Combined with the pulsating beat it hypnotised the girls seductively as they sipped the most delicious cocktails that had touched their lips.

'This is great, a little more chilled than Greg's soiree. Shall we go for an exploration? It's meant to be on three floors. I'm bound to get lost so keep sight of me,' lisped Gina who was now slightly tipsy after her cocktail had been guzzled down way too quickly.

Leaving the quiet oasis of the bar, the main corridor was heaving as members moved from room to room. Gina yelled out after spotting a fellow colleague.

'Peter, over here! What are you doing in a place like this? Not the kind of venue I thought I'd bump into you. How's it going?' It was aimed at a rather heavily built guy, who certainly knew how to look after himself. In fact as Zara scrutinised him she felt rather unsure of the lad all together. But as Gina seemed to be on first name terms with him she assumed he might be ok. She wondered what he had paid or done to get entry into this exclusive venue.

Standing awkwardly between them and Peter's friend, Zara felt rather uncomfortable. Hating long silences she knew she had no choice but to make stilted conversation with the stranger, as Gina was by now in animated chat, oblivious that they were standing in the corridor blocking the way of every clubber. The jostling was now every second.

'Hi, do you know Gina as well?' Immediately Zara cringed, blushing at the cliché sentence she had spouted. She could have thought of something a bit more original. Her mind crashed backwards and forth for some trivial anecdote to blurt out.

'I'm afraid not. Your mate's right, it's not the kind of place we would normally frequent. More a spittle and sawdust kind of bar you'll find me in. I like the traditional Scottish bars myself. You're not from round here though, that accent is definitely not from this neck of the woods?'

Zara was acutely aware of the young lad's gaze now it was fixated on her. His eyes framed by long, thick lashes. As he smiled, his eyes disappeared behind them as they crinkled up with genuine happiness. Scanning his face quickly she took in how boyish it was, not tanned but the most gentle and soft trace of fine freckles graced the bridge of his nose. This tended to make him seem younger than ever. His face was framed by a tousled mat of dark wavy hair. Not long enough to be unruly but if left to its own devices it would be a wild mass of tight curls.

He leaned in closer, gazing down towards her. Zara was aware of the height difference and regretted her rather low cut outfit. Not normally concerned with leering males, she had become well practised at ignoring this less attractive feature of the male race. But this time she felt a little on show. Not victimised, but strangely embarrassed for his sake that she was so provocatively dressed. Certainly she didn't want him to get the wrong conclusion about her. Although the scantily clad females that glided past, made her pretty well respectable in comparison.

Conversation was constantly interrupted by the pushing and shoving, until Gina finally focused on the pair of them again. The lad suggested they move out of the way of the corridor to somewhere quieter.

'We're just going for a drink in the next room. Do you want to join us? He looked directly at Zara, hinting strongly that he wanted the answer to be a yes. His eyes were friendly and welcoming, not indicating he was going to seduce, this being the agenda on most of the male fraternity's mindset in a club like this.

'Great idea, come on Zara I've got loads to tell Pete.' Gina walked arm in arm with her new found companion towards the next intriguing room before Zara could utter any protest. Having no choice, she followed the pair and his friend into the adjoining bar.

'Here let me get you a drink. What do you fancy?' enquired the lad.

'I've had rather a few by now, just a soft one thanks. By the way what's your name? Seeing as we've got to get to know each other,' asked Zara politely, trying to sound casual. She didn't want the guy to think she was coming on to him.

'It's rather weird, you might not have heard it before, it's Brett; bit American I know but my grandparents used to live out in California before they had my mum. She was born out there and must have picked up some of the trends and kept them, before she moved back up to bonny Scotland. Why they came back to cold and rain from the hot shores of the USA I'll never know. Just think I could be surfing the golden coast rather than the freezing north east sea, funny how your life can turn out with just a twist of fate.'

Zara stifled a grin. What with Gina and this guy talking karma, she wondered what the next conversation was going to be. They sat chatting fairly easily. It was nice, no strings attached and strangely no uneasiness at all.

As the evening wore on Zara was aware that Brett was starting to get closer and slightly more intimate; was he going to kiss her? She wasn't too concerned for her personal space like some people, if she warmed to them, sadly others if you tended to get anywhere within three feet of them would be backing off or getting twitchy. Always a slight problem when body contact was required with Zara's job. What she was acutely aware of was she felt no attraction to him at all. Cute and not exactly unappealing, but on no accounts the kind of guy that would make her take notice of him in the street. But his close presence was creating a strange underlying chemistry to kick in; a strong sensation of sexual yearning was rearing its ugly head. It was a weird situation to be experiencing. Normally if no visual attraction Zara would be shifting uncomfortably away from someone if they got too close for comfort. Now she actually desired his contact.

'So who's the lucky lad in your life?' probed Brett, inquisitively looking as if he was trying to read her mind correctly before she even replied. How should she answer? Even Zara wasn't sure if she really 'had a lad' as he put it in her life. Tyler was clearly a casual affair.

'I'm not sure how to answer that.'

'Oh, are we being underhand and playing the field and keeping more than one option open?'

'No, no nothing like that, it's just complicated.'

'Umm, tell me more, I like complications, makes life a little more exciting don't you think?' Brett moved in even closer, encouraging her to open up a little. Zara could now feel his breath as he spoke sending a shiver up her spine as it grazed her neck.

The pair became locked in conversation for some time until Brett decided to apply some flattery to the situation. In the hope she would open up a little more.

'I don't believe he deserves you, must be mad to string a pretty girl like you along.'

'Flattery will get you everywhere but my feet are killing me. Can we sit down for a while?' By now they'd been standing for some time and killer heels were not designed for her fragile feet to withstand for too long a period. The previous dancing at Greg's had nearly finished them off.

The only place vacant was a tiny alcove, barely room for one, but before Zara could object, Brett slipped in beside her. It was a tight squeeze but the relief just to take the pressure off her feet was bliss.

Rapidly Brett edged closer to kiss her. She felt at this stage reluctant, unfaithful but also mildly inquisitive. She was obsessed with Tyler, looks wise, and boy did she remember how sexy he was. Commitment was not one thing he probably considered, so why should she? Tyler's presence made her feel nervous. Many times she had wondered why he gave her the time of day, let alone took her to bed. Not normally of low self-esteem, he brought out the worst in her. With Brett there appeared to be no problem. He moved in closer as she predicted, his lips brushing against hers softly and hesitantly, teasing her for a response. Within moments Zara did respond, her control and will power seemed to have vanished. Brett kissed her more seductively.

At first Zara felt nothing, it felt unreal and strange kissing a complete stranger who she assumed she had no desire for. Comparing it with Tyler's kiss it was definitely different. The seconds passed developing to more than just a quick dalliance with tongues. Zara felt a need and desire for the kiss to feel good, a welcoming distraction from her obsession with Tyler. It might just release the clutch he had over her. His nonchalance and non-committal attitude was now driving her insane.

Slowly the knot of sadness dissipated and a new sensation swept through her body. Brett's tongue probed deeper into her mouth. His fingertips ran slowly up her back, causing a spine jarring sensation to ripple down her body. Her mind drifted from her surroundings and she started to enjoy the kiss a lot, in fact too much. Zara couldn't believe it - Brett was actually stimulating her deeper internally than anything Tyler had achieved. It seemed when in his presence her nervousness and awe of him, seemed to cut her body in half, with no connection to the parts that needed it. Maybe she should do what the adverts say and drink some Guinness. What did they say? It reached parts that the other beers couldn't. This put a smile on her face and Brett allowed her to come up for air.

'Wasn't so bad, was it?' he beamed, sensing her uncertainty at the situation.

'No it was rather nice actually,' sighed Zara.

'Nice, is that all, I better try a bit more if I've only scored a rating of nice.'

'I didn't mean to offend you, in fact it really turned me on,' blurted out Zara. As soon as the words had come out, she regretted it. Whoops bit too much information for a first kiss. Brett grinned from ear to ear.

'Did it? Well you know how to make a guy feel proud.'

He leant forward to continue the good work. By this time, Gina had spied where Zara was. Looking up rather sheepishly Zara was still feeling the after effects of the kiss. Feeling even more embarrassed that her best friend was checking up on her.

'What's been happening over here? I can't leave you alone for one minute without you seducing young men.'

'Not so young thank you. You're not that young are you?' enquired Zara, a look of horror on her face, alarmed at the consequences and her seduction so quickly.

'Depends what you consider young. I'm twenty two. I think I can say I've passed my teens and able to drink legally,' laughed Brett. Zara gulped. Here she was a ripe age of thirty two and pulling a guy nearly ten years her junior.

'Sorry to break up the party but we've got to get a taxi, as I'm slightly past it now and don't fancy walking back to my pad,' Gina proclaimed as she staggered sideways, leaning rather heavily on Brett's friend.

'Don't worry we'll help you back. It would be courteous to do so after meeting such gorgeous ladies.' Brett focused his gaze on Zara.

'Very charming, what are you hoping for?' chuckled Gina giving a wicked grin. Zara glared at her friend. A compromising position was going to happen if she wasn't careful. Gina wouldn't notice a thing in her state.

The lads guided the girls through the crowded club. It was jam packed and soon all and sundry would be streaming out onto the streets for the homeward journey.

The night sky was clear and the air crisp, causing their breath to emerge in wisps of foggy smoke. Edinburgh was truly a sight to see, with its twinkling lights beaming out like lanterns from the tall austere buildings that towered above them. Brett grabbed Zara's hand and hung back from the other two.

'Don't suppose you fancy a nightcap at my place? Got some mega pricey cocoa to try.'

'Isn't that what old ladies would have after the bingo? Are you implying that I'm too mature for coffee after a night on the tiles?'

'No, the complete opposite but I didn't want to push my luck seeing I've just met you. Honest I'm not like all the rest, really!' Zara could see he was trying hard to be genuine. She mellowed slightly towards him but was determined not to be persuaded, even with a girl's best friend of a mega chocolate fix. Besides she probably wouldn't see him again. How many times did she get to see Gina? Not many a year. No, it was just a nice evening. Best leave things as they were.

Deep down it had unfortunately set off a chain of reactions that Zara was feeling a little uncomfortable with. Looking back at Brett, she found her stomach churning with a touch of excitement and pride she could attract such a young guy. Maybe she was selling herself short with Tyler.

Before long her mature principles came storming out when Gina ahead of them decided very elegantly to semi-pass out on the shoulder of Peter. Zara stepped in and supported her friend.

'I think I better get her home pronto,' secretly a little relieved that she had an excuse to politely decline the offer of the warm beverage.

'Looking at the state of your friend, I better get a cab for you both. Shame though, thought I might succeed in the persuasion tactics.' Squeezing her waist he gave her a peck on the cheek and proceeded to simultaneously hail a taxi, open the door and scoop up the inebriated Gina and laying her down in the back of the taxi with such speed Zara didn't have time to even think of getting his number. The taxi trundled off leaving a lonely and somewhat frustrated Brett staring after the receding vehicle.

Chapter 6

TOUR DE FORCE

The clock ticked slowly round towards 9am. A fan whirled frantically moving the already hot and humid air in a gentle ripple over Zara, as she sat at her desk trying hard to catch up on her workload. The break up north had done her the power of good and she felt stronger, ready to put the world to rights: well maybe her first customer, which wasn't an easy task. The woman was the most taxing of clients Zara had on her list. Ms Lintel loved herself to bits. Generally, she wanted whoever happened to be her chosen therapist to be at her total beck and call. On many an occasion, Zara had to act as her PA answering a mobile whilst in treatment time or requested for a home visit, which was strictly only for the infirm. Ms Lintel somehow, and to this day Zara didn't know how she managed to do it, was able to twist Zara's manager, the chief physiotherapist of the practice, around her elegant and richly attired little finger.

Money obviously talked in Roger's case. Zara never had that effect over him; he was fair but could at times be somewhat difficult to work for. Loving the power he had over his workforce, Roger's traits over organising, stubbornness and being the biggest perfectionist around were dominant in the handling of his staff. His constant note taking and policies drove Zara insane at times. Nonetheless she had learnt a lot and he did have some great contacts in the sporting arena.

Ms Lintel was not one of them; the most exercise she probably performed was shagging the plumber or whatever handy man had graced her presence. Cost had never been an issue. If it involved spending, Ms Lintel would be top of the list for indulgence.

Secretly Zara was sure Roger thought that in time, he might be a conquest. It was a vision Zara didn't want to picture. Why he chose to be manipulated by the woman when more important customers needed to be focused on was a problem at times.

Her mind returned to the job when the sudden vibration of her mobile caused it to leap across the desk violently. Grabbing it quickly before Roger's head could appear around the door, Zara glanced at the caller ID. Not one to receive many texts, she still enjoyed the intrusion when one came through. Her heart leapt as she saw the name light up; it was Tyler. Zara's face didn't remain so excited once the short but sweet message had been read: 'Hi, not sure if this is going anywhere for me so going to call it a day.'

Zara sat stunned, suddenly winded by the surprise and harshness of the message. That was it. No 'sorry to break your heart' or 'thanks for the sex.' Nothing; she'd been dumped by text - the ultimate get out of jail card for a coward. He might have played a gentlemanly sport but his manners were zero in her view.

Furious as well as bitterly disappointed, she could only assume the spark clearly hadn't been there for him. Feeling like a teenager every time they met, her nerves had got the better of her on a few occasions. The unequal balance of being a little out of her league in his company and the uncomfortable sensation of feeling privileged to be in his presence, didn't exactly bode well for a mutual relationship. The sex hadn't been that bad though, had it? Not on her part. She'd worked hard to please him in every way, but his attention span had obviously wandered to some other female company. The pressure to keep a guy like that into you was maybe not worth the hassle involved.

That was the trouble with highly charged sportsmen, too much adrenaline in their veins. Testosterone shooting all round them. They couldn't be happy with one woman; they had to prove themselves, for their own ego, to hundreds.

Well she was just gonna have to get over him. It would be hard; he had become not dissimilar to a slight drug addiction. The high was pretty dramatic when she saw him, followed by angst and a drop in mood afterwards. This probably outweighed the good parts. But the high normally made up for it. Tyler had certainly used her for a few female charms and that was about all it probably boiled down to.

Letting out a deep regrettable sigh, she deleted the message and stared out of the window. Shaking slightly, she grabbed the hot coffee next to her. She tried hard to savour the flavour and allow the caffeine hit to penetrate her foggy brain and the bemusement of what had just happened. Holding back the tears of emotion that were now starting to kick in, Zara tried hard to concentrate on the many files she had left to plough through. But her mind played games and drifted off; reliving the time Tyler came charging into her life, quite literally.

~ ~ ~

'Come on Zara, it will be fun. We're free, let's go and watch the game for a laugh.' Pinching her waist, Amber dragged Zara towards the main entrance gates of the impressive Cowdray Park estate.

'You're just a snob. We won't mix in at all. Besides what do you know about ruddy Polo for starters? When have you last sat on a horse for that matter?'

'When I was five years old actually, my rocking horse so there, I can say I know more than you,' retorted Amber. Laughing hysterically she dragged the reluctant Zara to purchase the tickets.

'We're a little under-dressed. I thought you're meant to dress up for these occasions?'

'No, half the country folk just wear jeans and wellingtons most of the time. We'll fit in easily.'

Zara mumbled under her breath. 'Maybe, but I bet they'll be designer ones, not your £10.99 wellies from Asda.'

The girls walked across to the main grassed area set up with amenities for the event and headed for the large bar. The weather was bordering on an early seventy degrees. The grass was lush and green still untouched by any heavy drying heat. Summer had suddenly arrived.

'Don't you think this is idyllic? I could get used to this. Touch of summer sunshine, gin and tonic on the rocks, and a superb country location. We better get acquainted with a few of the rules. I want to know who we should be cheering for,' gushed Amber as Zara stood confused scanning the rules and regulations from the official programme they had been given at the gate. Immediately Amber decided to order two ridiculously large drinks. Her excuse was it would help focus the mind. Clasping her drink, she scanned the set up and spied a nearby marquee, where the smell of fresh seared meat was wafting towards the girls' nostrils.

'I'm starving. Let's see if we can have some of their barbeque? Amber marched off in the direction of the burly minder, standing like a bulldozer on the marquee entrance. He looked meaner than some of the usual bouncers in town. Zara didn't fancy trying to slip past him uninvited.

'Amber, wait! I think it's for the players and relatives, not Joe Blogs like us.' But Amber was on a mission and nothing would come between her and her stomach. Zara wasn't sure how her friend achieved it, but she'd blagged their way into the VIP area within seconds.

'Now, I do feel I should have dressed for the occasion. I don't know what you do! But you seem to get away with it every time.'

'Confidence, sweetie. Any man, job or desire can be yours but you need to send out the right vibes,' Amber replied with a twinkle in her eye.

Mingling amongst the spectators and players, Zara's eye became drawn to one of the riders. Trying not to stare, she was aware of his confident and definitely cocky manner. He stood towering above the other players, six foot two in height - his persona clearly showcasing someone in complete control of his audience. Trying to put a stamp on what was so attractive about him was hard. His portrayal of complete arrogance on the surface strangely was not a negative, it enhanced his appeal greatly. His domination off the pitch with his peers and colleagues only drew the viewer in more; to want to break down his exterior to see what was underneath. What made this man tick? It wasn't a trait that was endearing to Zara but he was too charismatic to ignore. His raw sensual attraction seemed to be emitting to all and sundry. Discreetly she edged closer, guiding Amber to a vacant table nearby and conveniently eavesdropping to zone into some of the conversation. From what she could detect amongst the general background noise – which was muffling words - he seemed to be bragging of some stunt job he was required for. He didn't look famous or familiar but who knows. People do look different with a bit of lippy and a dusting of powder. Though this guy would set the camera alight without the need of any subtle lighting or gloss.

Before she was aware of what Amber was doing, her voyeuristic observation was rudely interrupted as Amber clocked the group of riders.

'Zara, honey I'm going to get you a little prestige work of your own. This is too good an opportunity to miss with your expertise. Wait here for a moment.'

'What? No wait don't.......' Her words hung in the air as Amber ignored her completely. Zara cringed sitting further back in her chair wishing it would swallow her up completely.

The one player Zara had been intrigued by looked over and for a moment seemed more than interested in what Amber was saying. Hesitating before replying he glanced over in Zara's direction. Running fingers through his hair, he seemed to be inspecting her from afar. Distraction interrupted their conversation when the tanoy system shrieked into life, requesting the players to mount shortly for the start of the match. Zara strained to hear what was being said. Lounging sideways slightly as if rummaging in her handbag, she just managed to pick up the conversation again.

'I've got to prepare for the match but maybe,' he paused again fixing Amber with a flirtatious grin, 'I'll catch you later. Interesting proposal, I like your style. When we've had a chance to crush the opposition, I'll talk further.' With this final comment he placed his helmet on, squashing the blond tousled locks that cascaded down around his face. He rotated his body to the right and then left, clearly loosening up, ready for the impending match.

Maybe she should consider watching a little more regularly; sure beats viewing a load of egotistical footballers on a Saturday afternoon. No wonder the aristocracy frequented the game,' thought Zara. It was all very reminiscent of Mr Darcy and Jane Austin. A little reminder maybe of when the class system really was separated. Smiling seductively in Zara's direction the player swaggered off towards the horse enclosure with his team following.

96

Zara sat fuming at Amber's antics, feeling now highly embarrassed at what she'd done; she shot over to join her, 'Amber, what possessed you to do that? He'll think I'm some sad fan who can't wait to get my hands on him.'

'No, we're in the connected marquee silly. Probably thinks you work for one of the other clubs. Blag; it's the only way in life, you never know where it might lead. Come on; let's see what he's made of.' Amber was clearly now getting into the swing of things and no protest from Zara would make a blind bit of difference.

Managing to grab two seats central to the pitch, Zara listened to the names as they were read out. Number three was Tyler Montgomery. In the programme a humorous pitch was presented below each player's photo, with their main role in the game. Zara sat staring at them disconcertingly.

'Quick, what does it say about him?' Amber grabbed the booklet from Zara, scanning the literature to clock Tyler's details.

'Thirty one, single, devilishly handsome, part-time stunt co-ordinator, keen show jumper, blah, blah, blah...not bad. He's obviously a bit of a daredevil and connected in the film world. No wonder he's cocky as hell. What do you think? Do you like him? He's about your age, toy boy by one year. He plays position three. Hey up, normally the play maker of the team. The one in charge well that befits him definitely. I noticed he liked to turn on the charm.'

'Yes he seems to fit that role perfectly and I appreciate you trying to be my personal romantic booking agent, but I'm sure I can manage without you doing the dirty work and fixing me up.' Zara snapped back. Sensing he was a somewhat dangerous proposition, she wasn't going to allow Amber to lead her into hot water however determined she was. 'Besides, I thought it was work you intended drumming up for me, not dangerous liaisons? Fraternising with clients is not how the job works. I'm not on some film set where the leading actress gets her knickers off for her co-star. I can get into a lot of trouble.'

'It was work and I think I've got it in the bag. But hey, with a hunk like that if he offers himself you can't say no.' Zara huffed a bit more but had to agree the temptation would be hard to say no to.

The match getting underway to the delight of the crowd distracted the girls' disagreement. The ringside seats provided close action viewing. Although the rules were hard to understand for a novice, they started to work out that a chukka was a section of play, crossing the line in front of the ball was the most frequent foul, (which Mr Montgomery's team seemed to prefer more often than not) and any fouls allowed a free penalty hit. This seemed to cause no upset to Tyler's players who all seemed to enjoy and relish the defence required on any free shots awarded, due to their underhand playing.

'Not very polite, his team, are they? Seem hell bent on annihilating their opponents,' said Zara as Amber stood rotating her arm above her head, booing one of the player's blatant tactics for retrieving the ball, nearly causing the rider to fall and lose his stick at the same time.

'Amber you can't boo his side even if he is well out of order; it doesn't bode well for winning a contract. It resembles a vicious hockey match on horseback; I can imagine the girls back at college playing this. They would definitely give them a run for their money. I can still feel the bruises from many a match inflicted on me just thinking about it.'

'Yeah, they were a mean lot that team who played against us. I think our Tyler likes a challenge. If he sees we aren't impressed and falling at his feet, he may well negotiate better with me. I have my ways Zara babe; I know what I'm doing. I think it's time to tread in the divots.'

'What?' exclaimed Zara, thinking her mate had gone mad.

'It's tradition. We walk over the pitch treading in the loose turf. Don't you watch anything posh on the telly?'

'Ha, ha, you obviously do. I think you've been spending too much time with the ladies that lunch. Or did you read it in the subsection which I haven't got to yet?'

Amber's husband was rather aristocratic but had a heart of gold. She had never needed to think about supporting herself in any way. Career wise though, Amber had an underlying talent for design and fashion which was sadly going to waste; Zara knew she could go far if she wanted to. Her nature hadn't changed much; she was still a true friend: clever, always there for support and great fun to be with, even if Zara cringed at her impetuous traits sometimes.

'Right, enough of sitting on our slowly drooping backsides, let's go and take a peek at the horses. Might have to take a few lessons, learn a few tricks of the trade. Do you fancy joining me if I do?' asked Amber.

'I'll think about it. My times on horses if you remember rightly when we did venture out on four legs, didn't always work out that well.'

'Oh yes, I remember. Skippy who wasn't so skippy when you wanted him to be. Or the incident of the ducking in the river, that really made my day.'

'Thanks, can't say mine was quite as enjoyable as yours, took me days to get the river cretins out of my hair after that dunking.'

As the girls approached, they could see the horses were beautiful specimens, elegant and proud. Each one dancing around restless for the game to begin, their tails bound high in braiding, coats as sleek as any smart limousine.

'How can you say you don't want to get back in the saddle? Those would be off as soon as you were on them. It must be so nice to feel the wind in your hair and be totally in control.'

'It probably takes years to gain control of one of those horses. The lovely nags we had down Turner's yard were nearly fit for the French meat market I think, knackered from carting fat Prudence or podgy Edward around the yard.'

'Yes, do you remember they always had that private school before we had our session? Right stuck up lot they were.'

The girls returned to their seats when the tannoy burst into life, sending the horses into a jittery dance at the sudden noise. Tyler's team were now way ahead in the scoring department. He clearly relished the adrenaline rush as his performance was outstanding. Pounding the turf, the skill of controlling the horse in whatever direction he needed was sheer magic to watch. His strong forearms guided the reins, body raised from the saddle as he swung his stick to hit with such power, the opposing side had to ride fast to get anywhere near the ball. Swerving around his opponents he claimed victory fairly quickly as the score rose steadily. They cheered the team on to the foregone conclusion of a staggering win.

'Phew, he's a hot mover. Nice style; now do you want me to pursue him more on your behalf? Don't say you don't want me to after seeing him in action. I know underneath you're dying for me to do more.'

'Ok, ok I'll let you, but I really don't think he'll be keen. He looks as if he practically owns the polo club; they probably wine, dine him and offer him anything he wants without him lifting a finger.'

'Poppy cock, he's just a mere mortal, pretty stunning mortal I must say but human and in need of a body session, way more than the normal guy that plays on this turf. You wait and see.' Zara knew now that Amber wasn't going to be shooed away this time. The look of determination on her face said it all.

The commentator requested the crowd to gather round the podium for the award ceremony to take place. Grabbing a couple of cool beers, they jostled to get a good position, slipping in amongst the dense crowd. Each team were duly presented with a smart jacket and the usual polite handshake to each team player. A few team photographs were taken to capture the moment and probably used in the official marketing merchandise. Until finally, the main attraction: the prize trophy and cheque presented to the winning team captain.

'No surprises of course, none other than the leading man, Tyler Montgomery,' said the President of the polo club. His name echoed out loudly amongst the throng.

'I think our little Tyler is obviously the local team's heartthrob, as support from this crowd is pretty impressive for one player. Look out, a femme fatale is about to seduce him,' commented Amber giving Zara a nudge playfully in the ribs.

A very leggy blonde approached Tyler, planting a slow kiss on his lips before offering him the cheque of £10,000 his team had just been privileged to win.

'Ten grand; worth getting out of bed on a Saturday afternoon, don't you think?' chuckled Amber.

'He probably wins that amount every game for the club. Probably seems like pocket money to him. Well that's that, we may as well go now,' Zara sighed glancing one more time at the player. He was very attractive on the eye. But his surroundings made her feel very uncomfortable. Amber seemed non-fazed and launched into her attack with zeal.

'Nonsense, the fun has only just begun. We've got the tiny matter of securing some work for you. Follow me. You're not going to get out of it that easily.' Grabbing her arm she dragged a rather reluctant Zara back towards the marquee. Amber sidled up to Tyler as he stood chatting to his team. Interrupting him smoothly, she professionally steered conversation into her sales flack immediately. Her talent was not wasted; her negotiation skills were second to none. Any boardroom would happily embrace her if the need arose.

'Nice game, congratulations on the win. Now I'm sure you're in need of some remedial treatment after a game like that. Have you considered your own personal therapist for your team? Why wait for the organisers' of an event to sort you out. As I mentioned earlier, we could come to some arrangement with you for future games. A body in its prime needs to be looked after, don't you think?' Surveying his torso in detail her eyes scanned up and down hovering at chest level, and then coyly dropping her lashes, she tilted her head slightly showing the line of her neck. Having drawn in Mr Tyler Montgomery, she leant forward whispering gently in his ear.

'From what I can see, I think some professional hands are required for someone of your calibre.'

Tyler was hooked. Adoration was what he thrived on and Amber was giving it in bucket loads. Zara was more hesitant, she may have the contract but Amber was probably more attracted to what he was interested in. Surprisingly he smiled over at her and after some brief discussion left Amber to make his way across to where she was waiting.

'Your agent is a sweet talker; she's done a good job of selling you to me. When can I have my first workout with you? It has to be a pretty intense one as we do already have a guy for the team. But hey, I never turn down a pretty face unless I have good reason to.'

Zara blushed deeply. She wasn't sure he was entirely talking about her work. Charm he definitely had, but was he toying with her just a little? Zara was falling for the biggest and most flirtatious player on the field. Much to her heart's discontent this was not going to lead to happiness long term. But for now she may as well entertain the idea and see how it panned out.

Reality returned and Zara found herself staring hard at the clinician's notes in front of her just as the excitable and unnerving Roger entered her office. Zara left the dilemma behind in the recesses of her mind for later; clearly Roger had more important work for her to attend to. How she would avoid any polo work in the future she was unsure. Seeing Tyler and not being romantically involved with him was not a cross she would bear easily. Mixing business and pleasure was always a bad idea now leaving her in this dire predicament.

'Good news Zara. Is your passport up to date? I've sponsored one of our client's relatives Steve, Jack Mcnara's brother. He's entering the Tour de France this year. I feel the prestige of this sponsorship will enhance this practice many times. My plan is to send you and Jamie out to France to work on some of the stages. It will be great fun for you both and beneficial for us and the team. You'll be flying out this weekend, so get packing.'

Before Zara could protest in any way he flounced out of the office in search of Jamie, leaving Zara reeling in a double shock. Well it wasn't a bad one and did kind of compensate for the disappointment of Tyler's bombshell. Out of every bad thing comes some good, thought Zara. She felt she had to believe this as life could be bloody daunting otherwise. Within minutes her files were pushed aside, and jabbing numbers rapidly into her mobile she was on speed dial to Gina.

~ ~ ~

Airports always are a hive of bustling people from all walks of life, dashing to far flung places. Zara wasn't a big lover of them, being a somewhat hesitant traveller. She scanned the lounge for anything to take her mind off the impending flight, delayed as usual. Jamie had been sent off to see what the problem entailed. Zara wasn't keen to know really as this would only worry her further if it was a mechanical delay. She hoped if it was a technical problem they might be offered another plane quickly.

Sitting opposite was someone whom Zara admired, the frequent flyer. The woman obviously flew business or first class every flight. If she had the opportunity to do the same, maybe she too wouldn't be so daunted by the process.

The woman appeared to be around fifty; surgery could have shaved a few years off. Her attire was classy and particularly expensive, from her clean and crystal white slacks to gold Gucci sunglasses perched delicately on her refined chiselled nose.

Even if there was sunshine outside rainy Gatwick somewhere between the cracks of dense cloud, there sure wasn't any inside the terminal. Zara deliberated on what her view of the world was. No bright colours to stimulate you or raise your spirits, everything in monochrome. The woman was most certainly a seasoned jetsetter and totally chilled.

Across from her was what Zara termed the eco-warrior type, a complete contrast to the bejewelled and elegant woman. Birkenstock sandals, which everyone knew did nothing for man, woman or beast for that matter in making the legs sexy. Even Brad Pitt would look a geek she was sure, if he adorned them on his gilded legs. For this traveller, it was the uniform as anoraks were to the train spotter. His rucksack was part of his anatomy. With wild unkempt hair poking out of the obligatory beanie hat, he looked like he was attempting some new caveman look for the catwalk.

Nearby a commotion had started. A poor harassed mother was trying hard to calm her overactive brood. A screaming baby was strapped into its buggy with a multitude of items hanging from it. You had to look hard to see the little thing, but sure as hell could hear the young babe.

Zara knew before even stepping on the plane that this was going to be her plane buddy for the entire journey. A little uncertain of how she would handle kids of her own, let alone other people's kids, this journey might give her the opportunity.

Zara became aware that while watching her fellow companions, she too was being observed. Glancing over to where the presence of eyes bored into her was a guy lounging opposite, clearly interested in what she'd been doing too. He appeared vaguely familiar but she couldn't place where from. Smiling faintly, as a little unsure how to react, she decided to avert her gaze and pretend to read a magazine. As she looked up again furtively, the guy seemed to have lost interest and was stretched back in his chair. Clearly he was as bored as she was waiting for his flight to take off. Leaning back further still, his shirt rode up exposing a substantial chunk of bare flesh. Zara was drawn to the tanned physique and then it clicked into place where the familiarity was - an area of the body that was unmistakable. It was Abman from her past jaunt visiting Gina in Edinburgh. How could she have forgotten a stomach like that, perfectly formed, rippling like sand on a beach when the tide had withdrawn. In fact, a pretty nice specimen all round for any anatomy class. She wondered how many more top marks would have been achieved if live models such as this guy were brought in for revision aids. No bunking off whenever an opportunity if he was scheduled on the timetable.

Zara immediately leapt to find her phone and texted Gina. She wouldn't believe that he was actually two feet away from her in the flesh. A beep returned with a rapid reply.

'You lucky sod! Don't you dare get your hands on him, find out some info, love G.' Zara laughed. No way was she going to accost the guy in broad daylight but how the hell do you suss someone out?

The main passenger intercom announced in a very polite tone that passengers could now pass to the departure gate for Nice. Jamie came instantly bounding back with his long gait.

'Come on, let's go. We're off. Aren't you excited?' he exclaimed, bouncing around like an enthusiastic three year old. Zara now was contemplating if the seat with the wailing brat wouldn't be a better option, than coping with an over excited Jamie all the way. Travel plans had got in the way of aiding Gina's request. No time to delve now that she needed to rein in Jamie rapidly, as he started picking up speed towards their gate.

Once on the tarmac and sitting down on the mode of transport, she relaxed and started to feel more excited at the prospect of some sun and a change of scenery. It wasn't everyday she got an all-expenses paid business trip abroad to work with some top athletes; it might be more fun than she thought.

Before she could settle, a rather large rucksack came crashing down in the seat next to her. She froze, thinking it couldn't be, could it? Eco-warrior didn't look the type to fly to a posh place like Nice, though looks can be deceptive as we all know. Hesitantly Zara looked up as the rucksack's owner heaved it into the overhead locker like a sack of potatoes. Then she gulped feeling slightly nervous at her new companion sitting right next door to her.

The passenger noticed Zara and grinned broadly. A row of white gleaming teeth met Zara's surprised and rather hesitant grin in return. It was the ideal companion, Abman. Now this might be a perfect opportunity to delve deeper into his life but Zara felt strangely coy knowing Gina had her on a private mission. A whole journey to Nice making small talk, yikes what do you talk about. He appeared friendly but she still felt uneasy as if she was walking a fine margin of helping Gina and being disloyal at the same time. Why couldn't Gina be the one to bump into him? She was the one smitten, though Zara was finding it hard to stay neutral at the moment as he leaned over to take a look out over the runway.

'Sorry, like to look at the land just prior to take off. Hope I'm not squashing you?'

Zara felt pretty ok at being squashed under his torso; she could think of many fates but that one was rather attractive. His skin smelt heavenly of an aftershave vaguely reminiscent of the sea. Touches of sandalwood and cypress floated beneath the main body of the scent. Breathing in sharply to take in the full aroma, its strong undertones started to make her giddy, unsure if it was the ingredients or the pheromones the guy was kicking out at top speed; but whatever it was; it was making her pretty lightheaded.

After take-off he settled down and started to make conversation. His voice was fairly posh with a southern drawl to it. Maybe a touch of a country Somerset accent thought Zara.

'What brings you to the continent, business or pleasure?' his tone was husky and his question had hidden undercurrents.

'Business, I'm working away for my clinic at the Tour de France bike race, pretty lucky to be chosen; and yourself?'

'You must be well trained, only the elite therapists are normally chosen for working at an event like that. Well done for getting the position. Myself, I'm on a personal vacation,' he seemed to hesitate and looked as if he was going to say more but stopped in his tracks. Zara tried hard to draw attention to Gina and keep the conversation focused but Abman was having none of it.

'Tell me a little about yourself. We've got plenty of time to waste. Are we travelling solo or a partner in tow?' he enquired again searching her face for any hidden information she wasn't relaying. Shuffling in his seat, he appeared to edge in closer. Not that that was difficult. Flying Ryan Air, the space capacity between seats was at a minimum anyway. You half sat across your fellow passenger without even trying. Trust Roger to book economy class at its lowest. Zara felt Abman was obviously keen to get to know her better, placing her in a rather awkward position.

Changing tactics, Zara tried hard to concentrate on him being just a fellow business colleague, never mixing business with pleasure. She needed to remember this rule in future after her Tyler predicament. She attempted to make the conversation more formal but it ended in disaster. She couldn't do it. One wink was all that was needed and the intense longing to devour his body became stronger and stronger. The tingling between her legs increased infuriatingly.

Squirming on her seat and feeling a flushing occurring across her chest she decided to excuse herself. Nodding, he smiled keeping her gaze for longer than was necessary. He drew back and raised his body up from the seat to allow her to pass by. Zara rose gingerly and attempted the ungainly process of scrambling across her neighbour's lap.

Moving into his personal space while squeezing by was like foreplay in itself. She was trying very hard to extract herself carefully over him, due to the severe lack of space. Getting her foot entangled in some luggage beneath the seat well didn't help and she fell back squarely onto his lap. Zara felt mortified; scrabbling to get a hold on the seat rests, she supported herself a little and tried to extract her foot.

'If you wanted to swap seats you only needed to ask! At least you had a soft landing; I can't say it will be like that when you return.' He looked at Zara closely for a reaction. By this time Zara was so flustered she murmured a 'thank-you it was lovely' and charged up the aisle to the restroom at breakneck speed.

Inside the tiny cubicle she worked hard to contain her sensations of longing, but other than a cold dowsing of water from the sink they weren't going to disappear that easily. The desire was so strong she felt like joining the mile high club there and then, dragging him back up the plane to do it that instant.

Looking at the dimensions of the restroom, she wasn't sure how anyone did the deed at all especially anyone the size of Abman. There wasn't room to manoeuvre an inch and you would definitely want to move with that guy. Cringing at her parting comment she prepared herself to return with some dignity intact, trying hard to cool the flushing in her cheeks with the tepid tap water.

As she approached he stood up to let her go by, possibly sensing that she was starting to feel uncomfortable by her speed of escape. Her mind raced back to Gina, she'd never been in a situation where they'd had to compete for a member of the opposite sex. They just didn't like the same kind. This time it might be different. It was probably a chance in a million she was on the same plane. Once landed they would both head off to whatever destination they were meant to be at, and that would be that. With this thought she settled down to enjoy the rest of the journey as best she could, trying extremely hard to ignore the sensations of fire down below.

Abman continued to stoke this fire more than Zara could cope with as he proceeded to lean frequently across her to look out the aircraft window. Zara could feel his breath at times skim across her chest, making her catch her own with nervousness. Certain he was aware of his untimely effects on her, Zara tried hard to remove herself from the situation and concentrate on the novel she brought hoping for a little escapism during her working break, but it was nigh impossible to ignore what was sitting so close by. In the end admitting defeat, she closed her book gently and allowed conversation to carry on. On approach to the runway looking down over the coast line of Nice Abman leant forward and whispered in her ear,

'Give me a ring sometime. I might be working closer to you than you think,' he grinned, pressed a business card into the palm of her hand and before she knew it was heading off with a group of passengers out of the plane and out of her life. She looked down at the business card. This was for Gina and her intended mission. If she kept thinking like that it would be fine. Hitting the terminal she rounded up Jamie with a loud command.

'Come on Jamie, let's get cracking otherwise we'll be knackered for the race tomorrow. I definitely need a cool shower.' Jamie looked at her rather curiously.

'You haven't worked up a sweat yet sitting on your backside for three hours.'

'That's what you think,' replied Zara. She smiled secretly wandering off across the terminal with a rather puzzled Jamie tagging behind.

Chapter 7

FUN IN THE MOUNTAINS

The mountain air felt thin and light. Zara was finding herself out of breath quite quickly. She would have to pace herself a little as the day wore on. The views were spectacular beyond anything she had ever seen before. A panoramic scene of the mountains glistening in the early morning sunshine lay sprawled around her. All colours of the rainbow were bouncing off in a hazy sheen, extending high up into the sky which by now was turning from a soft pinkie grey, to what would probably be a glorious pale blue by the time nine o'clock arrived. Getting up had been a strain, catching the mini bus to first camp worse, but after seeing that view, it had been well worth the trouble.

Many of the crew members were by now bustling around checking supplies. Food and drink was being laid out in some nearby tents, camera crews milled around trying to get set up in the best position. Throughout was a sense of excitement particularly for the newbies. For some of the regular staff they were just on autopilot, displaying a sense of calmness for something they did routinely. Zara walked towards the tent that Jamie and herself had been assigned to work in. It had no front panel to the carcass for easy entry.

The tent walls at the rear flapped in the breeze. It was an idyllic way of working. You didn't get this back in the big city, thought Zara.

Everything was to hand: oils, talcum powders, lotions. Alongside the main essentials lay an army of tools to pummel and seduce the body into submission or rev the powerhouse up for the next leg of the journey. Zara could feel the excitement rising now.

'I can't believe we're here; glad we drew the short straw. I'm still uncertain why we were chosen over the other guys at the clinic? But I will be eternally in debt to Roger.'

'Don't you be letting Roger know how grateful you are, he may decide you need to pay him in some weird unconventional way and it may not involve clinic work, if you know what I mean,' Jamie raised an eyebrow to stress his case.

'Jamie! He's not that bad. Besides I'm not loaded enough for Roger to consider blackmailing me for favoritism he's shown me. He knows how much I take home. It isn't enough to wine and dine anyone.'

'Well just remember what I said, play it cool otherwise he may decide he wants a bit of the action next year if we get invited back. He'd be a bloody nightmare with his anal ways. I half think he's bisexual, no straight guy is so pedantic.'

'Ok, ok I'll play it cool.'

They both emerged from the tent as the manager in charge came roaring up the mountain road in a very minute buggy. Jamie looked on in awe, obviously summing up the attraction it could instill if he had one.

'Don't go thinking you need one of them Jamie,'

115

sensing his thoughts, 'Looks a bit too play-boyish to me, but hey, maybe that's what they drive up here.'

The crew gathered round to listen to the various instructions to be remembered. Some helpers listened politely but knew the course of action by heart. The newcomers were all ears, some appearing nervous and anxious not to make any mistake, lest they may never get a return invite.

'Right, listen up,' bellowed the manager, 'by ten thirty the first of the pack will be approaching the base of the steep climb. The work station has been set up here to tend to any injuries sustained in that long hill climb, back breaking that it is, a lot of thigh and knee problems can rear their ugly heads, as you all very well know from experience. If you don't you shouldn't be here.

I need you to be quick and precise with the work. No delay in sorting the problems out; the riders will be keen to pursue the pack as soon as they can and not lose their positioning.' He paused for breath and surveyed his audience.

'Once the majority of the riders have gone through, half the team will to be taken to the next station for the latter stages of the day. The riders that come through there will be for the wind down sessions, designed for relieving muscle tiredness and as this will be the end of the race that day, longer work can be performed. A follow-up team will also arrive for the slower riders later on. Does that clarify all you need to know?' He stared beadily at all the crew. Quietness ensued, everyone waiting in anticipation of the first to raise a hand. Nobody did.

'Ok, let me inspect you all look up to scratch.' With a few cursory nods, and brief acknowledgement to some familiar faces, the chief jumped in his buggy. With a loud wolf whistle, he charged off down the mountain road to the start of the stage.

Zara glanced at Jamie and twitched her eyebrows in acknowledgement that the guy probably got carried away with his position. They proceeded to get prepped for the day, swigging a gallon of water to avoid dehydrating too early, and be set up for the strenuous work ahead.

Sure enough the first of the riders came up over the hill bang on time. The sheer strength of these guys was incredible. Heat was already rising and sweat glistened all over their bodies.

Several leapt off their bikes. A whirlwind of activity ensued. Biker and bike were given a full MOT and service in double quick time, to ensure the next leg of the race went smoothly for them. Zara had never pummeled so many limbs in her life; she felt she'd performed this stage of the race herself.

The day flew by in a complete whirl; the crew had no time to chat hardly, as one athlete to the next leapt on the couch. The crowds that came out of nowhere to support the competitors were awesome. It certainly wasn't a relaxing experience but one she wouldn't have missed. Any lingering thoughts of Tyler had vanished. Zara didn't have a minute to think.

In her break, she decided to get to know a few of the other helpers. Wandering over to the rest area she sat down next to a young girl.

'Hi I'm Zara, how's it going? You've been here

before on the job?'

'No, first time. I'm here to support my brother whose racing. I thought it would be a good combination to offer my expertise and allow a bit more interaction with the event, rather than just watch it all on the television.'

'Where's back home? Enquired Zara.

'I'm from Russia, my name's Natalia,' she extended her hand towards Zara.

'Wow your language skills are perfect, I didn't detect anything to say you were from Russia.'

'Yes we learn from an early age to perfect our English; my mother is part Danish so I am a slight blend,' her mouth broke into a wide grin. 'Have you had any oddball customers so far?'

'Not yet, but sure I will do by the end of it. I'm enjoying seeing problems firsthand after the body has gone through some grueling exercise, rather than when the client arrives stiffened up a few days later. It's a completely different way to approach the treatment on the job isn't it?'

'Yes, I think I will learn much on this trip. I work with gymnasts back home so this is a little different. Would you like another drink? I'm going to grab one.' Natalie stood up leaning back to extend her back and stretch.

'I'll have a coke if they have any left thanks. I'm drinking loads of water but fancy a caffeine boost,' beamed Zara wiping her brow with a towel. The afternoon heat had risen to a high 80 degrees. It was a bit too much but the mountain breeze just helped cool them enough to make it a little more comfortable.

Circling overhead an eagle swooped high, diving down in the distance to its prey. The work station had encroached on its life and the bird was unsettled at all the commotion. It was finding it hard to hunt now. The easily startled prey was eluding it on a frequent basis.

Zara looked out at the changing hillside. Shadows had started to form as the sun beat down on the trees and scrubland that could be observed as far as the eye could see.

The camera crews had moved on now ready and prepped for the next stage. Zara puzzled how they'd managed to get past the race pack. There must be a back route that could be taken. Once the pack were on the road, no passing space would be possible. Time was approaching to get on the bus for the next stage of the day. How many days she could do this, she was a little uncertain. Four days might be her max; otherwise she would be on the couch for treatment herself. They had two weeks contract so she'd better pace herself.

The bus was air conditioned luxury indeed. Zara sank back in the seat and glanced out of the window. She loved doing something a little different and challenging and this was certainly unusual to her pretty mundane working life, though the bohemian lifestyle wasn't something she fancied getting used to long term. In fact after today's workload her little treat that was prearranged for Jamie and herself, was going to be bliss indeed.

Their new destination was gradually coming into view as the bus rounded the hairpin bend. Cactus & cypress trees littered the side of the road providing a dark evergreen contrast to the scorched earth. Pulling

119

into the layby, the team piled out to survey the next location. A few shot off to their stations to get prepped up early. Jamie smiled.

'Well, let's get cracking. I'll see you in the bar later once those knuckles have worn thin.' Zara grinned back mischievously.

'Ok, but make sure you can summon the strength to lift the pint to your over confident mouth.'

With the sarcastic comment fresh in the air, a slow procession of cyclists started to arrive, exhausted from the stage they'd just completed. The look of pain mixed with sheer happiness knowing their achievements had been accomplished for now, seemed etched on their faces. The riders collapsed on the nearest couch for the demon team, (a nickname the therapy team had decided on calling themselves for raising morale) to work their magic.

Zara heard footsteps crunching on the loose shale leading up to the tents. Swiftly preparing her oils ready, she spun round to welcome the weary rider. A shock awaited, her gaze transfixed on the rider standing before her.

'Oh, err! Hello, pop up on the couch you must be exhausted, is there anything I can do for you?' Her voice quavered a little. This was not what she'd expected. Feeling a little unsure of the situation and trying not to become too unnerved she steadied herself discreetly. It wasn't as if the guy was royalty or something, just a client in a normal day's work.

'Hi, it's my lucky day I may not have the yellow jersey but I've struck gold now.'

'Didn't know you were actually competing? You're

a dark horse not telling me you were racing.' Zara could feel herself getting worked up in defense. Her cheeks were slowly changing an insane colour of rosehip, bright red from embarrassment. Knowing there wasn't any way to avoid treating the guy, she'd have to knuckle down and be professional.

He looked a little sheepish at this stage and smiled, trying hard to ease the tension that was sparking between them. Zara felt a strange sense of anger and indignation at him. Stirring underneath was the strong pull of sexual desire again. Her hormone control must be totally haywire. Maybe a serious, steady relationship would be a good idea, as this seesaw effect of desire with the male species was beginning to get ridiculous. She now had a fair idea what a love-hate relationship could be like. Composing herself she plunged straight in to get on with the job, politely guiding him onto the couch.

With speed he unveiled his body lest she changed her mind. His lean and now rather moist torso was revealed from the shirt that had clung and highlighted every muscle on his frame. Mesmerized, her jaw dropped slightly, having not really taken a lot of notice the last time Gina and herself had first clapped eyes on him in the spa.

Now after viewing his entire body close up, not just an odd tantalizing glimpse beneath clothes as at the airport, she was completely taken aback. The guy was perfect. No, not perfect but a complete Adonis. She hadn't seen a body like that in all her years of working on the human frame.

Gingerly she draped the towel over his torso

covering some of the bare flesh to avoid being totally distracted, and prepared to run the oil blend over his back.

Each drop seemed like foreplay to her and she wondered what he might be thinking. On reflection it was better she didn't know, desiring to cool the situation. Gliding her hands over the lightly tanned skin, her fine-tuned hands detected a slowness of breath as he relaxed into the couch. His heartbeat continued to pound into her fingertips but diminished in intensity as the oxygen levels rose slowly returning the body to balance after the hard exertion he had just pushed his body through.

Her mind and body reactions became confused and rather than slowing down in tune with her client's rhythm, her own heart rate started to increase. She was unsure if it was due to his presence causing heightened sexual desire or nervousness. Either way Zara had to remedy the situation rapidly. On no accounts did she want him aware of it through her touch.

As her hands glided over his legs she imagined what Gina would be thinking if she knew what was happening. Better it was never to be mentioned. It was one secret that she couldn't divulge, damage limitation was best.

Zara consciously tried hard to relax, as her increased heartbeat was having a detrimental effect on any willpower to center herself. Forgetting time constraints her treatment was taking longer than her peers.

Every stroke she found was electric to her fingertips. She fought very hard not to imagine herself in bed with

122

the guy. It was starting to make her feel slightly uncomfortable having such untoward images flashing through her mind. Now it was time to work the front of her client. It would be very bad practice to do half a session. It was going to be a tall order trying to hide her feelings when he would be staring up at her.

Zara brushed some hair from her forehead, which was becoming annoying. Working so intensely combined with desire was making her perspire more than normal. As she worked upon his hands he responded by squeezing her palm gently.

'Thanks for not passing me onto anyone else, you're a pretty damn good masseuse, even if you are annoyed with me,' he winked and watched for her reaction, goading her to retaliate once again.

Zara now felt very uncomfortable. She was aware that if anyone suspected the way she was feeling about him, it would be instant dismissal and a possible ban from her career. Ethics had gone out of the window. You just didn't fraternize with the customer; she should have indeed passed him on and he knew it as well.

Her heart pounded at the situation she was in. Being given full permission to touch Abs' body and being paid for the privilege was not something you turned down. Gina would be doing somersaults by now. The mess she had fallen into with Tyler was bad enough; she didn't really want to fall back into another situation so soon after that one.

Sliding back the towel over his midriff she oiled her hands that were shaking by now and they drifted over his stomach. Her fingers now nuzzling softly at a line of blond hair leading down to an area Zara was trying not to be drawn to. It felt like silk tufts to her fingertips as she moved across the torso, skimming over the ribs and skirting down over the raised six pack of muscle.

At that precise moment Zara felt a strong familiar urge that she had experienced on the plane, to just leap on him and be done with it, though the fact she was in a crowded tent with numerous other work colleagues was not the appropriate time or place.

As the treatment finalized Zara stood behind him, easing tension from the neck. However loyal she was to Gina it wasn't going to be easy to move on from this scenario. She sensed something more might happen if she bumped into him again. Any willpower from the temptation in front of her was running at top speed in the opposite direction. On completion she advised him to dress ready for her to resume work on the next rider waiting.

Abs moved to swing round and lever himself up. With one swift lunge he guided Zara towards him and whispered subtly in her ear. Zara tried hard not to show any reaction. Jamie glanced over and looked worryingly across at her, his frown portrayed it all. Zara pulled back and tried to look more official but the high flushing and bounce in her step as she tidied her work area couldn't be disguised.

Mr. Abman poured himself back into the now, somewhat dryer racing top and with a brush of his lips upon her cheek left Zara reeling from the last hour she had experienced with him.

On the bus back to the accommodation quarters Zara was lost in thought. Jamie felt compelled to say something.

'Hope you're not getting into trouble, we've got work to concentrate on. I couldn't help notice the effect he had on you today. Wasn't he that guy you sat next to on the flight over? Seemed a bit slimy if you ask me.'

'You're only jealous Jamie as you haven't met any totty yourself,' Zara joked. She was trying hard to distract Jamie, now he had cottoned on to the dangerous situation.

'That's as may be but be careful, remember your work record. Don't abuse it for an inflated muscle bound poser.' With his parting comment Jamie burrowed his head in the latest lads' mag.

Zara sighed thinking it was some insult after what he had just come out with to leer at the classic stereotypical woman plastered all over the magazine. Alright for him to be distracted by the lure of large breasts and pouting lips, but she couldn't be affected by a perfect set of abdominals. She was aware she shouldn't be entertaining such thoughts, but didn't want to accept it, for a few hours at any rate. Maybe she should have chosen a different career, where the option of bare sporty flesh wasn't on show in front of her all the time. Or total avoidance of high end events where the candidates were of course going to be in their prime.

After a meal and shower Zara felt ready to forget her altercation for the time being, avoidance maybe the best choice. Fingers burnt once with Tyler was more than a deterrent; she should have learnt her lesson by now.

Jamie's words echoed around like a pinball machine in her head. The night air was cool and soothed her troubled mind a bit. The moonlight left strange shadows upon the fields dancing and ebbing as the clouds swept across the night sky. The breeze was strong now. Leaves of the nearby forest rustled and seemed to whisper in Zara's ear as she sat quietly on the swinging chair nestled in the grounds of their current hotel.

A little hedgehog emerged and started to snuffle for its supper amongst the undergrowth. Zara felt alive for once despite her punishing work schedule that had gone on before. Letting her mind drift like the clouds across the evening sky, thoughts of her best friend sprung into focus and what fun she had had. It didn't sit well with the pain she would cause Gina if she ever found out what had been running through her mind today.

~ ~ ~

The next few days of work flew by. The weather stayed warm, and she managed quite successfully to avoid Abman, making life a whole lot easier for Zara. Though he would have been a rather nice distraction from her constant thoughts of Tyler, whose image flashed at inopportune moments way too often, much to Zara's intense annoyance. Why she couldn't just let him go was pathetic. He was out of her league and not worth the trouble.

On reflection the assignment had been perfect. The social scene at the end of day allowed them both to expand their horizons. The range of nationalities working close to the base was broad, Jamie even managing to learn a few choice foreign words that weren't all obscene.

The crew knew not to drink heavily. The high temperature they were working in and the manual labour required, did not mix well with a large consumption of alcohol. Enduring the hassle of a hangover next day wasn't one any of them relished.

Jamie, to Zara's astonishment, managed to attract the attention of a very attractive Swiss girl, her affect reducing him to a lovesick puppy whenever she came within feet of him.

By the end of week two, the teams were moving further north. Zara was sad to say her goodbyes but it did mean they were now leaving for a welcome treat of a few days in glamorous Cannes. The glitz and glamour of the southern resort of France was going to be great, she had always wanted to visit and now was the perfect opportunity. Two holidays so close were unheard of in Zara's calendar but she was going to enjoy every damn second of it.

Once their goodbyes had been said they headed off with their hire car and motored south along the coast to Monte Carlo and Nice. Prices in Monte were a touch prohibitive so Cannes was a nice compromise. Although Jamie was feeling a touch disappointed at missing out here, he wanted to be viewed with the jet set, swaggering around the harbour, leering at any bikini clad babe who languished on the decadent yachts as they sauntered past. Zara relented and stopped off for the afternoon but had to tell him off on a few occasions to behave, as the locals were starting to think he was a danger to their female folk.

'Will you behave Jamie, what happened to that

doting boyfriend of Maria two days ago?'

'Guy's gotta keep going.'

Zara rolled her eyes at him thinking that men and women were definitely from different universes, let alone planets. There she was pining over Tyler, the distraction of Abman had helped a little of course, but she had at least tried being a little reserved. Jamie on the other hand would be well taken in if so much as a wink came his way.

They strolled up to the Palace making sure she was dressed appropriately and praying Jamie would be also allowed in, so she could keep a close eye at all times. Zara definitely didn't trust him to go wandering off alone. Dreading what untold trouble he might get into. Once Jamie had had his fill of Monte they ventured off down the coast again towards Cannes before nightfall set in.

Arriving at their destination for the night they started to find it was nigh impossible to find the hotel. Not having a good street map, each street looked exactly the same to the foreigner. Once in the one way system they became completely lost.

'We're going to have to ask otherwise we'll be sleeping on the beach at this rate,' declared Zara to Jamie, who had the map upside down at this point.

'Ok, how's your French?' enquired Jamie.

'Probably as weak as yours, my forte was biology, languages a bit of a no, no.'

Pulling over and grasping the map, Zara approached a young couple with the aid of a few arm gestures which made monkeys look normal, a smile and head scratching, the kind couple decided trying to explain the

128

route would be way to difficult, and gestured they would get their car and guide them to the hotel personally.

'That wasn't too bad was it? Very friendly folk, can't see what the English mean when they don't like the French,' exclaimed Jamie. 'Seem alright to me.'

'You would say that having been undressing them all day in Monte,' laughed Zara.

The hotel was family run and right across from the beach - a private one at that. Settling in for the night, a good sleep was in order. As morning broke Zara awoke fairly early, keen to embrace every minute of the day and allow enough time to really explore the local area. Waking Jamie was more of a struggle, resorting to practically manually dragging a reluctant Jamie from his bedcovers.

'Psst Jamie, come on wake up you sleepyhead. Let's not waste any time. Come on, let's go.' Zara in her annoyance rocked him roughly. Dragging the light duvet with Jamie wrapped up in it onto the floor, lest she exposed him completely, unsure how Jamie slept - commando or clothed.

'Can't a guy get some peace on his day off, we've been up early every day for the last two weeks. It's my first day off.' Groaning he rolled over clutching the pillow around his ears.

'Jamie, don't be such a big wuss. Just think of all those golden babes just waiting for you on the beach, they don't waste time here lying in, when the hot rays could be christening their seductive bodies.' A few persuasive tactics were in order thought Zara otherwise they wouldn't be hitting the town till after lunch at this

129

rate.

Jamie opened an eye, glaring at her, 'I suppose that's your way of blackmailing me to get up, rather tacky to say I'd be tempted by such trivia. On the other hand you may be right. Strike early before those lazy French bastards get down there.' Zara grinned, 'so easily led' she must use that tactic a few more times,'

Breakfast was taken on the terrace with the sun glinting softly on the crystal blue sea. The hotel positioning was ideal for quickness to shopping or the beach. She had chosen well. Zara was now in her element munching on croissants and apple pastries. Her figure would be expanding quickly at this rate but they were so moreish. Jamie peered over his shades eyeing her expectantly in case a crumb would be left for him.

'What! You had two croissants yourself,' blurted Zara as she popped the last morsel in her mouth rather quickly.

'Just thinking of your waistline, know you'll only regret it once home in Blighty. Besides I'm a growing lad - my need is greater. Not much chance of sharing with you I notice.'

'You really don't understand the female race do you? Never come between a female and her food. Whether it's a measly salad or slice of gateaux you do it at your own peril.' Jamie grunted and grabbed the last piece of fruit from the platter.

Once completely stuffed and satisfied they went up to the top floor to check out the view and inspect the rooftop pool. The scenery stretched out for miles along the meandering coastline towards Saint Tropez. The pool looked inviting but the excitement of exploring was more enticing.

They decided to have a walk along the beach first, particularly as Zara had torn Jamie from his beloved bed with cunning persuasion, he was going to pursue the idea, whether she liked it or not. Only once he had had his fill of the foreign delights would he entertain the idea of the shops. It was Zara's turn to be leaping about like a puppy when the shops beckoned.

Everything seemed new and different to back home. Restaurants thronged the beach front, capturing the beautiful view of the ocean. Big picturesque windows slid back to allow alfresco dining. All looked inviting at any time of the day, not the kind you get on Eastbourne seafront with lashing rain or winds eight months of the year.

Zara looked into one of the restaurants they passed. Clearly it must be of high caliber she thought, as a bronzed waiter polished cutlery to a gleaming mirror standard. Stripped to the waist, tall and dark as most French were and of course the clichéd, handsome beyond words. Zara wondered if the cheaper restaurants offered only clothed, overweight waiting staff. Memories of the debonair Markus back in Edinburgh came to mind. He'd be the perfect job transfer.

The French possessed an epitome of elegance whatever age. Most women they observed appeared slim and fashionably dressed. From the rear, age was undetectable; on closer inspection, facially the ravages of the hot Riviera sun hadn't done much justice to the complexion. Jamie seemed disappointed as yet another bronzed female came within eyeshot only to be less hot when he took a second glance from the front.

'Has that calmed you down a bit? Looks can be deceptive. Must admit though, the state of the bin men look a bit more appealing than our lot back home,' commented Zara as she scanned the side streets.

'Yeah, can't see any overweight, fag ash blokes. Bit unshaven, though I have been told a girl can like a little bit of stubble. Might consider it myself when I get home.' Zara stifled a laugh behind her hand.

As they neared the main harbour, several of the local gendarmes lounged casually at the barrier. Though appearing to be uninterested they scanned the locals with venom hidden behind their dark shades. Even in seventy degree heat, they still wore tall black boots with not a speck of dust on them. Their ensemble complete with smart jackets oozed authority. Probably from Armani or some designer assumed Zara.

'What is it with the obsession with tiny dogs, don't they like a meaty Rottweiler now and again,' Jamie commented. 'It's somewhat disturbing to see them prancing along the promenade like poodles on display and I'm talking about the owners not their canine buddies.'

'Jamie, for Pete's sake, stop it someone - will hear you.'

'I'm sorry they all seem a bit fancy for me, some of these French chicks need a real man. We Brits can show them a thing or two.'

'Yes ok, I admit the male population although sexy does portray a certain feminine air. I could be home in Brighton walking along here, but a bit of French work wouldn't go amiss on a few individuals.'

'Glad you agree with me,' muttered Jamie trying

hard to appear casual as they sauntered past the gendarmes. Sadly Zara's comment had floated over Jamie's head completely.

'How about we hire one of those boats? Get a chance to see the coast line a little. What do you say?

'Ok, but I'm not driving the bloody thing. Unless they have a speed boat - more my style.' Jamie replied.

'Deal! I'm not embarrassed. Besides, I wouldn't trust you with speed and power behind the wheel.'

Setting off along the coast watching the emerald waters lap gently at the coastal inlets, the choices of moorings along the coastline were vast, some pristine beaches, some wild and natural. On the return journey the current caused a fair few large waves to rock the boat up and down, a little too much for Jamie and his face started to turn a sallow shade of green.

'Are we nearly there yet? It seems to have taken far longer on the way back than when we went,' he proclaimed in a slightly weak and high pitched voice.

'Not far to the next bay, good thing I've had some boat skills from my father. You'd have been rubbish for navigation with your head over the side,' sneered Zara. She wondered how Jamie ever got anywhere in life; he seemed to be in a perpetual daze.

'You won't be taking any flaxen haired maidens out on your proposed launch parked at Monte will you? They may just want you to take them for a spin. That lovely shade of green doesn't really match your shirt I'm afraid.' Zara felt a bit mean saying it but Jamie was looking a very weird colour by now.

Guiding the vessel slowly into the harbour, Zara knew she would have to dock herself as Jamie was now fit for nothing. Once the rope was secured on the harbour wall the insistent rocking of the boat subsided. Leaping out onto dry land, Zara helped the somewhat unsteady Jamie up the sharp steps to safety.

'Terra firma for you from now on my boy.'

Back at the hotel they settled down to relax by the pool, it being a much safer and calmer choice where Jamie was concerned. The late afternoon sunshine warmed the terrace nicely. A few last minute sun worshipers lay out their already bronzed limbs, trying to gain a deeper shade of dark leather. Zara could never understand why.

She looked up to scan the horizon as one of the bodies decided to adjust their position. His legs bent up, strategically splayed wide open. Zara was sure the sun was shining on parts that really didn't need a tan. Luckily the way he was exposing himself, nobody but someone with very long distance binoculars would catch him from the front, there were some benefits for sunbathing on the roof.

After a while he turned and stood up casually leaning against the railings to look out to sea. Zara imagined he may have felt a somewhat singeing effect of the sun on his most personal areas. They did say ten minutes and sun block might be required. She was aware of his vanity, seeming to enjoy a little showing off to the other clientele sunbathing. Stretching up and then casually leaning forward more, his backside stuck out at a most precarious angle. 'What a poser,' thought Zara as she watched him discreetly behind her sunglasses. Bella was missing out here, she'd love it.

The young guy started to get dressed. He wore very

smart jeans obviously worth a bit of money. Worn well in certain areas but in that cool distressed look, proceeding to slip on his shirt which was very unusual, adorned with large pink rose blooms. Set against his jet black hair and leather brown skin he carried it well. Any other guy Jamie particularly, would have their sexuality questioned at once but he seemed different. Probably a model or actor she thought.

A little girl who had been playing at the poolside looked up seeing his flamboyant shirt immediately shrilled in a very loud voice.

'Mummy, look at the flowery shirt. Only girls wear them.' Her mother hushed her, embarrassed that the young man may have heard her daughter. He seemed unfazed, smiled and sauntered off leaving Zara to suppress her own giggles beneath a towel.

The peace of the terrace was interrupted by Zara's mobile. It made her jolt bolt upright, she hadn't received a call for so long. Rummaging quickly she pulled it from its holder so as not to disturb the other resting, leather handbags next to her. Jamie raised his head for a second and then settled back to the land of nod, still recovering from his boat ride from hell.

'Hello, how are you? It's lovely to hear from you, what's this surprise call for?' Zara whispered trying hard to be discreet, aware of every ear pricking up to eavesdrop. Within seconds her cheery expression faded and Zara looked close to tears. She found it hard to speak again, as a lump blocked her throat. 'I can't believe it, look, I'll come straight back, I can get a flight tomorrow. I'm sure first thing. I'll be there for you. Don't worry.' Jamie woke again aware of the

135

reaction Zara had to the call, before he could ask Zara who it was, she had leapt from the sun lounger and grabbing her belongings headed towards the lift leaving Jamie behind in her wake.

Chapter 8

THE BEAUTY IN YOUR EYES

The rain dripped relentlessly down the windows of the limo, trickling down in long spirals and eddies like the rivers crisscrossing Europe. Zara looked out as the passing scenery whipped past too quickly to see in the foggy mist. The world outside became just a blur, like her mind felt at this present time.

Arriving at their destination she elegantly stepped from the limo, dressed rather inappropriately for the weather. Pulling her light coat tighter around her body, Zara felt damp and chilled to the bone already. After all the heat of the south of France she was noticing the drop in temperature more than the others.

Familiar faces of friends started to appear from other cars. Handshakes and polite conversation flowed but Zara didn't really hear what was spoken, her mind distracted. She searched frantically for Amber amongst the crowds, such a lot had happened whilst she'd been away. A situation that now she felt totally distraught about, unable to reverse. For once in her life she was quite useless to know how to help.

Through the gate emerged Amber, her head held high, she looked serene and composed as usual whatever the circumstances. Greeting other members of her family and a few close friends she led them through the archway into the church.

As the music struck up, Zara gripped Amber's hand, a token of a lifelong friendship and tried very hard to relay her thoughts that she was there for her.

The congregation bowed their heads in respect as the coffin was carried slowly past them. Zara felt Amber stiffen, holding on tight to her grasp as a tiny trickle of a tear welled up in Amber's eye. Zara tried extremely hard not to get upset too, but she was useless at this. Swallowing hard in an attempt to quell the lump developing in her throat, she placed her arm around her friend to give her a comforting hug.

The service began as the vicar looked out over the sea of faces before him. Each member of the congregation was transfixed on his every word. Beautiful roses and late summer flowers cascaded down the walls and pews, lighting up the dimly lit church with colour and fragrance, bringing a little lift to the damp summer weather that lay outside the cold stone walls.

Halfway through the service, Amber made her way to the lectern and proceeded to read a very special letter. For a moment she stayed silent focusing on the words before her. Finally she spoke with a strong clarity of voice. Her words echoed throughout the tiny church, each guest bowing their heads in respect.

You remind me of the taste of summer
Of sweetness and delight
You came into my dearest dreams
With a fire in your soul and heart

The way your beauty and integrity shines
All those gifts you gave to me
You are my soul and saviour
Your lips I will caress forever
Although not by my side
You are within me forever growing
With passion and sincerity
I will continue on this life's path
For without your judgment and guidance
I would not be the woman I am today
As I see the raindrops falling
The seasons changing
A part of you will be with me forever
As our offspring arrives
Amongst the new spring flowers
I will remember our time together
You are my eternal friend
My soul, my life

The audience stayed hushed as Amber slowly returned to her seat. Close family nodded and laid a supporting hand upon her arm as she glided past them. The soft, deep notes of the organ echoed around the high rafters of the old church. Standing, the final hymn rang out as the pall bearers prepared to lift the coffin and lead the congregation out into the church yard high up on the hill behind.

There was not a dry eye in the audience as Amber led the procession. Zara sat shocked and reeling at the news, on top of everything else the words of her final reading became clear. Amber was going to have a child. It was wonderful news but so cruelly twinned with this tragedy. Her thoughts were only of her dearly departed husband. Why such sadness had to happen, to someone so good and full of the joys of life, just as they had moved to the next adventure. It seemed such a vicious blow that her best friend had to endure such a loss at such a happy time in her life. Amber hadn't mentioned anything when they last spoke. Maybe she hadn't even known of the news herself.

Stepping out from the pew, Zara walked behind Amber and the other mourners. Each guest slipping in one by one discreetly to slowly follow the procession up the gentle pathway that led to an old wrought iron gate.

Pushing the heavy gate gently open for the coffin to precede through, the vicar marched steadily over the damp spongy grass, until he reached a small clearing amongst the gravestones. Some were clad with lichen, more yellow and smudgy green. Their faint lettering faded and worn from the weather that hit the hillside over many winter months.

The last rites drifted on the air as Zara looked on grimly, trying to remain composed for Amber, who was staring down at the vast hole that lay gaping in front of her.

As the last prayer was said she stooped forward to place a single lily upon the coffin. It lay glistening with the faint moisture that was enveloping every surface. Standing, Amber smiled and turned to hold her father's hand to which the party walked silently back out to the awaiting cars, treading gently in the faint footprints that had been trod into the soft grass. Every guest slowly fallin into line to follow.

The wake was a splendid affair. Amber's in-laws were affluent and knew how to run an occasion like clockwork. Canapés were beautifully laid out on gold platters, offset by variegated ivy. Shots of yellow and gold highlighted the food as it lay upon them. Once all the guests had been catered for and everyone dried off from the showery weather conditions, goblets of wine were handed around for the parting toast. A hushed silence proceeded after Dean's father tapped a knife to one of the crystal goblets, the tiny bell ring vibrating through the air.

'I would like to say a big and most sincere thank you to all of you for attending today. We are of course shocked and raw from this sudden passing of our son. Our only wish is to extend our most heartfelt gratitude and support to you Amber, at this time of sadness. We are here for you in every way. My son met you for a reason, now so cruelly taken from us; we must remember the good times we shared with him as he looks down on us. Dean would want us to embrace life as he did. Not to live in sadness at our loss. His legacy is your new child. We will all be very proud to help in this new life that you will bring into this world shortly. Dean was a fabulous son. Both I and Irene could not have faulted him. Hardworking, kind and generous to a fault, his pleasure in having you in his life was everything, Amber.' He paused, regaining his composure,

'For now I would like you all to toast our son. Never forget but learn, life is for now and the present moment. Support and cherish the loved ones you have: to Dean our beloved son.' Overcome with emotion he hugged

141

his wife, smiling weakly at his audience, he sipped some wine to steady his nerve again.

Zara glanced over at Amber who slowly walked forward to kiss her father-in-law, turning to survey the guests, she spoke quietly,

'I too am very grateful. I cannot say how numb I feel at present to my situation but hope you will all not forget Dean in our busy lives. I am looking forward to being strong for our new daughter or son. My only regret is Dean will never get to experience or see his offspring. But I will do my best to bring them up with the same moral standards and fun they would've had with him. Thank you so much for being here.' Amber bravely raised her glass, her hand shaking slightly.

When the routine rituals had been completed, one by one the many guests left with their sincere and best wishes for Amber. Everyone struggled not quite knowing how or what to say, one of joy for a new child or one tinged with such a loss of a fine father.

Zara helped tidy the house removing the leftover food and placing the many cards upon the mantelpiece, adjacent to the loving and sentimental photos of Dean. Red rose petals fell onto the fire hearth, as the heat from the burning logs wafted a hot breeze, towards the fine flower display nearby. A present from Dean as Zara caught sight of the card propped up.

'To my darling wife may we be blessed with a child as sweet and caring as you, love you always D.'

Zara swallowed hard, she still felt this had been a dream, walking on auto pilot since returning from France, how on earth was she to make life normal for Amber ever again? Things had changed so much overnight.

Dean's mother emerged from the kitchen wearing a worn and very tired expression.

'Oh, hi dear I think we are done now. I believe you'll be staying with Amber tonight? Thank you for all your help. It's friends like you that she needs at a time like this.' Her eyes glanced at the card that Zara had placed neatly on the side, a dark shadow crossed her face and she turned back to the kitchen calling for her husband to hurry, Amber would want to rest in her condition.

The house had an eerie feel once everyone had left. Normally it had a relaxed Sunday morning atmosphere about it. Dean's golf gear scattered around, the two dogs bounding about, causing havoc amongst the financial papers Dean had to scour regularly. But now all items of this nature were hidden. The house now seemed like a show home, soulless and far too neat to be lived in.

Amber came in from seeing the last of the guests off and collapsed into the nearest chair and looking up at Zara she declared:

'I think I need a strong drink.'

'Do you think that's wise in your condition?' Asked Zara not sure what to suggest as she needed one herself by this stage.

'Oh, I forgot about that, the drama and stress of the day has made me forget everything. No, maybe not, although a small red wine can't do much harm, I need some iron, my body feels it's going to collapse soon.' With this comment Amber trembled. Her fragile frame seemed unable to cope anymore.

143

Zara sat down next to her hugging her close, 'We'll survive this. It may take a while but I'll be here for you, we all will. Let me run you a hot bath and put on some music, light stuff to relax to, come on.'

Leading Amber upstairs, Zara busied herself in the en-suite whilst her friend undressed. The bathroom still had bottles of aftershave and the many myriad of toiletries that Dean used to slap on. They were cascading out of most of the cupboards and stood lining some of the shelves.

Amber had clearly not wanted to sort this out probably due to the strong connection of smell that reminded her of him. Givenchy, Dior, Calvin Klein, there were more bottles than Zara had bought in a life time. She couldn't remember any exes that wore much aftershave. Most seemed to have the impression it wasn't macho enough. Maybe that was where she'd been going wrong all these years, they were too darn heterosexual for a lasting relationship.

The bubbles filled the deep oval bath slowly, brimming up to the edge of the golden rolled sides. Everything was opulent and Zara was quite envious of the house Amber lived in, but in her circumstances a lovely lavish lifestyle was empty if you had no one to share it with. It seemed that they were rattling around in it since Dean's accident. It was too quiet and lonely now.

Zara tried hard to set the scene, placing candles to waft soft scents near the bath, hanging some soft, deep pile towels on the radiator to warm, finally scattering a few rose petal flakes in a bowl for washing. By the time the bath had filled, Zara was quite pleased with the result. Leaving Amber to relax she busied herself checking the last of the funeral food had been cleared and the place resembled a less formal home.

Once Amber had slung on a warm robe after her bath, they both settled downstairs in front of the fire. Zara had tried to maintain its flame from earlier but it wasn't her specialty in life. Generally not having the opportunity to dwell in a big mansion or castle, it wasn't on the agenda normally. A switch of the button and hey presto the electric fire lit. Not the same ambience, and definitely not as romantic she had to admit. But this was the least of her problems, being more concerned at how Amber would carry on.

The flames flickered more as the fire took hold. Both girls became slightly hypnotized as the shadows danced across the room. Cupping the warm mug of tea as she sipped slowly from it, Amber turned and looked at Zara intently.

'Zara, don't waste any chances you get in life. If anything this has taught me, even if you find the one, your soul mate or whatever you like to call him, grab the opportunity by the horns. Even if it's only a small chink in time that you can experience the closeness of feeling at one with somebody, enjoy the moment. I have had a good time with Dean and know I was privileged to be with him even if it's disappeared so quickly.' Her eyes drew dark and started to water. Zara drew close and hugged Amber to her.

'I know what you're saying. It's you we need to look out for. Would you like me to stay for a while? I don't mind, I can still commute from here and let you get used to the difference in everything that's happened.'

Her friend looked again at the embers of the slowly decreasing fire. Dancing shadows drifted up over the creamy walls appearing similar to dancing fairies gliding gracefully across them.

'Maybe for a while, I've got to get used to the quietness some time. You've got your work to see to and now I've got a little one on the way there's plenty to sort out. I had wanted to leave so much to later. The nursery Dean and I were going to sort out next month, now I'll have to make those decisions I suppose. Then there's Dean's work to finalize.' Amber started to appear bewildered at the many jobs to complete.

'Don't you worry about that, Dean's dad will sort out most of the finance and work commitments, you just focus on baby. I'll get Bella to pop down regularly to check you're ok and help; she's very good at nest building as she calls it.'

With this statement Amber came back to reality and seemed to panic immediately.

'Bella, help no, no. I'll be ok, I'm not sure my vision will be the same as hers. I know she's close to you but I tend to find her a bit strange. She'll be trying to get me to talk to Dean or something; you know what she's like.' Amber's eyes drew wide with nervousness.

Maybe Bella wasn't such a good choice for rehabilitating someone who had just lost the love of their life thought Zara. She was a little weird at times; actually weird was too good a word, more on another planet.

Thinking back to how Bella had been at college, in particular her fundraising escapades for the student union were beyond the pale. Physic match in heaven she had named it. Her aim was to pair off as many people as possible with their astrological match.

The combinations had been frightening. One guy, a devout vegan of the persona no leather wearing or eating flesh of any animal, was so set in his views, he'd been on a charge for activist work already at the local cosmetic company. He very kindly released quite a few of the cute albino bunnies into the wild out of the goodness of his heart. Did this trait come into Bella's mindset when making her match in heaven? No, not one little bit, good old Bella found his match in heaven alright, oh yes, with the only chain smoking, leather clad Goth, who happened to hate anything remotely veggie, preferring her steak semi-raw, if she was to extract any iron from it. This might have allowed just a little flush of pink to grace her near white complexion.

Unfortunately most of the beautiful shading that graced her delicate features was make-up derived, from the lovely cosmetic company that Mr. Vegan despised so much. The fireworks flew in that match. It went on for weeks. It sent shivers down Zara's spine.

'Yes, I have to agree. I'll come over myself. My schedule isn't overly busy at the moment, just regulars. The posting for the Olympics is next summer, so it'll be fine. We'll have that nursery sorted in no time.' Zara noticed the relief in Amber's face, colour seemed to return and her eyes relaxed focusing on the dancing flames of the fire once again.

'Remember what I said Zara, take every opportunity. Don't just sit there and be controlled, move on quickly, life goes by like a flash. I can't even remember what Dean and I did the last time we were

147

together. It seems like another life time ago already.'
Zara clutched Amber's hand and holding it tight they
sat in silence taking in the moment, before both girls
drifted asleep from the emotional strain of the day. The
clock ticked softly in time with their breathing, the
embers dying slowly in the hearth. Silence finally
descended on the house.

Chapter 9

SECOND CHANCES

A loud screech of brakes approached the flat and Gina's little car came to a sudden halt. The wind was howling and rain was just starting to fall from the heavens. Welcome to bonny Scotland thought Zara. So much had happened since she was last up it seemed like a decade since she had been here. What with the death of Amber's husband, Tyler's departure from her life and work, she had felt her head was spinning. This was one break she needed more than anything prior to Christmas.

Hesitantly she approached the car. Gina had only just passed her test. Having been a student for so long, cars weren't a priority for her strapped for cash lifestyle. Now surpassing all expectations with flying honours at University only a few months back, Gina had walked straight into what was a reasonably paid job. Not exactly the ideal one but still the money was very attractive when she had struggled for so long.

'Hop in, it won't bite. I'm a bit late and the Christmas shopping traffic is going to start soon. Come on, we've got to get going.' Gina's high pitched voice yelled from the confinement of the compact vehicle.

Zara strapped herself in securely. This was going to

be a ride of her life that was certain. Gina wasn't one to do things by halves. She had a passion for living life to the full. Speed wise and social wise. No time for being shy or nervous with Gina about.

Speeding off into the dark night, a whirl of twinkling lights streaked past. Zara was unsure if they were car lights or Christmas tree lights, as the rivulets of rain water started to wet the window screen, distorting the bright lights to a blur.

Once on the motorway Zara gripped the sides of the seat quite intensely. Her knuckles started to go white with the pressure. One thing she wasn't going to do was drink heavily tonight. Free to do so, the beckoning late journey home was going to be rather interesting. Zara was still unsure why Gina wasn't drinking. Probably her detox for the festive period, though it was only the second of December mind you.

As they sped on, Zara had visions of being vacuum packed up the exhaust of the truck in front. She was starting to feel they were in a Mr. Magoo car with the Tasmanian devil as driver. Due to the mileage Gina was tearing up, they arrived at their destination on time. The venue being the Harbour Club and Gina's first ever works' Christmas party. Now in employment, the perks of the working world were now for her to enjoy. Zara knew one party and she'd be racing to sign up for the nearest university course available. On paper it sounded very plush but as the norm, a little bit of photo shop and marketing talk can make any dive sound like the Ritz. This location the girls knew was no Ritz once they arrived at the front entrance.

Walking in it was clear it was no more than a jazzed

up public bar. Definitely no private Harbour Club. Beer, cigarettes and way too much glitter everywhere; mostly adorning the workforce, greeted them immediately. A lively looking singer took center stage, belting out mostly archive songs that should have been relegated to gathering dust, from the past twenty years. His repertoire was varied credit due, from Bond movie theme tunes to Celebrate tonight, finalizing in a little Agadoo. It was going to be hard to know which foot to move first once the dancing began. Zara smiled weakly at Gina attempting to show enthusiasm.

They seated themselves at one of the larger tables. The crowd seemed reasonably young so it could bode well for conversation. Cherry red paper napkins and jugs of beer jostled for space amongst the balloons and garish Christmas crackers. Two bottles of solitary white wine were left untouched. They were obviously beer drinkers, thought Zara and began to assume the women might be as well, as she leant forward to retrieve a glass, noticing not one wine glass had been touched.

The meal was edible and well presented, if you ignored the tackiness of the surroundings that didn't do it much justice. A hushed silence came over the room. Zara looked up from devouring her tenth Christmas pudding in the last few weeks to notice all eyes were now riveted on the main table for the big raffle, everyone sitting in anticipated suspense.

Zara glanced over at Gina having a private grimace as the first few prizes were called out. A day in lieu, not much use to her, a bottle of sherry. (Did people still drink this? It reminded her of good old Babycham that her mother used to knock back in the holiday season,

151

well anytime there was a celebration. Practically most weekends if her mother had an excuse.) The scintillating prizes carried on: a desk fan not once but twice.

'Kindly donated by our in-house electrician,' declared the Managing Director of Gina's department. Much reveling followed this comment. Zara at this point was biting her lip so hard that it was close to drawing blood, lest she giggled out loud and offended Gina's colleagues.

Not all the staff were completely enamored by it all. Leaning sideways, Zara's neighbour (who by now was a little worse for wear) lisped gently in Zara's ear.

'Not much good winning that prize, my George brought his own fan in this summer, was told to remove it for health and safety reasons. Bloody cheek if you ask me. Now they're giving them away.'

Zara tried really hard now to suppress herself from giggling out loud. The woman's hair she noticed had a life of its own, reminding her of a large bird's nest. By now Zara could only picture it being entwined in the whirring blades of the so called fan, as she tried to seduce her George over his work station. She really needed a stiff drink to get through tonight. Having lurid thoughts of George who was seated opposite in a somewhat compromising position with the missus was not a happy one, even if it did pass the time.

The corporate clerical world wasn't Zara's idea of a job for life. Most jobs had their cringe factor and hers definitely had this in Roger, a boss you really didn't want to introduce to anyone you were on personal terms with. If Rodgy did care to have a raffle at their rare

Christmas night out, Gina would probably have hysterics herself, as good old Roger, would without doubt be offering the pleasant delights of a large tub of extra warming massage balm, for those little stubborn areas in need of lubrication, (probably having bought a job lot at the cash and carry) or a pair of snazzy signature towels.

Zara eyed the bar. Sensing she needed to escape rapidly she excused herself as politely as she could and shuffled over to order a stronger liquid to numb the brain. Any plans of alcohol avoidance had been dispelled by now. The journey home would be exhilarating for her psyche compared with this. She just hoped Gina's working day had more highs than tonight was having. As she propped up the bar, the DJ started an attempt to rev up the action.

The attraction of any groove master to grab dance talent from an event like this was always going to be slow. Out of the corner of her eye Gina was heading across the room straight at her. Zara gritted her teeth. The next stage of humiliation was about to begin. Signs of protesting went unheeded as Gina dragged her onto the floor, allowing enough time for one quick swig for Dutch courage.

Feeling like she was auditioning for the X-Factor, she felt all eyes were now planted securely on her fancy footwork. More than likely they were secretly commenting on her dance ability, being zero most times. Whether Lambda or Rumba, Zara had never mastered the correct rhythm. Hip swiveling was one feat she had never achieved however many times she'd gone to class.

Within the hour even George was whipping his shirt off with the best of them. Zara swiftly grabbed Gina when the music slowed down; she had no intention to be anywhere close to the dance floor for any slow numbers. Fearful for her dignity and wanting to remain polite for Gina's sake, she was keen to avoid any stray office gigolos, who by this time were well under the influence of the copious free alcohol being dispensed at the bar.

As the evening drew to a close they emerged into the damp night air. The rain had ceased now and the tap, tap of the mast wires on the neighbouring boats repetitively clicked away as the strong wind whipped across the harbour.

Zara in her haze of the evening had forgotten about the trip home. Not a fond lover of water she now found the boats a lot more appealing and attractive than being squeezed into Gina's car again.

'Did you enjoy yourself?' asked Gina.

'Yes, it's been err… a somewhat unusual experience, a little eye opening. I'm not sure I'm cut out for office life.' Her eyes rolled to the heavens but Gina was in full throttle mode, totally oblivious and ready to hit the road again, unaware of her friend's expression.

'Hold on tight, get ready for takeoff.'

Zara prepared herself grabbing the handrail above her head and pressing against the foot well with her feet. With a slight over revving and clunky gear change, they swung out of the harbour club car park back onto the open road. Zara shut her eyes tightly in the hope that not seeing the landscape pass by so fast, would allow her to feel less of the speed of Gina's driving. Sadly this didn't have much success. By the time they did reach the comfort of home Zara's face was a fetching shade of green, tinged with a white hue of fear.

'You ok? Too much sherry if you ask me. You're looking the same shade as my car, pistachio green. Here, let me give you a hand.' With this less than considerate comment Gina manhandled Zara up the stairs to her flat. Leaving her to lie comatose on the couch and hopefully return to a healthier glow.

By daybreak Zara had started to feel a little more normal from the after effects of Gina's driving and the alcohol induced hangover. Another day of Zara's precious break had passed by in a blur of activity. Gina's life never seemed to stop. How she fitted in any work she would never know.

Today Zara was on her own, able to wander the streets and take her time over the usual decision making of what to buy Aunt Ethel. She seemed to be permanently ninety, never appearing to age anymore, but alas, no spring chicken.

Zara pondered on what to get the old dear? Whisky, whether vintage quality or not was a bit strong for the liver. Then on the other hand why worry if you've got to nearly a century, your liver's done pretty well, whatever you'd dowsed it in.

One thing Zara was irritatingly slow at was making the right choice in men, work, anything. The more she thought the more she couldn't make her mind up. 'Well, follow your gut instinct so they say. Mine happens to be mega hungry so I'll buy it,' thought Zara. She was certain the nurses in the care home would have a tipple anyway.

The shops, due to the approaching season, were now a riot of festive fancies. Each window glowing spectacularly with multi coloured merchandise, tinsel and lights, some more traditional, unlike the majority of commercial and garish delights of London and the south. Zara adored the history and the whole feel of Edinburgh. It had nearly inspired her to study at degree level in architecture but her yearning for all things scientific had led her onto a different path. She skipped from shop to shop, relishing every new one she came across.

The smells of the specialist shops from haggis to spirits were making Zara's taste buds tingle and water. She really needed to stop and have a snack. Wandering amongst the shoppers, she spied a narrow alleyway leading down some much worn stone steps, adjacent to the castle.

A sign swung in the light breeze advertising hot coffee. The door was framed by twinkling yellow lights. Frosted panes of glass sprayed in snow dragged the mind back to how it must have been a century ago when snow in December was not amiss. So much for climate change, maybe they should consider altering the date thought Zara.

A slight frost still permeated the air around the alleyway. Music from a nearby flat could be softly detected, adding ambiance to the place blocking out any noise from the main street behind.

The bell tinkled above the door as Zara entered. Tiny wooden tables bestowed with holly and candles were crammed into the minute shop. Hot coffee beans ground away behind the counter and candles lit the back counter. It was a beautiful sight to behold and quite unexpected.

Zara spied a table near the corner and sat herself down. Flinging off her heavy coat, having ordered fairly quickly she studied the local paper, relaxing in the coziness of the café.

Suddenly her peace was interrupted by a young man enquiring to sit at the same table. The place had filled up all of a sudden and it was now a tight squeeze to get anyone else in. Every nook and cranny was filled with a body.

'Do you mind if I sit here?' enquired the lad, 'I'm dying for a cuppa.'

Zara looked up and stopped in her tracks, 'Yes, no problem. Please sit down,' she stammered shocked that she recognized the lad and to meet him in such an out of the way place.

'Well, well, well fancy bumping into you. This is a local gem of a place, not many outsiders know about the location. What's dragged you to bonny Edinburgh again then, gorgeous?' The young lad stared like a laser into Zara, a smile twitching at the corners of his mouth.

Staring back she absorbed his features once again, trying hard to remember what he was like the night they'd met from memory. She was certain he'd been slimmer and lankier in appearance. Scanning him now he was far from under developed. It had been only a few months, but he somehow seemed so different, she was surprised to recognize him at all. To avoid appearing fazed by her guest she offered to buy him a drink and replied quickly,

157

'I just popped up to see Gina and do a bit of Christmas shopping.' He glanced at her very sparse purchases.

'See you only came for the whiskey, you dark horse, I should have offered a bit of the amber nectar instead when you wouldn't take up my offer of some specialty hot cocoa, last time we met.' He smiled and nudged her playfully.

'No, that's for my Aunty, she likes a tipple occasionally and you can't get better than a nice malt can you?'

'Right, so the whole family's into the grog. I'll have to watch out. You might give me a run for my money on a night out.'

'Who said we were going on a night out?' Zara declared somewhat startled at his forwardness but enjoying the banter and his flirtatious attitude.

'A gorgeous girl like you up for the holiday season, in my own personal coffee shop, no foreigners invited. I think it's only right I should extend the hand of friendship, and cordially take you out for a night of fun and games. Scottish style of course. Are you up for it?' he enquired, leaning closer his hand brushed hers as he leant in to sip his coffee.

Zara felt strangely excited at his presence again, just as she had the night they'd met in the club with Gina. Feeling a little adventurous she accepted the offer. Time sped by and closing hour was approaching. She still had purchased no more than a couple of presents all day.

Another steaming cup of cocoa arrived and Zara knew she really must make a move. Gina would be home soon and they were sure to be chucked out shortly. Brett laughed at her concern.

'No worries here, they don't conform to time. Live above the shop so really we're in their lounge. They won't chuck us out unless it's bedtime. We can finish this and I'll take you on a moonlit walk around the streets. The city will be well lit up by now. I'll keep you warm.'

Aware of his raw sexuality even more now, Zara found she wanted to edge a little closer. His long thighs touched hers. He appeared quite a strapping six foot; his arms were muscular, not boyish, with long slender and soft hands. She'd never noticed this before, just focusing on his facial features but his frame was one that could cuddle you, making you feel protected within its grasp.

Laughing inwardly at being influenced by such a young guy she was beginning to feel like a teenager again having a date in the local café. Nowadays women desired hotels, dinner, and the whole package. A walk wasn't normally on the agenda, but it seemed more romantic when she looked at the simpler things.

Outside darkness had descended on the streets lit by the glow of the streetlights. Very ornate gas lamps in the past would have shone over the uneven cobbles beneath their feet, leaving dark shadows in the passageway. Sadly nowadays the harsh electric lights stole the effect. Elsewhere the Christmas lights shone from numerous windows. The large multi layered buildings sheered up towards the sky, each window gleaming with a tree or fairy lights draped elegantly across their ledges, softening the grayness of the stone.

Brett grasped Zara's hand and guided her up the street stopping to point out various areas of interest. She observed the city in a totally different setting, more serene and atmospheric than in harsh daylight where commercialism tended to take over a little.

Cold shafts of air bellowed out every time one of them spoke. Climbing up the steep steps in the direction of the castle, Brett guided Zara into a doorway. Pausing, he grinned and asked very softly to a rather bemused Zara,

'I can't wait any longer. I've tried being a gentleman but now feeling as we are somewhat more acquainted, I need to graciously request a kiss.'

Although appearing calm, a certain urgency and longing was detectable in his tone of voice. Zara was impressed with his courtesy and she did fancy, just a tiny part of her, to revisit the effect of their last kiss. Just to prove it wasn't in the heat of the moment. She was certain it was just that, the occasion and a desperate yearning to give her a boost. But Zara was in for a surprise, as he leant forward, their lips brushing closer together.

Brett hugged her closer. His body felt warm and inviting. With the gentlest of touches he grazed her cheek and entwined his fingers through her hair caressing each tendril, sending tingling down her spine again, as his touch came to rest at the base of her neck. The effect was more like the full national grid.

Zara pulled his body closer to her, tucking her hands deep inside his coat. Feeling the taut curve of his back drifting to the dip of the lower spine she felt strangely shy and didn't feel she should venture lower.

As they came up for air Brett smiled.

'I've been dying to do that the moment I set eyes on you again. You kiss pretty well I can tell you.'

Gazing down at her, he suddenly appeared even taller than in the cafe. Zara leant in and breathed deeply. Brett smelt like marshmallows: she felt the urge to kiss him again. The sensation experienced on their first meeting was the same. Having no control over how her body was reacting chemistry-wise, Zara moved in closer pulling Brett's head nearer to her lips. Without hesitation she kissed him long and hard. He may have been a fleeting stranger as such but she defiantly wanted to gain access to more of him as quickly as she could.

Brett seemed unabashed at her complete abandon of lunging at him; with a twirl he grasped her waist and lifted her from the ground. Zara gripped tight at his waist. He felt warm and so nice between her thighs.

'Wow, what do you do for regular exercise, your buttocks are like buns of steel?'

Zara burst out laughing and the moment was lost, as Brett stumbled on the cobbles and they came crashing down to the floor. Zara grabbed the handrail nearby to control the fall. Unshaken by their sudden landing Brett picked her up and hugged her close.

'Come on, let's hit the bar. I'll show you how to warm up the Scottish way.'

Staggering being the only way down the somewhat slippery street, they made slow progress towards the bar of Brett's choice as the frost was starting to form beneath their feet. Peals of laughter rang out each time their footing ran away from them. Within minutes Brett

161

had sought out a tiny gem of a pub, not dissimilar to their previous haunt Zara had stumbled upon by accident.

Built into the hillside a set of spiraling stairs led to a door so small it looked like a tiny cottage. Brett stooped to go in, his tall frame filling the tiny entrance, pulling Zara behind him.

The pub was warm as toast. Solid oak panels decorated the walls from floor to ceiling making the atmosphere welcoming. Brett maneuvered them a pathway to the bar and Zara was aware of many a local eyes upon them. Her cheeks were smarting from the contrast of air and they felt tingly and warm.

Music echoed around the room. A steady beat ricocheted from the rafters. Squeezing in between Brett and the bar she felt him hug her close and nuzzle her hair. His breath sent tingles along her neck again.

'My treat and I won't take no for an answer. How about some Scottish liquor to warm your throat? I'll choose a good one.' Two tumblers were planted sturdily upon the bar as the glistening amber fluid trickled over ice.

'No ice for me mate, I like it neat, no fancy diluting,' he turned and smiled at Zara.

'For you, I think you may need it. I want your throat in good working order not smarting with fire.' His hand brushed her bottom finding the small of her back he pulled Zara in closer.

'I'm really proud to be here with you. I can imagine what those old boys are thinking how a guy like me, pulled someone like you.'

'I don't know, you're not doing yourself justice.'

More the other way round thought Zara deciding not to say it out loud, keeping it firmly between closed lips.

She took a swig of the drink and it was indeed like fire water, smooth but very strong. Immediately Brett came in to kiss her, she had barely swallowed the drink before his tongue probed her mouth, dipping gently into her mouthful of drink. As he moved back, she swallowed what was left. A bit intimate she thought - not one to share her drink normally let alone once in her mouth.

'Umm, that was nice. An alcohol laced kiss. I can highly recommend it. Not bad.' Again as she sipped her drink he came in for another. Zara giggled and pushed him away.

'You'll get the locals chucking us out for indecent behaviour.'

'Nice idea, I've always wanted a reputation as a gigolo.' But he took heed and stepped back allowing her to finish her drink in peace.

The music upped in tempo and by the third drink the place was rocking with all walks of life, from beard clad bikers to young students popping in for one on the way home from. Zara glanced at her watch.

'Crikey! Look at the time. Gina will be back by now and wondering where on earth I am. I should be going back,' she said very half-heartedly.

'Sure, whatever, I'll walk you back. I know Edinburgh well so I'll take you a quick way. Where does she live?'

'Robinson's Row, down from the posh part of town as far as I can gather, if my bearings are right,' stammered Zara. Her navigation skills were poor and she could only go by shops she'd passed when walking in.

'No problem, it will be an honour to escort you to your door.' With a flourish of his hand Brett whisked her out of the pub and proceeded to head up the steep hill back to Gina's. Gripping her hand tight he squeezed it gently. The journey didn't take long. They were standing outside the flat before she knew it.

'Well this is goodbye again. I wish you didn't have to go,' declared Brett as he moved in closer to kiss Zara goodbye.

'If you ever pass by again let me know.'

Zara sighed. She really wished that she lived closer but the opposite ends of Britain was not good for a friendship, let alone the start of a relationship. If that was what it might be?

'How will I get in contact with you? Zara was aware she knew very little about Brett, not even where he lived or surname for that matter.

'Here, this is my mobile, the flat phone I share with some girls so it's a bit hard to get a message there, always goes amiss. I might be out of contact at times as my family live out in the country side. Bit short on masts but I'll get a message sometime.' He peered deep into her eyes cupping her face in his warm fingers and a sense of mischief lit up his eyes.

'I'll miss your cute English ways, but do let me know how Aunty likes the whiskey. Sounds like my kind of girl.' Leaning in he brushed Zara's lips gently again. She shivered in the cool night air; a sense of sadness gnawed always. It was a shame it could all end now. Maybe it was better to let things pan out, within

164

seconds he had disappeared over the hill, his long shadow striding in the distance. Earlier her mind had become somewhat hazy and Gina would want to know what she had been up to all day. It felt more like a dream, or was that the effects of the drink. At this moment the facts were a blur.

Slowly she ascended the steep steps to the flat. Her mind whirring with questions unanswered about him. Acutely aware he shared a flat with the opposite sex, a small amount of jealousy trickled in. The lucky cows, she thought wondering what they were like; were they young students or older? What did he do for a living? She could have kicked herself for not asking at the time.

Entering the flat she found Gina full of energy, bounding around like a happy puppy. A pile of ironing stood on the side, with music blaring from her stereo as she shimmied around the room dusting in her very tiny underwear. Gina had no shame about her body, unabashed completely. Zara was sure she wouldn't have blinked an eyelid if Brett had come upstairs with her. Though Zara was sure she herself would have felt a slight twinge of fear. Gina was very fit and it wouldn't have gone unnoticed in Brett's eyes she was sure, a close shave indeed.

'You must have shopped and explored till you dropped. Where's all the Christmas shopping then? Demanded Gina eyeing up Zara's rather measly bag clearly confused at the lack of purchases.

'Err! I kind of got distracted by something.'

'You better tell me more? It must have been one hell of a distraction. You've been gone for hours and with

165

the flushing in your cheeks I will need to know everything.' Gina laughed with glee as she could see right through Zara who was attempting to be discreet about the situation.

'Tell me more?' With that she bounded over the back of the couch duster in one hand, 'Come on spill the beans.'

Chapter 10

THE LAST SEDUCTION

The winter months seemed long and tedious to Zara having spent time at home with the family over the festive period on returning from her northern jaunt. Life was now back to normal but in the background her concern for Amber was still very evident, attempting to be buoyant and uplifting whenever she was with her - all in a vain bid to make life seem a little more normal once again.

Christmas was, she knew, the hardest period for her friend to pass through, so close to the event of losing her husband. Now Zara was starting to feel totally exhausted from keeping up such a cheery persona for so long. Family had driven her to distraction with their petty squabbles that seemed so trivial to Amber's situation.

The saving grace was work plans. These were going into overdrive. The practice was getting some very good contracts now for various sporting events and seemed to be going from strength to strength. Zara had to work seriously hard now to gem up on theory and attend workshops to keep up to date in furthering her skills.

This was the perfect distraction she needed to keep

the mind active as well as the body. The stimulus and buzz from expanding her knowledge of the body was fantastic. She had a fair few ideas that the work team were now putting into action, with the promise of more control in her section, perfect timing. Jamie was one guy who Zara could bounce off a few of them. His mindset seemed to think along the same tracks.

Roger was obviously pleased, as a steady stream of revenue was coming in, racking up the money so much that they were now shortly moving into some swanky new premises - equipped with one rather flash in-house physiotherapy pool. Zara had been trying so hard to push for support with some of her disabled work. The pool was going to make life a whole lot easier. Working with the local disabled school had been fulfilling, but the hassle booking time at the local Hospital pool was proving more and more difficult.

One feature of their own gym meant the staff could also train if they desired and be on hand for more personal training. Thus opening a whole doorway to some diverse customers at all levels. It was a great opportunity for the clinic. It had fired up a little excitement. Work was not such the restricted slog it had been.

The park was misty creating a soft muffled effect to the crisp crunching sound Zara's feet made on the gravel path, as she ran around the perimeter. Determined to get a little fitter, the run was the start of an extensive workout plan. The effects of stodgy food in the holiday season had made her feel like a puffed up doughnut. In fact she was certain she resembled one as well in certain lights.

Stopping to take a deep breath and stretch her legs on the wooden bench nearby, Zara took some time to look around properly. There was hardly anyone present at this time of the day. The solitude was great to focus the brain cells. Which in her case were always in overload mode. The peace was shattered all too soon when the shrill sound of her mobile penetrated the air.

'Oh ruddy hell, it was probably Roger wanting her in early or something. I knew I should have left the mobile at home.' Her mood changed instantly from being still and collected to on edge and grumpy. Putting the receiver to her ear, she heard a voice that was familiar but definitely not Roger.

'Hi, how're you doing? A soft dulcet and very Scottish voice echoed down the phone.

'Fine how are you?' Zara's mood instantly lifted and she could feel her heart beating quicker. A sense of nervousness crept over her; she'd completely forgotten about Brett with work and family issues, certain it was going to be Roger. Since visiting Gina she hadn't heard anything and had put it to rest, trying hard to focus on other things that were obviously more important than pathetic affairs of the heart.

'You sound a little flustered. Have I called at a bad time? Or is it my sexy voice that's causing such a rampant effect?'

'You wish, I was just having a run in the park you know, usual New Year mission to get the butt into gear.' Zara prayed she didn't sound too breathless as she felt at that moment her oxygen levels were lowering somewhat, with physical exertion and the thumping of her chest at the same time. It wasn't a healthy combination throwing her body into overdrive hearing from him so out of the blue.

'Shame, I must be losing it.' he laughed making it clear by the sound of his voice he knew otherwise.

'I found myself back at the bar that we hit on with some friends after Christmas, when you were up visiting. It brought back some memories. My New Year mission was to track you down, hence my call at this unearthly hour. Thought you would be tucked up in bed describing your most innermost thoughts to me. Never mind I'll catch you next time.' Zara chuckled to herself. How could she be nervous of Brett, he was too beguiling and funny. He'd make anyone feel comfortable.

'You're teasing me and why would I let you into those most innermost secrets? I hardly know you in that way just yet.'

'True, but if I do get the opportunity to catch you, will you divulge them? Otherwise my offer on the table may not be put forward.'

'Offer, what offer? I'll need to know the goalposts first.' Zara was rather inquisitive now. Surely he wasn't coming down to visit her. She could hardly believe he would. They'd only met twice and although intense not exactly long in duration. There were a thousand and one questions to ask, which took some time to enter conversation; dating was a game from what she could see, a process of elimination each person scoring points in the eye of their beholder before they could continue on the path of the dating cycle.

Flashbacks to her flat projected in her memory. What would he think of it? Was he a slovenly laid back

170

kind of guy, anything goes or was he anally tidy, everything in its place? Some days her flat looked as if a kindergarten had run amok.

Her motto was always be prepared for guests, but allow a time frame of at least an hour to discard wet undies from bathroom radiators, hide anything remotely personal from teddies to ladies accessories, (Gina had insisted she return with some of the merchandise resent as replacements for the unfortunate stolen items. Talk about costly she really didn't need to purchase the gold and rather garishly tasseled vibrator). True she definitely didn't have an alternative to it. As Gina so rightly said, keeping up with the new technology was important if she was to have a fit and healthy love life. How this would impact on her near extinct sex life she wasn't clear. I suppose it keeps things in working order, kind of takes the romance out of it but maybe it wasn't such a bad purchase.

Hiding the offending article was rather more difficult. The flat was short of storage. Open plan in design, it made storage problems a big issue. When an unexpected visit from her parents arrived, it culminated in coming up with an impromptu and very quick explanation of the said item. Describing it as a tribal artifact she'd picked up in the south of France with Jamie. Her mother bought this well but she could see her father was not so gullible and was clearly keen to investigate further.

It had been an effort to distract his attention, one saving grace being Ms Godfrey, the neighbour who happened to live directly opposite. Her most recent hobby was belly dancing. Ms Godfrey was now intent

171

on practicing this recent pursuit on a more regular basis, generally in full view of her picturesque window, having a preference to showcasing the delights from her most recent class. Being of ample proportions she was quite a spectacle to watch and clearly her father thought so too. Mum was hurried into kitchen to talk Christmas food lists, whilst her father stood transfixed to the spot, watching the curvaceous silhouette of a sixty year old woman. Zara focused on Brett's voice once again.

'Well, I'm on a training course for skiing and climbing in snow conditions.'

'You are? Umm, nice - not your usual course then.' Zara was now really intrigued. What the hell did he do for a living? Why did she always meet super fit blokes? The thought of chucking herself down a mountain didn't come up on her wish list of things to pursue before she died. In fact if it was, she was pretty certain that is what it would entail, a death wish for sure.

'Yeah, so I've got a couple of days to get acclimatized before starting. Just wondered if you could make it up to the Cairngorms for a flying visit? It's next week, I'll take you up the mountain if you fancy it for some skiing yourself, you look as if you could look after yourself on the slopes.'

Zara nearly choked, this wasn't an idea that made her dance with glee. She could make a right fool of herself; standing would be a feat in itself let alone sliding downhill. Before her mind knew what her voice was saying she spluttered.

'Yes I'd love to, but I will have to come clean. I've never actually skied much. When I have I'll be honest, I kind of don't get the hang of it that well, might dampen your enthusiasm.'

'That's fine, I'll be there to hold and guide you. Ring me back as soon as you get to work with your decision and let me know, gotta go the trains in.'

The phone went dead and Zara was left reeling from the invitation. Her legs started to feel cold from standing still so long. Jogging gently round one more time she headed off back towards home. Funny how one second life sucked, now there was a thousand and one reasons to get fit in one week, not to mention what she was to wear in arctic conditions. How can you look sexy in an all-in-one with thermal undies? This needed some serious thought.

Trembling inside Zara started trawling through her wardrobe, her mind trying to piece suitable items together. Panic was setting in early and she hadn't even got on the train yet. Before Zara knew it the weekend would be here and she needed to be packed, booted and hopefully appropriately suited for the mission ahead.

Many thoughts had lingered on her mind at how she would feel meeting Brett again. Would she still be attracted to him? It had been a while since she had seen him and she was finding it harder and harder to recall his looks. A rosy image was all she could visualize and she was sure she was kidding herself.

Well nothing ventured, nothing gained. Amber's words etched the back of Zara's mind. She was going to take every chance she was offered, even if it went nowhere. So what? She was a modern woman, and was sure she could think of some excuse to avoid any compromising situations. If indeed he wasn't what she'd been hoping for. With this thought she continued to plough through her rather dire wardrobe for last minute items of importance.

The weekend approached surprisingly quickly, giving Zara no time to fret at what she was to encounter. In fact she woke nervous but very positive. She busied herself before leaving. Zara surveyed her luggage, as usual having packed a tad too much, but hey she needed to be equipped for all eventualities. In this case it was a winter expedition. Though what Brett would think she wasn't sure. But she set off with a frisson of anticipation at what lay ahead.

Once Zara locked eyes on Brett immediately the memory of his face, body: every detail came flooding back. But she was still uncertain he was really her type. At every chance encounter with him so far, she had been somewhat surprised by her reaction. Silently cautious she was feeling unsure if any frisson of excitement would happen, maybe it had been a one off when they'd met in Edinburgh, the romance and intrigue of the big city taking over. Zara did wonder if she had just imagined the connection they'd experienced together, having a bad habit of building up something that wasn't there. Look at Tyler; they'd hardly seen each other but she still thought she'd meant something to him over the brief dates they had touched base.

Since Brett's sudden meeting with her, she hadn't let him prey on her mind. In fact being so wrapped up with life, Brett hadn't even got a mention. So why had she been so enamored in coming up to see him? For what was only a weekend of fear and embarrassment? The skiing was going to be one hell of an ice breaker.

Walking slowly across the concourse Zara's heart mellowed and some of the many fears that were shooting left right and centre in her mind calmed and dissipated as he smiled a warm welcoming grin. Stepping forward he wrapped his arms around her holding Zara gently but firmly, planting a huge kiss upon her lips.

'Hi gorgeous, so you took up my offer, I must be irresistible.' Brett laughed mischievously.

'Let's pop in a taxi, it's not far where we're staying for the two nights.'

Zara breathed a sigh of relief at least they weren't hiking to the accommodation. She just hoped it wasn't some modern communal hostel which probably was the new 'in' thing for the under thirties.

As they approached the resort, the taxi turned rather abruptly up past a lake onto a tiny, single track road. As they trundled down the path the wheels skidded occasionally, as every bump and dip lurched the car from side to side. It was definitely going to be remote by the looks of it. Zara was certain no hotel or B & B could possibly be allowed access like this. They wouldn't get much repeat business.

Fir trees of every type stretched as far the eye could see. A hazy mist clutched softly at the tops of the jagged mirage in front of her, enveloping the surroundings and muffling any sound emitted.

Zara emerged from the cab, her long limbs suddenly feeling rather cold and somewhat underdressed for the damp climate. Brett appeared rather quickly from the other side of the cab and held out a hand for Zara to take. Noticing his eyes sliding south she was fully aware of his gaze settling on the rather short skirt, which at this precise moment in time wasn't covering what it should have been properly.

He was either thinking that she was particularly stupid to wear such ridiculous clothing or imagining he had died and gone to heaven. Either way she was sending out all the wrong signals for a first official meeting.

Zara felt she'd hit a midlife crisis early and may have to play this one rather coyly. The thought of being shacked up with a guy who she didn't fancy however comfortable he was to be with, was going to be hard. What would she do if he became even more amorous with her and she wasn't keen?

Zara's feelings were conflicting, deep down she felt excited at the prospect, the newness of what might be, but alarmed at the problem if it didn't stir up any initial feelings that had arisen on their last two meetings. 'Well there was nothing for it but to await kick off.'

Feeling Brett's warm hands gripping hers she glanced at him. He still seemed relaxed, confident and boyish. Maybe he just might be worth learning a little more about.

He rummaged in his pocket retrieving a large iron key as she followed him through the woods towards a clearing. The poor taxi driver was struggling far behind with Zara's expedition clutter. Brett turned and beckoned to the guy behind.

'Wait a minute; I'll give you a hand. No need to struggle.' He turned to Zara and smiled gently, 'We do like to come prepared. You wouldn't need half those things if I'd packed.'

176

Zara wasn't quite sure what he meant by this. Was he scorning her or anticipating they would be undressed most of the time? She still couldn't read his mind yet but his courtesy and respect for other people was rather appealing. Tyler would have ignored the driver expecting him to be his lackey. Not a trait Zara approved of one bit.

They emerged into the clearing having been showered by the tiny raindrops cascading from the trees, which kept brushing their heads as they stooped beneath them on the tiny path. Zara for the first time saw their accommodation clearly. Before her was a wooden chalet very akin to a chocolate box design. A balcony overlooked the lake; a large pile of wooden logs lay to one side of the door. Looking up, a spiral of white smoke drifted lazily into the misty sky.

'Umm,' thought Zara this might be rather fun. It wasn't a smelly hostel after all thank goodness. Something to rejoice about she thought.

'Do you like? Enquired Brett, 'It's a mate's family pad, they like to come up here regularly to ski and do what most Scottish locals love: enjoy the fresh mountain air. It's great in the summer too, barbeque heaven if you're immune to the midges. I'd imagine you have sweet blood, so might be rather preferential to their dinner, but we could have some fun applying the midge repellent.' nudging her playfully Zara smiled back hesitantly.

Entering the chalet Brett left her and went back to help the driver. The air smelt nice of wood resin releasing from the fire's burning logs. Zara wandered towards the hearth; it was roaring well. Her hands

177

edged closer to the flames warming and tingling her bare cold flesh back to life. Glancing around the room she noticed a bottle of wine on the table, some muffins and a scrawled note presumably from the owner. Inquisitive Zara walked back towards it and tried discreetly to read the note before Brett walked in.

'Hi, you old dog, hope the pad is up to scratch for you matey? Just a little pressie for you and your beau, don't do anything I wouldn't do.' Andy.

Zara smiled. His mate knew more than she knew about his intentions. He seemed friendly from the language of the note and obviously was a close friend.

Brett returned and closed the door on the damp mist. They were finally completely alone for the first time since they'd met. Brett read the note and chuckled tossing it aside into the fire.

'I think we should get this chilled ready for tonight. I'll cook, Andy should have left me some items in the fridge I hope or otherwise we'll be catching our dinner from the lake.' Eyeing the cases he hurled them up the wooden stairs with Zara following slowly behind. Approaching the bedroom Brett dumped the luggage down on the bed.

'I better get out of these wet things. Trust it to rain but hopefully the snow will come in again up high tonight. We should get some good skiing in then.'

Zara was distracted with what he had said as he peeled the brown jersey from his body. Having not seen much of him up to now, she was very surprised at his physique. It wasn't as developed as Gina's Abman but wasn't something you would turn away in haste. Brett became aware of Zara's eyes boring into him.

'Here come over, I think you may need to warm up and get dry yourself.'

Zara hesitantly went closer feeling strangely excited. Was this going to be it so soon? They'd only just arrived, surely he wasn't intending to seduce her just yet. He pulled her close lowering his long lashes eyes and gazing transfixed down at her. Fingering her top at waist level, with one clean sweep he pulled it slowly and precisely up and over her head. Leaning forward she could feel his breath on her neck as he slowly undid her bra. Brett had obviously had experience in the past, no fiddling required here.

Zara could feel his lean torso mould to her body. Warm and very inviting he stroked her gently down the spine as he unbuttoned her skirt, gliding it seductively down over her hips till it fell softly at her feet. She felt comfortable but slightly embarrassed at her nudity, so feeling compelled to even the stakes she reached down and undid the thick metal buckle of Brett's jeans. The next challenge was the buttons. She loved the style but was she going to be as professional at undoing as he'd been.

The tight buttons fell open revealing nothing but Brett in his full glory. Zara swallowed hard. She certainly wasn't expecting this but strangely was getting turned on with anticipation more than she thought. Was it just because it was with someone new? She was unsure, feeling way too forward for being so quick in being seduced.

The yearning within her grew as Brett fingered her briefs; slowly and gingerly probing deeply he playfully rubbed and stroked her intimately. Like slippery silk his

179

fingers grazed her, the sound of heavy breathing filled the room. Zara was very aware of her body's reaction to his touch. Arching closer to his body she felt him stiffen and harden beneath her pelvis.

Delicately he cupped her face as he'd done on that cold evening in Edinburgh and kissed her hard, his tongue probing all corners of her mouth. Zara gasped and the tingle of electricity she'd felt started to mount within in her. Brett felt very compatible indeed. Feeling the rim of Brett's jeans she slid one hand beneath the hard fabric glancing over his buttocks that felt taut and smooth to her touch.

He moaned gently as her hand touched his skin. Nuzzling her ear he tenderly kissed the lobe. Suddenly the intensity of the moment was rudely interrupted by a sharp banging on the Cabin door. Brett smiled and hastily started to make himself suitably attired to venture down the stairs again.

'I'll finish this later, get some warm clothes on and I'll see who it is. Don't worry; you won't be disappointed I can assure you.' He cupped Zara's face in his hand and planted a delicate kiss again upon her now moist and wet lips.

It happened to be one of the local neighbours just checking in that all was well. Zara was sure if they knew what was going on yards from their front door, that they would indeed know all was going well.

It was just her luck to have a nosy neighbour come knocking, in the remotest part of Scotland and at the vital moment. Interrupting her first time of getting down and dirty, with a hot new guy, she prayed the moment wouldn't be disrupted again. As from now she clearly had her mind set on enjoying the moment.

Once Brett had politely spoken and assured all concerned he was in control and close friends with the owners, they left Brett to promptly close the door. Breathing a sigh of relief he leant heavily against the wood panel rolling his eyes to heaven.

Zara could hear Brett's hasty retreat back upstairs as he bounded up the steps two at a time.

'Nice couple, I've met them before once, very briefly. Give them an inch and they'll take a mile, if you slightly beckon them in. They would probably settle in for the night and that isn't what I had in mind for us. Making small talk and discussing the attributes of the lesser spotted something or other would have driven me crazy.'

'Bird watchers I gather are they?'

'You could say that in a big way. So if you see a guy with binoculars strutting around focusing on the chalet, just be careful you don't flash yourself at the window. I'm not sure if his old ticker could cope with it after seeing what I've just seen. I want to keep you under cover for myself.' He walked over to Zara and tweaked her from behind.

'Dinner will be served in a short while. I'll just stoke up the fire first; get it nice and cozy in here, so we can snuggle down. Exercise of the external variety can wait till tomorrow. You get some warm clothes on while I sort dinner.'

When suitably dressed again, Zara sat down and watched Brett as he busied himself. He seemed so much in control. None of her ex's could have even known how to light an open fire properly. They would have

181

been either smoked out or froze to death unless they sat on the ruddy thing.

Before long a delightful smell was erupting from the kitchen area, she obviously wasn't going to starve either. With a flourish Brett appeared laden with two steaming plates of food. As they sat down the light became softer as dusk approached. Brett lit some candles and the mood of the chalet changed to a soft warm glow. His face seemed even younger in this half-light and extremely fetching. Zara hoped it had the same effect on her features as the age gap she was now starting to be slightly aware of.

The food was delicious dowsed down with some copious full bodied red wine. Zara felt pleasantly relaxed and dreamlike in quality. After putting the world to rights in their own way Brett stood up, shoving the plates into the centre of the table he led Zara over to the fire.

'Here, make yourself comfortable, I've bought some marshmallows to toast over the fire, a favourite of mine.' The sweet smell reminded her of when they'd met last time.

The fire had started to die down to a red warming glow. As Brett twirled the gooey sweets over the heat, Zara sat watching his every move. Although years apart, he seemed more intelligent and worldly wise than Zara felt herself. Offset with his youthful charm she was inexplicably drawn to him.

'Here try this,' as he trickled the mixture slowly on Zara's tongue. It felt very sensual as he leant forward breathing closely into her space. The electricity between them was stirring again, sending shivers down

182

Zara's back.

Brett's eyes scanned Zara's body in great detail, as the fire flickered softly silhouetting her outline perfectly. He shifted uncomfortably feeling the heat and urge increase in his groin. How much longer he could resist this girl he wasn't sure.

Lazily he traced a finger over Zara's shoulder gliding slowly and hesitating as it hovered gently across the crest of her chest. She shivered and Brett half pulled back unsure of her response to his caressing. She truly was stunning, he couldn't believe his luck that she would be half interested in a guy like him. Was it a shiver of anticipation or of nervousness and reluctance to his touch?

Her bodily cues indicated it was not the latter and with a smile and tilt of her head Brett continued his exploration beneath his fingertips. Zara's body shuddered softly again.

Damn it! He really was finding it hard to be the perfect gentleman. The desire for her was kicking in big time, there was no way he could resist her tonight. There was something about this girl he couldn't stop desiring and he was sure he would want more once this break was over.

He hesitated in opening Pandora's Box. Brett's plans for the next two to three years didn't involve a static location and a girl on his arm. If he slept just once with her it would cause major problems. He didn't want Zara to think of him as toying with her affections or using her for her bodily charms, once more, even twice, then an unspoken agreement was always assumed on the girl's part, that they were indeed possibly an item by then.

Brett's stomach clenched at the thought. Too many of his close mates were now entwined with a woman in some stage of development. His memory already haunted by a recent Ikea experiment he'd had to endure with his best mate Ed. What a sad loss to society he was going to be. Now married with the usual 2.4 kids in tow, Brett endured hours of social hell looking after two screaming brats from Nightmare on Elm Street. The mind numbing sense of loss at being entombed in what was a DIY handy man's paradise was hard to eradicate. What was their achievement? A coffee table and one set of cutlery. It wasn't something he wanted to repeat in a hurry.

Zara turned and sat up. Her profile looked even more alluring outlined by the rosy glow of the fire. Examining her features he looked longingly at the shape of her neck. Flaxen gold hair shone rich with the many hues of orange and red glinting perfectly in the half light. It was the one thing Brett had noticed when he'd first encountered this living stunner from out of nowhere.

Appearing by his side he'd been in awe at first but Zara had been so open and easy to communicate with, he liked her style immediately. It made what was a rather iffy night into one with some great potential.

Although Brett's chat up lines had failed miserably at the last moment if he recalled, it was probably for the best as the amber nectar had taken its toll on his body by then and he was pretty certain the evening wouldn't have lived up to his own standard of expectations that tonight might well do. Who was he kidding, with this one he may have to work a little harder.

Brett had had many a girl in his past, younger and older but Zara was somewhat different. A certain air and charm that enticed him in. She hypnotized and charmed him in a way no other girl had before. The lure of her lips devouring his body was one hell of a turn on. Brett decided he was being well and truly intoxicated in the heat of the moment if he desired something like that.

Zara turned towards him, and he decided to make his move. Slowly and seductively he stroked her face and as he felt the soft dewy texture of her skin, he lowered his lips to hers. Each time had been better than the last and this was no exception. Zara was one hell of a kisser.

Lost in thought Brett languished in heaven as he drew her closer to him, feeling her curves beneath his chest. He wanted more and more to be within her now. Flashbacks of earlier when he'd glimpsed Zara's body undressed and beckoning, it had taken all his control and willpower to pull away when that doorbell had rung. He was secretly cursing but it had helped to quell the situation at least until now.

Zara moaned softly as he explored her mouth and gingerly stroked her body. His fingers now circled Zara's smooth taut belly. Warm and pulsing beneath his touch he ventured lower, gliding down across her hips and then the most pleasurable part to Brett encompassing the sloping curve of a girl's inside thigh.

Feeling his heart beating harder than ever, his breath deepened at the thought of moving closer into Zara. Caressing further, Zara arched forward her pelvis pressing very clearly against him; he was in no doubt that she was now fully aware she had his attention, as nothing was going to hide his ardour now. Moving gently against him Brett felt more excited by the minute.

Seconds later the deft unbuckling of his belt and the great precision of one swift rip of buttons which impressed even him, Zara had more style than he had with bra territory. Before he had time to decide what move was to be next Zara sat astride him, staring gleefully into his eyes. She peeled his shirt undone, stroking and massaging his chest. Her pelvis rocked and pressed repeatedly on a most personal area.

Brett lay back and enjoyed every pressure and turn. When he could bear this no more he rolled sideways returning him to power and lay astride Zara.

Smiling he leant down and delicately lifted the tight sweater that encased her form, kissing butterfly kisses slowly over her exposed tummy. Nuzzling lower he pulled the taut fabric of Zara's skirt easing it over the gentle curve of her hips. Brett viewed the most desirable part of Zara. Kissing slowly once again he glided his head between her thighs as a fine frond of hair framed her tight underwear.

Brett absorbed and worked deeper with his lips, removing the fragile lace from her form. Even he gasped at the beauty of what he saw. His loins clenched tightly fingers gliding and tongue exploring every cleft and inch of Zara he felt her quiver at his every touch.

Soon he couldn't withstand the heat of her reaction to him anymore. He moved upwards penetrating her fully, his breath taken away by the sensation he was experiencing as he entered Zara.

The waiting had been worth every agonizing second from his first encounter to the chance one in his secret cafe. Brett's mind didn't want to consider the consequences of where his actions would lead; he just needed what was between them now, this instant. Gliding deeper with every thrust of his fired up body, Brett looked deep into Zara's green eyes that lit up in the half light. He couldn't think of a better moment he'd experienced.

Zara moved rhythmically against his body friction warming him like fireworks on every nerve ending, until exhaustion and satisfaction ensued. Brett could hold out no longer, every stroke and clench finally had their way. Zara trembled and groaned feeling her stiffen gripping in waves over him. He finally let go, sinking down into the most luxurious sensation. He smelt Zara's intoxicating scent at the base of her neck, taut nipples pressed firm against his now heaving body. Trying not to crush Zara, Brett supported his body up and without hesitation kissed Zara full on the lips whispering in her ear tenderly. Zara melted, inching closer into his body. The fire crackled gently in the hearth, sending soft shadows over their naked bodies as they lay closely entwined.

Chapter 11

SNOWY ESCAPADES

Zara lay dozily stretched out over the bed, her mind a little hazy from the night before. Flickers of recognition drifted lazily in and out of the deep recesses of her mind. Turning, half expecting the sleepy body of Brett to be slumbering next to her, she was surprised he was nowhere to be seen. Surely she hadn't scared him off that quick. Her body melted into the warmth of the duvet, just remembering Brett's touch and seduction methods sent shivers down her spine.

The alarm clock perched daintily on the wooden cabinet showed it was still quite early - about seven thirty. Far too early to be gadding around just yet, besides she was on holiday, a welcome break from the ardors of heavy pounding on many a neglected body. Now was definitely the time to wallow, or so she thought.

A loud slam echoed around the chalet as the front door swung open abruptly, crashing against the wall, twinned with a shrill and very upbeat whistling. The sounds drifted upstairs towards Zara's muffled ears, as she lay under the snug thick duvet. A quick pattering of footsteps leaping up the stairs followed. Zara was met by an exceedingly happy and very cheery Brett.

'Hi gorgeous, you awake now? I'll bring some breakie up if you are, then I'm hounding you out into the balmy fresh air to tackle some outdoor pursuits.'

Zara's mind remembered the real reason they were here - the dreaded mountain and skiing expedition. The one thing she'd been most uncertain about and now had finally arrived.

'Umm! Lovely can't wait,' feigning enthusiasm. At this precise moment she was keener to drag Brett back into bed but she could see he was itching to be going.

'You're a morning person aren't you? No one can be as full of energy as you after what we drank last night.' Zara grinned at Brett as she poked her face above the covers.

'You bet, it's fabulous out there, perfect conditions. The mist has lifted and you'll enjoy it once we reach the top. The views are out of this world.' With this he yanked the covers back and gave Zara a playful slap on the behind, 'Get that butt moving. I'll pop breakfast on and bring it on up.'

Before Zara had a chance to pursue his already dressed body, he was down the stairs before she drew breath. A mad panic rushed through Zara's body as she leapt into the bathroom to hastily try and make herself half decent. It was one thing hiding under the duvet looking sultry and alluring, but in the harsh daylight her disheveled appearance was not to be desired. Quickly brushing her teeth and running a brush through her hair, she decided a slick of lip gloss and mascara wouldn't go amiss as well. Looking at her reflection in the mirror she hoped that Brett would be satisfied. She had to protect the mystique of the thirty year old brigade.

Within minutes Brett was climbing the stairs with a tray laden with goodies. Zara leapt back into bed as if she'd not stirred at all. There was a long pause as Brett set down the tray and a slight hint of a smile crept up the corners of his mouth. He leant forward and kissed Zara on the lips, taking time to savour them slightly longer than a quick peck.

'Amazing minty lips. How do you women achieve that?' Zara cringed and smiled.

'Amazing, I have to admit,' leaning forward for a second kiss that Brett duly gave with a bit too much passion for so early in the morning - breakfast forgotten in the heat of the moment. Brett rolled back leaning up on one elbow he traced his little finger along Zara's arm and across her breast. A yearning could be seen in his eyes.

'However much I enjoy the delights of your body, and it is hard for me to say no at this moment, I can tell you. We better eat, as you'll need some fuel for keeping the cold out.' He swiveled round to grab the bowl of porridge which had lost some steam by now with the delayed wait, from the breakfast tray.

'Ok, you're boss, I'm totally in your hands so I'm not gonna protest,' Grabbing his inner thigh and squeezing gently. Zara inched herself up into a sitting position. Brett focused on her naked body inches from his face.

'Looking at the choice of lukewarm porridge or your hot body this isn't an easy option.' Brett clearly feeling the effects of being stimulated again as he hesitated in considering placing the breakfast bowl down again.

'No, we both need to get out there in that bracing

190

cold weather. Sizzling sex beneath the sheets can be done anytime,' Zara took the bowl from Brett's reluctant grasp; she smiled coyly and tucked in. Brett's face dropped looking bitterly disappointed. He grabbed a shirt from the side chair.

'You better pop this on, I don't have the willpower to eat and see what I could be missing.'

'Ok, if I must.'

He helped her into the shirt buttoning it up for her slowly enjoying each second, until finally all exposed flesh was covered. After devouring most of the food Brett had Zara packaged up, clad in her snow thermals, and dragged out into the bracing weather, before his resistance broke down.

A taxi approached the far end of the track, prompting him to escort the now suitably attired Zara to the awaiting car. The journey to the ski area was dramatic with the true beauty of the resort appearing as the mist unfolded, dissipating into thin, crystal clear air.

As they approached the mountain centre Zara noticed how high the mountain seemed once up close. Her gaze caught sight of the chair lifts heading up to dizzying heights, far up into the clear sky. Zara's stomach lurched and she wished she hadn't consumed quite so much breakfast. This meant putting on a brave face.

The heavy ski boots were tightly strapped around her slender legs. The weight of them seemed heavy enough and then to be armed with two poles and skis the size of a couple of planks of wood, Zara just knew she hadn't done enough serious training for the weekend. The muscles in her legs ached before she'd even got on the chair lift. Last night had used quite a few muscles within her anatomy she didn't know existed but they'd been worth testing out. Now her thighs were politely screaming for mercy.

Brett helped her onto the skis and before any nerves could kick in they were being whisked up onto the chairlift, high up the sloping mountain that lay before them. Their feet were dangling in mid air. Vertigo was not an option in skiing. Zara reached out tentatively to grip Brett's hand. Tiny puffs of steam erupted from her mouth as she decided chatting may distract her somewhat of the tiny, tiny issue of the expanding gaping space that was developing beneath their swinging chair. Zara tried hard to remain optimistic but it wasn't her idea of a perfect date.

Nearing the end of the lift, the difficult part was how to alight gracefully without falling flat on her face or a less attractive option of going round for a second tour. Brett leant forward and with one swoop guided Zara forward as their skis hit the slippery slope. Unprepared with her dithering Zara felt the firm surface beneath her skis but the slippery ice layer caught her by surprise, nearly causing her to lose her footing on the left ski too quickly. Her back arched violently. Before she could fall Brett steadied her and managed to glide down safely towards the start of the first run.

The area was crowded with skiers all dressed in some pretty bright skiwear. At least she was going to see whoever she careered into, well in advance! 'Nice thought,' murmured Zara as a fluorescent, very orange, leopard print ski suit sped past, practically taking Zara prematurely down the mountain before she was semi prepped for takeoff.

To start with, Brett demonstrated the snow plough and how to skid to an abrupt halt. Zara fancied this maneuver as more advantageous to trying to do the splits in reverse, which is all she could remember from a one off college expedition. With some practicing she did at least come to a kind of stop without falling flat on her backside. After having done so on a few occasions, she found getting up was nigh on impossible without the strong hand of Brett, coming to the conclusion falling over was an option best avoided. Lest she found herself alone and abandoned, with no helpful individual to gallantly haul her upright once the snow embraced, she had better learn to stay upright on her skis. With visions of Brett sailing off down the mountain, she didn't think he would be too impressed if he had to crab walk up again to rescue her. One passionate weekend would be ruined for eternity!

The morning progressed well, except for a few moments of fear, laced with some rather natty antics by Zara, processing two left feet when it came to any technical maneuvers. Brett was an experienced teacher allowing Zara to feel safe with him by her side; to be let loose on her own was another thing. After one spectacular fall, Brett lay in the snow, a tangle of skis and poles intermingled with Zara's who had by now collapsed back onto him. Gazing up at the vast blue expanse above her head, the strong arms of Brett grasped her waist.

'You've got no chance to ski for Britain. Just warn me if you ever sign up on any expedition I might have to go on, as I will be resigning straight away.' He kissed her neck softly, hugging her close before pushing her forwards to try and untangle his right foot. Levering up by the aid of his poles, he reached forward with a helping hand to pull Zara up onto her feet again.

'I was a little ambitious in bringing you here, wasn't I? But don't worry. I can always arrange a place in the kindergarten section next time.' Zara retaliated to his comment and shoved him straight back into the soft snow again.

'Ok, as you're so talented then, see if you can teach me to a respectable level of competence. At least I'll know you're as good as you say you are then.'

Brett lay back weighing the situation up. Leaning forward to heave himself up again he retorted, 'No, I think I'll call it a day. I haven't got enough padding on me to keep falling down with you. I'd much rather fall back onto a soft warm mattress if you're going to be on top.' Zara's reaction was a little taken aback at first, then seeing the humour in what he'd said she leant forward to help him.

'Ok, but maybe we could attempt just a few more goes. Practice makes perfect and you are a good teacher. Honest! I've just got no balance when it comes to hovering on top of slippery surfaces.'

'Hmm, remind me not to take you ice skating if that's the case, as I would like to keep hold of my toes for a little longer.'

'Yeah, yeah come on lead the way. I'll try my best to mimic your every move but only if you're sensible.'

'As if I'm not,' wiggling his hips, Brett pushed away gliding on one ski and with one leg up precariously bent to the side. Zara cursed him and moved off rather

194

cautiously at first trying hard to stay in his ski track due to his antics. This time she found it slightly easier after overcoming the fear of falling over, managing to carve a few half reasonable turns down the semi steep incline, culminating in a wobbly stop at the bottom. Brett skied swiftly over to join her and leant in to kiss her chilly nose tip now representing a glowing red orb. Zara responded grasping him closer, his skis now gliding between hers. This outdoor activity was becoming a turn on and she had every intention of finishing the day with some warmer activity off the slopes. Nerves had started tingling with the exertion expended.

~ ~ ~

Inside the cozy wood interior of the chalet, Brett started running the shower for them. Steam soon started billowing out of the door, drifting lazily along the landing.

'Come on, strip off. You need to keep your circulation moving and warm the muscles up as you'll seize up later, especially as you're a beginner.' Smiling he worked diligently at removing the many layers that clad Zara's figure.

'You're telling someone to suck eggs really, I tell my clients that every day. Not that many take much notice, probably why they're always back on my couch complaining,' Zara sighed.

Feeling suddenly self-conscious she grabbed one of the towels draped nearby as Brett removed the last of her garments. Wearing just a pair of tiny briefs she climbed the steep stairs to the walk-in shower room.

Steam cascaded from the shower head, allowing drops to condense on the ceiling, clouding the vast mirror that framed the far wall. The warm water felt like razors glancing off her shoulders, aching from the combined effort they had performed. Lathering the shower gel over her body it felt heavenly to have all her exhaustion washed away. She hadn't felt this good for a long time.

A gentle click of the door was heard and Zara turned to feel Brett slide in behind her, softly stroking her shoulders and tracing a lone fingertip down her back. He took some more gel and smoothed it delicately over her back, massaging and probing any sore spots. Grasping the nape of her neck he kneaded the taut muscles to the base of her hairline and then swept down over her breasts to caress and stroke her with the soapy bubbles.

Zara could feel Brett move in closer behind her. He felt hard and firm, pressing into the cheek of her buttock. His hand moved smoothly down over her tummy and nudged ever closer to her pubic area. Inside she felt a burning sensation of sexual tension and yearning. Deftly maneuvering her round in the small cramped space he guided her hand down to grasp him. Taking heed she moved it over his erect penis, the slippery soapsuds allowing her to slide and masturbate him perfectly. Tiny droplets of water framed Brett's lashes as he closed his eyes savouring the work Zara was performing on him. When he could bear it no longer he lifted her back against the far wall of the cubicle and with a little difficulty pressed up inside her, thrusting powerfully until he came hard and strong. Gently lowering Zara, he kissed her apologizing for being so selfish. Zara embraced him holding him closer, relishing the sensation of the strong surge of water cascading down over them. She whispered in his ear,

'I'll let you relax while I go and see if I can produce something to eat. You can please me later. I've got no energy left, completely zilch.' Brett's eyes looked slightly alarmed.

'I don't know if I've got anything left myself,' seeing Zara's look of disappointment he hastily added, 'but I might have some reserves after a bit of substance.'

'You better! No way can you parade your gorgeous body in front of me and expect me to not become a little addicted. It's like putting kids in a candy store with all the goodies locked behind a glass door. One of the kids is bound to smash and grab some time.' Brett grimaced.

'I'd better put myself on awareness surveillance in case I get attacked at short notice.'

'You'd better, as I might decide to use unfair tactics to get my fix.' Grinning from ear to ear Zara left him to raid the kitchen cupboards. Scanning the shelves she wondered how she would rustle up a meal for two, showing ingenuity and flair, which sadly she lacked when culinary skills were required.

Brett sighed under the warm shower, letting the sharp rods of water ease his tired muscles. A strong feeling of not wanting this weekend to end was knawing away at him. He felt seriously attracted to Zara and now actually enjoying the intimacy. It was going to be hard to cool off and get his mind straight. Where he was going, there wasn't going to be time in pursuing a partner. No, his focus had to be on the end game.

Maybe this hadn't been such a brilliant idea. Looking logically he may as well enjoy the moment while they both had the chance, though he knew he was now diving in far too deep.

~ ~ ~

The lads leapt up the mountain trail, hardly out of breath. Strong and lithe like as any mountain goat, they sprung from one uneven rock and boulder to the next, practically bounding over the uneven terrain. Once reaching the ridge they paused for breath, lugging the huge rucksacks from their shoulders. Brett's friend sat down on the nearest boulder.

'The high altitude training is going well, not long before you'll be off for the real stuff. Man, I don't envy you stuck up a mountain in freezing temperatures with just your own body warmth. Give me a hot bit of totty any time.'

Brett laughed and retorted, 'There's a time and place for that, and up a mountain is not one of them.'

'By the way, how did your little shenanigan in the lodge go? I understand she's quite a stunner.'

'Good, but skiing wise she hasn't got the urge or confidence. I certainly enjoyed teaching her some techniques mind you.'

'Yeah, I can picture you now with your suave techniques. But how did you get on in the bedroom department? If it had been me, I would have skirted the skiing and stayed holed up for the entire weekend. Especially as you've got plenty of time on the snow soon, why bother?'

'Well that's where we differ. I'm surprised I managed to get you up here you lazy git.'

'I've got the stamina, just use it differently than you. More a quiet, laid back exerciser.'

'Laid flat on your back more like, with some woman on top of you,' scoffed Brett with a wry smile upon his face.

'You can scoff but you've got to admit, it's a great way of doing a sit up. Now back to the subject of the southern totty how did you leave it?'

'Normal, said goodbye, see you some time. I'm tied for most of the year as you know and she's off to the Olympics for work, so we're kind of not up the same mountain at this moment in time. She's cool about it.'

'No woman is cool about a bloke's plans, unless she made them and she is part of them. You sure she will be around? If she's that fantastic I might be giving her a call myself or are you still running away from the past? It's been two years mate since Tanya. Open up and let somebody in. They're not all like her.'

Brett shuffled uncomfortably from foot to foot scraping the loose soil and gravel under his well-worn hiking boots. Tom could sense his uneasiness in the subject but was determined to tackle it head on.

'I mean, it wasn't your fault she decided to bat for the other side. A good looking lad like you couldn't have done more for the girl. This Zara doesn't seem too disappointed with your bedroom skills.'

'Don't say it like that it sounds so sordid.' Tom recoiled a little but could see a grimace of a smile cracking at the corner of Brett's mouth.

'Yeah sorry, probably not quite what you want to

hear, but we lads are no competition to the delights and skills of the rampant bunny. The other half informed me there are dozens of tricks she can use with it. I can tell you, I've sampled some myself and it isn't half bad.'

Brett spun round and roared with laughter, 'You're telling me you've used one on yourself or the Mrs.?'

'Look, it can get lonely when she's out on shift and the urge arrives, besides it was research if I ever need to use it on a woman. May as well know the competition inside out. Never know when you may need the expertise.'

'I don't think a woman would need one with me. I'm sure she would prefer the real deal.'

'Possibly but you can't vibrate and I'm sure you can't damn well rotate it clockwise at the same time!! If you can, you better teach me. I'd even consider going to bed with you myself.' Brett lunged towards Tom tussling with him and uttering some unsavory names into the bargain.

'Zara's different. She wants stuff out of life and her career as well. The sex was great, mind blowing at times but I can wait. It will be the last thing on my mind when I'm training.'

'Yeah ok, I believe you. Just make sure you pop it in the diary to keep in touch with me when you're back on home ground. Because I'm damn sure I'll miss your sweet little ways no end.'

Chapter 12

THE SHIELD

The tight white coat was tied tight behind the buckles secured all complete and ready for action, bar the metal head piece to be placed over the face for full protection. A gleaming metal instrument was placed in the right hand. The padded gloved hand grasped tightly the pronged handle. Electronic wires were placed to the rear of the coat. Combat was to commence.

A hushed silence prevailed as the buzzer indicated play to begin. The room was filled with many age groups all brandishing a lethal weapon and identically dressed. The bright white linens gleamed clear and pristine in the lighted studio.

Zara wiggled within the confines of her suit. At this moment in time she felt like a trussed up turkey, feeling deep sympathy for any poor soul who had psychiatric problems and had to be confined by a straight jacket. As this was indeed how this outfit felt like.

Wisps of sticky hair fell across Zara's eyes as she passed the metal head piece over her head. Viewing the outside world as an insect would, peripheral vision was not ideal now. It was a damn good thing combat was only in front as how you defended yourself to the side was anyone's guess.

Yes, Zara was now the unwilling recipient of an intensive course of fencing, her mission to learn the precise problems that the average fencer would experience in their sport. The preparation for the unlikely choice of her allocation to work with the Olympic fencing team.

Roger had chosen each person randomly to be assigned to the various sports the clinic had been asked to support, within this very important contract.

No chances were to be taken. Each member of staff was to breathe and live the sport, so every angle could be assessed. Then problems that may arise from over training or injury in the events could be tackled professionally and quickly.

Zara was uncertain if her choice was all together random; she had a sixth sense Jamie had bribed Roger into choosing her for this. He had the cushy job of the badminton team which she could actually play anyway. Jamie knew this as did Roger.

No hassle for him in being spot on but for Zara this was a whole new ball game or point as there were definitely no balls in this sport, just some horrible flexible (so they say) pointy instruments. The said items designed to poke through several layers of padded fabric, with the chief aim to strike your opponent on the arm or body more than the other guy on the receiving end.

Zara took her position. She had learnt some techniques to circle the opposing sword away from her and then execute an elaborate lunge forward and attack her opponent, ultimately striking his body. Slightly difficult when your partner was six foot and his arm's length was so long, that you nearly ended up doing long jump to get anywhere near his body and strike. Several times she ended up impaling her own armpit on his sword without her opponent even moving.

It was good she wasn't on the team because there would be no medals for Great Britain if she happened to be competing. The buzzer sounded far too many times on Zara's side much to her annoyance, lighting up like a belisha beacon.

The saving grace was she felt every little muscle that was being used. Zara was beginning to feel the control required along with the expertise in co-ordination of eye, shoulder and arm that was required. Indeed this was not a mamby pamby sport. Her legs and upper body hadn't done such an intense workout for a long time, well not in usual sporting techniques, as her mind wandered back to the Cairngorms with Brett.

Boy did she miss him but work was to come first. He was dedicated to his career so she better be to hers. His long lean torso swayed in front of her eyes, causing major distraction and loss of concentration. Before she could do anything her opponent was lunging forwards, swords clashing. She could only defend herself as she was pushed backwards to her start line.

Once twenty minutes had elapsed Zara began sweating. It was hard work and when the buzzer finally sounded for end of play she breathed a sigh of relief, pulling the mask off to allow some fresh air to flow over her hot sticky skin. Instantly noticing Jamie standing nearby smirking quietly in the shadows, she wandered towards him eager to take a break before ridding herself of the uncomfortable attire.

'Hi my little musketeer, how's your fighting skills coming along? Seems you like the sound of the alarm a little bit too much on your side, but I do like the trendy trussed up look. Just wondering how you get out of it all?' Jamie grinned and tweaked her bottom, well what should have been a bottom, now resembling the well-endowed cushioned look now.

'It enhances the cuddly aspect of your body shall I say.' Though all he'd felt was a handful of wadding. Zara glared at him with contempt.

'You may scoff but I'm actually improving. So watch out as I might learn some more disarming moves before I complete this course. You better be wearing your cricket box if you get close to me in future.' Zara flounced off to the changing cubicles to have the weekly fight in trying to get out of her bodysuit which was some feat in itself.

Removing the heavy helmet was one thing, her hair matted and sticking to her forehead, she then endeavored to try and undo the zip down her back. This was a very intricate and delicate process. Too fast and her hair always got stuck in the zip, too slow and she ended up nicking the zip in the fabric. A dire move as the only choice was to limp out and ask some poor soul to help, rather embarrassing when everyone on the team seemed to whisk off their outfit with one flourish

The sight was quite comical; Jamie would have been in hysterics if he was watching. Zara managed to undo the required zip line and peeled off the sweaty garment, to then unbuckle the next specially designed garment, meant to protect the arm that held the sword. It tied on the opposing side with a buckle and loop.

204

Zara at the beginning always put this on the wrong way and forever got poked through her clothing until she clicked that being right handed meant protecting your right side.

Now for the wonder buster that protected her ample bust. She felt very much like Madonna when wearing this fetching garment. This was probably why she resembled the Michelin man when fully dressed. Zara sat down as she finally peeled off her breeches, not wanting to fall flat on her face trying to remove the skintight garment.

How the team was going to cope in eighty to ninety degree heat in Atlanta she wasn't sure. Barbequed more like by the time they got out of their suits. She stood quite exhausted, by now red and puce from the exertion of it all.

Once refreshed and less bound up, Zara emerged from the changing rooms to find Jamie in the wings, watching the training commence with the more professional athletes.

'Don't think you're up to that standard?' Jamie laughed.

'Yes ok, don't rub it in. I'm not aiming to be. I'm dropping in to Amber's to see how she's doing, do you fancy coming with me? I'm sure you can take the piss some more at my expense. Amber will be in need of a pick me up by now. It's not long to go before the big day.'

'Yeah ok, I won't say no to chatting to your gorgeous mate whether they have a bun in the oven or not.'

'Jamie, have some decorum, that's my best friend

you're talking about.' Zara snapped back as she did feel Jamie was very near the mark some times.

'Yes I know, but you can't say I discriminate who I insult now can you?'

'If you say so.' Zara decided to stomp off to the car clearly wishing she was not in such a bad mood. Was it the enforced fencing that she had to endure or missing the calming influence of Brett, still unsure if she would ever get the chance to catch up with him again?

Zara hoped it wasn't going to be a flying couple of one night stands. Maybe good enough for Jamie to have but she really felt she should be looking more long term now. With a graceful sigh she opened the door to Jamie and beckoned him into the buggy mobile that many friends frequently teased her about.

'Cool wheels, didn't know you had one of these?'

'As yet I can't afford anything flash. It's just a form of getting from A to B at present. It's reliable although a bit eccentric looking. It was my college friend Bella's. I haven't had time to re-spray it yet and she was selling it at a good price.'

'I don't know, these old fashioned beetles are quite collector's items. Especially ones that are rather individual. I'd keep it like it is,' enthused Jamie. Zara was unsure about this, it certainly attracted attention when driving but it was not an image she wanted to portray long term. Hippy wasn't her scene.

Before long they were pulling up at Amber's long driveway. Parking close to the main entrance they both alighted.

'Gee, nice pad your mate has but must be worth a packet to live here?'

'Yes it's pretty big, but does cost a lot to maintain. Now Amber's on her own I'm not sure if she will stay here long term. I don't like to ask about her financial situation too much. Nice having it but doesn't come cheap.'

'Do you think she could do with a handy man or little light gardening? Can see myself part time with the clinic job pottering around, shirt off, looking macho, it would cheer her up no end.'

'Jamie, since when do you know anything about pruning or DIY? You've been watching too much of that series Desperate housewives. We Brits aren't that swayed by muscle. More than likely we would get on down and do it ourselves, though have to admit her tree surgeon who popped by the other day was pretty hot. Amazing what a man equipped with a chainsaw can do for the libido.'

'I could do that, half the price. Bit more masculine than a gardener don't you think, more my style?'

'No way, you'd be a major health hazard to yourself and nature. Stick to what you know best.'

'Oh you old killjoy, you've no faith in me. I might have some multi-talents underneath this good looking exterior.'

'Maybe, but I haven't come across any yet.' Zara just looked at Jamie as if he was slightly mad, and pressed the buzzer.

The doorbell chimed echoing around the large house. For what seemed an eternity they waited patiently on the door step. Finally Amber opened the door apologizing profusely for keeping them waiting.

'I'm so slow now, can't think how anyone copes

207

with twins or more. I feel I'm carrying a mammoth already and got another four weeks to go.' Amber grimaced and smiled at Jamie. 'Hi and you are?'

'Oh yes, this is Jamie, one of my work colleagues. He's just been watching me fence or rather taking the mick out of my endeavour to fence.' looking at Jamie intently.

'Nice to meet you, come in and I'll get you a drink. It's always nice to chat with Zara's friends. I haven't been out as much as usual. The hunting grounds that we frequented are off limits at present, can't exactly look stunning in the tents that I have to wear now.'

Zara watched Jamie closely at this remark just waiting for him to say something insulting. She was uncertain how sensitive Amber had become with the pregnancy hormones escalating in her body, especially at a most crucial time when Dean should have been here to share each moment.

'On the contrary you look stunning. Would be interested myself if you were not with child. It would seem a bit crass of me to try and seduce you at a time like this.'

Zara cringed and wanted the floor to swallow her up immediately, but was surprised when Amber laughed mischievously and grabbing his arm swanned off towards the kitchen with Jamie in tow.

The three of them chatted and put the world to rights in the spacious conservatory, enjoying the last lingering light as the sun set in the distance. The view was lovely from Amber's back garden. With the doors thrown back, the soft chatter of the dusk insects had now started, creating a slow steady hum in the background. A heady scent of jasmine entwining the pagoda close by wafted a fragrant breeze into the house. It was definitely one place to spend a relaxing evening.

The atmosphere was interrupted with the shrill ringing of the landline. Amber excused herself and went off to answer it. After some time Zara looked at her watch as Amber had been quite a while and not returned.

'I'll just go and see if she's alright.'

'Ok, I'm fine here. Your mate has a great place, really idyllic. You better get me an invite back soon.'

'It might not be so idyllic when child comes along,' laughed Zara. Jamie flinched and decided he better enjoy the moment while he could.

Wandering into the lounge Amber was nowhere to be found. Cautiously she stepped upstairs calling for her friend. As she pushed open the bedroom door she stopped dead in her tracks. Amber was kneeling and breathing deeply, clutching her stomach.

'Oh my god, are you ok Amber? What's the matter? Is it the baby?'

'Whoa, one question at a time, I was just feeling a bit weird when I came off the phone, put it down to the wine I'd had, shouldn't have had any really. Then I started to get some contractions. They're probably only the Braxton Hicks to get me psyched up. I'll be fine in a minute,' uttered Amber, standing unsteadily, leaning out to steady herself on the cabinet.

'I think I better stay. Jamie can get a taxi home.'

'No, I can always ring Dean's mum.'

'True, but I'm here now. I'll get you a drink of water first and settle you down.' Zara rushed off to the bathroom when she heard a cry from behind her.

'Oh dear, I think you're right, it's D-day time.'

Zara sprinted down the long landing to where she had left Amber to be met with the sight she really was not prepared for.

'I think my waters have broken. It's a bit early for labour, baby obviously wants to come out quicker than intended,' gasped Amber.

Zara then became like a headless chicken running back to the bathroom she grabbed some towels to help clear up and yelling for Jamie at the top of her voice, headed back to the bedroom.

'We've got ages yet, don't worry I just need to contact the hospital and get my birthing bag from the study.'

Jamie appeared his face falling when he saw the commotion Zara was making, as she scurried past him to the study, then being faced with the sight what was clearly only meant for your nearest and dearest to see.

'Not sure what I can do, but may I be of assistance?' Jamie's look gave it all away, that he was hoping there wasn't anything he could do but just make a cup of tea and pray silently the girls sorted it out quickly.

Zara peered around the study searching for the new, very trendy birthing bag. Amber had been indulging in some gorgeous items for her newborn. This was one that oozed style right down to dainty silver zip tags in the shape of miniature dummies. They were so sweet, but at this moment Zara was more keen to check what was in the bag than admire the outside.

She delved deep into the base to extract a bottle of Bach flower remedy and some Lavender. Having gone through all that was needed, including Amber's birthing plan with her, she felt fairly gemmed up on the procedures but now it was the real deal she was in need of being a touch calmer.

Emerging from the study she caught Jamie's eye as she sprinkled drops under her tongue and sniffed violently from the bottle she was clasping. Immediately she sighed and drifted back into the bedroom. Jamie was clearly impressed and seized the bottles from Zara.

'I think I need a bit of that, looks pretty good stuff with the effect it had on you, how much do you take?' As he attempted to nearly drink the bottle.

'No, no! Only a few drops, less is more in natural medicine,' snapped Zara. While all this had been going on Amber looked in complete amazement at the proceedings playing out in front of her.

'Excuse me, but it's me that's in pain here and about to have a baby. Some help you two will be in the labour ward. I thought you both….,' Amber stopped to catch her breath as a contraction started to kick in. Clearly things were moving faster than she thought, 'I thought you both were good with injuries and first aid.' Jamie's face went white with fear.

'Err, what do you mean help in the labour ward? I'm not cut out for birthing procedures. I only came along for the ride. Besides we only deal with the injury once all the main trauma and gory bits have been dealt with. If I'd wanted to be a doctor I'd have become one.' Amber tried hard to be discreet in laughing; even Zara now calmer saw the funny side of the situation.

'Yes, fair play that's kind of true. Can't say I'm not a touch squeamish as well. You can do the phoning and

211

maybe drive us to the hospital. I can concentrate on Amber then, deal?' Zara locked eyes on Jamie as he squirmed on the spot. He sensed there was no way out of this predicament.

'Ok, but if I see anyone I know whilst driving your old car, you owe me. It's not too bad as it does have trend appeal but I draw the line at the painted daisies. My street credibility will nose dive after this - we better take the back roads.'

As they argued, Amber clutched hold of Jamie and they proceeded cautiously to negotiate the stairs. Once manhandled into the rear of the vehicle, Jamie decided to practice his rally skills as a worried frown developed, causing Jamie's brows to grow closer the more Amber panted away.

In the safe haven of the hospital walls, Jamie was allowed to be released home as the girls were directed to the maternity ward.

'This is it Amber, don't worry I'll be here for you the whole time.' Clutching Amber's hand she held on tight trying hard to portray some confidence and support to her longtime friend, knowing that she was here only to replace someone who would have been a fabulous birthing partner and a very proud dad indeed.

The ward was busy and after what seemed ages Amber was finally shown a private room, after a precarious ride by wheelchair to the next level. A lot of cursing was uttered mid travel. Zara was now seeing another side to Amber's personality, who was by now somewhat short tempered. It must be the contractions pondered Zara as she hurried to sort out what they might need and prepare the room.

212

'Here let me help you onto the couch, you might feel better lying down.'

'I don't think any position will make much difference. It bloody hurts any which way I move.' Amber was getting impatient and snappy. Her face grimacing with the discomfort, finally letting out a loud groan, she struggled to find a comfy position, eventually leaning over the back of the delivery couch, hanging on for dear life. 'I think this is it. I can't wait any longer. The head must be coming now, please get someone? Boy I wish I'd had time to have some pain relief.' Amber puffed quickly the timing and practice that they had both achieved on the birth plan had gone completely haywire.

Zara leapt out of the door frantically scanning the corridor for what looked like an efficient and in control nurse or midwife but as usual never one when you needed them.

Swiveling back into the room she noticed the alarm button, why hadn't she thought of that. Deep meditative breaths were required for her, let alone for Amber if she was going to be of help. The soft ring rang out down the corridor, praying that the unit wasn't too busy to notice otherwise she would be delivering the newborn herself. The thought didn't appeal, even being up the more desirable end was somewhat a squeamish situation for Zara, and the idea that she may have to go through this sometime in the future was not a very enlightening thought.

Amber's breathing slowed for a few minutes but before long the contractions increased once again to crescendo level. Her hand gripped Zara's for support.

'If I knew it was going to hurt this much I'm sure I would have reconsidered this.'

Zara smiled weakly trying hard to reassure her that it would be all over shortly and how brave she'd been up till now, but her face was not in agreement with what was coming out verbally. Minutes later one of the very harassed midwives arrived, taking charge immediately.

'Now Amber, I want you to relax and try to not push just yet. We need to just expand a little more for your baby to be born. You're doing really well. Now pant slowly.' Amber rolled her eyes and looked in despair at Zara.

'I can't stop the urge it feels so powerful,' she moaning so loudly that Zara was nearly put off for life. How could this be natural, surely the genetics of evolution must have made a complete and utter hash of the design, producing a billiard ball through a hole the size of an orange was not advanced design by a long way.

'Now pant, follow me.' Zara said as calmly as she could, 'We are nearly there, and then the big push can begin.'

Amber gritted her teeth and some very strong and not very polite swear words uttered around the room. Zara detected a little frustration with the situation and was now wishing it was indeed Dean here holding her hand but she snapped herself out of it, telling herself not to be such a wimp. It wasn't her going through the pain. Amber would probably have forgotten it all by tomorrow. Especially as she wasn't sure how she would react to giving birth herself. Shuddering at the thought again, she concentrated really hard in not looking at the busy and very productive end, focusing on the beads of sweat forming on Amber's brow instead.

The minutes ticked slowly by, within five the midwife was now encouraging Amber to push and with four mighty shoves, plus two nails dug into Zara's hand, a bonny and rather large baby girl was born. Whisked quickly to the side of the room she was checked over and swiftly handed back to Amber's breast. Her soft light skin showed translucently in places and a shock of dark hair crowned her scalp.

Zara peered closely at her. She had tiny rosebud lips and her face crinkled up as the lights in the room dazzled her.

'She's gorgeous, wasn't she worth all that hard work?' Zara looked up at Amber but she appeared not to be listening just staring intently at the bundle within her arms. Emotional and exhausted, Amber started to cry. Tears flowed one by one down her flushed cheeks. Zara bit her lip trying hard not to join in but her lip quivered with such intense effort. It was a perfect and proud moment but for the noticeable absence of Dean. He would have been so chuffed, the perfect dad. Venturing forward, Zara sat alongside Amber on the bed and placed an arm round her,

'You did it. It will be ok. Dean will have been looking down on you I'm sure. I'll let the family know while you rest for a moment and then we can get you settled and cleaned up.' Kissing Amber and her newborn each on their forehead, she exited the room quietly leaving her friend to bond with her new child.

'Hi it's Zara, Amber's friend. I'm at the hospital. A little early I know, but Amber has had the baby. It's a little girl, eight pounds nine ounces, with a shot of dark hair just like Dean. Congratulations you're now proud grandparents.' In the background Zara could hear Dean's mum sobbing with delight, shouting out to her husband the good news.

'We'll both come straight up to visit. Tell her, will you? Thank you for supporting her Zara, thank you.'

Chapter 13

OLYMPIC STANDARDS

'Tyler Montgomery.' The name rang out as the lists of various riders destined to compete in the horse jumping were relayed live on screen. Zara suddenly gripped and tensed her hands in surprise at his name shrieking back into her sub-conscious mind.

'Oww! Slacken off a bit it's really tender there,' groaned an immovable body beneath her fingertips.

'Sorry, I'll be a little gentler.' Zara tried hard to relax but her heart was pumping so hard with sudden adrenaline at hearing Tyler's name. She'd completely forgotten he was a talented and first class show jumper. Obviously he would have been chosen for the UK team. It'd never crossed her mind he would be here close by, whilst she was on assignment. 'Damn, this was not good, not good at all,' she mused to herself.

It had been well over a year since she'd seen Tyler. Staring hard at the television nearby relaying the events in the main arena, Zara hoped secretly it would stay on the Equestrian section and not suddenly zoom off to the swimming or some other mundane sporting event.

Working diligently, her heart froze in a flash as one of the riders came into view. Tyler, as dashing as ever was cantering forward, professional and devilish

217

looking. A knot of sadness developed in the pit of her stomach.

It had been an eventful year but her one wish, and probably her only one, was not to be so traumatized by Tyler. Why did he have such a hold over her? It wasn't as if he was ever that good in bed. Her thoughts swam back to the few sordid occasions when she had succumbed to his charm. They hadn't been overall dedicated to her enjoyment. Tyler was a man of lay back and think of England. Relishing the work of any willing female who fell into bed with him, she was certain it should have been the other way around.

Tyler would definitely be the perfect specimen to live in the Far East, with a few nubile nymphs attending to his every need; she could just picture him reclining on a chaise lounge while grapes dropped seductively into his pursed lips by the female of choice. Zara shuddered; she felt jealous even of this fantasy. Especially as she knew Tyler would have loved every moment of it.

A woman was just a smart appendage to have on his arm, certainly not one to fawn upon. What you would call a 'full on flirt'. On many occasion, Zara had been fully aware of a pretty face being a major distraction for Tyler. She could have evaporated into thin air most of the time. It had been a constant worry to look devastatingly beautiful all the time, particularly hard when it wasn't your forte in life to have blue blood Sloane looks as a natural attribute. Zara sighed heavily. She was tired of feeling inadequate and fed up to the back teeth with her heart doing somersaults every time he was mentioned.

218

The year had passed quickly. There had been plenty of friends to distract her from the break-up including Brett, to which she really should be more concerned about. She just couldn't understand why she was so distracted and upset at seeing Tyler again in the flesh. It felt just as raw now as the time of the aloof text she'd received.

Glancing again at the screen and simultaneously trying hard to concentrate on the job in hand, Zara managed to position herself with some difficulty, to work at an angle where both she and the client were satisfied at the same time.

The horse Tyler was riding was a perfect specimen of power and agility, prancing into the arena with his rider competing for control. Zara was never exactly into equine activities, having hurt her back in the past from trying to do the usual pony pursuits that young kids enjoy. On most occasions she ended up with the horse that nobody desired to ride. Either so frisky she was unable to control them and just held on for dear life, or so slow a good kick up the backside still didn't get them into trotting mode.

Tyler was definitely not compatible with Zara if mutual skills were a factor of everlasting desire, but looking at him in perfect shape controlling half a ton of horse muscle, she well wished she was a keen horsewoman.

Six foot in height, with a lean muscular body showing through his polo shirt, Zara nearly went weak at the knees as she diligently tried to concentrate on working. The camera zoomed in close searching for expressions of the riders prior to this very important competition. Tyler's steely grey blue eyes were calm and relaxed, absorbing the atmosphere around him. Laser like in quality, he scanned the opposing riders watching their every move and how their horses performed in the warm up, fully aware of any weaknesses that might be displayed.

His forearms strong, powerful and tanned allowed him to maneuver the horse skillfully around the course. Zara watched as he leant forward, guiding the horse with control of his thighs as he took the perfect position to clear the jumps with precision. He still had what it takes, definitely for the ladies, as a roar of approval sounded out around the arena. All Zara could do was watch wistfully at what could have been. Sometimes you just know a guy was out of your league and she knew that this one certainly was.

Feeling like some lovesick groupie waiting for a crumb of attention, Zara tried hard to distract her mind from the screen. After watching half the entrants competing against Tyler, she felt more upset by the minute. It was the last thing she needed having Tyler swan back into her career. This job was important and she couldn't afford to muck up now.

Eventually the screen changed events and Zara was now aware that Tyler was within sprinting distance of her somewhere on campus. There was a very strong chance she would bump into him unexpectedly, which was a slightly unnerving proposition. Zara's back tingled with fear and anticipation. She was unsure of the reception she would receive. Would it be a warm or frosty one? Most likely a cold front or total oblivion. Crikey what could be worse, that he wanted to avoid her at all costs or to have completely forgotten her like some trailer trash? Zara swallowed hard; that would hurt more than anything. Maybe it was best to avoid the situation completely.

At the end of the session, Zara collapsed with exhaustion from nerves. Deciding the best option was to meet with Jamie for a refreshing beer at the local bar, the only place where alcohol was allowed and that was severely restricted for the workers. No staff must be intoxicated on duty or turn up in a less than satisfactory state. She felt the need to be on red alert with Jamie in case he tried to overindulge, but today she felt she deserved a reprieve herself.

The cold beer slithered down, cooling her parched throat and calming her nerves after the close encounter she'd experienced. Jamie detected all was not hunky dory in Zara's mood. The slight pensive facial features, constant tapping of the foot against the table and an irritating habit of rolling her right shoulder back made him feel obligated to make a remark.

'What's up? You look as if you've had the fright of your life!' laughed Jamie looking enquiringly at Zara.

'Never a saying so true, I have kind of.'

Jamie leaned forward, 'Yeah, and you look as if you didn't want to one little bit. Come on, you can tell Uncle Jamie.' Zara looked at Jamie with a wry smile, cocking the edge of her mouth up.

'Since when have you been a soothsayer? Normally it's me that has to do the listening to tales of woe.'

'Yeah, but I've matured a little in the time you've known me. I can help out with my male perspective you know.'

'Oooh! Err! Where have you gained that legendary intelligence?' Zara teased.

'By the way, changing the subject for a minute, how's the flamboyant fencing team doing? Are they ultra-sensitive on the couch, as they sure look right pansies on the circuit?'

'Don't be rude; someone will hear you. They're a great bunch and not mamby pamby.'

'Well they look like a right lot of feminine charms dressed up in breeches, skipping about.'

'Jamie, what are you like? Now let's see how you fair in the consultation department.' Zara started to explain what had happened earlier. She tried extra hard not to spoil the moment and laugh when Jamie gave her the insight of a life time.

'As a male I would, if I were in your shoes, just shag him for old times' sake. Use him as he's used you. A guy can't bear a woman not needing them and one that seduces you is even better.'

'Great, I can see myself doing that and what happens if he runs scared at the sight of me?'

Jamie looked closely at Zara, 'And you think he would do that? I think not. He's obviously as cocky, pardon the pun, as ever. Wish I could be as cool as him. No, he loves himself too much. He'll remember you alright; haven't forgotten one of my notches on the bedpost.'

'Yes, but you've only got about four to remember, not hard really is it?' Zara punched him in the ribs playfully.

'Speak for yourself; I have had many a conquest under the belt that you don't know about, quite a ladies' man in my day.'

'What day, at kindergarten?'

'Funny ha, ha, so are you going to take my advice man to woman? At least you can remind yourself how crap he was and move on and get a kick out of being in control for once. Boy would I like a girl in control of me.' Jamie's eyes glazed over as he retreated into some wild fantasy, leaving Zara to ponder on the idea that Jamie had left with her.

As they relaxed, the subtle effect of the alcohol took over, and Zara slowly let moral responsibilities to the job lax. One more beer had turned into three or four in the case of Jamie. Zara slowly disintegrated into a giggly wreck trying to keep up. Jamie always loving a partner in crime certainly wasn't reining her in to behave with decorum. The loud laughter from the both of them attracted the odd look from several drinkers. Zara was now oblivious to their stares.

'Come on mate, let's go for a walk, it's such a nice night.' Jamie grabbed Zara's hand, yanking her up and heading off in the direction of the practice areas. Spectators were milling around all over the place. Life in the Olympic village never rested; there was always something going on even after the main competitive events had ended. Practice makes perfect, as always the mindset of the keen sportsperson, clearly set on the gold emblem.

'How about you showing me some fencing moves? It should be a doddle. You can show me some of that fancy footwork you learnt.'

'No! Don't be silly.' Zara gripped his arm trying hard to pull him back from the training studios.

'We can't, if we get caught that's it for us.'

'Don't worry, no one will know if we're professionals or not. We're allowed entry as you're on the team's personal staff. So who's going to quibble?'

The hesitant look on Zara's face said it all. 'I don't know Jamie.' Even though the after effects of the hops were lulling her mind, her usual old habits of being responsible and sensible kept flooding back.

'Oh, what the hell,' she had to learn to let go some time. Giggling, she responded to Jamie's goading. 'Go on then, I'll show you where to pad up.'

The escapade in getting the kit on was no different to when Zara had gone to classes back home. Getting Jamie in the gear was even harder. His long lanky figure looked quite hysterical when finally clad all in white. Zara's face puffed up and exploded in hysterics when she saw the final product.

They crept out into the big hall where the practice sessions were held. It was quite late now. Most keen athletes had gone home for a well earned rest prior to the next day's competition. The freedom of space allowed Jamie and Zara free range to leap about practicing the various moves. Jamie was no talented swordsman, sadly.

'What the heck are you doing?' shouted Zara as the gangly Jamie jumped all over the place, flaying the foil everywhere but where he should have.

'What! I'm copying what you did, aren't I?' replied Jamie looking baffled. Zara was totally perplexed at how his mind comprehended anything.

'I don't know what you've been analyzing, but you look more like Darth Vader and his glowing Mojo than a swashbuckling pirate.' They both collapsed into a heap laughing like idiots on the floor.

'Yes, I admit it's not as easy as it looks, but I still think any bloke who wears this garb must be short of a few male genes, whatever you might say.'

As they larked about, a solitary figure stood in the wings watching them quietly from the shadows of the auditorium, taking in their every move.

Back in the dressing rooms Zara felt hot from the excess alcohol consumption and exercise. She tried vainly to release herself from the rather constricting garments again.

'Here, let me help.'

'Thanks, as I've said before it's a nightmare getting out of this stuff.'

'Umm, I can see, but it's more than a pleasure to help.'

Zara stopped suddenly and detected it wasn't Jamie's voice she'd heard. Spinning round she was confronted with an obnoxious grin, a slight tilt of the head and a very direct stare that bored straight into the core of her heart. She stood shocked, rooted to the spot.

'How did you get in? How long have you been here?' she stammered.

'In answer to your first question, same as you and yes your moves are somewhat attractive to watch, so decide from that how long.'

Zara felt instantly mortified; this was not what she had expected to happen. Before she had time to cringe anymore Jamie returned from the showers, surprised at first at the unknown visitor then looking a little concerned. Uncertain if this stranger was welcome or

225

not, until a look of faint recognition swept across his face.

'Hi, you must be one of Zara's ex's yes? Heard a lot about you; any chance of letting me in on some insider information about Zara? I need some stored ammunition.'

Zara just wanted the ground to swallow her up; it couldn't get any worse, she'd been hoping for some moral support, but no Jamie had to put his foot in it more than ever. Tyler's gaze swiveled slowly towards Zara again.

'Talking about me, yeah? Thought my ears were burning earlier, nice to know I hadn't been forgotten in or out of bed.' His voice mocking, waiting for her to react.

Zara's mind was completely stunned and she was unable to react in any manner. Cool had just gone out the window. Jamie noticed something was wrong as he'd never seen Zara lost for words. Feeling slightly guilty, he distracted the situation.

'Right, I think bed is beckoning, so I feel we better say our goodnights and slip between the sheets, as I'm dead beat now. Fit for nothing.' Zara knew now things could get worse and Jamie had just put his foot even deeper into a massive hole. Tyler laughed and whirled round to Zara.

'I think I might have just been enticed into a threesome, though I might be enjoying myself more than others.' The look on Jamie's face was a picture and was the only saving grace throughout the whole situation.

'No, I didn't mean that at all, just it's late and we're

on duty again in the morning.'

'Sure, I know what you meant. But if ever the choice arises, let me know.' With this statement hanging heavily in the air Tyler grinned cheekily.

'I normally prefer the company of two of the same, if you know what I mean,' winking at Jamie as he strode out. Zara turned on her heel and stomped over to her clothes. Yanking them on, she glared at Jamie.

'Right, I'll shower back at the flat. Only you can make a dilemma ten times worse. What possessed you to say that statement?'

'It kind of came out all wrong. I agree it didn't really gel well with your past history with the guy. Though I have to admit he's good, really good. I'd never have thought up a line like that.' Zara's eyes rolled to heaven.

'Men you're all the bloody same. Some help you've been.' Leaving a bewildered Jamie behind Zara turned on her heel and stomped out of the room, huffing deeply.

The next two days passed rapidly. Zara managed to avoid any more encounters with the past. Painfully aware that she may bump into Tyler again when she least expected it wasn't a pleasant thought, but at least the difficult first encounter in a year had passed.

~ ~ ~

Jamie came bounding up the steps to the flat Zara had been appointed to share with another massage therapist. Banging loudly on the door a bewildered Zara emerged, clutching hold of the door frame her face

227

screwed up against the harsh sunlight that was streaming through the doorway.

'Yes, what do you want at this unearthly hour of the day?' squinting blankly at Jamie and not fully awake yet.

'Have you got a free evening tonight? I've got an invite to a fab party. One of the sponsors is holding a bash at the Berkley Hotel downtown and I've just buttered up the guy to get a special pass. Wall to wall glam and glitz, your cup of tea; all I ask is don't step on my pulling power. I don't mind arriving with an escort but I'm hoping to be leaving separately.'

'Really, you don't say, my diary is pretty free. Dinner with the president isn't till next week so I just might be able to fit you in as your pretend date.'

'Great. I'll meet you here at nine tonight - it's smart casual attire.'

'Oh is it? That might pose a problem but I'll find something.'

'Smart casual over here means little more than a bikini. It's summer in the USA and eighty odd degrees so don't fret too much.' Jamie bounded off to annoy some other half asleep individual. Zara just frowned and closed the door gently, sinking back down the other side in a tired and crumpled heap.

~ ~ ~

The night of the party was muggy and humid. Air crackled with an electric undercurrent, accompanied by the gentle hum of a mosquito that was now threatening Zara's exposed flesh. She had acquired a light tan

228

which she decided to show off for once. No damn insect was going to stop her.

As they arrived, a stream of stretch limos glided towards the main semi-circular forecourt in front of the Hotel. Smart uniformed bellboys attended to each one, as a spectacular attendance of very nubile and elegant women emerged, hanging off the arm of their accompanying male conquest.

Zara looked down at the cocktail dress she had slipped on. It was a deep emerald green colour and was clinging closely to her toned body. But for Zara, all she could see was a normal run of the mill girl at a function, which was probably going to make her feel like a fish out of water. With a determined look on her face she steeled herself prior to entering the fray.

The entrance hall was lofty. Spirals of long chandelier droplets cascaded down into the lobby above the many guests. The marble steps rose up in a long curve beckoning you to follow the gilded line and curve of its handrails. Zara felt like Alice in Wonderland. Glistening glass mirrors reflected the light from the crystals. She tried hard to glide up the steps as graceful as some of the women who were attending. But her tight dress was preventing her moving elegantly; twinned with high heels, the combination made it a little difficult.

Her eyes were drawn to the roof top terrace where the party was being held. As they neared the top of the staircase, French doors opened up onto the vast terrace. Huge cactus plants and miniature palm trees lined the entrance in vast steel pots. Tiny red fairy lights twisted & turned around the rough bark, leading the guests out

229

towards the dimly lit swimming pool.

'Wow! Told you it would be a hot place to be. This is going to be fun.' Jamie looked about as if he was to leap into the pool fully clothed with the anticipation he was portraying.

As they approached the pool area a funky vibe could be heard, drifting across the enticing expanse of blue water. The beat immediately got the feet moving and already semi-clad individuals were dancing at the far end of the terrace. It was a sight for sore eyes as Zara watched the fit guys moving intimately with any female that passed by. Jamie's eyes were on stalks by now, practically champing at the bit to be part of the pulsating mass.

'Come on, let's dance,' he shouted. Grabbing Zara by the hand he dragged her as quickly as she could manage, with the restriction of her attire, towards the centre of the dancing throng, neatly sandwiching her between two very gorgeous young men. His ploy being of course, not for Zara but another young filly he had eyes for close by. Not that Zara minded. She soon found herself twirling around, assuming a very close position to one of the dancers, who was now leading her into the most intimate lambada move possible.

The heady scent of Honeysuckle wafted through the air, mingling with the smell of warm sun kissed skin. This tinged with evocative cologne emitting from the guy she was now practically on intimate terms with by now. It sent Zara's hormones into a heady frenzy. Maybe, just maybe, this had not been a bad idea of Jamie's to come. Take her mind off things.

Within the hour Zara left the terrace to cool down,

leaving Jamie behind who was now trying his hardest to out dance the cool customers, still jiving and twisting away. On walking past the pool an area led off into a luxurious lounge. Whoever designed the hotel was pretty up to date in style and architecture. The long, clear glass windows blended into a soft, red glow, creating a stunning effect. It was as if the floor was fading away into the distant sunset.

The atmosphere had stepped down a little by now. Iced cocktails were available at the long bar that lined the far wall of the adjacent studio. Zara stepped as daintily as possible amongst the many sofas and cushions placed around the room. Its high ceilings allowed the air to cool. Twinkling stars could be seen through large skylights edged with red orbs. Her eyes were drawn to stare upwards as if looking through a long telescope. Suddenly she knocked herself sharply on a corner of a low lying table.

'Steady, we don't want you ruining that stunning body before anyone gets a chance to enjoy it.'

Zara flinched at the pain in her shin and the embarrassment of walking straight into the ruddy table. Turning round she took a sharp breath once again, and composed herself looking steadily at her new acquaintance.

'Tyler, we meet again. I should have known you would be here. Never one to miss a smart set up like this.'

'Now, now we aren't jealous are we? How did you swing a ticket? Or was it your sweet minder that escorted you here, who acquired the golden invitation. Still unclear why you're with him? He seems to have

231

been abducted by two very, and I say with the utmost of approval, lithe like brunettes the last time I saw him.'

Zara was acutely aware now that Tyler must have been watching as she arrived. At this moment she felt very out of her depth. Tyler's presence was digging in where it hurt, deep inside; the feelings of jealousy and inadequacy were surfacing again.

Trying hard to appear unflustered and making sure he understood she was not with Jamie, she made her excuses, smoothly and as carefully as she could and made a sharp exit towards the landing.

Hating the uncomfortable sensations he produced in her, she tried to dissolve the emotional pull. Staring hard at her reflection in the vast mirrors of the washroom, resembling more a spa pod than a normal restroom, she splashed herself with the cool water cascading from the touch sensitive taps. Trickling the water gently through her fingertips the words of Jamie rang through her head.

Maybe she needed to remind herself of what a dire and bloody awful shag he had been. Looks were not everything. Compassion and gentleness were much more important.

Her mind trawled back to her night with Brett and she relaxed a little, savoring the memory. The high screech of two drunken females brought her back to the reality of where she was. Drying her hands on the delicate tissues and slathering the rich hand cream over them, the soft scent of ginger and lemon clearing her head. Zara felt ready to step back into the party.

Strutting purposely she headed into the long studio again. Tyler had vanished, probably now moving onto the next slain victim of his choice. The ranges of cocktails were too numerous to read through. Zara decided to just flick the dark leather menu open and jab blindly at whatever came up.

'I'll have a Black Russian please.'

'I bet you will.' Jamie's comical and rather puce face appeared hovering over the menu.

'Enjoying yourself? I heard on the grapevine you were being enticed by two very lovely brunettes.'

'Yes I have been, but afraid lost out to two top damn athletes. Baseball or something; they obviously knew them and that was me ousted.' The lost look on Jamie's face said it all. For once Zara felt quite sorry for him. He always seemed to lose out at the last minute.

'Come on, cheer up, there's plenty more fish in the sea.' They both surveyed the room swiftly from left to right and with a smack of two hands together, Zara dragged Jamie back towards the pool and terrace. Once bitten, twice shy but tonight that wasn't on the agenda.

The party had increased in pace somewhat since they'd both been occupied inside. The dusk had turned to an inky blue. The clear night sky sprinkled now with tiny stars. The pool looked as enticing as a cool shower and many guests had come prepared. It was now filled with splashing beauties, gliding and diving like mermaids beneath the turquoise waves. The array of skimpy costumes flashed quickly before the eye like rainbow lights.

Zara found herself drawn to stripping right there and feeling the coolness of the water but a little self-conscious of her attire. Jamie looked at Zara as if to say, 'we may never get another chance.' They both took

233

the plunge.

Discarding her emerald dress she felt strangely exposed in her matching bikini against the starlets that had attended the event, but once in the dimly lit water she melted back, enjoying the gentle caressing of her skin from the water that enveloped her. Floating calmly, staring up at the night sky above, the muffled sounds of the party now seemed far, far away.

Before long she was rudely interrupted as someone dived in close by. Droplets of spray splashed over her face causing her to grimace and rise back to the hub bub of the outside world. Turning sharply Zara swam over to the side and brushing the water from her eyes she stood up. The vision slowly returning, luckily waterproof mascara was her saviour otherwise she may have resembled a bedraggled panda by now. Her gaze met with the shadowy form of someone so close she was breathing in their closest inner space.

Startled she stepped back only to bump into another gliding mermaid. Losing balance she plunged back under the water and emerged gasping for breath again, having swallowed a mouthful on the way back down. Strong arms grasped her waist and dragged her back to the side of the pool. Choking, Zara managed to gasp a polite thank you. The kind rescuer held her tight, not letting go even after she had composed herself. Zara turned round slowly and attempted to grab the side of the pool for support. She was met with a broad tanned chest.

Glancing upwards and preparing to offer her thanks again towards her rescuer, the half-smile that had broke forth from her lips froze in shock as her eyes met

Tyler's once more.

'Don't look so surprised. I wasn't going to let you drown on me was I. Haven't had the pleasure of your company yet tonight, although feigning drowning on me was one way to get my attention.'

'I wasn't feigning it. I was actually choking!' Tyler pressed a finger to her lips.

'Yes, I know and I was very near to giving you the kiss of life. You were a pretty good option to practice on. Maybe I can try now, you still look rather breathless.'

Zara knew that that wasn't from the water but the image of him so close and naked clinging to her bare flesh. That was harder to handle. Tyler grinned relishing the power he had over her. Removing himself from the pool in one swift move, water glistening from his frame, he held out a long tanned arm for Zara to grasp.

'Come with me. I'll show you where you can dry off. It's way too busy now to enjoy the watery delights.'

She felt herself being lifted gently from the pool. Before she knew what was happening, the firm pressure of Tyler's arm was pressing around her waist, leading her away from the poolside towards a second terrace adjacent to the party. Here lines of striped tent like cabanas were set up. Their sides swagged and draped ready for privacy to be upheld at the drop of a sash. Tyler's arm guided her inside and as she looked back the curtain of soft white muslin shut out the dusk. The only sound was the heavy breathing between them. After several seconds, she became aware it was coming mainly from herself. Swallowing hard she attempted to quell the rate, but the sight of Tyler in such intimate surroundings, undressed at that, was hard for her to remain neutral.

Rivulets of water trickled down his chest. Moving forward Tyler stroked Zara's shoulders. The only light was from a single Turkish lantern that emitted a soft amber glow to the striped interior of the tent.

Zara was aware now of Tyler's fingers caressing her neck from behind loosening her bikini top, the wet neck tie slipped slowly down her shoulders, exposing her breasts that were rock hard from the chilliness of the evening air. Tyler ran a finger delicately over and around one of them. His body stepped forward and pressed up close. Zara could just make out his slate blue eyes boring deep into her soul. Fear of the past resurfaced, entwined with the passion of lust she always experienced in his company.

A smile ebbed slowly from his motionless face, like a wolf ready to devour its prey. Leaning in the warm tangy taste of his lips and mouth surrounded Zara's tongue, her heartbeat thumping close against his warm and silky smooth chest.

Feeling the tie being released, hands brushed down to her waist; first one tie then the second of her bikini briefs, exposing her completely. Tyler skimmed across her bottom. The heady sight of Tyler's body slowly emerged into Zara's head; flashbacks of when they were an item seared her memory. She needed and wanted him badly, her defenses screaming out to be broken.

Tyler, forever the dominant alpha male, laid her back upon the cushions, piled high at the rear of the

236

tent. The softness against her skin felt cooling and comforting. He appeared silhouetted in the half-light against the soft muslin curtain that wafted in the evening breeze. Tyler stripped naked and without hesitation Zara leant forward kissing him softly upon his thigh. Moving closer until embracing him, she took him firmly in her mouth sucking slowly, teasing him, her tongue swirled and taunted. Her manner in control, Zara rimmed and caressed every part of him. Although still feeling slightly inferior she felt more enlivened and liberated wanting him for her sheer enjoyment. A faint groaning emitted from Tyler's lips, feeling his buttocks tighten beneath her hands, Zara pulled away lest she wouldn't get a chance to enjoy him fully.

Tyler pushed back; devouring her breasts, he cupped and sucked each nipple hard. Moving his hands firmly along her thighs he cupped each buttock and slipping a finger inside her teased gently. Moving on out he circled her clitoris, returning to press hard and sink deeper inside, probing her g-spot, spreading juice as he stimulated her harder and faster. He slid and maneuvered himself into a comfortable position. Beneath him, Zara felt his body weight lower and press firmly between her thighs, his hand guiding himself into her. Gasping she flinched at first, Tyler was never inadequate in size. The firmness and neediness she felt from him took her by surprise. It was strangely intoxicating. He thrust deep inside, angling himself to hit just the right place. Feelings of warmth aroused her after several minutes.

Zara felt herself rolling and suddenly she was astride and on top. Sinking deeper down into his shaft, he melted into her body. Zara rocked back and forth riding slowly at first. Tiny shock waves started to send tingling around her vagina, producing an effervescent sensation like drugs hitting the body. They began to merge welling up more and more. Tyler thrust harder and faster, her pubis hitting hard against his pelvis. A wave of ecstasy enveloped her as a soft tingling shot over her skin, each pore electric to Tyler's touch. As it descended she was taken by surprise once more as the sensation rose up again, deeper, stronger and more exhilarating than the last time.

Tyler's mood changed and he detected and felt Zara grip harder. Moaning he grasped her hips tightly, pressing her harder. She moved against him until they both merged and came once again feeling the gentle pulsating sensation ebb slowly away.

Sinking down over Tyler's chest she rested her head, feeling his heartbeat pound into her cheek. Clearly Tyler had improved in some areas and she didn't want to imagine how. Pushing down a wave of jealousy that sprouted its ugly head, Zara edged up to kiss Tyler strongly on the lips.

'Thanks for the double ecstasy, it was pleasant to touch base again but I better make my departure. We don't want people to get the wrong idea what's been happening in here do we?' Zara laughed nervously and prepared herself to walk out of Tyler's life. She didn't want to feel awkward after such an encounter and her pride and self-esteem needed boosting. This was the way to go. Tyler looked at her bemused, not sure why such a swift exit. Rolling up he grabbed Zara by the arm,

'You haven't lost your touch. I'll have to catch you around.' He rolled back again with a satisfied grin. Zara knew she would have to turn the tables and managed to reply with some dignity.

'It's always nice to teach you some new tricks. You were ok for a carnal pastime but I'm required elsewhere I'm afraid.' Zara grabbed one of the snowy white robes that hung near the entrance to the cabana and blowing a kiss back to Tyler, she exited before she succumbed to him again.

As she redressed in one of the free cabanas Zara felt much more in control. She had laid some ghosts to rest. The empowerment of taking the lead and using Tyler for herself for a change felt good. She just might be able to move on this time. Grabbing cool refreshment from the bar, Zara attempted to find Jamie and tell him her leave.

As she departed from the party she noticed the white billowy shirt Tyler was wearing in the distance. He stood tall and proud laughing and joking with some of the team he rode with. Zara's heart missed a beat again and she had to force herself to be distracted lest she crumbled again.

Bending down, she adjusted the strap on her shoe which was digging sharply into her ankle, and on arising her eye caught Tyler as he headed off in the direction of the cabanas for a second time. But this time he was being led by the two willowy brunettes that had been seducing Jamie earlier on. Her breath stopped completely, this time stunned to the core at what she was witnessing: her self-esteem plunging to the floor again.

Tyler was danger in capital letters. His red hot looks were just a magnet to any wanton female. He would clearly never say no to any attention. Zara turned on her heel and with tears stinging her eyes she exited the party as quickly as she could. She tried hard not to focus on what Tyler would be doing in the next hour.

The cool night air made Zara shiver. Looking back at the venue, the tiny stars high above the terrace and the faint sounds of the party ringing in her ears, she vowed to banish Tyler for good. He had broken her heart too many times in the past year. This was the final ultimate insult to experience. One she could bear no longer, trying to win against Tyler would never happen.

Chapter 14

ABANDONING ROOTS

Zara rummaged through her desk feeling a little nostalgic at leaving so soon. Looking around her office she recalled the many customers she'd met over the last few years, the highs and the lows of working with Roger and the fun with her colleagues.

The desiccated plant that had seen better days definitely wasn't on the packing list. Scanning the shelves, she grabbed her massage tools and after filing the last records, she closed up her account on the work laptop. No more incessant clerical work. No doubt some other mad boss would be taking over where Roger had kindly stood down. But that could be dealt with when the time arrived. Zara wondered how the Americans did business in the therapy world. They definitely knew the muscular-skeletal system inside out. The latest trends and treatment were always available much quicker than here on her home turf. It was going to be interesting how far ahead they really were.

Patting the desk behind her, she struggled to lift the box laden with her accumulated items. What the hell had she put in there? Backing out of the door, she heaved the box round so the door would swing shut ending up careering straight into Jamie.

'Going so soon? Can't believe you're leaving me to man the ranks with old Rodgy. I've got nobody to blame now if I cock up or fancy an easy life.'

'There's always Felicity. I'm pretty certain she can cover up for you.'

'You are joking! She's more of a control freak than Roger. More likely I'd be the one covering for her. No, I'm gonna miss you big time.'

'Before you cry all over me will you help me to the car first? This box is cumbersome and I'm about to drop the damn thing.'

'Come here, at least you can rely on us Brit boys to be gentlemen. Not sure what those arrogant jocks will be like?'

Zara frowned. She hadn't thought of the difference between the two countries. There was no turning back now, the job was accepted and she would be shortly winging her way to good old U.S of A. Since returning from their Olympic positions, life had rapidly changed. Opportunities had materialized from all directions. Zara pondered on why Jamie hadn't ventured away from the confines of the clinic. He plonked the box squarely in the boot of the flower mobile. Stroking the car gently he seemed to be wistfully looking at it. After a few seconds he glanced at Zara.

'What's the plan for the wheels?'

'Not sure yet, I may leave it stored at mum's or have to sell it. Obviously if I stay a long period of time there's no point in keeping the vehicle. Can't see my dad driving the flower power mobile, can you?'

'I don't know, he likes to be a bit of a cool customer and it could make him more appealing to the ladies.'

242

'Jamie, my mum has enough trouble with him. He doesn't need encouraging, besides the way you were just ogling my wheels, I'm wondering if you have a secret fetish for cruising down the promenade. Remember we are in Brighton, it won't be female birds you pull in this thing.'

'Yeah, may have to do some spray work and jazz it up a little in places but I must admit, if you want to give it to a good home I'll take the baby.'

'Really! I'll have a think about it.' With a loud thud Zara slammed the boot down and indicated for Jamie to follow, 'Got a moment, shall we have one last bevy across the road for old time's sake, before I see you for this big send off you've arranged for me?'

'Thought you'd never ask.'

~ ~ ~

Returning to her flat, the heavy task of packing was on the agenda. What was she going to leave behind? Certainly the winter woollies could be abandoned. Cossie for sure, that had to be packed, though surfing wasn't her thing, she may have to have a little sample. When in Rome, as they say. The beach lifestyle was very attractive, but in Brighton it seemed only fun for a small part of the year. When faced with February winds and driving rain whipping up the waves, the thought of wading out to sea wasn't such an appealing idea. Though there were always a few mad nutters who did.

Sitting on the suitcase she leant down to secure the locks. Done, and now a few more jobs and the goodbyes could begin. The doorbell rang urgently echoing around the stairwell. Rushing downstairs two at a time Zara opened the door to be greeted by a very welcome face.

'What the hell are you doing here?' Zara stood stunned, her eyebrows rose in a comical clown appearance as she stared at her unexpected guest.

'You didn't think I would miss out on a party of a lifetime? No way was I going to let you fly off without me saying a proper goodbye. Besides I needed a good excuse to cop off work. It's driving me nuts at the moment.' Gina hugged her tightly practically squeezing the breath out of her. Bundling past, she dragged what appeared to be a body bag and sat down demanding the kettle to be put on.

'What's it to be? Normal Tetley or black bush tinged with sage or something like that?'

'Tetley will do as I know you don't have anything else, let alone that concoction you said. It's red bush actually.'

'I'm learning slowly. Still can't get a liking for the weird stuff just yet.'

'You wait until you're in L.A. It will be all that whacky coffee, latte stuff or mega juices. Hope you're up for embracing the ultra-fit obsessive lifestyle out there?'

Zara sat the two steaming cups down. Offering a high calorie digestive to her friend she shrugged her shoulders, grinned and stuffed two biscuits in her mouth immediately.

'Gather you're not starting just yet?'

'No, plenty of time to embrace their fitness trends, I'm aiming to take it slow. The settling in will seem hard enough. Bit scared of what I've let myself in for combined with of course a bit of the wow excitement factor. No more Roger or having to cope with the trials and tribulations of Jamie.'

'Well, I think you'll love it once you find your feet. Besides it's only a plane ride away. Few hours I admit, but if you ever need a bed to sleep in back home my put-you-up divan is always vacant.'

'Nice to know, but please don't be offended if I favour the Travel Lodge instead.'

'Thanks a bunch; thought you were a friend?'

'I am, but that camp bed looked pretty uncomfortable last time I was up.'

'So, does that mean I have your luxury bed for tonight or have I got to endure your put-me-up bed as well?'

'Err, hadn't thought about that. I'll let you have mine and I'll have the futon. Just in case when I do return, you can't make me have the creaky old bed. I can hold you to ransom then.'

'Who needs enemies when I have a mate like you?'

~ ~ ~

By morning, Gina woke bleary eyed and surveyed the floor allowing her sight to register the world around her. An array of holiday and travel items was strewn across the floor, abandoned by Zara when she had arrived on her doorstep the day before. Rolling over onto her stomach she noticed the full paraphernalia that actually brought it home Zara was leaving for good.

245

Her passport and e-tickets lay alongside a purse displaying travellers' cheques and dollars. A neat pile of scanty underwear, bikinis and toiletry items littered the floor nearby. This was it, Zara was going. Earning more may have to be realised if she was to get a chance to visit a few times.

Heaving herself up, she swung her legs over the side of the bed trying to avoid trashing the neat pile of garments stacked next to it. She stepped delicately across the floor to be confronted by Zara's head popping round the bedroom door. Grinning insanely she asked her guest how she'd slept.

'Fine, but gee you have some packing to sort yet. No way will you get through customs with that lot.'

'Yes, I do need a bit of streamlining. It's so hard to leave stuff behind.'

'I can see that. When you came up to visit the first time you met the intriguing Brett, I thought you'd come for the month. I'll help you be ruthless later but now I need my caffeine fix.'

'Deal; one espresso coming up.'

Gina seemed quiet as they ate breakfast. Noticing the change in her persona compared with when she first arrived, Zara enquired what she could do to make her leaving any easier.

'I'm only a plane ride away. I probably won't stay the three years anyway. Can't see me lasting out permanently in sunny California can you? Think of the Botox I'll be seduced into having. Living on carrot sticks. Mind you it won't be short of some hot bodies. Brighton never really had it going for me, too many tight shorts for my liking.'

Gina let the corner of her mouth flicker into a grimace. Toying with the sugar bowl she hesitated and looked as if she was about to say something. Swallowing hard she paused and stopped herself.

'If you have something to tell me, I'm listening?' Zara seemed concerned. It wasn't like Gina to go quiet on her. Reaching out she squeezed her hand, trying hard to allow her to open up a bit.

'I have got something to tell you before you go, but not quite sure how to put it.' Zara was now intrigued waiting with bated breath.

'Go on, what is it? Don't keep me in suspense, you know me, got no patience if there's some gossip to tell.'

'It's gossip alright but I'll be the subject of it.' For what seemed ages Gina sat quietly saying nothing, taking another swig of coffee to steady her nerves.

With frustration rising Zara let out a yelp, 'Gina! What is it? The suspense is killing me, come on.' Shifting nervously in her chair Gina licked her lips and replied.

'I'm in a new relationship. It's very new so not going to introduce you to them just yet. It feels right, but I want you to understand why I've chosen this person. We met at one of the clubs back home. She's my age, totally different career than me. Bit of a brain boffin in fact. But we understand each other. She knows what makes me tick.'

Zara couldn't quite take it all in. Pausing she tried to correlate what Gina had implied.

'Run this by me again, you said 'she,' did I hear right?'

247

'Yes you did. Please don't laugh, I'm deadly serious. I've had so much grief from the opposite sex and when I hooked up with Jenny she opened my eyes to a different world.' Zara couldn't quite believe this but was trying to put the thought out of her mind and remain tuned into Gina. 'You can experience more respect, love and bloody great fun with another woman than I've ever had with a guy.'

By now Zara's eyes were bulging, too embarrassed to ask what she meant in detail of 'fun'. Confused at why she had never discussed it before, she sat opening her mouth like a puffa fish trying to string some words together.

'Um, when? How? I'm a bit bemused and shell shocked that's all. Don't get me wrong, I'm not judging you. It's a world I don't understand a lot about. Did you just change affections overnight or what?'

'No of course not silly, I just slowly found my patience with men dwindling. Constant let-downs, leering at other women, being unfaithful, bad tempered, disgusting habits, need I go on?'

'No, no you've painted a pretty appealing picture to swing away. I might be thinking about it myself at this rate, though the delights of meeting Brett again may keep me batting for the opposite side,' sighed Zara, 'Tonight Jamie has arranged something via the clinic. I dread to think what it is, normally it involves copious amounts of alcohol and mad dancing. Think you're up for it? I can't guarantee what the ratio of men to women will be. Pretty certain he won't know any woman on speed dial that doesn't always desire him; likes to try being the centre of attention as you very well know.'

248

'Of course I will, I'm not on the look out to hook up with every female that comes my way all of a sudden. Besides who said I haven't considered being 'bi'? More choice then!'

'Gina that's just being dead greedy; I'll be watching you now all night.' Zara sat with her mouth gaping at the audacity of her friend.

'Oh! You old prude, Once you hit LA you'll be changing your mind I bet.'

'Doubt it, I've been holed up in Brighton for many a year and it hasn't changed me, with its many powers of persuasion out on the streets at night. So far, I've been pretty immune,' declared Zara grinning with pride at her resilience.

~ ~ ~

By nightfall, the girls approached the secret address Jamie had sent them earlier that day. The taxi dropped them off in what was one of the seedier areas of Brighton. The tall regency buildings at either end of the street stood like white guards, causing wayward tourists to hesitate in entering the side street. A selection of swinging signs swung from the few austere town houses lining the road each side, (the cheaper end of the bed and breakfast market). Lying central to these few businesses was an unusual doorway framed in gaudy pink. A gold panther knocker held centre stage enticing any stray traveller to succumb and indulge what secrets may lie behind.

249

Zara looked a little perturbed at the setting before her. Gina on the other hand, was excited, immediately leaping up the steps to rap tartly on the knocker.

'Oh bloody hell, what has Jamie got lined up for me tonight?'

'Can't wait, this is so different compared with up Edinburgh way. You know without doubt it will involve kilts, no briefs and a fair lot of whisky swilling but here it could be dolly mixtures, drag queens & strawberry Manhattans.'

'Yeah, that's what I'm worried about. Fingers crossed I survive this.' Stroking her hair down and adjusting her dress she stepped up to the door as footsteps could be heard approaching.

As it swung open, they were met with a cheery, over-made-up face of a lady, who wasn't their first choice to meet on such a dark evening. Towering above the girls, she was in platforms so high any accident or trip would have been serious. Her eyelashes gave the false lash industry a real run for their money, framing deep blue eyes and she or he greeted them with dulcet tones.

'Hello my darlings, I'm Marlene, your host for tonight. Come in and I'll make you comfortable in our boudoir. Some of your other guests have arrived already.' On turning his or her fishnet clad derrière, led the way; the image enhanced by an extremely tight scarlet leotard. On frontal examination, it left the imagination to ponder on the logistics of how a man could hide his vital organs in such a figure enhancing costume

Gina nudged Zara sharply in the ribs whispering, 'Hey up she seems a friendly sort. Now I'm in a right dilemma who to go for: Marlene, Bob or Sally?' Zara looked aghast again. Not entirely sure her friend was actually joking or being half serious, with the bombshells she'd divulged so far. This evening was certain to get a whole lot worse.

The town house was decorated with decadent cornices crowning the high ceilings. Quirky light fittings dangled down, casting a subdued pinky glow over everything. A staircase swung up to the second floor. Its worn handrail was smoothed to a rich mahogany. Black and white pictures littered the walls. Luminous faces stared out; some with flamboyant messages scrawled across them. As the girls followed Marlene up to the second level, soft music drifted down beckoning them towards what lay elsewhere.

'Here we are. Your personal show will be around nine o'clock, so let me grab you some of our best cocktails to get you in the mood.' Marlene wiggled her tight arse over to the tiny alcove bar, smiling seductively at the bartender, who looked totally unfazed at his colleague's outerwear or lack of it. Pouting her scarlet lips at him she indicated towards the girls and whispered in his ear.

Zara was getting more uneasy by the minute, 'Trust Jamie to book her leaving event at a drag queen venue. Only he could think of that.' As they prepared to sit down a raucous voice emerged from the adjacent room.

'Zara come in here and join us. What do you think of the place? Cool huh!' Jamie was surrounded by several of her work colleagues including Roger.

251

Grabbing Gina securely by the hand lest she lose her, they joined the rest of the guests.

Once the bewitching hour of nine approached, Marlene appeared wearing a very nifty red number with a plunging neckline. It was now Jamie's turn to be baffled by the statistics of a bust cleavage that only a false breast enhancement could achieve. Leading the party down to the basement floor, Marlene guided the visibly excited entourage through the plush velvet curtains that draped the double door entrance. The space opened out into a vast room with a centre stage. Oval tables scattered the floor space like jewels. Each one was finished with a ruby red tea lantern.

Jamie led Zara to the main front table, beckoning a few of the other girls to grab a place alongside. He looked really pleased with himself which worried Zara more than ever, never quite sure how his mind worked. Gina was revelling in the potential show to come, knocking back another fancy Sex bomb cocktail garnished with half a pineapple and cherry, with what appeared to be half a ton of foliage.

'They do some mean drinks in here; so glad I didn't miss this event.'

'How many cocktails have you had off the menu?' enquired Zara, having had three herself.

'Let me think, the brain is going a little fuzzy at the moment. Had the Screw me on the Beach, this Sex Bomb, Tiger Lilies Delight and possibly the Pink Orgasmic froth.'

'Urgg! That sounds disgusting, what was in that one?'

252

'Pink gin, apple juice, raspberry liqueur and a dash of Champagne I think.' Zara screwed her face up pursing her lips, still not impressed by the ingredients.

'I'll get you the sick bowl tonight after that lot.'

'No, I'll be fine - used to mixing my spirits. University training, remember.' Before Zara could comment, the music boomed out loudly and in sashayed Marlene, centre stage. Loving the adoration of the crowd she whipped the audience into a frenzy.

'We have some comical delights for you this evening, some sexy dancing with our lovely chaps who will please all of you present. Our final event tonight is laid on by Mr Jamie Anderson. Sit back and enjoy.' Wiggling her hips and with a final pout, blowing a kiss towards Zara's table, Marlene exited the stage for the show to begin.

As the night progressed, the audience were baying for more as the show got raunchier and the jokes more extreme. The drag queen madams dressed in Vivian Westwood, made Fashion Week in London fade into the background in comparison. Raucous behaviour followed every act as the tables became weighed down by further empty drinking vessels. The lights eventually dipped as the final curtain call came. A hushed silence developed as the music changed to Night Fever. 'This was it,' Zara gritted her teeth to what delights Jamie was to bestow on her.

The lights went up illuminating five raincoat clad figures, all stood with their backs to the audience. Turning suggestively they tilted their trilby hats acknowledging their viewers. With the music beat building, one by one they rotated to greet their guests.

253

Clad in skin tight leathers they gyrated suggestively to the music.

'Oh crikey, this was it. Stripper hell and she was the target for the night.' Zara gritted her teeth in reluctant anticipation. Gina was rubbing her hands together hysterically laughing at Zara. 'Thanks for your support,' murmured Zara trying to keep a smile on her face for Jamie's sake.

Within minutes one by one, the trench coats were discarded and five male chests exposed; muscles flexing, they dived from the stage to surround the front table. Zara's face once having clocked their faces was memorable, instantly recognising one of them from the local rugby squad.

'You sods, how on earth did Jamie suggest you do this?'

One by one each player performed their own personal dance routine for her. Geoff the largest of the squad did them proud as he gleefully stripped to his G-string. Clad only with a slither of leather for his modesty, that was now starting to strain with the pressure it was under. (Geoff being a fond lover of a few after match beers had begun to offer for defence - sheer bulk rather than skill and power). Zara found it difficult to know where to avert her gaze. Noticing Geoff was enjoying the exhibitionism more so than others.

Next to delight Zara was Zeb. She was aware of a strong blush now tingeing her cheeks as he sat to face her. Lowering his body onto her lap slowly and very seductively he drew her face into his chest. Grabbing both her hands he placed them against each leather clad buttock. Zara was now grateful her face was buried in his pectorals as she knew everybody was watching her avidly by now. He felt smooth and soft to her cheek, smelling of the fresh scent of Escape by Calvin. Being the youngest on the team, he was a mere baby in comparison to Geoff. Hair free, his lean form sat neatly on her lap as he wiggled and circled gripping her hands hard against him. Leaping up after what seemed like an eternity to Zara but a pretty pleasant one at that, the squad returned to the stage to retreat behind the curtains for a brief interval and costume change.

The blaring sound of 'I'm too sexy,' set the stage for how low the delights of the evening were to stoop. Clad now in rugby gear they swung into a dance routine that impressed Zara by the agility of the larger guys in the team. Not to miss out, the last three members prepared their own personal send off. Mike the captain now suggestively beckoned Zara with his finger. Leading her on stage, he sat her down gently on the reclining chaise longue. Whipping off his shirt with a tug from each side, (very professional thought Zara), he stepped forward; how Roger had allowed this she would never know. Mike proceeded to grab a bottle of spray cream placed amongst a variety of potions laid out in preparation for the act. 'Oh gaud, here we go,' Zara knew with any show like this, cream of the whipped variety had to be produced at some time in the proceedings.

But Mike didn't offer her any before he tossed it aside. Grabbing a spray bottle of massage oil he glazed his chest with the pale lemony coloured liquid. Zara knew instantly what was to come now. Immediately her hands were placed on his taut stomach. As she glided them around his midriff Mike writhed in mock ecstasy. The audience were all now practically falling off their chairs, bawling with laughter. Zara was glad she wouldn't have to face them all on Monday, now finding being the centre of attention pretty excruciating.

Her final send off was to be Brian and Lucas. Strapping lads who appeared as sheer muscle and power in the squad, nobody got past them. Any brave soul was normally tackled instantly or eyeballed into submission. Zara swallowed, not quite sure what would follow with these two. Turning the tables on her was one such delight she hadn't expected.

Lifting Zara from the chair they carried her high above their heads. By this time she was squealing as loud as the audience, as the lads lay her face up on a high table draped in fabric. Each took turns to glide a finger slowly and seductively up each leg. Gently stroking her dress up inch by inch, 'Thank god I'd thought to shave.' Zara breathed a sigh of relief, 'I don't fancy the humiliation of roughened stubble on show.'

Removing their black tuxedo jackets to avoid ruining them, they poured a slow trickle of the silky oil over their hands, proceeding to glide all four hands simultaneously up her slender legs. The sensation of numerous palms and fingertips, twinned with two muscular guys venturing closer and closer to her crutch was something a lot of women might want to place on their wish list for Christmas.

Not happy to finish here the guys rolled Zara onto her front, covering her pretty dress with a light towel, only to oil up for a second time and offer a little smooth hand work to her rear. Both guys were not shy in gliding higher and higher, to reveal more of Zara's buttocks than she would have liked to place on show in a public arena. To finish they flipped her over. Lucas kissed her hand and draped her arm around his shoulders, grasping her around the waist he lifted Zara as if weightless, allowing her legs to nestle in the crook of his arm. Carrying her towards the audience he lowered her softly back down at the table she was sharing with Gina. Kissing her delicately on the lips and winking, he leapt back on stage to do a final suggestive dance with the others. The audience rose and gave them a massive cheer. Other lads in the team were present and their roar of approval became deafening, nearly causing Marlene to beckon security in case it turned nto a full on riot fest.

Chapter 15

REKINDLING LOST EMBERS

'How are you, darling? Hope you're ok after that long flight? I was worried the whole time. These constant travel larks you do for work; where it's inherited from I just don't know!'

'Mum, I'm fine the trip - is fab. I could hardly miss an opportunity to not come here. It was enroute anyway and it's a nice rest from having to be in charge of Jamie. Every time I'm in a foreign climate, he's normally tagging along.'

'Yes, he's such a nice boy I don't know why you two don't get together. Very respectable; you young women always wanting something you can't have. I would be proud for Jamie to be my son-in-law.'

Zara tried hard to bite her tongue. If only her mother knew how Jamie was twenty four hour seven, she might not think he was such a knight in shining amour. Smiling sweetly down the phone, she decided to distract the situation.

'No worries mum; I'll consider it if all else fails. How's dad anyway?'

'I really wished I'd sent your father with you. He could have done with a break. It certainly would have got him out from under my feet. A little late now though. Thinking about it, maybe all those wild and extreme sports wouldn't have been a good idea. Ted would only have had to show off and join in.'

Zara had visions of some rather hilarious consequences of her father upside down doing a bungee jump and it wasn't a pretty sight.

'At the moment, your dad is seeing too much of Glenda's husband. He's nothing short of seventy and both of them out on those bikes trying to compete with these young lads from the race team. How Glenda lets Ray out in those cycling shorts in public I shall never know. It's a good thing he isn't a young man and wanting any more children as fatherhood would be totally out of the question, the amount of hours he's encased in that lycra. At least your father hasn't been talked into wearing a pair himself yet, thank goodness.'

A loud mumbling could be heard from the background. Zara presumed it was her father muttering some insult back in defense.

'What was that mum?'

'Nothing, just your father being childish in his comments; anyway have you met that young man yet? You make sure he looks after you whilst you're there. I can't believe I haven't been introduced to him. I thought you said you've known him years now. I haven't heard the slightest hint of wedding bells. Make it clear he doesn't use you like a lot of these bachelor lads today - only after one thing.'

Zara tried to allay her mother's fears but it was rather difficult. Even she didn't know how to explain her relationship with the one and only Brett. Sensitive and caring, he would be ideal marriage material. Sadly it never seemed to get off the starting blocks long enough, before he was darting to some wild destination totally and infuriatingly elusive. Maybe that was what was so desirable; the passion, the long distance yearning and firework sex when they eventually touched base.

This was one item on the agenda she really didn't want to divulge with her mother. Best to say they were just platonic friends, rather than explaining the sexual laws of the modernistic age of casual sex partners. No way could Zara visualize her mother just dating for some bedroom antics. Her father yes, but mum no, frigidness was her middle name.

'Mum, I've got to go. I'll ring tomorrow as the money's running down a bit too rapidly. Give my love to dad.'

'Yes I will. Don't do anything I wouldn't do and ring soon darling please.' A loud good bye from her father echoed down the phone and a short but sweet parting comment.

'Zara, just enjoy yourself. If you only do what your mother would do you'll never see the world, let alone enjoy it, have fun.' The long beeping of the ring tone rang out as her father disappeared from the end of the line.

Zara placed the phone down on its cradle and walked towards the main water front of Queenstown. The lakeshore lay before her surrounded by high mountain peaks. New Zealand was truly magnificent in all its winter glory. Back home it was near eighty degrees and her new LA home that beckoned was nudging the mid-nineties. Here the air was clear and crystal cool she felt alive and sensual. Just thinking of seeing Brett made her excited.

Any trauma of Tyler had faded into the background now her life had moved on dramatically. The new position that was soon to start was going to be a great opportunity for her. Leaving Jamie and her colleagues had been a massive wrench but she couldn't have said no to the offer. Now utilizing her plane ticket to have a stop over this side of the world was well worth the journey and decision. Visiting New Zealand was one wish that could be crossed off her to do list. A chance like this combined with Brett, well what was there to complain about?

A whole year and a half had passed since she had been intimately acquainted with him. The trip to Scotland had been magical, but all too soon it had come to an end. Brett's training had taken up a lot of his time. A couple of long phone conversations and one passionate meeting after Zara returned to England from her Olympic assignment, was definitely not enough for a sexually distressed girl.

The same old insecurities started to creep in. Would he be the same? Time does alter people's perspective of you. Would the caring and fun loving Brett still exist? Zara hoped so; if he'd grown up and become mature and boring she would be beside herself.

Glancing over towards the jetty she watched the yellow jet boat zoom out towards the open water, sending cascades of white foam in its wake. The shrieks of laughter and fear intermingled with the roar of the engine echoed around the shoreline. Yes, Zara wanted some fun experiences to send adrenaline through her veins, but she did balk at the thought of chucking herself off a small ledge thousands of feet into space, on the end of a thin bit of elastic. There was excitement and there was sheer stupidity.

Lost in thought, she was unaware of the presence of Brett coming up from behind her. Suddenly she felt strong arms wrap around her middle and the gentlest of kisses on her neck.

'Hi gorgeous, been waiting long?'

Zara stopped breathing for a moment, her heart in free fall at the strong Scottish lilt of Brett's voice. Spinning round she met his dark, brown eyes still laced with the longest lashes, making Zara's insides leap fifty feet. He locked lips with hers before she could reply, and kissed as passionately as the time when they'd met in the snowy cabin so far in the past.

Zara nearly passed out with the joy of being there, holding him, and being so close. The layers of clothing they had on didn't restrain Brett in the least. Even Tyler hadn't had this effect on Zara's sex drive. Coming up for air Brett grinned.

'Glad to see me I gather. Got two choices: lunch or catching up for lost time?' He looked at her and winked pulling her body closer again.

'We could always do both at the same time.' Zara replied wickedly. Eyeing him closely and biting her lower lip eager for him to say yes.

'Funny you should say that, just what I was thinking.' He led Zara purposely away to the local market grabbing a large amount of delectable goodies to devour. Hugging her playfully and guiding her back to where he was staying, he pointed out areas of interest on the way.

'You're a bit forward after such a long break. A formal cup of tea would be in order. Remember, I'm an English lass at heart.'

'True, but the Scottish way is more grabbing it while you can. We never had time for niceties on those wild moors up my way. Too bloody cold, by the time we would have made the stuff we'd have gone off the idea.' Zara laughed. Brett's sense of humour and silliness was still apparent.

'Don't you like me being so raw and animalistic or do I have to be a reserved gentleman like those lily livered, feminine southerners?' He stared ruefully at Zara tentatively teasing her. Knowing the answer full well would be the former.

The next few hours certainly made up for lost time. In fact Zara couldn't recall any experience so enjoyable in a long time. The late afternoon sunshine dipped slowly behind the mountain, casting long shadows across the lake. Zara came up for air with a most satisfied smile on her face. Pulling herself up she turned to grab her clothing but with a shove and a playful slap Brett declared, 'I'm afraid I still haven't caught up fully for the last few months. Dinner will have to wait.' Zara fell back on the bed dragging Brett across her. His broad chest smothered her, feeling him press down his pelvis firm against her thigh, indicating he had other plans.

'Ok, which month are we catching up with now?'

'Not sure, but whatever it's going to be it will feel like Christmas that's for sure. I haven't even started yet.'

Zara wondered how Brett got his energy. His body shape had now filled out slightly to become more angular, muscular and stronger. It was driving her wild more than normal. Any young boyish charm was wearing away and he was a challenge and a half for any girl to resist. Whatever training he'd done was working perfectly. Zara lay back in seventh heaven.

By the time they'd both devoured each other including the lunch which had merged into dinner, Zara insisted they get some clothing on and maybe hit the town. This was what living was all about, thought Zara: seizing the moment as it came. By midnight their raucous laughter was waking the neighbours as they both staggered back to Brett's digs.

No questions were asked; both knew that she was staying the night. Zara wanted to enjoy every moment that she could. Banishing the thought of how she would feel when it was time to say goodbye, to the recesses of her mind. Now was the present and she was savouring every drop.

Waking to the bright light of the early sunshine trickling beneath the blind, Zara rose slowly and as quiet as she could, sneaking a look out over the mountains in the distance. A soft swirling mist lay close to the surface of the lake, its long tendrils curling and enveloping the shore. Projecting like clear dominant statues raised the majestic mountains bathed in the warm yellow glow of the sun. It really took your breath away, which was what Brett did as he hugged her from behind suddenly.

'Argg! You made me jump,' exclaimed Zara glad that he had woken so soon.

'Not bad for a morning view is it? A little bit different to city life. Who wants to be a city banker tied to your chair when you can get into nature out here?'

Zara could see quite clearly why Brett liked the travel bug. He was no suited and booted kind of guy. The passion and relaxed spirit he oozed from every pore just made Zara even hornier than she had been the day before. Catching him unawares, she twisted and flung him backwards onto the bed.

'I'd like to get back to nature with you for a moment; any chance?' she whispered seductively into his ear.

'Every chance, you don't even need to ask.' He smiled and playfully rolled her over so he became the one in control again.

'When you've had your fill of nature I'm going to excite your senses in a different way.'

'You are?' Zara looked confused but excited at what he might have in store. Then a shadow crossed her face and she felt extremely worried.

'You're not getting me on a bungee jump. I don't need that much excitement to my senses. Just being with you is as much as I can handle.' She pinched him playfully.

'Trust me it doesn't involve any heights, speed but no heights.' He grinned mischievously and dragged her out of bed pushing her into the shower before she could question him further.

The start to the morning was clearly just the beginning and a warm sensuous shower with Brett was winning hands down. Zara couldn't help but relax as he ran soapy hands gently over her body, skimming her hips and gliding smoothly over every contour.

Once dressed, Zara reluctantly allowed Brett to cover his fit body, which only slightly dampened her ardour for him. With clothing on, Brett still oozed sex appeal. It took all her willpower to allow him to drag her outside into the cool air and down to the jetty on the lakeshore.

The town had come to life by now. Traffic was snarling through the centre. All manner of four wheel drives and passion wagons (as Zara called them) were snaking away out of town towards the mountains, ingeniously laden with skis and paraphernalia. All in pursuit of the thrill of allowing their passengers to gleefully hurl themselves off the snowy piste, competing for the fastest speed, only to return to top base and repeat the process all over again.

A hot soup kitchen was offering rich warm broths. Grabbing a bowl they both sat out on the jetty for a light but warming breakfast. Brett lured Zara over to the end of the promenade towards the area of gleaming yellow speedboats. Cuddling up to her, he decided now was the time to pronounce his surprise.

'Today we're going for a once in a lifetime spin in one of those babies,' announced Brett.

Zara eyed the jet boats suspiciously unsure of what to say.

'Don't look so worried, they're quite safe. I've got friendly with one of the lads. I've been for a spin on many occasion. It's great fun. I'd love to be as good but you need some skill to drive the way he does.' Brett laughed as Zara's face said it all with the comment he'd just come out with.

Before Zara could hesitate or kick up a protest they were both being bundled into more professional attire for the trip to keep warm due to the speed of the boat once out on the open water. First a strong, black, waterproof jacket with the jet boat logo, light but extremely robust, topped by a meaty looking life jacket, which Zara was a little concerned about eyeing the icy, choppy water out on the lake, hoping that a watery bath wasn't in order. Finally thick gloves and a fetching woolly hat, sex appeal went out the window after that. She felt like some sumo wrestler. At least she would be concentrating on the ride and not sex which was probably a good thing if life jackets were in order.

After a primary chat and a few photos taken of the group, they were directed out onto the small wooden stage next to the speed machine itself. Zara's attention was caught by the rather dashing driver that swaggered over to bid the party directions on where to sit; now he did ooze danger. Clothed in exactly the same damn attire but minus the life jacket which was probably the deciding factor, offset with a fine pair of dark Ray-Ban sunglasses; the look became much more appealing. All that was visible was a strong, tanned jaw line. Zara was now mesmerized and putty in his hands.

Their dashing driver helped each passenger onboard by hand personally. Zara was aware of Brett's stare as she melted slightly. Two gorgeous males on one trip of a lifetime; she was one lucky girl.

No straps or belts were required in the boat, but a firm hand grip was advised to avoid falling overboard, particularly once speed was achieved and the three sixty degree turns were to be executed. 'Great,' thought Zara.

'Not only am I head over heels with excitement at being with Brett again, I've got to cope with being flung round at top speed in a circle. She hoped her constitution was up for it. Being sick all over either one of them would be the most embarrassing event of her life. Breakfast should have been missed.

The jet boat fired up. The driver revved the engine to check all was in good order and with a cursory glance and nod to his passengers, they sped out and round the jetty into the open waters of the lake. Picking up speed he aimed straight for the wooden jetty, where a line of floating buoys were attached indicating the start of the open water and the entrance to the main bay.

Zara stared ahead and fear was creeping in as she wondered if the guy was insane or an adrenaline junkie. The solid structure was getting too close for comfort; it crept up fast, meters away. Just as she was certain they were going to hit it, they swerved sharply to the right.

The boat twisted on its side as spray showered down on them from above. A loud cheer erupted and Zara let a stream of expletives out under her breath. Brett laughed and kissed her on the cheek. The jet boat headed off out into the choppier water of the bay. Bouncing on the waves, flinging its passengers up with a rather sharp landing each time.

The scenery sped past. The air moist and chilly was bringing a tingling warm glow to Zara's cheeks. The hand signal was raised and seconds later the first of the 360 degree turns were executed. Zara gripped on tight to the hand rail and with a very precise hand movement their driver dropped the throttle. Sharply turning the wheel, the boat spun around, and the spray this time

268

coming down on the outside passengers in an icy deluge. Now they all knew why the protective gear was required.

The driver grinned and checked everyone was ok, before revving up once again, slamming the boat out against the ripples of water created by the spin, careering back along the far side of the lake towards the canyon region.

Here the water narrowed considerably. Loose shingle could be felt hitting the under surface of the boat as the water depth lowered to just inches beneath them. The river that the lake emerged into ran fast over the smooth pebbles.

Huge rock walls enshrouded them, topped with tall, woody and very dense pine trees. The speed of the boat intensified as the sides of the canyon whizzed by at top speed. Any images were a complete blur. Just as the speed became breathtaking, the jet boat slowed with a sharp turn. They spun round once again to face the way they'd come, the boat rocking gently to a standstill. Turning towards his audience, the driver sat on the edge of the boat. Calm and collected, one leg up to support himself he faced his crew and explained at length some of the history and background of the area they'd passed through.

Zara sat agog; she hung on every word. Intelligent and competent with such a mean machine, she felt slightly embarrassed to be sitting there like any other tourist hooked completely. Brett squeezed her thigh bringing her back to reality.

'Do we have a little crush going on? Does that mean I might have to compete with a bit of heavy arm wrestling? There's no way I'm competing with the guy jet racing,' Zara blushed strongly.

'No not at all, how can you say that?'

Brett knew her far too well. He hadn't forgotten some of her little traits that we are all infallible in exposing when our defenses are down.

Before Zara had time to wriggle out of her predicament the jet boat was off again, careering along at breakneck speed, back towards the open waters. After several 360 degree turns that were getting more and more exhilarating by the minute, a very soaked but gloriously contented crew sped back to the home jetty for disembarking.

Unsteadily Zara needed the helping hand of the driver to disembark. With Brett holding her from the rear she was spoilt for choice for whom to swoon over first.

On dry land the driver helped everyone out of their safety gear with the aid of several young girls who sold and promoted the trips. Brett fumbled with Zara's. Grabbing hold of her waist and ushering her away from the jetty he raised a solitary hand to his friend and a cursory nod of thanks, proudly steering Zara back towards the town.

'You were in a hurry to leave, weren't you?' piped up Zara glancing at him to try and read how he was feeling.

'Too right, I wasn't going to let my mate man handle you, knowing how much you might enjoy it.'

'Do I detect a slight essence of jealousy in your remark?'

'No never, me jealous, there was no competition. I'd

have won hands down, you can't resist me.'

'You arrogant sod, you don't know that. I might have very well been tempted if the offer came up.'

'Umm I'm not so sure. But I still wasn't taking a chance. I saw you wistfully looking. I could have fallen overboard and you wouldn't have noticed. Backfired on me a bit, didn't it?'

'No, it was lovely and I wouldn't have been tempted. I'm only teasing.'

Zara did notice that Brett still seemed rather concerned with her last remarks, and held her closer to him over the next few hours. As the long shadows of the late sun started to emerge, both Zara and Brett were beginning to flag and sustenance was required again. They cornered a couple of lounge chairs outside a rather decadent bar. Complete with two roaring, outdoor fires at either end of the front entrance, huge umbrellas provided shelter from any rain.

The warmth of the logs with the panoramic view of the mountains and lake was a perfect combo combined with a warm hot toddy. Zara melted under Brett's touch as he played softly with her hair and kissed the nape of her neck.

'Brings back a few memories, doesn't it?' Zara gripped his body a little tighter and a pang of sadness knotted her stomach. She really didn't want this to end; for once she was cursing the commitments they had. Brett picked up with his sixth sense something was wrong. He sighed.

'It's great here isn't it? Makes wet and dull Britain seem a million miles away. Shame it can't be like this always. I'm really grateful you managed to come over

271

this way, it's meant a lot to me. I knew you would love it here.'

Zara snuggled up closer, her hand nestling on and between his thighs. The longing to be embraced and back in Brett's bed permanently was a little too much to bear, knowing her time was short lived.

'Yeah, it's gorgeous, but it's the company that makes it so perfect.' She looked wistfully at him wishing that he was more open with her, upfront about his plans and what she actually really meant to him. Hating having to ask him outright, but needing to know now before it was too late.

'So where do you go from here, back home or back to Australia?' hardly bearing to breathe as she waited for his response. Brett paused for a moment trying hard to phrase what he was to say. Uncertain of how to word it in the best way, he was aware of Zara feeling vulnerable and wasn't keen to spoil the moment they were experiencing.

'I've got to go back to Australia; my contract is for another year at least. Now I've signed up and completed my certificates, I need to get the experience of working in all climates. We work with a lot of gap year students, all ages really. My first assignment is working the outback on a survival course. My climbing skills will be useful so some expeditions will include that, along with some ski work at the mountain sites. That will give me some all-round skills. Then the world will be my oyster. I can travel and work in most places. My expertise will be up to scratch. It's what I've always wanted to do really, travel, live outdoors. I'm not one for the mortgage and drudge of society. It's living so close to the hills back in Scotland; I blame my ancestors.'

Zara laughed. She couldn't be sad with Brett, he was only living the dream and well organized he was too, just what she was doing really but unfortunately on another continent.

'Maybe we will meet at a mutual point some time and can enjoy a bit of life like we are now?' Brett turned to hold Zara's face cupping it within his warm fingertips. He leant forward and kissed her delicately on the lips staring directly into her eyes. He found himself feeling for the first time in ages a deep yearning and a subtle tinge of sadness that he wasn't going to see her for some time and it was of his own doing.

He couldn't ask her to give up the fantastic opportunity she had in LA to travel with him, and besides he was going to be self-absorbed with his training. There'd be no creature comforts where he was travelling. He couldn't quite see Zara sleeping under canvas in the hot arid desert for weeks on end. No, he would have to be tough but looking at Zara he was finding his weaknesses surfacing up pretty damn fast.

The fun they'd had on the past few occasions of meeting were etched in his memory. He was succumbing to being seduced by the opposite sex and it wasn't what he had on his agenda. Too many mates had fallen by the wayside and left all their dreams and ambitions behind. Holed up in some two up, two down terrace, their freedom curtailed. Their only highlight being one bender a week, if the other half allowed them the freedom of the city. He didn't want that. Besides whoever he ended up with, he wanted to at least have

273

something to offer them and know that he'd achieved everything he had aimed for. Unresolved dreams were not a good start to any relationship.

The urge that was rearing deep between his loins was like a wave. His sex drive was screaming at this precise moment. In fact he'd felt horny ever since he clapped eyes on Zara. The memory of their session in the Cairngorms kept drifting across his mind. The excitement of making love to her was still indelibly inked on his brain. Just touching her naked body sent him bloody wild with desire. Trying to forget about her after this week might prove a massive challenge. He'd not spent such a long time with her as this and they did get on pretty well, he had to admit.

Zara slipped her hand further up the inside of his thigh. By now he could feel the pulsing of blood shooting forward and was beginning to feel rather confined in his constricting combat trousers. Zara sensed he was feeling aroused and grinned a mutual knowing between them.

'I'll just have to wait until the time is right, won't I?' There was a strong questioning to the remark she uttered.

Brett sighed deeply; this was going to be one hell of a slog. But on a lighter note, they could make the most of the time they did have together. Always an optimist he moved forward to whisper in Zara's ear and slowly slid his hand teasingly up Zara's thigh, this time his erection hitting an all-time high in anticipation of what he was feeling. Zara moaned beneath his touch.

'I think we better finish off this soiree away from here, don't you? Otherwise I may be arrested for indecent behaviour in a public bar.' laughed Brett, breathing hot air onto Zara's cold nose.

'Not sure what the penalty is in New Zealand!'

~ ~ ~

The next few days flew by in whirl of hedonism. The early dawn light crept eerily up the vast mountain expanse as Zara peered sleepily out of the window. Blearily she rubbed her eyes and longingly looked across at Brett. Now was the final day of departure and goddamn it! She was not prepared.

Padding quietly over to her bags she sorted any last minute items into the awaiting suitcase. Her new independent life crammed into one box and the one item she wanted to keep close to her was going to be thousands of miles away.

Now she just wanted to chuck everything out and squat there until Brett allowed her to go with him, but she knew that wouldn't happen. Standing up, she was aware of Brett embracing her body with his strong and comforting touch.

'Morning gorgeous, I hope you weren't slipping off without me saying goodbye? I'd have been heartbroken if you did.' Zara turned and grasped his waist tightly.

'As if I could do that, in fact I nearly unpacked and was thinking of sitting it out but I know I can't.'

Brett's eyes focused deeply on her, his breath soothing her forehead. She felt lightheaded with the intensity of her feelings. Wanting the moment to hold forever but prolonging the goodbye made her feel totally vulnerable to him. He grazed her cheeks with his

275

soft lips and in seconds she was kissing him, locking on to his body feeling every tremor and heartbeat between them. His thick lashes laced with a faint glint of moisture.

Zara had always laughed at romantic films when they showed long lingering goodbyes, harmonious and soulful music always playing in the background. She would cringe. It became embarrassing to watch, but now she was in that moment it felt like a knife plunging deep into her body. Fighting back tears Zara tried hard to smile.

'I better get sorted, otherwise we'll be late to the airport.'

Brett half smiled, and squeezing her hand he reluctantly wandered off to the kitchen to prepare them some breakfast. Zara tried hard to finalize everything passport, luggage, tickets but she kept being distracted by the presence of Brett only feet away. She was trying hard to memorize every nuance and part of his anatomy, the long line of his back, the soft but taut curvature of his buttocks, his gentle profile and cute button nose. It was all there in her mind but she was scared it would fade. Photos were fine but they never captured the true personality and soul of that individual.

~ ~ ~

The airport loomed large and noisily into view; walking the concourse to the passport control was the hardest thing Zara had ever had to do.

'Well this is it. New lives beckoning, it's been fantastic being here and seeing you and please, please remain in contact.' Zara's voice faded silently, her voice drying up unable to articulate any more words.

'Here come on, don't worry. You know we'll keep in touch somehow. It's just the way it is. Who knows, things may change a year down the line. Me stuck out with only a sheep to shag, pardon the terrible crassness, and you in hip L.A., the bodybuilder paradise, how can I compete with what's over there? It should be me having sleepless nights wondering if you want to keep in touch. I'll probably be just a playful memory of a guy you had some fun with.' Zara laughed, her mood lifting momentarily squeezing him softly.

'If you put it like that, I better be going straight away,' pausing she hugged him close.

'But somehow I don't think that will be the case.'

'Yeah, glam babes like you have no hassle in pulling. My next invitation will be sitting in the wings at your big wedding wishing I'd never let you get on that plane.'

Zara couldn't withhold the tears any longer cascading down her face like pearly beads. They flowed constantly. Brett wiped them with the back of his hand.

'Zara don't cry, you'll start me off and I can't be some wimpy Pom can I, compared with these macho New Zealanders.'

'And why not? I think it's lovely when a man shows his emotions.' As she glanced up, Zara felt the warm moistness of Brett's own tears as he kissed her.

'Go, you must go, you'll be boarding soon. Ring me when you arrive, I'll be looking forward to it.' He backed away brushing a hand against his eyes clearly trying hard to compose himself and waving madly in the process. Zara turned and forcing herself to put one foot in front of the other she passed through the gates of passport control. To a new life; one far, far away from Brett.

Chapter 16

FOREIGN SHORES

Touchdown, Zara breathed a sigh of relief. They had landed. Flying was not her first passion in life, but it was unavoidable if you wanted to stray further than the good old UK.

The cabin crew unbuckled and walked slowly up the aisle, checking relevant documents for the passengers before disembarking. Customs was not something Zara really looked forward to after such a long flight. She prayed it would be quicker than last time when Jamie had accompanied her. One look at Jamie lolloping towards the scanner and she wasn't surprised they were nearly strip searched. His sense of humour had made a routine search into more than a mammoth procedure.

Cringing, she approached the checkout hall. Luckily the queue was pretty rapid; no drug smugglers, irate passengers or loopy grannies bringing in their homemade produce. Zara was looking forward to collapsing in her hotel room and having a rest. Though what time it was back at home or even New Zealand was a little uncertain. She had lost the plot a little. Too many time zones had passed by.

Feeling emotionally raw after her brief stay with Brett and the jetlag combined had made her feel rather hesitant about the choices she'd made. New horizons may be beckoning, but it had been one hell of a wrench to say goodbye.

Wandering towards the main exit she scanned the awaiting crowd for a glimmer of recognition of the guide she was to meet. Laptop photos were never that clear and amongst the sea of faces it was hard to distinguish any that were familiar.

A woman was waving frantically in her direction. Probably the pale, whitewashed female staggering towards her with too much luggage was a pretty safe bet she was the English pickup. Zara pushed the heavy trolley, laden with half her life on it towards the woman. Smiling, she welcomed her with a very cheery American twang.

'Hi are you Miss Hinchcoombe? Miss Zara Hinchcoombe?'

'Yes I am thank you for meeting me. It's a pretty daunting place, LA, I have to admit.'

'Oh, you'll soon get used to the big city. I can give you a tour over the week. I'm Caprice. Your new company have assigned me sole charge to help you settle in. I've arranged a couple of viewings for some condominiums. You'll get your first month's salary upfront to help towards your rental and to live on, as well as a small bonus. It does mean your second month may be a little tight on finance, but LA is a healthy city, food is pretty reasonable. I'm sure you won't starve.'

Zara grinned a little falsely. Caprice seemed a little robotic in her attitude; maybe it was just her way. She'd make a note not to get on the wrong side of her. Compassion probably wasn't her strong point.

'There is some legal work we have to sort out with your working visa and health insurance but...' Caprice noticed Zara's weary expression and hesitated in her tracks.

'We can sort that much later once you've caught up with the jetlag. I can meet you tomorrow and show you round, get your bearings of the city, meet the company's staff and visit your base.' Smiling, she led Zara towards one of the waiting cabs. Maybe she did have a teeny drop of compassion under her professional persona.

Zara's brain was thinking only of sleep at this moment in time, although the bright sunshine of LA was hitting the serotonin and melatonin levels. The body was still not sure what it was meant to do. Sitting back in the rather hot leather seat, Zara leant her head against the window watching the busy traffic flow past. Hypnotised by the flow she drifted off, momentarily blotting out Caprice as she babbled on about the key areas they were passing through.

A sudden jolt of the taxi cab stopping woke Zara from her slumber. Turning towards Caprice she looked a little bewildered as to where she was, then recollection returned and she wondered if her guide had been aware she was off the radar for the last thirty minutes. It appeared not.

Stepping out into the bright hot sunshine again, the hotel loomed up at her. Boy, they did do things large over here. A bell boy immediately had her luggage sorted and she was being whisked by buggy this time towards her accommodation on the far side of the hotel grounds. It was going to be some walk in the morning for breakfast. Maybe it was the norm in keeping the lithe-like figures intact, enticing the guests to do an early morning jog before hitting the breakfast table.

Zara was hoping the buggy ride would be complementary each day but her finances may restrict her with the constant tipping business they liked to do. Strolling was going to have to be the order of the day.

Entering her room the welcome sight of a massive queen sized bed and ensuite the size of her flat back home, nearly made her jump for joy. Turning she looked out over a balcony terrace towards the golf course. She was in seventh heaven.

'Well, I think my duties are done for now. Have the rest of the day to chill and recuperate. I'll meet you at reception at nine. Breakfast is from six so enjoy.' Turning on her heel Caprice, left Zara to collapse on the bed in a weary heap.

'Six! She'd be lucky to be up by six. Maybe with the hour changes it was a lie in compared to New Zealand time.' Zara decided the calculation too difficult to work for now, the mind needed to be recharged. The last twenty four hours had been pretty wild and traumatic. The new life would have to be put on hold for the moment. Turning over she lay her head on the soft pillows, silky in texture they reminded her of Brett's soft touch and a tear slowly rolled down her cheek. Swallowing hard she distracted herself with thoughts of what LA would be offering before she drifted into oblivion.

~ ~ ~

Up earlier than normal due to her disjointed sleep pattern, Zara felt ready to embrace what LA had for her. Meeting the lovely official Caprice was not too daunting after some shut eye. Even the tedious paperwork that had to be sorted was over before she had time to wilt.

The work base was interesting; on first impressions it was nothing like her premises back home. The building loomed up in front of her, all glass and modern architecture. Entering reception, its glossy marble floors and friendly reception staff were a far cry from Gwen who used to be their receptionist. Unless you were hobbling, she was not one to be over friendly on greeting. Here the American bubbly persona was constant.

Once shown her work station, Zara smiled. It was a pretty deluxe clinic, beyond her wildest dreams. If Jamie could see this he would be champing at the bit to be joining her company as well. Overall it was the height of efficiency, climatic air control, electronic couches that looked as if any position could be achieved at a flick of a button. No heaving some big woman over, praying she didn't flop over the edge of the couch.

Before she could take it all in, the ever efficient Caprice was bustling her on to the staff room to meet some of her new colleagues.

'Hi everyone, please meet your new work colleague Zara. She will be joining next week once I've settled her into our community. Please show her the routine and protocol as you go. Any questions, Zara?'

Zara stood looking a little uncomfortable as all eyes swivelled round to focus on her. 'No everything's fine, looking forward to joining the group. Just need to check out where everything is and ready to start.'

Glancing round she noticed the staff had a fairly equal male to female ratio. A couple of guys looked like the stereotypical sporty jocks. Straight out of college, muscle bound, crew cut hair with a certain whiff of a competitive nature.

The women looked friendly, not dissimilar to the girls she worked with back home. One girl stood out. Clearly on a level with the jocks, as her demeanour was all out cheerleader material. Swinging ponytails, white charismatic smile and long lean limbs, gently tinted a golden brown. Zara was noting not to stand too close if she ever wanted to be noticed by the opposite sex. This girl would take centre stage where ever they were.

'Now if that is all, I will leave you in the capable hands of Crystal my colleague, who will escort you around the city more to get a feel for it, I have to meet another client at the airport sadly.'

A snigger from the back of the room broke the quietness and one of the lads piped up.

'You are cruel. First day and the poor girl won't know what's hit her. By Monday you won't remember what you looked like.'

Zara was unclear what he meant. As if on cue the door opened and in sashayed Crystal. Zara noticed that she was even more the stereotype of the all-out Californian girl. Dressed in the most revealing outfit that showed her figure off at every angle, her skin lightly tanned and hair sun kissed with soft highlights, Crystal would turn heads any time of day.

'Hi sweetie, on time today but it was a miracle.' She embraced Caprice with a hug and air kiss to both cheeks. Turning she surveyed Zara,

'So this is Zara, lovely to meet you. We're set for some fun today. That's why I like my job so much, the ideal opportunity to show off and visit the best of the city. What is there not to love about it?' Flashing more thigh than was legal, she sat perched across from them flashing a pearly row of pure white teeth. Zara started to feel she rapidly needed some catching up to compete with the female race over here.

Caprice made her excuses and left the girls to proceed without her. Crystal scanned Zara up and down. Her critical eye seemed to bore inwards analysing every part of Zara's anatomy. Why was she feeling a little hesitant? It was just tour guiding she was assigned to do. Why did she feel she was being scrutinised for surgery?

'Darling once we have seen some of my favourite haunts and there are a few, we may need to make you a little less English looking. A little tanning might do wonders for your complexion.' Before Zara could protest indignantly, the rear view of Crystal was sashaying out of the staff room doorway beckoning her to follow.

What a cheek, thought Zara. She quite liked looking a bit different from the usual crowd. Scuttling after the cool Crystal she was going to have to reserve judgment for a while. Finally encased in their transport for the day, which resembled a sports car like nothing Zara had seen before, Crystal popped her shades on and allowed the car to purr into life. Releasing the clutch they were off as she slipped into the main traffic stream, deciding to compete with the nearest saloon driver to the next traffic lights.

Zara again had flashbacks to Gina's wonderful ability of scaring her rigid whenever she got in a vehicle. Moving into the flat was one such incident she chose to eradicate from her mind. Today it was coming back rapidly. Gina had no conception that a large van needed more room to manoeuvre than her tiny old contraption. After two wing mirrors and one near miss with a cyclist, Zara had no choice but to drive and relegate Gina to directions.

Crystal seemed to have that dogged determination that nobody should be on the highway but herself. Oblivious to the looks of disdain and rage that were directed at her, she cut up a third driver in less than five minutes.

As there was no top to the car, this meant Zara could only keep her head down or smile apologetically. Deciding to join forces, she placed her own sunglasses on to at least hide some of her embarrassment.

Distance between places in LA involved a fair stretch of highway driving. The heady delights of Sunset Boulevard approached and Crystal slipped the car left into an underground car park. With a flick of a button the roof sprung up and descended down into place.

'Right then, let's get you California initiated,' shrilled Crystal as she grabbed her keys and bag.

Zara wasn't sure how much this involved, but the end result probably wasn't what she would feel comfortable with. Smiling weakly she followed Crystal to the lift, adorned with posters proclaiming the enhancements that Wonder Glamour could do for the woman of today.

'Hello darling, brought another protégé to you. This is Zara she is due to work at the clinic downtown. Now I need you to do your magic in making her feel more at home. Forget the nails, this one has to work for a living,' she smiled kindly at Zara, 'I don't mean that in a rude manner, just some of the girls I bring here are only on business with their other half. For them, using the hands are just for the bedroom if you know what I'm referring to. Don't normally have to lift a finger unless it's tea at Beverley Hills' latest cafe.'

'No offence taken,' replied Zara. Looking at the nails that adorned the girl on reception, she was pretty sure she wouldn't be doing much to initiate her into the Californian look either. Tapping out a phone number would have proved difficult with her talons, particularly on the tiny keyboards of modern technology.

After being eyeballed a few times in an attempt to see what delights were needed for this venture, Zara was led into a tiny room adjacent.

'Now, all I need you to do is to pop on the paper underwear, make sure you wash any deodorant off and make up. Otherwise you might go rather streaky,' pausing for a few moments the young beautician analysed her facial features, 'that is if you use any of course.'

Zara wasn't sure if she was being sarcastic or impressed that she didn't need any. It was hard to tell in this city what was implied. It was going to take some getting used to. The girl exited the room smiling sweetly.

'I'll give you five minutes to get sorted.'

The door closed silently with a tiny click. Standing alone in the room Zara rapidly stripped naked, looking at the brief and rather skimpy paper knickers with disdain. How on earth had she been talked into this? The G-string was barely covering her female area. No wonder they did Brazilians over here. By the end of this she would be no longer a soft auburn but a dark mahogany down below. Or it would be silhouetted in a burnished brown. Neither look sounded very fetching. But she would stand out from the crowd in the changing room.

Shortly a polite knock at the door caused Zara to grab something to make her feel half decent. Clutching a towel to cover her essential area of breasts, she stood feeling very vulnerable at what was to happen next.

'Hi how are we doing, ready for me to start? All I need you to do is step into the cubicle and place your hands up high to begin with. I'll then spray the first coat on and show you the new position. Please close your eyes and breathe gently out rather than in as I spray.' The therapist looked friendly enough but armed with a spray gun that looked something out of Robo Cop, she wasn't sure if the image would stay in her mind.

As the spray tan shot out, the coldness took Zara by surprise very nearly causing her to take a deep breath in. She could feel her nipples standing on end and was thankful it wasn't a guy doing the job, gay or not. The misty spray seemed to hit every millimetre of skin.

'Lovely now I'm going to need you to stand sideways on, one leg forward as if you're walking. Great.' Aiming the gun again, the spray hit every angle of Zara. The minute particles of lotion exploding on impact creating a fetching sheen over her skin.

Finally the rear side made her judder and brace herself as the cold tan lotion hit her back. Visions of a past experience at the German health spa, when Bella had so kindly enticed her to attend came roaring into her mind. Standing in the long cold corridor, an icy jet stream of water had been politely aimed at her derriere. The purpose to dissolve any cellulite was one memory she would rather not return to. Standing on the back patio with Bella using the garden hose would have sufficed. At least she could have sworn at her and saved fifty pounds into the bargain. A smacking with a rolling pin would have been more pleasant. Those Germans definitely like to go one step further in the quest for perfection.

Zara did wonder what extremes of pleasure the beauty conscious Californians would go to in their quest for perfection. Her German counterparts were pretty vicious in their quest. The frequency of cold herbal baths and foul smelling water tonics had not attracted Zara to pick them out of the tourist guide for any other little European jaunts.

'Fabulous, we have finished. Just take few moments for the tan to settle and dress lightly. Avoid the bra, as it will cause you to have streaks where you don't want streaks.' The young girl smiled obviously trying to crack a joke. It sadly fell on deaf ears with Zara, as the intention of showing half her breast area off to all and sundry, wasn't on her list of 'to do's'. They liked to flash it around out here by the sound of it, thought Zara. Smiling meekly in return, she tried to do a gentle dance around to air dry the tan liquid quicker, praying there were no surveillance cameras lurking.

Luckily, Zara had brought her loose fitting summer dress which she could just get by with no bra under. Being a fair thirty two D cup she normally needed one, but having a little support in the dress did help. Emerging from the room Crystal immediately looked up from her pedicure station. One hand clasped elegantly around a glass of a strange looking green liquid, the other flicking through one of the latest glossies, whilst her feet were carefully attended to by a robust Mexican lady of about fifty. This was hard for Zara to ascertain as the woman had a lack of wrinkles showing anywhere on her smooth olive skin.

'Oh, there you are, all finished. Perks of the job, have to amuse my time away somehow.' Beckoning the lady to finish, Crystal plonked the evil looking glass on a mirrored cabinet close by and flung the magazines back into the holdall, attached to the reclining seat she laid sprawled back in. The salon was pretty flash by any standard. Something you might find in Knightsbridge. Not that Zara had ever had time or inclination to spend half her salary in having a treatment, but Amber had on a few occasions left the odd pamphlet around at home, assuming she may have had the privilege to indulge.

As they returned to the car, Zara was intrigued by Crystal's fantastic lifestyle. It seemed all she had to do was meet and greet occasionally. Check out any hot sights worth showing her client and then relax and enjoy, whilst she shuffled them into a revamp on the pretence it was a complete necessity for the job. Personally she felt Crystal just made most of it up. Taking the clients to where ever she wanted to hang out for the day, throwing in a few tourist attractions on the way. It was hard to dislike the girl though irritating at first, over time you found her less and less comical and ditzy on the surface, enticing you to delve deeper where first appearances let her down.

'Now I have two lovely condos to look at for rental. I'm pretty sure you will find both to your liking. If not, I do have a few more but financially they are a lot pricier and with only the therapy salary, you might struggle,' she looked a little embarrassed to have to say this reddening slightly. 'Are you ok with your jetlag to pop over now? It saves having to do it tomorrow.' Crystal obviously had her own agenda for tomorrow, thought Zara.

'Yes fine, glad to get it all sorted as quickly as I can. Then I've time to get used to it all.'

Crystal's face brightened. 'Good let's go then.' Slamming the car into gear once again she sped off like a demon possessed. Surely there couldn't be too many Gina's out there who love speed so much when behind the steering wheel.

The first pad was nice but the view from the balcony was dark and oppressive, looking over the back yard of several apartment blocks that lay behind it. An array of floating washing attached to make-shift clothes lines draped the balconies of the opposing apartments. No,

291

she couldn't see herself here. Crystal turned her nose up straight away on entering the lobby, even before she had shown Zara the fetching view.

'Urgg! I'm not sure how they put this on my list. First time I've been here and the last. I'll be getting it crossed off immediately. Apologies, wait till I see Sheldon back at the office. Wasting our time, and the rent isn't that cheap either.' Huffing, she clattered her high heels down the stairs not wanting to risk the lift.

The second condominium was way better. Zara on stepping out of the car, immediately felt more at home with the area. It appeared to be quite close to the beach. The foyer and lifts were smart, newly renovated by the look of it. A concierge was situated on the ground floor which meant safety was paramount. The whole place had a cheery, fresh persona.

As Crystal opened the smart oak door, Zara knew this was the one. It was part furnished, a modern art deco looking cabinet lay to the left of them in the short hallway. Entering the lounge, an open plan set up showed off the large u-shaped sofa in cream leather segregating the room nicely from a tiny kitchenette leading off the main room. 'Umm, flash,' thought Zara. Soft peachy chiffon curtains billowed into the apartment from the open patio door. The girls passed through the clouds of fabric to be met with a very enticing view of the sea in the far distance and a small balcony just large enough for a couple of recliners if you didn't mind being toe to toe.

'Now this is what I like, definitely worth the journey. It fits the bill perfectly. Whatever the cost, it's the one. I'll just have to get a second job if the rent's too high.'

'No, it should be well in your range,' replied Crystal clearly relieved she had produced one option that was desirable.

Zara took one last look around the premises, inspecting every nook and cranny. The bedroom had a wow component of a floor to ceiling window. Venturing forward to place her nose close to the gauzy curtains, she peered through noticing instantly nobody overlooked the building at all. She had visions of awakening and having breakfast in bed with a view to kill. It certainly ticked all the right boxes. The ocean scene in the distance was very attractive. Another tick on the list, it would remind her of home hopefully in a comforting way rather than creating homesickness. Adjacent to the main bedroom was a smaller room but still adequate for a futon or small double. At present, the room was used for dining in. Zara had other plans visualised already for it. Which meant moving the glass topped table into the lounge where the view was so much nicer. It wouldn't impose at all on the space. Not envisioning having vast dinner parties it would only be herself for a while. There was no need for it to be tucked away in its own room. The space could then be utilised for visitors. Having Gina or Amber over was on her list as soon as possible.

'Yep, I'll take it whatever the price. It's ideal.'

'Well, Miss Hinchcoombe, we have a deal hopefully on the cards. I'll ring them now and sort out deposits. You could be in by the end of the week.' Swallowing hard, Zara found her heart beating slightly faster with nerves. Everything had happened with such speed. This was it.... she would now be a citizen of LA.

Chapter 17

NEW BEGINNINGS

Her heady welcome to the delights of Zara's new home had now come to an end. The settling in period had gone by in a flash. This morning was the first of many more at the new clinic. Zara managed successfully to bike to work as she found this would be one way to get fit and enjoy the sunny climate at the same time. Most importantly she wanted to save a little cash that would otherwise be spent on taxis. The trek home if walking, would be a little arduous after a long day. Biking less so as at least she was sitting down. The locals did seem to favour transport of some kind. Good old fashioned walking was clearly frowned upon. Transport could be limo, rollerblading or even skateboarding but never two legs. If you did remain on two legs, you were deemed to be keeping fit by jogging and that didn't seem to involve a gentle saunter.

As she entered the clinic, a rather over friendly receptionist greeted her. Rummaging under the desk she produced a locker key and a smart work top. All were freshly packaged complete with a mini roll-on deodorant. Hadn't they heard of the new cologne a la sweat? It may be a nice gesture or a persuasive hint to smell delicious at all times in the near permanent summer outside.

'Thanks,' murmured Zara unsure of what the refreshing products really implied. Remembering her recent visit, she wandered down the main corridor to the far end where the staff room was situated. Zara changed rapidly in the nearby locker room. It was a change from her past job, where a quick brush and polish had to be perfected in the toilets. Make-up would be applied haphazardly in the misty old mirror. Although the new premises she'd left behind were marginally better, not by any accounts as swish as this setting.

Back at reception, she checked her rota for the day. Four hour massages back to back. Zara flinched. 'They must be trying to kill me off straight away,' she thought. Observing the locals, the public ranged from ultra-fit, zero size to well into double figures. Road testing the couch with one of the larger specimens would be an interesting case. As she noted down her work, a young lad sidled up to peer over her shoulder.

'Hi, you're the new girl aren't you? I'm Patrick. Looks like they've given you a packed schedule for your first day. Some interesting clients, just be aware of Mr Glenshaw. Has some peculiar ways. A regular so treat him nice, but not too nice if you know what I mean.'

Zara tried to pick up a few clues in what he was implying and was just going to enquire further when her first customer arrived bang on time. She'd have to wait till they finally met later on. Having some ammunition before she had to deal with the customer

296

would have been useful but never mind. By the time Mr Glenshaw was ready to be tackled, she was firing on all cylinders. The morning had flown by whether it was adrenaline or excitement of the new position, she wasn't sure.

Mr Glenshaw seemed on first appearances to be a respectable type of guy; smart appearance, clean shaven, around fifty. On first meeting Zara, he greeted her with a winning smile and a hearty handshake. She prepared to leave and allow him to undress but he motioned her to stay.

'No need to leave. I'm happy to strip off. Not got anything you haven't seen before. I'm no prude.' Zara was certain he wasn't but hesitated unsure to insist or to politely ignore him as he undressed. Deciding to busy herself elsewhere in the room Zara turned her back to her client and prepped up an oil blend. On hearing Mr Glenshaw declare he was ready, she turned round to be met by the apparition of her client standing there stark naked. Gleefully asking,

'Where do you want me?'

Zara assumed it was pretty obvious, especially as he was a regular. Her assumption of his personality was he either liked playing tricks on any newbie or was an exhibitionist at heart. Pausing, she rapidly thought through what to do next. In all her years of working in the job, this was a first time for blatant nudity. Most sportsmen weren't shy by any means and happy to strip off in public, but they did at least try and cover their private region. Attempting to remain in charge, Zara decided to show she hadn't been flummoxed by his audacity. Making sure her eyes didn't scan lower than his face she replied in a brusque manner,

'Right then I think we know where to lie down don't we. I understand you're a regular here so let's get on and I'll cover you up decently. Don't want anyone walking in by accident and exposing ourselves to them, might offend some people.' Zara tried to give him a condescending look but Mr Glenshaw seemed indifferent to the meaning behind her words.

Once Zara had covered anything that shouldn't be on show publicly, treatment progressed well. Mr Glenshaw slipped into a stupor, snoring deeply as she worked into his many rolls of fat. Yes, they sure saved the heaviest session to last. There must be some muscle somewhere under all this flab, thought Zara.

After manhandling most of the front of the body, now was the fun bit. How was she to awaken the comatose body and turn her client over successfully, without a tragic accident of him falling off the couch? A gentle nudge sufficed in bringing him round to reality. Engineering the movement was harder. The couches, although wider than back home, still appeared small when her client lay on it. Zara was careful not to press the wrong button on the remote control. One was for increasing height, one for lowering but a couple had options for tilting the back or leg sections. Visions of casting her client in a slippery heap head first onto the floor didn't bear thinking about.

'I need to turn you over onto your back Mr Glenshaw. Be careful as you roll round as the couch is a little narrow. Don't want you falling off the other side as you're so sleepy now.' More the fact she didn't fancy having to save the guy if he did. Knowing full well that she could be grappling with god knows what under the towel in the process.

On turning safely, Zara made sure her client was comfortable and worked diligently on his legs. As she prepared to work his upper body, Mr Glenshaw suddenly seemed more perky and chatty after his snooze and interacted a little more. Though Zara was wishing he'd stay asleep.

'You wouldn't be a dear, like Isabella and massage my stomach. Normally does a grand massage the best here. Always good for the constitution I find it the best part of my session.'

'Yes, of course.' Zara exposed his abdomen and went to mix up some more oil; being a large body he seemed to be swallowing it up quicker than she could mix it. Turning back she stood frozen to the spot, eyeballs practically bulging at the sight she was confronted with. Mr Glenshaw seemed oblivious to any offence he was giving; eyes shut firmly, a smile lacing his lips in a contented smug manner.

Her neatly draped towel across his midriff was now slewed to the side, as his erect penis stood proudly to attention, causing Zara to nearly drop her oil in surprise. She was stunned how the guy could think he would get away with it. Why wasn't he banned from booking in if this is what he got up to? Or was she looking vulnerable enough for him to think he could take advantage? 'Ruddy cheek,' uttered Zara under her breath. Even the gorgeous Abman never exposed his desire outwardly when being treated. She was bloody fuming.

Approaching the couch she decided to carry on and not let on her disgust. Treating him in a nonchalant manner, she acted oblivious to the games he was attempting to play. He was either out to shock her and get some kick, or thought he might get some additional handiwork. Shame she hadn't brought her tools for deep massage, a nice bit of pain might be in order at this precise moment, an excellent way to distract the situation.

Avoiding the erection was difficult. For an older guy his genitals were working pretty well. Zara was surprised he had any blood left coursing his veins. Discreetly she applied heavy pressure skimping over any skin below the navel, lest she would brush against the offending item and give him more stimuli than he could cope with. With some fetching sound effects from the mouth of her client making the situation worse, she cringed inwardly. Deciding to finish as rapidly as she could, she moved up to the shoulder and head area with speed, purposely avoiding any eye contact. Mr Glenshaw still remained unfazed and oblivious to anything going on around him.

Leaving her client on finishing to rest and pay at reception, Zara darted from the room as fast as she could. Entering the staffroom, a few work colleagues were lounging around relaxing on their breaks. All eyes immediately focused on her.

'Can I ask you a question on protocol? As I have some issues with a situation with Mr Glenshaw and need to know if it's just me or regular feature with him.' blurted Zara aiming the question at the two female colleagues in the room, as the response from the jocks wasn't going to be worth listening to. The girls glanced at each other and looked concerned. A slight facial twitch occurred on one of the girl's face.

'Don't tell me you didn't get warned about him. Who booked him in with Zara? That was pretty mean without letting on.' The girl swung round to the guys jabbing a finger at them. 'Shaun did you? Or was it bloody Jack, thinking it would be a joke? You wait, I'll have it out with him when I see him next. He can apologise to you Zara. It's bang out of order.'

'Do you mean to say he does this every time, stripping naked and getting a hard on?' Zara was now really annoyed. Not only that they let him get away with it, but she did at least need to be told in advance. The young lad Patrick tried to reassure her,

'I did sort of mention he had some funny ways.'

'Yeah, but that means nothing. A bit more info would have been appreciated. I could have been prepared to approach it differently rather than being put on the spot.'

'What, beat it with a stick? Or you would have had a hissy fit and refused to do the guy. Someone has to have him. I've had him four times in the last two months. You girls can have the bloke for a change,' piped up the other lad.

'You're not telling me he does the same with you as well. Urgg! That's gross. What's the matter with the guy?'

'He's got some problem with his circulation. The slightest stimulus can set it off; wouldn't mind the condition myself. Don't worry we've had words. But he

301

says it's not intentional. He's unaware half the time it's happened.' Patrick explained trying to be diplomatic.

'Strange he always wants his stomach done though isn't it?' glared the other girl. Her stare aimed at both the boys, 'Particularly as he knows of his so called problem. You'd think he would avoid us going anywhere near that part of his anatomy, out of embarrassment. He must be thick skinned as far as I can see or secretly enjoying it.'

'Well I hope I've had my initiation ceremony after today. I haven't got any more to come, have I?' Zara looked pensively at the group.

'No, I'll make sure of it. After lunch I'll fill you in more on the dodgy ones that grace our tables. Sadly we do get a few varied clientele through here. But, not as bad as Mr Glenshaw,' the girl smiled at Zara. 'Don't worry, I'll make sure you're ok.'

'You better not forget Adrian; she might freak if you don't mention the pink frilly panties he likes to wear,' uttered Patrick keen not to upset Zara again and be blamed for withholding vital information. Zara looked on in amazement. Eyes agog she thought, 'What kind of job had she applied for. Come back Jamie, all is forgiven. Maybe good old Roger wasn't such a bad boss after all.'

'Well at least he wears some. You've got to at least give him credit for that.' Patrick's colleague smirked, 'Though they are crotchless sometimes. Must be the latest fashion in the undie world.' A moment of silence entailed then a grin spread across Zara's face.

'Well I won't be homesick for Brighton for long with your colourful characters. Just fill me in and I'll be happy. For now I need a stiff drink for recovery.'

'Strongest we have is coke or fanta. If you'll wait till six o'clock when I knock off for the day, I'll treat you to something stronger as way of an apology, deal?' Patrick looked pensive waiting for her reply. Zara dropped her defensive front and shook his hand, 'Deal.'

Chapter 18

THE JET SET

'Right, roster for today guys is pretty intensive. We have two clinics that we are operating. One at the half marathon; it will be mega busy today there. As you know, a fair few celebrities will be participating in this event so please, no ogling, or trying to get autographs. They are going to be set on the race itself. They definitely do not want some sad losers like you trying to get rich, and selling some half developed picture on EBay. Especially as they lie exhausted with no decorum left after completing what is a pretty tough run for some of them.'

Max looked up at the sea of faces waiting for someone to retort and put him down, but strangely nobody did. He was a little taken aback, unsure they had fully absorbed what he'd said.

'That's good, no wisecracks to be had. The second event is down at Malibu beach. We have a local surfing championship going on, new to the list. We are not sure what work will be needed as those surfer guys never cross our doors much, but we have been asked to attend and offer our service. I know which ones the ladies will want to work at. Sorry to disappoint a few of you but I've chosen who goes where. Don't want to have a riot on my hands. I will be at both events at some stage but really on a supervisory role, any questions?'

Max scanned his staff clearly relishing his role of manager and able to kick ass if he wanted to. He looked expressively at Doug who lounged casually in his chair chewing gum; many a time he wanted to really push this guy but fair to him, when the pressure was on he did come up with the goods and gave a mean treatment. How he passed his physio examinations Max was unsure. Probably paid some other guy to do them, but he worked well if he was keen on the job. Today he would have no choice. Malibu was on the list for him. He couldn't afford for Doug to embarrass the clinic in town, not at a prestigious event like this one.

Zara glanced down at the roster memo; she was listed to work at the Surf site and she could hardly contain her excitement. Warm sunshine, beautiful views and a beachside location to work at. It couldn't get much better than that.

Since joining the Maple Leaf body clinic on the outskirts of Santa Monica she had settled in great. Meeting some great new friends and now located in a rented apartment, moments from the beach.

Zara had embraced the California lifestyle with relish. The work's van drew up out the back and in bundled the crew for the event. Bags loaded and couches placed in the adjoining trailer the size of a mini car, nothing came small over here.

Working on site for a job like this was a doddle. Weather always permitting, unlike rain sodden Blighty, where outside venues were harsh and barely adequate to provide a half decent treatment. Over here, luxury was the name of the game. Zara could see why so many who had privilege to work or live in California couldn't bear to leave.

The warm haze shifted rapidly over the surface of the tarmac as the ocean road slid like a gentle snake in front of them dotted spasmodically with large fronted villas. Palm trees wafted high above like tiny umbrellas. Throngs of spectators were already jostling around the parking zone as they neared the main arena set out adjacent to the judging area.

In the haze, tiny figures were gripping their boards, heading out for a few practice breaks before the timed event took place. Zara had never seen a competition like this up close. It was quite spectacular even from where she was situated. The surf looked pretty fierce out towards the main surfing channel. No wonder you needed to be a 'pro' to get in there.

Suddenly, Zara heard the shrill coyote tones that only she knew best; 'Crystal,' there was no mistaking it. Crystal had arrived and everyone was going to know about it. Zara scanned the beach until sighting the pagoda where the main event work was performed.

Waving frantically and dragging some poor guy behind her, along with a small entourage who struggled wearily with various items of luggage, Zara braced herself for the onslaught. As they got nearer, she recognized some of the party that she had previously met before at one of Crystal's many social soirees. They certainly knew how to party over here. Crystal was one friend she was not allowed to forget. After her funny ways of introducing her to LA lifestyle she had become a close confidante. If you wanted to know something or get to know someone Crystal would have the connection.

'Zara darling, knew I'd find you; can't believe you are so lucky to be given privileged access to the hottest guys in town.'

'I wouldn't call it that, I'm pretty sure the true professionals won't be interested in a session with the team. It's more the amateur coming to watch and copy some of the pros' skills.'

'Nonsense, it's LA. Here everyone wants a piece of freebie stuff. Everyday those lads fall over themselves to show off. Especially if they've come anywhere on the league table, so get those hands warmed up.'

Zara immediately noticed the guy who had accompanied, or rather been dragged behind, Crystal. He seemed sheepish and unsure of how to introduce himself. But not for long Crystal aware of the sudden atmosphere, swung round and shoved the poor unsuspecting male forward.

'Zara meet my long time friend Bruce. If you want to know more about the California region, Bruce is your man. I've told him so much about you; he even has some distant relatives back over the pond on your soil, so you could be practically related if you think about it.'

Zara smiled inwardly trying not to let the corner of her mouth curl up. If that wasn't the most obvious date set up she had ever come across. Bruce shifted from foot to foot in the hot sand and tried hard to appear relaxed and interesting but Zara could see a wave of nervousness. Not liking atmosphere, she stepped forward to shake hands.

'Nice to meet you, hope you enjoy the day. Sadly I'll be working most of it but maybe Crystal can give me your details and you could be my guide for the day sometime?'

'Sure that would be nice.' Bruce smiled and Zara felt a little more at ease with the difficult situation. Hoping and praying that he was a little more talkative if she did utilize his tourist skills.

'Right, let's get settled down. We will leave you in peace for now.' With a knowing look and a nudge she pulled the poor guy further down the beach with Jed, Veronica and Ella tagging behind.

It wasn't long before the first heats of the day had started. Work was slow at first but as the day wore on a small queue had formed, eager to chill out before the real party started later that night. A massive beach barbeque would be held for the many competitors and helpers at the event.

The competition went remarkably quickly and as they were packing up for the day, Zara heard shouts from across the beach. Ella came running at top speed across the sand beckoning for Zara to come.

'Zara quick, Crystal needs you. We need a first aider.' Running hard after her, Zara was a touch worried what she was to find. As they rounded the far side of the beach back up towards the breakwaters she could just make out the silhouette of the others. As she approached the group she could see clearer, and made out the stooped figure of Bruce clutching his lower calf grimacing in pain.

'Oh my god, thank goodness you can help. Bruce slipped badly on the rocks. It was my entire fault, you know what I'm like, wanted to muck around on the rock pools. Bruce gallantly wanted to accompany me and took a massive tumble on the slippery rocks. Is it broken?'

Crystal for once looked as if the wind had been taken out of her sails. Zara stepped forward gingerly, clearly not wanting to come to the same fate noticing the tide coming in quite quickly, as the late haze of afternoon sunshine was diminishing. The area was getting more and more hazardous as the minutes ticked by.

Glancing down at Bruce's leg she noticed a huge gash about two inches long oozing blood. Not one for the sight of blood at the best of times, she took a deep breath and opened the first aid kit quickly.

'Let's get a tourniquet on the leg first. It looks like a nasty cut. We will need to carry him off these rocks rapidly. Don't put any pressure on it just in case there's something in the wound. I need to flush it out first. Where's the other guys? I think we're going to need some help to carry Bruce back up the beach.'

'They left about half an hour ago for a drink. We decided to have a muck around down here till the event closed, bit stupid really seeing what's happened.'

'Accidents happen, shame but we will have to manage. You take one arm I'll take the other and see what we can do, Ella.' Bruce seemed extremely embarrassed but was wincing too much to try and be macho.

With the help of Ella and the hindrance of Crystal, who wasn't much help at all, they managed to stumble back across the vast expanse of sand towards the clear coast line and car park. Most of the stragglers had departed by now and the beach was becoming deserted. Placing Bruce on the floor of the tent that was still erect, Zara managed to examine the leg better.

'I feel a bit of a fool, sorry. I'm not normally such a wimp but it really is giving me some major pain now.'

Zara tried to reassure him, but the bleeding was not stemming and a quick hospital stitch up was going to be required. After flushing the wound, she applied a tourniquet to suppress some of the bleeding.

'Crystal get my cell phone and ring for an ambulance, we need to get Bruce sorted. A cab won't take him and I haven't got any transport as I came with the team from the clinic. You're in too much of a tizzy to drive and I'm sure the others aren't insured to drive your vehicle anyway.'

Zara was quite surprised how organized she was. Normally the sight of blood made her very peculiar. Bruce was clearly also very affected by it. His face was now draining of colour and he was starting to feel quite lightheaded, as if he was going to pass out any minute. Leaving it for Crystal to sort would be an utter nightmare that wasn't worth thinking about. At this moment in time she was a nervous wreck, but not having enough hands to do everything she had no choice.

Zara looked up impatiently at Crystal, not wanting to get annoyed but needing to stress the urgency of the situation, she decided to be a little more firm.

'Crystal please, I need you to ring now not in five minutes after you've had your mini stress. Time is essential - if not I'm going to have to slap you.'

Crystal was still running around like a headless chicken but the threat of a slap did seem to bring her to some sense, and she rustled through her shoulder bag for the cell phone. After what seemed like ages, she finally retrieved it and rang the number.

'Ten minutes...will he live till then?' At this stage even Zara was feeling faintly hysterical and was not in the mood for Crystal's brainless comments. Snapping she retorted,

'Of course he'll live but he will require some help pronto. You'll scare the living daylights out of Bruce at this rate.' Crystal went very quiet and looked close to tears.

'Sorry I shouldn't have snapped. It's been a long day and I really am a little concerned we get Bruce seen to quickly. Here, help me to keep his leg higher than his body.' Bruce was now half woozy and paler than ever, he squeezed Zara's hand.

'Glad you were my angel of mercy when I needed you.'

'Grateful to be of assistance but my bedside manner could do with a bit of working on, don't you think?'

Bruce smiled weakly. 'No you'd have to be Saint to cope with Crystal in an emergency. You appeared very much in control, thank you.'

Zara looked closely at Bruce as he leant back on the sand; he seemed exhausted suddenly and she was now a little worried he was losing more fluids than she thought from the gash he'd experienced. What seemed like an age the ambulance appeared up high on the beach. Beckoning to them, Zara breathed a sigh of relief as help was now close by.

'You're in good hands now. I'll find out from Crystal how you're doing.' Bruce's eyes flickered as a response.

~ ~ ~

Steaming lightly from the hot shower, Zara wrapped the only towel around her slender frame hoping it covered everything it should do to answer the call button of her apartment.

'Hello.'

'Hi, it's Bruce here, could I come up and have a word?'

'Yes, hang on I'll do the buzzer for you.' With the press of the button and a frantic dance to try and dress half-decently ensued. Her skin still damp from the shower made it nigh impossible to get her top on before she heard Bruce's feet shuffling along the corridor from the lift. 'Oh crikey I wish I'd stayed in the towel.' thought Zara.

The doorbell rang and grabbing a sarong she hastily tied it around her bust. Opening the door she was taken aback by a massive bouquet of flowers hiding Bruce's face.

'Hi, are you in there somewhere?' joked Zara. From behind the flowers emerged Bruce's grinning face. He seemed less shy today and mildly cute.

'Yep, hope you like them as they're for you. I did have a few jibes as I walked from the limo I can tell you.'

Grabbing the flowers Zara beckoned him to come in with one hand on the door the other clasping the bouquet. Zara was aware of a slight slippage occurring.

The knot she had hastily done of the sarong was loosening. Unaware of the delight he was to experience any minute, Bruce sidled past into the apartment, his coat dragging the fabric further down leaving most of Zara's upper torso barely covered.

Turning he was met by the spectacle of Zara chucking the flowers at him and the naked apparition of Zara fleeing towards the bedroom leaving a trail of shimmering fabric behind.

'Sorry, emergency! Won't be a minute,' spluttered Zara.

Behind closed doors Zara cringed. What a presentation to give to a bloke she hardly knew. How the hell was she going face him now? Grabbing a more substantial top and bottoms and checking everything was secure, she decided to brace herself and carry on as if nothing had happened.

Emerging back into the lounge, she apologized and offered the bemused face of Bruce a cup of coffee. Being a perfect gentleman he never mentioned the incident in their conversation at all, much to Zara's relief. Thinking of Tyler, she knew that some crude comment would be in order: offering her body before the coffee or was it a preview of what was to come.

'How's the leg doing?' enquired Zara glancing at the bandaged limb.

'Doing ok, a few stitches but told it will be as good as new in a while,' bantered Bruce. 'Because of you I might have bled to death, if it was just Crystal and myself left on the rocks, so I'm totally indebted to you and would like to thank you in some way. Maybe take you out for a meal on Saturday…would that be possible?' Bruce looked faintly worried as he awaited her reply. Knowing she couldn't refuse such an offer without appearing insulting, she put him out of his misery.

'Yes, sure that's fine. My diary is not exactly as booked up as the President's! What time?'

'Can we say five thirty? I know it's early and hope you don't mind. I will send a limo for you.'

A Limo? Zara was a little impressed by this, though in LA there was always a bit of showmanship. Most of the people didn't know how to be non-descript.

'Ok, I'll be ready.' She was a little surprised at the early time, maybe Bruce was not keen on eating late or had to be in bed tucked up by ten or something. She still couldn't make him out; he just seemed very conformist and uptight. How did Bruce really chill out?

~ ~ ~

The limo arrived bang on time of five thirty. Zara stepped out into the soft California sunshine. It still felt pretty warm now. In England, the shadows would be lengthening and a slight nip in the air would be biting at you, but here nearly every conceivable hour there was warmth available. Secretly, Zara still favored good old Blighty and its diverse weather system. It was much more exciting in some ways. It always provided an element of surprise each day.

The smooth leather interior enveloped her completely as she sunk down into its cocoon. The driver nodded politely and cruised off down the side street onto the busy main highway. The tinted windows

314

shielded Zara from the heat and she could watch the world go by in secret. Now this was one of the perks of being loaded. Discreet but still being able to do a bit of voyeurism in private, Bella wouldn't need her shades this way. A whole new game could be had with a limo like this. Wait till she rang her back home.

The roads lessened and they headed out to a sparse, barren area on the outskirts of the city. Zara wondered what little restaurant Bruce had had in mind; maybe he was planning a picnic next to the canyon.

As the many ideas whirled around, she noticed they had pulled through a check point and were now gliding across a vast expanse of tarmac towards an old aircraft hangar.

Bruce was waiting patiently for her as the limo pulled up; he opened the door and held out his hand towards her. Zara remembered the etiquette her mum had tried continuously to educate her with, the words ringing in her mind. 'Always act with decorum, like a lady in every situation, including never ever show your knickers off in public.'

Some chance of achieving that at this moment, the seats were so deep and low, trying to swing elegantly round with the tight clingy dress she had on, was going to be a feat in itself. Not that Bruce would make it known. She was positive he would avert his gaze; past conquests wouldn't have done, mind you.

With a strong grasp and heave from Bruce, Zara managed the maneuver quite well. He smiled warmly as she stood up leaning forward. He pecked her on the cheek and declared,

'Zara, I hope I haven't gone too far but I would like

315

you to accompany me to San Francisco. I need to drop an important document off enroute and thought, why not combine business with pleasure. Hope you don't object? Flying ok with you?'

Zara stood a little stunned. No one had ever flown her privately to dinner before; she was a little taken aback.

'No, it's a wonderful gesture,' half spluttering in the process of replying.

'Great, some women would be a bit overawed and think I'm trying to show off, which is not me at all. The jet is a friend's, well a business partner in fact. It's not my own sadly, just in case you think I'm being pretentious.'

Bruce seemed highly embarrassed now and Zara could see visibly he was trying not to show it. Hastily she tried to reassure him.

'No, I would never think that of you.' Zara was one hundred percent positive of that. Bruce didn't have it in him to be a pompous self-absorbed git, but she knew a few who could be.

Zara assumed he might be carbon print friendly, liking to cover two jobs in one. He probably wouldn't have been so flamboyant if he hadn't had to go for business, but hey what the heck, she may as well enjoy it while it lasted.

The interior of the jet was plush, very plush. To Zara it looked pretty gorgeous, not that it was her frequent habit flying first class. Bruce showed her to her seat and helped buckle up. A flight attendant handed her a flute of champagne and a small bowl of peanuts.

'Just in case you get a little peckish, madam.'

316

'Thanks.' Zara wasn't sure how to react as a madam. She had a feeling the attendant could see straight through her, but it made her more comfortable knowing he was probably at her level anyway. Grinning insanely she noticed a slight flicker of a smile and wink was returned, discreetly of course.

Bruce leant over and held her hand as the engines thrust into action. Conversation between the two flowed easily and the journey flashed by in an instant. Bruce was in fact, a very charismatic and captivating host.

Zara began to warm more to his personality; the only times she had come into contact with him was via Crystal, and with her strong and overbearing character Bruce had been firmly in the shadows. Too polite to take centre stage, he let her take the limelight.

San Francisco was everything Zara had imagined. The rolling, gigantic hills made her catch her breath. The chauffeur who came to meet them gallantly gave a whirl wind tour of the major highlights before dropping Bruce off briefly for his business matter.

The man who greeted him at the office door looked rather shady but Zara decided not to make a snap judgment, half of the east end of London looked shady and Bruce seemed far too straight to be on the side of dodgy business dealings. Even so she felt relieved that the chauffeur was with them.

Bruce returned to the car and before long they were drawing up to the main harbour area. Stepping out, he led her to one of the bay front restaurants. It was an idyllic setting to dine. They shared fresh lobster. Zara had never had the opportunity to devour freshly caught fish of this caliber. Bruce, under candlelight, was starting to become less square and austere, more alluring by the second.

Zara wasn't sure if it was the luxurious surroundings or the clean, crisp southern California wine they had been supping for the past two hours. Feeling strongly attracted to him, she was a little surprised. Bruce was not the type of guy she would have noticed in a crowd. Money could definitely woo a girl.

To finish the evening, Bruce had organized a late cruise around the harbour. San Francisco looked fantastic from the waterside, the myriad of twinkling lights silhouetting the night sky was a memorable sight.

By the time they were both aboard the flight home, it was gone twelve. The effects of the alcohol was causing both to be very relaxed and as she leant her head against Bruce's shoulder the smell of his aftershave and skin merged, sending tingling through Zara's nervous system. Bruce looked down and placed his arm around her, whispering into her ear tenderly.

'Have you enjoyed yourself? Apologies for the late hour you're going to get back home by.' Zara placed a finger upon his lips to stop him in mid flow.

'It's been perfect. In fact it's been the best date ever.' Whoops, had she really said that? Bruce grinned.

'A date eh!' Zara glanced back as coolly as she could but the alcohol effects were too much; unable to maintain a look of indifference she smiled. Leaning forward to kiss him squarely on the lips, Bruce responded immediately, cupping her chin gently he explored her mouth delicately, his fingers gliding softly over her dress. He stopped after several minutes and rang a buzzer. With a nod and a command by hand the attendant exited from the cabin and her seat reclined slowly. Zara tried hard not to giggle; it seemed all too much like something out of some Bond novel.

'And what do you suppose you are going to do with me Mr. Loxley?' He looked at her wickedly.

'Wouldn't you like to know? I might be a gentleman but when the time comes, I can be as much fun as the next guy.' He leant forward to toy with her lips once more. Zara snuggled back beneath his frame and enjoyed the rest of the journey with a pleasant and long lasting smile on her face. This was one date that needed serious competing with.

Chapter 19

IN THE PURSUIT OF PERFECTION

As Zara approached the house, it reminded her of her childhood. The lane led towards a three storey house reminiscent of a classic Jane Austin style; creamy and mellow its gravel drive spread out from the worn stone steps leading to a dark green painted door. A large wooden gate leant gently against the hedge worn to a soft silvery hue.

For once Zara felt more at home from the fast track and glitz of America she had seen so far. The house was framed by a close knit hedge. The lawn stretched out in a gentle arc to the back of the house, far into the distance an arbor and small pond could be seen twinkling in the half sunlight. Tall bull rushes wafted in the breeze. She smiled to herself, 'Well, well, well he had kept things under wraps.' Bruce's manner and education had indicated he came from a fairly affluent background but she still hadn't been expecting this.

Bruce was polite and engaging in conversation. Courteous to a fault and although she was not dumbstruck by his presence, as she had been in the past with many a conquest, he had drawn Zara in by his comforting manner. Zara was now weary of the dynamic, sexy males that loved only themselves; what she needed was someone stabilizing and supporting. Bruce might be that one.

Her eyes darted around soaking up the sights in front of her, trying hard to assess what Bruce's parents would be like: their background, preferences and dislikes. Peering further afield she noticed a tiny stream trickled past the side of the house spanned by a small moat bridge. The other side was dotted by stables and outhouses. A gleaming sports car sat elegantly within one of the stables; there were definitely some British undertones here. Bruce's accent was hard to decipher as it was without some of the harsh American twang that many citizens had in this area. Bruce's was softer, in fact a gentle lilt could be heard when he spoke. It had become a game reaching far back into people's history, hunting out clues from their demeanor, voice; even their political attitude could say a lot about their upbringing and the circles they mixed in. It was one project she'd been meaning to do for her own family but had never got round to it.

As they approached the door, wafts of scented blossom stimulated Zara's nose making it tingle slightly, whomever was the gardener here knew their stuff. The front of the house was cushioned by foliage green and ripe; bursts of bright flowers erupted from the many climbers adorning the house like strands of multi coloured hair. Zara felt she had been transported back to an English summer's garden, a twinge of homesickness settled in her stomach. She hadn't thought about home for some time, now suddenly feeling it had been a long time since she'd touched base with her own family. Her work having taken her

321

everywhere was fantastic, but in the last year or so it had become somewhat draining. Zara did like her home comforts. The U.S.A was a fabulous place though sheer size and razzmatazz wherever she went was becoming pretty exhausting. Before she had time to think, Bruce's mother answered the door immediately.

Zara glanced shyly at her. Surprisingly young at first glance, but on closer inspection small lines etched her face; expertly disguised with a fine veil of make-up. She greeted them both with enthusiasm.

'Darling it's so nice to meet you; Bruce has been telling me so much. I've been keen for Bruce to let you come over for ages. I'm Vivian. I understand you're a very talented young lady. Most of my brood are sports oriented in some way or another. Though Olympic standard they are not, I'm afraid. Frederick is more into his cars; speed is all he seems to be keen to beat, as you may have noticed the metal specimen residing in the stables is his. Cost a fortune to ship over but Frederick is my baby and I didn't want to disappoint him, once he was of age to drive here,' she hesitated and looked at Bruce. Back-tracking slightly and laughing rather brusquely she added.

'But Bruce has so many fine attributes, being my eldest.'

Zara glanced at Bruce, but he seemed to be unaffected by his mother's open favouritism to his younger brother. Maybe he had become accustomed to it over the years, blocking it out.

The hallway they passed through was long and wide. A stairway led up to a wide landing area. Oak paneling lined the staircase. The walls were littered with photo frames of the family. A room led off to what probably might have been a study and the one opposite a drawing room in English circles.

Zara soaked up the atmosphere. Feeling that she could have been looking at a Homes and Country shoot, it was uncannily similar. What took her by surprise was the stag's head placed ceremonially above the door of the lounge they were heading towards. Zara knew hunting was done in some parts of America but here it wasn't the norm. 'Oh well,' she thought, 'They were definitely not vegetarian inclined if they had stuffed dead animals adorning their place of residence. Bella wouldn't be impressed being such an eco-friendly girl at heart. Some scathing remark would sure to be uttered from her pursed lips if she ever met them. Shuddering at the thought of how she would ever introduce the family if it got really serious. She pushed this situation to the back of her mind. Bruce's father stood up as they entered.

'Hello, so you're the young lady Bruce has been escorting around town. I can see why his head's been turned.' he winked at Zara sending a cursory look to his wife in case she'd noticed. Luckily there was no reaction or if she had noticed, she obviously was well used to it and was not in any circumstances being drawn into reacting on this occasion.

Zara had the impression Bruce's father was a bit of a cad, a flirt possibly and of the old school attitude. She wasn't sure if she liked this or not but it didn't mean Bruce had inherited the same traits. In fact he seemed the total opposite, quite stuffy. She wondered what Freddie was like. Probably he had quite a few of his father's genes, and maybe that was why Bruce's mother pandered so much to him, a reincarnation of her husband.

They sat chatting politely. Zara probing gently with her questions to try and build up a bigger picture of what Bruce was like. Having only known him a month, as with any new liaison a lot was always held back to create the perfect illusion to their date. From what Zara had managed to extract from her interviewing techniques (not very Parkinson-like though) was pretty limited. She would never make a journalist by trade.

Once polite conversation had been exhausted and before a lull in the meeting could develop, Vivian moved the proceedings to the lunch table. Zara was aware that Bruce's mother liked to do everything by the book, from the formal meeting to total perfection and etiquette at the table. Thinking into the future to a situation when they may meet her parents, what opinion would be assumed of her family? It was being a bit forward to even imagine anything like that.

A laid back approach was more of her mother's making and although she liked to keep up appearances with the neighbours, she was not the one to stand on ceremony all the time. Supper in front of the telly, slippers on and as for her father, pomp and fussiness was not his strong point, although Bruce's father would probably love to let his hair down once in a while. Zara had a sneaky suspicion that he did quite often, but not when the wife was around.

Lunch was just about to begin when a loud bang and crashing sound came from the direction of the kitchen. Bruce's mum Vivian raised her eyes to the ceiling and within seconds the dining room door flung open.

'Hi everyone, sorry for the late arrival, heard your latest was getting a grilling from mum so thought I better drop by for a look myself.'

'Frederick what time do you call this? Don't be so impersonal. We have company as you very well know.'

Zara looked slightly embarrassed as Frederick bounded around the table flinging his arms around her shoulders and giving her a huge kiss on the cheek.

'Hey Brucey, you've pulled a little corker here. No wonder you haven't brought her home earlier. I might have had to fight you for her. No contest darling. Bruce has never won in any contest between us.' He looked cheekily in Bruce's direction.

'Yes but that could be as you never play by the rules.'

'True, but I normally win the girl or the game; now who's the fool?'

Bruce scowled at him. Obviously past history between them was still annoying to Bruce. Zara found a protective arm slung over her shoulder. Frederick just grinned even more, noticing the effect he'd had with his comment.

'Don't worry I'm well and truly taken for at the moment. Seeing a raunchy little number from New York; met her at the race track last week. Nothing will distract me at the moment, you know what I mean?' winking at his father.

Zara was beginning to get the dynamics of Bruce's family quite clearly now. Poor Bruce was too plain obliging and Freddie the alpha son was led very much by his father. She could see Tyler in Freddie so vividly it was starting to bring back memories of her last fling with him, much too clearly for her comfort.

Lunch progressed along at quite a pace. Zara was again bombarded by questions from Freddie and had to remain on guard at all times. Freddie wasn't easy to pull the wool over his eyes. He'd seen and done most things by the many tales he was relaying. Embarrassment was not his weakness. Zara warmed to him slowly but noticed a certain coolness between Bruce and his sibling.

As the warm sunshine started to wane and the afternoon wore on, Bruce made strong gestures to Zara that they were going to make a discreet exit. Freddie hardly noticed as he plopped himself in front of the telly to flick between every channel that had some fast adrenaline sport relayed on it. Vivian had probably given up trying to control her younger son; she seemed unfazed by his manners and chose to ignore him completely once the meal had finished.

'Zara it's been a pleasure to meet you. I hope you haven't been put off by my family's funny little ways,' and she looked rather sharply at her husband as he made advances towards Zara to kiss her goodbye. Luckily for Zara, he was apprehended at the vital moment by Bruce who very professionally escorted her out of the door and harm's way.

Back in the car, Bruce turned to look at her. He seemed concerned that she might have been put off now she had met the family.

'Are you ok? I wasn't expecting Freddie to come barging in. Sorry to put you in the midst of it. They

326

mean well just a bit overbearing at times. I should have eased you in gently.' Bruce seemed to be rather embarrassed of his family and clearly doubted his judgment on bringing her home. Zara held his hand and squeezed it gently.

'They were fine, no different from any other family. We all have irritating brothers or sisters that we are reluctant to release onto society. I'm sure I'll get used to them.'

Zara put on her most reassuring face. Secretly she was still a little traumatized by the grilling she had had to endure. At least she had a little more to work on about Bruce and his home life. Yep, he was not the go-getter but a more calm, deep and dependable type of guy. It wasn't anything Zara had come across before; even Brett had a wild card up his sleeve. It was going to take some getting used to.

Playing the lost maiden might be fun. She needed to give Bruce some time to open up. Maybe there was a hidden side to him that just needed some tweaking to reveal. Either way, it was nice to be wanted and desired. Bruce slid the car into gear and smiling nervously at Zara he glided the vehicle slowly across the gravel and away from the mad house he called home.

Chapter 20

COMPROMISING POSITIONS

'Damn, my back's jammed. What the hell am I going to do now? I knew that yoga position was way too advanced for me, contortions are not my best party attribute.' Zara winced and staggered over to the stool in the kitchen. Clutching it tightly she grimaced, heaving herself up by the kitchen top one hand leaning heavily on the stool to gain some support. Crystal grabbed the phone sharply.

'No worries, I'll ring the clinic where you're working. At least you'll know you're in good hands.' The dial tone rang out for what seemed ages to Zara.

'Hi,' Crystal chirped, 'Zara, one of your work colleagues, has kind of injured her back in what was a rather advanced yoga position. Any chance I can bring her in for a quick once over, see what she's done?' The muted babbling from the other end of the phone was somewhat stressed and Crystal's face fell. Zara knew that it wasn't going to be today. What a hell of a predicament. The thought of getting down the stairs and into a cab was going to be a feat in itself. Crystal rang off.

'Well, not a lot of joy there. They seem really manic but I think I've got the solution. Have you ever tried

Oriental medicine? We're very multi-national here in LA, all styles embraced. Noah from the yoga studio will have the number. He sees a really great guy in the suburbs. He knows the body inside out and will put a smile back on your face. I'm certain of that.'

Zara thought over this option and was a little hesitant. What Crystal meant by a smile was a little perturbing. After seeing most Eastern movies it normally involved endurance and a little bit of pain, sharp javelins and smelling herbage, frequently drank luke warm, and reminiscent of an old laundry. Just give her a Tens machine any day.

Before Zara could protest, Crystal had done her networking LA style with much kissing and promising of favours, placing the phone down she turned and grinned.

'Right then baby, let's get you to him.'

The slow arduous trek down from the apartment began. Each and every step or knock Zara felt it jar though her body. Boy, now she knew what some of her clients must have felt like when they staggered in for a session.

'Crystal, you will drive gently? I don't feel I could cope with your usual style of speed and stab braking.' Zara clutched the door frame to gingerly lower herself as best she could into the front seat. Being an American car it was pretty big and spacious, so lying out at any angle was possible.

'Sure I will. I always do. Just you English aren't acquainted with proper driving skills. I can see why though. With your teeny country lanes and no overtaking rules every ten yards, it must be a bit of a

329

pain in the arse. Two lane roads must be a joy to behold?'

'They can be but at this present moment, I have my own pain in the arse and not keen to make it worse than it already is.'

As they approached the venue, Zara noticed it was very unusual: set in a large warehouse. On entering reception, the girls were met with a welcoming and serene backdrop, a soft pulsing fountain trickled over roughly hued rocks in the centre of the room. 'Here we go,' thought Zara, 'Designed to send you into a false sense of tranquility.'

A very buoyant and charming receptionist rushed over to help. Zara was thankful but the extreme over-niceness from their host was making her feel a little uncomfortable. She wondered how much this was going to cost. Niceness usually came at a price. Before there was any time to make a bolt, (which was unlikely in her condition, but the urge was starting to take place), her appointment time arrived and she was ushered (cajoled?) into the vacant treatment room.

'Hello, my name's Sam. I can see you're in some distress. Can I enquire what you may have done to get into this position?'

'I was trying to retrieve something from under my couch and must have strained it in my yoga class; I'm not very experienced at it yet. I think it was a little too advanced for my less than supple body.'

Sam's eyebrows raised a little and his next question was, 'Can you reveal the yoga position to me. A description of where your limbs were will be ample.'

'Err! Where shall I start?' Zara was a little unsure

she could even remember the position. All she could recall was it involved a contortion of twisting at the waist. Assuming her waist had no spare tyre, but in this position she was fully aware that a slight bulge was hindering her action. Zara felt herself colouring up as she attempted to explain the mechanics of the movement. Sam's face crinkled up with laughter.

'Yes, I've seen many a woman complain of that. I think I can see the move in my mind. Have you ever had any Oriental style treatment before?'

'No I haven't, only a little acupressure.' Zara looked warily at him awaiting the delights he would come up with for treatment.

'Ok, we're going to introduce you to a myriad of ancient styles. Let's get to the lower back first.' He positioned Zara over a comfy padded plinth supporting herself on her hands and knees. Sinking down into position relieved some of the pressure on her back, helping Zara to relax. After much prodding and pressing, Sam explained the rest of the proposed treatment.

'I'm going to apply moxa heat to some key points at the base of your coccyx.'

'Right,' thought Zara, simple enough, until she noticed what was being prepared. A cigar shaped stick was being lit over a lighted candle. As it warmed up it started to glow violently in front of her eyes.

'Now please let me know when it's too hot and I'll move on. This is very important.'

'Yes, whatever you say.' Zara wasn't going to argue with a guy holding a lighted cigar close to her nether regions. The warmth was actually very soothing to

331

begin with until it penetrated deeper down. Then intense itching commenced after one second too long and Zara was ready to yelp. In certain places Sam rummaged around finding the correct point, delving deeper than she wanted him to. Is there really a point in the anus? She was slightly skeptical but unfortunately running out wasn't an option at this precise moment. Having a heated josh stick practically rammed up her behind, was something she might have to consider therapy for.

It was a novel treatment but weird beyond words. Just wait till she saw Crystal. Some choice words were coming to mind if she ever made it off the padded plinth, without her lower anatomy catching fire. She was just glad she never used hair spray down there. The consequences didn't bear contemplating.

Zara now felt somewhat intimately acquainted with Sam. It was one treatment she was pretty certain she wouldn't be able to perform on any of her British counterparts. Swear words may well have been uttered from the rugby lads if she'd flourished one of the sticks at any of them in a session.

Once treatment had commenced, Zara's spasms started to subside slightly and she managed to roll with a little hesitancy over and onto her back for further treatment, still unsure how she'd get upright again. Being at floor level, the comfortable option to just roll off the couch into a standing position wasn't an option let alone the bent double stance which she'd come to favour.

'Your muscle tone is a little weak in places. It's causing your back to over strain and it's not being well supported from the front. You need to avoid too much stretching and strengthen more of these key areas. Then, a situation like this won't happen again.' Sam prodded Zara's exposed belly and bottom. Alarmed that this was his polite way of saying she had the body of a sack of potatoes, she wanted a little further clarification.

'No, no, no you react like every female. You're not unfit, just using the wrong muscles. More internal ones are needed to support you, less of the laid back yoga and more fighting power and strength.'

Zara stretched out and relaxed a little. More sex possibly was required, intermingled with a little body busting combat. Maybe not at the same time; some might like it but she wasn't that type. Before Zara could protest, Sam started pouring a strong smelling and rather warm liquid onto her belly. It smelt incredibly unusual and intoxicating. He started to prod and move her somewhat loose stomach around like putty beneath his fingertips. She wasn't feeling so enlightened now.

'Your hara is very weak indeed; we will treat your Ren channel next time.'

Next time! Zara hadn't thought about revisiting his chamber of tricks again, but she had a feeling she might have to if she didn't sort out her weak hara. Sam methodically pressed and manipulated her stomach which felt quite uncomfortable under his firm touch. In places there was a barrier to his fingertips, probably something she ate last night. A huge plate of nachos hadn't been a good idea really. Still other areas, Sam's fingertips delved deeper. At one point Zara thought he must have been hitting her back bone; her muscle tissue seemed nonexistent.

Zara began to feel a little invaded as he probed closer to her pubic bone. This was an area she never went to with clients. There was a fine line between the base of the tummy and falling into taboo regions, male or female. Sam didn't seem to worry about this. Any lower and she would be having an orgasm. Involuntarily she tensed a little. Sam picked up on this and smiled.

'I think that is enough for now; remember what I have said and see me next week. We need to look further to prevent the back going again.'

Yes but how much further was Sam going to look? That was the issue contemplated Zara, but the relief of being able to move again was a pleasure in itself. Sam paused and looked intently at Zara.

'We haven't looked at what is the deeper cause for your weakness; be aware you do not need to go chasing your desires as they will run wilder and faster from you. Sit back, enjoy the view and wait. They will return when the time is right.' Leaving the profound proverb hanging in the air, Sam showed her the exit. It left Zara feeling a little perplexed that Sam seemed to know more about her than she would like to admit.

Returning somewhat slowly and carefully to her apartment, lest she upset Sam's work, Zara listened to Crystal bleating loudly in her ear of the alternative classes she could attend at the swanky local gym. It seemed to Zara as almost a religion, the dedication Crystal had for this style of therapy. After more slow and steady movements, they finally managed to get into her apartment safely.

Zara found LA life a tad weird. How Crystal found

time to make a living inbetween the many sessions of personal enjoyment was puzzling. From feet to personal training, hair, nails and not to mention her dermatologist and gynecologist, she swore blind something was going on. Who in their right mind needs such a regular appointment to see their gyne? It must be some American trend or something.

Crystal was ringing Bruce to come over for her as soon as they stepped back in the apartment. No chance for Zara to protest here. Crystal was on one of her missions.

'Sweetie, I've got Zara here and she needs you to pop over urgently. I dare not leave her on her own; she's hurt her back. I've sorted her out as best I can but over-exerting it won't help.'

Zara looked perplexed. She really didn't want to appear needy. Although their relationship had been some six months now, and yes it was going great guns, she was hesitant to commit too quickly. Old habits die hard. At this moment in time she wanted to appear Miss Independent rather than Miss LA who frequently desired most men to dote and fawn over them twenty four/seven. It didn't seem that attractive.

Within the hour, Bruce arrived. Zara was impressed at his speedy attention, trying to be the ever-gallant gentleman. Amber would be well happy with this response. Ringing regularly for full updates with the threat to come over and assess directly, Zara liked to take heed of Amber's advice, trusting her implicitly. Gina or Bella's love advice was possibly not such a good idea. Their track record of life in the love lane was way too traumatic and wild for good sense and decorum.It blew her mind what gems of advice they would have to say.

~ ~ ~

Over the next couple of months, Bruce was a perfect companion. Work had been sorted; cleaning of her apartment was arranged and trips out to the beach to relax and recuperate completed his agenda. For a while, Zara enjoyed the pampered lifestyle. Though all too soon she was champing at the bit to return to some order and self reliance in her daily routine. Bruce, on the other hand, was rather keen to delay her going back to work for a lot longer but she dug her heels in.

'Bruce, I can't live like this forever, I've got bills to pay. The job won't be covered indefinitely. Anyway, I like to be able to be in control. It's been lovely what you've done but now, I need to return to normal.' Glancing at the response of her outburst she waited for him to fight back. Reluctantly he just sighed and held her closer.

'That's what I love about you - that feisty blood that runs through your veins; it's such a turn on. Remember, I'm always here for you.'

Zara was a little taken aback by his personal endurance. Any past conquests would have reacted somewhat differently.

Once the back had improved enough, life returned to normal and the start of Crystal's new fitness regime was on the agenda. Zara found she was on the way to the studio rather quicker than she had envisaged, once Crystal saw she was nearly back to her old self. What she'd be letting herself in for was anyone's guess. After the therapy incident, she was a little hesitant to endure any more of Crystal's well-meaning fads of the local area.

Inside, the gym was rammed with lithe-like beauties glowing with fake and real sun kissed tans, blatantly preening in front of any available mirrored surface. There wasn't an ounce of body fat beneath their flesh, all long limbed and stunning. Most of the women wore their skin tight dance wear like a second skin, leaving little to the imagination.

Zara noticed that some wore bandanas and were wrapping their wrists tight with a type of black tape. This sight made Zara's stomach tighten at what the class might entail. Before she had time to become anxious, the buoyant and ever-exuberant Crystal appeared at the top of the staircase. Clocking her, she leaped across the gym to greet her.

'Hi, you made it, fab! Just wait, you'll die for this class. When you clock the instructor, no other class will suffice. He's half the reason why it's mainly women who attend. A pure delight to watch in action, I clean forget about the time and effort to work out.' she struggled out of her clothes to reveal just as skimpy an outfit as the rest of them.

Zara frowned looking down at her rather old fashioned training gear. Maybe she should have taken Bruce's advice and gone and treated herself whilst off work, but it seemed an indulgence when it was only going to get sweaty and dirty. What was the point? Clearly, now the point was pretty important. If you wanted to pull in LA, indoor gear was as important as outdoor gear.

Following the girls into the gym, she bit her lip. She could see the point smack in front of her. Warming up was an Adonis no words could adequately describe, crass thoughts of having gone to heaven was never a truer phrase. It made Abman seem way out of condition. Dressed head to toe in black, the tight combat shirt graced his body perfectly. A black and red bandana kept his blond tresses back to reveal the most piercing blue eyes. Zara became mesmerized immediately, feeling totally ditzy.

Aware that he was approaching her, the heart started thumping loudly. She attempted to take a large gulp of breath to steady her nerve, an irritating weakness of hers. Zara was used to being in awe of some guys like Tyler but no way could she make a fool of herself in front of the elite of LA.

'You must be new. Ever done some combat training before?' He grinned and waited for her to reply. Zara found her mouth run dry and unable to speak clearly she squeaked.

'No.'

'Well, don't worry I'll demonstrate any tricky moves; you'll catch up quickly.'

Crystal winked at Zara, 'Told you so.' All Zara could manage was a weak smile as she found her eyes drawn back across the room in the direction of the retreating figure. The class flashed by as Crystal predicted. Focusing hard to watch his every move she ended up nearly smacking herself in the face, not concentrating where she was punching. A trip to the dentist would be in order if she wasn't careful. Blood trickling down her chin with a gaping hole wasn't going to look too fetching.

Zara cringed at the thought of being in a real fight with the guy. He packed a powerful punch, but soothing his wounds would be attractive. The adrenaline rush started to kick in and by the end of class, Zara was kicking and punching with the best of them. Surviving the hour session, they were hot and sweaty by the end and both girls trailed out of the room physically exhausted.

'How was it?' quizzed Crystal.

'Not bad, at least I survived the pace. I can see why he has a big following.'

'Yeah you should see him in circuits. Boy does he make you work, if you want a butt made of steel, he's your man.'

'I'm sure he is,' Zara sighed wistfully. He'd eat Bruce for breakfast.

~ ~ ~

Dozing after her expenditure of energy with Crystal, the phone rang shrilly just after eleven. Picking up the receiver, quite expecting it to be Bruce saying goodnight, the dulcet tones of Amber rang through the phoneline.

'Amber, it's great to hear from you. How's your little one doing? Fine I hope. It's crazy out here, I'm missing you loads. Any chance you can come over for a visit? You've been threatening for ages and now I really miss not hanging out.'

'That's why I'm ringing. Chloe is now walking and

339

I'm near enough more confident with everything, so yes I'm going to be over next month. You've got to let me meet Bruce for a vetting session, otherwise I refuse to come,' quipped Amber. From her tone of voice, Zara knew she wouldn't be able to wiggle out of this.

'Yes, no way would I not let you meet him. He's been great, especially since I hurt my back recently.'

'How the hell did you do that?'

'Don't ask, yoga of all things. The only bonus is I've lost two inches in a few classes but any more and I'll be a walking chopstick, barr a little excess in places I didn't know existed.'

'You lucky thing, you've always been good at being supple.'

'So I thought, but over here we Brits can't compete with the yoga vixens of LA. I swear they have elastic bands as muscles. What they could get up to in the bedroom department is nobody's business.'

Amber laughed, 'I'm sure you can give them a run for their money.'

'I've been having a darn good go but Crystal's introduced me to another way of maintaining my ever decreasing fitness level: Thai fusion! Not to mention the treatment she made me participate in for the dodgy back I ended up with.' Filling Amber in with every detail, it wasn't long before she could hardly keep the phone to her ear as they both fell about in manic hysterics.

'You're telling me you paid someone to barbeque your bottom with a hot rod? What next, a josh stick to heat up your front nether regions? I ask you, no sane person would go for that.'

'Who said I was sane. No, honestly Crystal is great, it's just their style out here is a little unusual shall we say. The norm is boring to them. Thai fusion is the next big craze here. The instructor was to die for though, a California dreamboat. I couldn't work out why the women at the club were so gorgeous, done up big time with full make-up, the works. I don't even look that glam when I go out for a posh evening out. Now having been introduced to the delights of Kyle, I can appreciate why they make the effort. It made up for the back treatment I can tell you.'

'Who else have you been missing? I hope you haven't been affected by your wild clinch with Tyler again, he's not worth it. You better remember that. I wish I'd never got you chatting. I should have paid heed to the signs he was exuding from every orifice of his body.'

'Urgg, you make him sound gross.'

'What I meant was he displayed arrogance, mixed with a splash of vanity that he discharged left right and centre. It was pretty clear all he did was love himself.'

'I've learnt my lesson, bitten twice, never again, he's off the radar completely I promise you. Bruce and I are getting along fine. He's a nice breath of fresh air from what I've attracted before. Brett, as usual, is up a mountain somewhere blue yonder. Training kids or something, his path is not crossing mine any time in the near future. It's always off the beaten track. Plays havoc with my high heels I can tell you. It's been months since he last contacted me.'

'So what's that telling you, your path is aiming for Sunset Boulevard, not a mountain goat path?'

Zara was reduced to a heap on the floor. Coming up for air before she could continue the conversation, Amber always knew how to put things into perspective.

'I know, I know but he just felt so right. Bruce is lovely but he's not got that passion for life. I still think about Brett loads, though my last soiree in New Zealand seems a distant memory now; LA does distract you. There's so much going on. It never rests for one moment, a constant adrenalin rush. I've kind of given up on him some time back, which is why I'm keen to move on from everything. It's hard though.'

'Listen, do you really want your passion to be always out under canvas? You weren't born to be some wanderer. Good solid foundation is what you need.'

'Ok, ok my focus is purely on Bruce, steady and dependable. I know for sure there is no way he could light a fire, barbequing is a major catastrophe for him to achieve. He nearly set light to his mother's pagoda last time I visited.'

'Sounds a bit like Jamie, probably related in some distant past.' Zara shuddered at the thought.

'You are awful; I bloody well hope not, otherwise I'll be hiring the next Sherpa up the mountain. Now, I'll start making some plans and gemming up on the best places to take you.'

'Great, night life may have to be avoided as Chloe is now in tow. Sleep is what I dream about once the sun goes down.'

'Ok, maybe we can get you tied up with some movie mogul while you're here, nannies on tap everywhere.'

'My time for attracting the rich and famous has long gone. I'm finding motherhood quite enough of a challenge with Chloe now. Recruiting the energy to pamper another human, I think I'll pass. No, I'm content enough right now. Maybe in a few years I'll feel different.'

'I understand; I know Dean would want you to be happy. Just get your glad rags on and we'll have a whale of a time. I can't wait.'

After a prolonged goodbye, Zara sank back into the pillows. This was going to be fun. Having Amber over for a break would be just the tonic she needed. They could at least appreciate the same sense of whacky British humour; Crystal tried but failed on many occasions to see what Zara was finding funny. Some serious planning was on the agenda.

Chapter 21

AMBER NECTAR

The glam Malibu beachfront beckoned the three girls, as they raced as fast as they could go towards the waves. Clutching her mummy's hand the little girl jumped in the foaming water with delight.

Amber's athletic and gorgeously brown body received a fair amount of eye attention as she played in the shallows. A shout rang out and the girls looked round as Bruce headed towards them. In tow the tall build of Frederick was also heading their way. Zara let out a loud groan.

'Oh, not Frederick, I thought I could protect you from Bruce's brother but I've got no hope in hell now. Be warned, he's worse than any alley cat in heat so if you need to cover up do so, he has a bad habit of making you feel on display under his lecherous gaze.'

As the boys approached, Frederick's eyes nearly popped out of their sockets. Ignoring Zara completely, he took her hand and kissing it graciously stared fixated and lost for words.

'You ok, Freddie? You're not normally dumbstruck. Where's the one liner or the demeaning jokes?' Zara teased. He appeared to not hear and mumbled something in Amber's ear. Even Zara was a little taken aback by his reaction.

'I think with you Amber, he's met his match. You might just have tamed Freddie with one glance. I have total respect for you,' Bruce grinned at her, kneeling down to greet Chloe.

'Charming indeed, take no notice of my rather old fashioned brother and clearly tainted friend of yours, who may I add listens to far too much gossip. I'm a total gentleman at heart. Now let me show you the sights myself later; I'm sure Zara is dying to spend some time with your little one.' Freddie glanced sideways at Zara with a very wary look, waiting for her to shoot him down in flames but Zara was grinning at his audacity.

'Yes, I suppose I don't mind. But I'm warning you, no monkey business. I've invited Amber over for an enjoyable break, not to be seduced and used once or twice then passed to the wayside. She's far too intelligent for you to dabble with.' Zara shot a deadlier look at Freddie who gulped deeply, a look of mock fear crossing his face. Zara was the only woman who he showed any respect for and allowed her the upper hand. In fact, he felt somewhat sorry for his big bruv who was a pushover at the best of times.

'Ok, ok, I get your drift. I promise to respect your friend as I respect you. Please don't punish me like you normally do.' Zara's eyes rose in defiance as Freddie mocked her.

'Umm, just make sure you do!'

The afternoon flashed by as the boys joined them cavorting in the shallows. By late afternoon, they headed back to Zara's apartment to refresh for the evening. Chloe lay sleeping on the couch, the sea air having worn her out completely.

'Look Amber, if you want me to have Chloe you can go and have a nice meal out with Freddie. I don't mind, Bruce and I can stay in. No point in you missing out, as long as you want to that is?'

Zara was still a little unsure of letting Freddie alone with her best friend. Never totally trusting him, he was more than likely to take her racing along the coast road in his babe magnet sports car, and then try to seduce her at some romantic cliff top setting. But Amber was a big girl, she could look after herself if she needed to.

Freddie was a still a problem for her having far too many similar trademarks to Tyler. After her Olympic escapades, she shied away from anyone that came remotely close to this type of personality, but Bruce's brother was one guy she had no choice but to tolerate.

'That would be lovely. The sea air has made me feel great. I certainly don't want to bed down for the evening yet, so if you're still open to showing me the sights that would be perfect.'

Freddie's eyes glinted with mischief, 'No worries, I can show you the sights alright, but they may not be on the tourist list.'

'FREDDIE! Remember what I said earlier.' Zara nearly spat the words out, trying hard to make her seem more in control.

'Relax babe, I'll show Amber nothing you haven't seen before.' He waggled his eyebrow at her and winked. Zara had seen quite a lot of Freddie in the past, which was what she was certain he was referring to. In fact she had seen most of him at some point. He wasn't shy on many occasions, parading around at his parents with not more than the barest of threads. Yep, she had seen probably more of Freddie than of Bruce, her own boyfriend.

The door clicked shut and the echoing sound of their footsteps receded gently. The apartment seemed eerily quiet suddenly except for the soft breathing from Chloe as she slept. Her chest was rising and falling so evenly and peacefully, she looked like a tiny cherub.

'Don't you go worrying about Amber; Freddie will behave, and he won't take advantage. I know you're not sure about him yet, but rest assured he wouldn't dare. He knows I'd get mother to sort him out.' Zara knew that wouldn't necessarily be that daunting to Freddie. His mother tended to be somewhat soft with her youngest, but she wasn't going to upset Bruce by saying so.

For the rest of the evening Zara prowled around feeling extremely uneasy. Finally deciding the best option was to go for a run along the beach, she departed company rapidly. Bruce gallantly offered to watch Chloe for a while so she could let off steam, more so to stop her constant wandering up and down the apartment. It was driving him crazy and he couldn't wait for her to grab her running shoes and be off.

The cool evening breeze skipped delicately over Zara's scantily clad body. She loved running when she could, but only when the busy streets had subsided and the last holiday makers had retreated from the many miles of soft sand.

The loose, shifting floor of the beach helped strengthen her legs, easing the tension that would build up standing all day pummeling other people's flesh. The freedom of being by the ocean was really exhilarating. Zara had to admit LA did offer a fantastic quality of life.

With the breeze getting stronger, she headed back along the promenade, not wanting to totally abandon Bruce for the whole evening. The black silhouettes of the last surfers stood starkly against the rosy sunset forming across the ocean line. They seemed to have a similar mentality to her, wanting to squeeze and savour every last drop of air before nightfall and darkness dissolved the horizon.

As she climbed the steps two at a time to her apartment, she hesitated in her tracks at the door. Bruce was on the phone. Opening the door softly she entered and became aware that Bruce was very pleased with himself from the obvious backslapping he and the unknown caller were giving each other.

Trying to be discreet, she gingerly ventured across to Chloe to check on her but brushed against the cabinet. Zara's attempt to be quiet sadly failed, as down came crashing the delicate vase her mother had sent. Lunging forward she managed with sheer luck to catch the offending item before serious damage could occur. The commotion alerted Bruce to her presence.

'Won't be a minute darling, don't wake Chloe. I've got some great news to tell.'

Zara held on as Bruce made a polite exit from his caller. Beaming from ear to ear and leaping forward to swing her around which nearly took her breath away he declared, 'Babe! We're expanding. New York will be our second home. The business is going from strength to strength; we should be well established by then. Remember the guy Stephen I mentioned, well he's done the deal and we've got the premises sorted. His connections have paid off. I don't know how he's managed it, but I'm damn well delighted.'

Zara extracted herself from his firm grip of passion and excitement. She was a little taken aback by his buoyant attitude, 'Err! Sounds good, is this what you've been fretting about in the last month but wouldn't tell me what the problem was?'

'Yes, sorry darling. It wasn't worth me building up your hopes as well, just in case it didn't come off.'

Zara wasn't sure why she would be upset any way these were Bruce's ambitions, not hers. It was gracious of Bruce to consider her a part of everything though. She just hoped he knew what he was doing.

'Tomorrow you need to pop out and treat yourself with Amber to something nice to wear. Stephen wants us to meet for cocktails this weekend; seven sharpish, so don't be doing overtime at the clinic. The world is our oyster now.'

Zara cringed, detesting being seen as the lesser half of the relationship. Knowing it was simply how Bruce had been brought up, it was never meant to indicate this at all. For Zara, it was everything but respectful in her mind's eye.

It was way past midnight when Zara heard the key in the stiff door lock. A hesitant fumbling and scratching ensued until the key turned and muffled giggling broke the silence. Amber stumbled through the doorway clutching Freddie's arm.

'Shh! Zara will have my guts for garters if she sees

349

you like this.'

'I'm sure your guts would look very fetching as garters,' slurred Amber giggling by now and hanging on for dear life to the nearest table.

'Probably, but I don't fancy how she might extract them, if you know what I mean.' Freddie grinned lunging forward to support Amber who now was swaying a little too violently. 'Here, let me get you into bed.'

'Enough of that you've only just met me, I have a two night date policy before you can even touch base on the lips.'

'Only two…when do you go back to England? Might be able to slip another couple in; what do I get for the third date?' Freddie looked extremely interested at this prospect. He was leaning in close in the hope she might succumb, but Amber was no fool even though a little drunk. Waggling her fingers at him she extracted herself elegantly from his grip.

'Oh, you won't find that out. We won't make the third date for a while yet.' Amber fluttered her lashes at him, politely backing towards her bedroom, 'Thank you for a fabulous evening but now I must retire, before my body decides to collapse and that won't leave a very pleasant lasting impression for you, will it?'

'Depends if I get to bring you round,' Freddie was trying to the bitter end to seduce but knew he was in a losing battle. 'As long as you're ok, I'll take my leave reluctantly.' He stood beguiled by the figure of Amber as she silently slid behind the door.

Saturday evening Zara, consciously made a special effort to look gorgeous. Bruce obviously was indebted to this guy, so she'd better make a good impression for his sake, even if it did go against her principles.

'Amber, is it ok if I leave you tonight for this meal with Bruce? It's really important for him and I feel I should support him.' She looked anxiously at her friend. Zara felt loathe to leave her knowing it would be a while before they saw each other again, especially once Amber returned to England, but she felt she didn't have much choice.

'Of course it is. We'll be fine; sure a little early cable television will whet my appetite for the delights of the LA lifestyle, it might even tempt me to consider coming over more.' She smiled settling down on the cream leather couch, snuggled up to Chloe with the TV remote in one hand and a large glass of California white in the other.

'What more does a woman want?'

'Well if it's any consolation, I would rather be spending it in front of the box myself than making small talk with strangers but never mind, duty calls.' Zara wandered over to the fridge and opening it wide rummaged in the back. Grabbing a small silvery bar of chocolate she chucked it across to Amber. 'Enjoy!'

~ ~ ~

The car drew up alongside the Hacienda Resort Hotel. Stepping out they were met by the valet, who indicated to the concierge to guide the couple to the main reception. As they entered a tall, suave looking gentleman greeted them immediately with open arms.

'Bruce, it's so charming to meet your wife and see

351

what is behind the man himself.'

Immediately, Zara disliked him. She couldn't put her finger on it but something was amiss. Stephen kissed her lightly on the hand. He smelt of cigar smoke, laced with the pungent top note of too much cologne. Feeling the tickling of a sneeze occurring, she turned discreetly, but unable to control her reaction, she sneezed violently. Smiling meekly, she apologized explaining it away as hay fever.

After some more back slapping, which ignited Zara's contempt for the man even more, they all sat down with Stephen's current wife. By the conversation at the table, Stephen had led a colourful life before they married; she was one of several wives he had seduced over the years.

Zara could clearly see his charm appeal on the surface, that sadly was somewhat spoilt by the condescending remarks in the next breath that he so subtly entered into the conversation.

'Bruce, it's fantastic news that we can now go forward to greater heights, especially for you now you're supporting one of the female race in your quintessential homestead,' finishing his comment with a nudge and wink at Zara.

Yuck, thought Zara. Indignant at his referral to living off Bruce, a retort was required. Replying acidly, as she was keen to take a stance on this straight away she replied, 'I do actually work for a living; Bruce doesn't have to support me as such. Besides, we aren't married.'

'Yes, Bruce did tell me, but every woman needs a job to keep her out of mischief. Leaves us men to do the real work, that's what I say.' Stephen placed his arm around the new suffering wife's shoulders. Zara could clearly see she was mesmerized by him. Sad was not the word thought Zara. The poor woman; how could she not see through the guy?

The evening dragged somewhat as Zara tried hard to smile and fake conversation. Finding it harder and harder to find anything endearing about him, his initial charisma was rapidly disappearing in her eyes. As Bruce's business was unclear to her, she didn't really have a say in how he decided to expand or with whom. Now she needed to show at least some support. Her intuition indicated that something wasn't right about Stephen. It would show itself clearly eventually, she was sure. For the moment, she would just have to tolerate him as best she could.

By late evening, Zara excused herself to freshen up and have a minute's reprieve from the entertainment. Bruce was pulled aside instantly by Stephen.

'Lovely girl; why haven't you made an honest woman of her? You're way behind in the marriage stakes compared with me. Need to catch up. Some nice little tax dodging can be done when you're married. I can fill you in when we meet again. We might need to utilize it, so have a think about it.' Downing another brandy he leant back eyeing up the waitress that slinked past.

'Another one of these darling, make it a large one.' Zara returned just as Stephen very nearly slapped the waitress' rear in jest.

Chapter 22

REVENGE IS THE SWEETEST TASTE

Zara arrived at the clinic having left Amber to amuse herself LA- style, with no doubt Frederick lurking in the background. Their impromptu date had gone well, too well for Zara's liking. Frederick was hell bent on wooing Amber into his boudoir or lair, as far as Zara could describe it, having seen a fair few girls that came out of a morning, well practically lunch time. The girls looked mainly dishevelled, most certainly having put up a fight with his wandering hands.

There seemed to be a buzz in the clinic, some excited faces were busily tapping away on their laptops. Frankie the receptionist was applying more lippy than necessary for front of house greetings.

'What's up? You have a date or something?' enquired Zara surprised at all the fuss.

'No, I'd be so lucky. Haven't you heard the latest charity match at the Polo Club? They only have Tyler Montgomery playing alongside Royalty, your one and only Prince Harry. We have first-hand backstage passes. I am about to talk tactics with the trainers and organisers for the clinic's services. A girl has got to look her best of course.'

Zara's heart missed a beat; in fact it was verging on somersaulting completely. Her breath froze. A look of horror crossed her face. Frankie was oblivious, reapplying her blusher again even though it was only ten o'clock. Tyler had clearly been chosen to encourage more of the punters, who loved to be seen with a Celeb or two to attend the prestigious function, thought Zara now sucking fresh air through her teeth to allow at least a little oxygen to flood her shocked body.

Damn, it was only a few weeks ago she had declared Tyler was extinguished from her life. Then the hassle of Bruce's business partner last night and now this. Why did they all have to come together? She needed to know exactly what she would be letting herself in for.

'Are we assigned to this job or can we opt out?'

Frankie looked at her as if she had committed the ultimate sin and was losing her mind.

'Why would you not want to attend, Zara? Royalty will be there and the top players. Tyler is one gorgeous player. He is hot, real hot over here.' Frankie's eyes glazed over.

'Yeah, loves himself more like,' muttered Zara. How the hell was she going to avoid this job assignment? Having tried hard to banish the memory and move on from her past Olympic dalliance, the mere thought of embarrassment, indignity and anger of having to treat Tyler as his minion again was not going to happen. No way.

Meeting Amber for a brief lunch, she blurted out the bizarre situation that was scheduled for tomorrow. Amber leaned back sucking slowly on her Manhattan cocktail, embracing LA lifestyle very well indeed.

'It's a no brainer, you'll have to feign illness or pray you avoid having to be assigned Tyler, simple!'

'Easy for you to say, but my luck is normally in short supply. I don't on any terms want those feelings to surface again. My relationship with Bruce is going well. I feel safe for once, content in fact. I just don't want the past upsetting the status quo. I know seeing Tyler will unleash all manner of issues. I just can't go there.'

Amber glanced over her dark shades, with an air of total mischief and a glint in her eye, 'We could always swap places, one English physio looks like another, with my hair up in a ponytail and some glasses. Who's going to notice?'

Zara sat stunned. 'You want to be me?'

'Why not, I can give a quick rubdown quite easily? If it's serious the paramedics will treat them. I won't get a look in. You can look after Chloe. Make sure you are on the end of your mobile, in case I need some extra info; haven't had fun like this in a long time. Besides, I got you in this mess years ago in the first place. It will be fun to enact a little revenge on Mr Tyler.'

Zara mulled over this preposterous plan. Not having any solution to hand, reluctantly she agreed hoping not to regret the mad decision.

'Ok, but I hope I don't rue the day I let you. On another note I want a little feedback on how you found Bruce. Particularly when you have the dynamic Tyler to compare with, bit of a no brainer really.'

'Have to admit he is quite different to what I expected but that doesn't mean to say he isn't right. I do think a bit of stability and the lifestyle out here is doing

356

you the world of good. You're more confident and seem more settled than when you were back home. Bruce does seem to be grounding for you.' Amber twirled her straw around the glass, sucking the last droplet of cocktail from the bottom.

'You enjoyed that did you? I think you're embracing LA lifestyle more than I am. I feel a right bore in comparison.'

'I've got to enjoy the freedom while I can. The help you and Bruce have given me with the little one, like today allowing Crystal to have her for a while, is really appreciated.'

'Umm! Not sure completely how that will go. Crystal may be introducing her to Brazilian waxes, false nails and god knows what.' Amber raised her eyebrows a little alarmed.

'As long as she doesn't attempt to test them out on my daughter, I'm sure she will survive.'

'You don't know Crystal; no I'm exaggerating, she'll be fine.' Zara turned to beckon the waiter for another stiff drink. She was feeling in need of one with Tyler on the scene. She needed to brace herself for this little venture.

~ ~ ~

The polo grounds were cranked up to the highest security. Amber coolly pinned Zara's identity badge to her white shirt and sashayed into the main arena, heading straight towards the physiotherapists and remedial staff.

As in true California style the treatment area was outside under canvas, very bespoke indeed. No backstage, stuffy and vile smelling rooms were used over here. Her shades were perfect for avoiding recognition, and having tinted her hair back in England a soft hue of auburn it was now smoothed back into a neat chignon. Even she had to admit, she looked a dead ringer for Zara. Nobody would suspect a thing. Amber was relishing every second.

Scanning the fields that lay out immaculately before her, the first players were arriving for lunch, with some of the high society of the banking and super glam circuit of this sunny county. Oprah, Beckham and, oh my god, there was Cruise and more! It was like walking the red carpet. The place was brimming with celebs, eager to see the likes of Harry.

Once the usual fawning had finished after lunch, play began in earnest. Every two players were assigned a therapist. Prince Harry of course, had his own vetted staff, which was a great shame. Amber was keen to have been able to touch the royal thigh. But that was probably a wish too far.

Before long, the allocation process began. Amber was discreet but had managed to work out how the number system was to work, by holding back whilst lunch was served. Gliding over to the main reception desk, Amber glanced at the various numbers set out on the table, as Frankie fussed and flirted with the chief organiser close by.

Slowly and diligently she transferred Zara's name to number 3: Tyler's official player number, having originally been allocated number 6, a Portuguese player. Not as well known, but he would probably have been treated in close proximity being on the same team.

As the first chukka ended, the players came off to swap horses. It was a quick turnaround just allowing enough time for the treading in of the divots. A longer break was scheduled for a gap between the semi-finals and finals, chosen to allow more ludicrously expensive champagne to wet the lips of the already overspent pockets.

It was now that the players' one-to-one treatment was executed, if required. Of course Tyler was not one to miss out, particularly when a pretty female was instructed to work upon his prized torso.

As he approached, Amber smiled politely. With one deft hand she professionally guided him onto the treatment couch, immediately setting to work not in a calm gentle manner, but more with military precision. Watching Zara over the years she had picked up some key points that were none too pleasant.

Tyler winced at some of them. Bruskly ignoring his discomfort, Amber commented. 'Oh, Mr Montgomery! Surely a big strong player like you can cope with a little deep work. No pain, I am afraid means no gain. Your play will be sorely affected.'

Tyler shifted uncomfortably. A flicker of discontent scanned across his face. 'You seem very sure of yourself. How come I haven't been treated by you before on the circuit? Trust me I would avoid it, if I could. But you are pretty on the eye, maybe I could calm you down, show you a slower technique of working. Are you free after the match?'

Amber drew a long breath; he wanted some action did he? Well he was certainly going to get it. Smiling quietly to herself, her long slender fingers swiftly grabbed a pot from Zara's kit bag.

'Sadly, we have another job to go to. Now if you need a bit more of the gentle and tender touch, I think I better use some of our healing balm, brilliant for saddle soreness in any department.'

With a quick movement she slathered on the spicy liniment. As the paste melted with Tyler's body heat, Amber came very close to an area liniment should never approach. Designed for cramped muscles this fiery blend was most definitely not for delicate nether regions. The heat cranked up. With a yelp Tyler nearly hit the roof.

'Oh, Mr Montgomery please don't wiggle so much this must be applied gently.'

'What the hell is it? It's bloody burning me. You want to set my backside on fire, or are you getting some warped sense of fun out of this treatment?'

Swinging round to clutch his buttocks, Amber tried very hard to remain composed. If only Zara could see this now. Grabbing a towel, she offered to remove some of the offending balm. Tyler reluctantly allowed her to do so, as the smarting was bringing tears to his eyes by now. Not a good look in front of any woman, particularly a masseuse. His cocky attitude had disappeared. By now time was running out, and the tannoy was stating start of play to begin shortly.

Tyler removed himself from the couch. Glaring at her, he grabbed his trousers. Amber couldn't help but look as he pulled the tight fabric over his muscular thighs. Buttoning up he stretched across for his top, which Amber dutifully held in her hand for him.

Winking she commented,'A bit of warmth can always give zest to the game. I must check on the kit bag. I'm not sure how that balm got into that compartment. But a big strong guy like you, I'm sure it can only do some good.'

Tyler was lost for words, unsure of her sincerity or sarcasm. Tugging at his rear, he scrambled into his polo shirt. His broad shoulders filled it amply and many a therapist glanced over from their work station.

As play resumed Tyler seemed in a little discomfort, so much so his play was indeed affected, but not in the positive way Amber had portrayed. It was well below par. Agitated, he let rip at one of the grooms, demanding a new animal when his horse stumbled causing him to miss the perfect shot. The constant friction of flesh upon leather had worked it to a fiery combination.

Zara would be pleased once she could relay her actions, very pleased. Amber grinned like a Cheshire cat. One up for Zara! Revenge was indeed sweet.

Chapter 23

FUTURE HOPES & DREAMS

Bruce was pacing around the apartment, clearly agitated. A bead of sweat trickled down his forehead as he waited for Zara to emerge from the bathroom. He always found it incredibly weird how women took so long to get ready for an evening out. What did they get up to in the confines of the powder room?

He tried to have a sip of the beer he'd extracted from the fridge. Nerves were getting the better of him now and he was uncertain he could disguise them from Zara. Taking a hanky from his pocket he wiped the beads of sweat away. He shrugged his shoulders a few times, trying to remember the relaxation tips Zara had always harked on about when he came home stressed from work.

He surveyed the apartment Zara still resided in. He really hoped she would be happy to give this all up for him. He had a powerful family who were impatient for him to move forward. Zara was the ideal partner and he clung to the thought she would see this. He'd not let on a single clue of how he was to propose, lest she caught wind of his plans. Frederick had been ignored completely as one to confide in. He would muck up any chance of it being a surprise immediately. His ideas of romance would be way wilder than Bruce's. The competition was irritating at times. If Zara agreed, his years of competing and being second best might finally come to an end.

Being the sensible son of the family suited him, though a little more respect from some of the family members would be nice. His brother had always taken the limelight ever since he was born. The tussles they'd had since toddlerhood were too many to remember.

The bathroom door opened sharply and Zara emerged, a vision of feminine beauty. Bruce always thought she needed none of the potions and contraptions of pampering, which so many of the California girls seemed to be addicted to nowadays. They all ended up like over-inflated Barbie dolls in his opinion. Zara could wake after practically no sleep and still look ravishing in his eyes. Her natural dishevelled look suited her. Now she had followed the rules and resembled a glossy made up specimen, though still pretty natural looking, thank goodness.

The only saving grace with brother Freddie was he seemed to be attracted more to the glitz and glamour style of female. Easily distracted by a long leg or heaving bosom. Thankfully, on occasions this allowed Bruce a moment to step in and chat to the shyer and less extroverted girls they had been privileged to meet in the past. Not that Freddie would have noticed, these types of girls never passed his radar.

Zara looked over at Bruce as she picked her bag up from the couch, checking she had everything she needed.

'Right then, I'm ready to hit the town. What delights are we up to tonight?' she waited in anticipation. Bruce normally had some unusual ideas for an evening out, never wild but normally pleasant and luxurious. It was becoming quite a habit to dine at the Ritz Carlton or hang out at the Plantation Bar with a liqueur or two till the early hours. Life back in the UK was never like that, thinking back to her nights of hedonistic clubbing with Gina; gaining access to the top venues wasn't an option. Of course a little bit of flirting with the doorman when Amber accompanied them, did work on a few occasions to gain entrance.

'Tonight, we're popping over to a friend's house first, then maybe a bite to eat later.' Bruce tried his hardest to be nonchalant but was finding it hard to keep the appearance up, when this was the most important date of his life. Funny how after knowing someone so long, he still felt so uncertain who the real Zara really was. Would she take him as her husband? Or underneath, was she just enjoying the trappings of his wealth?

Zara didn't notice anything untoward, being more concerned to get on their way, having taken so long in dressing. She was aware Bruce seemed a little impatient tonight. Grabbing her light cashmere shawl and clutch bag, they exited her apartment and stepped into the old fashioned lift. Bruce pulled the heavy gate across. Although a modern condominium, they had retained some of the older features of the building before it had been revamped. Zara liked this aspect. It gave the building a feel of history. Modern was fine, but sometimes a little austere for her.

Once cocooned in Bruce's car, they headed out towards the Canyon to the west of LA. After thirty minutes of steady cruising they approached a Hacienda style house, painted in rich terracotta pink. Framed by several palm trees, it blended into the mountain rock that lay in the far distance, merging with the gorgeous sunset that was starting to form. Parking up under a slatted roof canopy, Zara stepped out noticing the house seemed noisy from the rear garden. Voices drifted on the breeze towards them.

'Seems they're having a right rave up,' commented Zara.

'Doug likes to throw some mean events. Part of the show business scene, kind of rubs off on him. Thinks he's in his own film. I'm surprised he hasn't tried to produce his own fly on the wall serial. Life is one long adventure.' Zara wasn't sure what to expect having only heard Bruce mention him occasionally. A nice bit of action would be a pleasant change.

Pressing hard on the door chime, its bell echoed loudly around the building. Vivid red geraniums reminiscent of holidays abroad, sat proudly either side of the entrance. The massive door, made of heavy dark wood displayed a huge wrought iron loop the size of a child's bicycle wheel as its handle.

'Wow, that's taken half a tree to make,' gushed Zara, staring in awe.

'You bet. I think his back extension probably took a few more up as well.'

Laughter rang out from behind the door as footsteps clattered towards it. The heavy door swung back exposing a pretty blond woman around forty, her hair tied up in a soft chignon. Dressed in a summery orange tunic, her bare bronze limbs extended beneath the dress ending in a twee pair of mules.

'Hi, Bruce and this is Zara I presume? Come on in. Doug is firing up his barbeque; not that he will be cooking much himself, we have our chef to do that. But he likes to look the part at first. Please stay for something if you can. Doug has a little surprise later for our guests so unless you have a better offering stay and enjoy.' As Zara entered, she was unaware of an exchange of winks and smiles between the woman and Bruce.

'Sure, depends on Zara. I've only booked a meal later it's no problem to cancel. What do you think, Zara?' He anxiously hoped she would agree, otherwise his plans would be somewhat slaughtered if she didn't.

'I don't mind, I like a bit of variety and meet some new people at the same time. Yes, I'd love to stay longer.' However nice Bruce's lifestyle was, just once in a while Zara fancied a little last minute hedonistic passion, but it just wasn't in him normally. He tried, but having fun without proper planning wasn't in his mindset.

Entering the back garden, the view was spectacular spreading from the infinity pool and out far into the canyon. Adjacent was a large decked area with a tanned thick set guy. Zara assumed this must be Doug. He stood proudly with hands on hips, a paunch of a belly protruded from his tight striped shorts, chatting to two younger colleagues, both dressed casual. One was tall and geeky, with tiny round glasses sat upon his face as he peered out like an owl. The other one was more stylish, dressed in white tailored shorts, twinned with a smart rugby style top, emblazoning the words of what Zara assumed must be the local baseball team. There were so many, she'd given up trying to get into the sport. The Americans seemed to be more fanatical about baseball than her fellow football fans back home.

As soon as Doug glanced across, he immediately left his guests to stride across the vast expanse of garden and greet them personally.

'Bruce, glad you could come over at short notice.' Hugging him close he whispered discreetly in Bruce's ear for a fraction of a second. Recoiling he then lunged at Zara, pulling her close and smacking a huge kiss on her lips. 'You must be the lovely Zara? Bruce is never one to visit often, always too busy. It's been some time you've been seeing Bruce, haven't you. I'll have to give him hell for not introducing you sooner. Come let me get you a drink. We'll be dining soon, just getting my coals warmed.' He hugged her again, guiding her towards a tiny bar area. Picking up various bottles to brandish in front of her he asked, 'What do you like? I'm sadly off the menu, but you can't have all the luck can you.'

'I'll try one of those beers please,' replied Zara thinking it would be better to start off slow, being in brand new company she hadn't met before. It was always a difficult one judging the relationship Bruce had with some people here in LA. His family upbringing and business meant many individuals were treated very formally, while others not so. It was frowned upon if you got it wrong for some reason. It seemed keeping up appearances was more important than genuine friendship in many cases. This couple seemed fairly relaxed and casual, so maybe she could kick back a little after she'd time to observe how the event was going.

It frequently put a strain on things with their relationship. Kicking back and chilling was not heard of in the Loxley household. Freddie did push a few boundaries. Maybe he wasn't a Loxley pure blood at all. Zara couldn't quite see their mother being unfaithful and frivolous, but it was always the unlikely ones that could be the worst. Maybe that was why she paid so much attention to her younger son, a forbidden secret. No, he was far too much like his father. But it did make her question the family dynamics a little. A smile traced her lips. She mustn't let her imagination run away from her. However, she might look at Vivian a little differently from now on.

Zara decided to mingle and try to gain some perspective on the rare business colleagues Bruce seemed to know. He kept a lot of them at arm's length, never mixing his business with pleasure. She still only probably knew a mere handful or so on first name terms. The American way was so different to back home. Doug appeared the complete opposite to the norm and not the type Bruce would usually partner with. He was definitely up Zara's street for fun and she was intrigued to learn more. She also was keen to know if he knew of the irritating Steve; or maybe not at all, which was more worrying.

'Well, Doug, how come I haven't had a chance to meet you and your wife before. I'll have words with

Bruce for that. Your place is spectacular. Did you build it yourself?'

Doug leaned in closer obviously loving the attention, and placing an arm around her shoulders he replied, 'I did, yes. On the other subject my darling, Bruce probably never introduced us because he was scared you might be tempted by my charm and good looks.' Zara stood back, loosening the hold he had on her.

'You might be right, but with a great wife like yours I think I know my place. Fill me in on how long you've known him? There are loads of close friends I don't know much about.'

'Let me grab a cool beer and I'll tell you some tales you Brits won't believe. We know how to have a good time over here and Bruce has been the guiding light on some occasions. He is a hard one to know how to let his hair down. But I've succeeded in persuading him on the odd occasion.'

'Really, I'm pretty shocked! You may need to give me some key tips, as I'd like to know what you did to loosen him up.' Doug rubbed his hands with glee.

'We're going to have some fun tonight, my partner in crime. Let's party and chat some more.' Flourishing his beer above his head Doug led Zara across the lawn to a few of his guests now languishing in the gazebo. Margarita cocktails garnished the table like dolly mixtures strewn haphazardly. Before long, the raucous laughter drew further guests to join the gathering. As the midnight was approaching, Bruce sidled up to Zara. Placing an arm around her waist, he pulled her in close and whispered softly in her ear.

'Doug's surprise is one of his fetishes. Fireworks and brimstone; loves to put on quite a show, as you can see. He's been doing this since college days. Shame he never went into blowing up buildings for a living. He would have known the trade inside out. Let's stand over near the woods, we can view the show better over there, away from the rest of the party.'

'Ok, if you want to.' Zara couldn't see why the main patio wasn't good enough, but she didn't want to quibble. Bruce led her out towards the wooded glade adjacent. A panoramic view lay in front of them far into the canyon's main body that sloped gently below the house.

'Some place to live, isn't it? Not that I'd fancy being out here alone at night. It's a bit isolated, but the views are impressive,' commented Zara

'Doug likes a bit of the high life, though he still craves some solitude at times. His wife is an artist by trade. Some of her work has been exhibited all over the city. Right now, cuddle in close. I want to enjoy the show - just you and me.' He stood behind her, nuzzling his face next to hers. Zara felt his strong arms nestling her waist, as they watched the first of the fireworks shoot high into the dark sky, cascading on explosion a curtain of pink streamers lighting up the canyon in a smoky hue. Rockets launched one after the other arcing over in a series of squiggles that faded into silvery dust. Blues, reds, scarlet - the sky a massive canvas painted as if by an invisible paintbrush.

Bruce kissed her delicately on the neck, pulling her even closer to his body. Colour after colour was backlighting the rocky outcrops of the canyon walls,

370

creating a spectacular waterfall of gold as the final fireworks exploded. Slowly the series of cascading glittery lines subsided and a silence prevailed. Darkness descended again on the vista until the eyes became accustomed to the subdued surroundings. A tiny pinpoint of light erupted beneath the gardens. Slowly, one by one, a series of pink tinged lamps blinked softly on, spreading out into a series of shapes.

Zara noticed the shapes take form. Letters developed, and one by one each light exploded into brightness. As the last few lit up, the words 'WILL YOU MARRY ME ZARA?' displayed boldly in front of them. A ripple of applause echoed around the gathering. It took several minutes before she fully comprehended the message was for her, even though her name was clearly there staring up in the darkness.

Bruce's touch increased; nuzzling her neck, he kissed her delicately on the cheek. Pulling away he took her hand. Crouching down on one knee he looked up anxiously at her. Half of his face was obscured by the dark woods to his left; the faint glow from the numerous lights the only illumination.

'Will you, Zara, Will you have me as your husband? I love you so much. You're my soul mate, my perfect partner. I would do anything for you. Just ask. I've searched high and low for a lover like you and nobody has ever come close.' Bruce's fingers clasped hers; an urge of dependency could be felt emanating from him. Zara stood very still; shocked and bewildered, she was trying hard to make the decision to answer.

Her mind mulled over the question. She had constantly chased dreams. Wanting, desiring, and

371

finally acknowledging the grass was never always greener the other side of the fence. It frequently appeared vibrant, fresh and smelling divine. But once you let your toes embrace the sweet new grass, its magic slowly ebbed away becoming the same dryer, insipid lawn that most people ended up with. Who exactly was her true soul mate? Was it the ones we never ever considered? The ones who sat patiently in the wings for a crumb of our attention, seen but not heard until we had lost them for good. Was Bruce her soul mate? Zara was confused. Hesitating, she smiled, stalling for time. The most important decision in her life and now a 'yes or no' answer had to be made within seconds. Feeling frightened lest she lost the moment and mortally wounded the one person that truly loved her, she frantically searched her brain for a reply. Even the President or Queen had time to mull over or liaise with close confidantes over any hot decisions to be made.

Bruce was shaking by now. The eternity of waiting for Zara's response was making him sick with nerves. He had no idea what her answer would be. Maybe it was too early and he'd pushed his luck by thinking such a proposal? The background noise of cheering and clapping merged in to the background as if the world had stopped momentarily. Suspended like a fairy tale, the viewer waiting with bated breath for the tale to proceed. This was well out of Bruce's comfort zone and he was slowly regretting his choice of public display for such a private question.

Detecting the quivering in Bruce's hand she squeezed it tightly, to reassure and calm him. Dropping down to kneel before her, Zara looked into his face. The friendly grin so frequently unsure at its recipient's respect stared back at her. His dark brown hair was immaculately cut, never a hair out of place, laced always with a slick of gel for perfection. Bruce lived his life like this. No risks, no drama. It wasn't in his vocabulary. Dependable, solid support, regular as clockwork, Bruce would never contemplate being late. If he said he would do something it would be set in stone.

Zara knew this was a door to a path she may not have walked before. But it didn't mean it was the wrong path. Just an opening to a future she wouldn't be able to know until she embraced it.

Bruce focused on her lips, full and moist. He so wanted to kiss her passionately, knowing his only hope and desire had come true. But still she held back, just staring. He could feel anxiety well up from within. Now was not the time to have a panic attack. He needed to show her he was what she had always been searching for. He was the one. Unsure still of Zara's past which had been glossed over, he'd been too scared to reveal or delve deeper. Did he really know how Zara thought or felt? He was starting to have serious doubts, feeling slightly foolish. He had never contemplated the answer could be 'no.'

A soft parting of Zara's lips allowed her to utter faintly the words he wanted to hear so much. Bruce hesitated before asking her again. Had he heard correctly? Was he sure, really sure she had said 'yes' to his question?

'Did I hear correctly? Was your answer yes?' Zara laughed; she couldn't help it. Even at a time of acute stress, Bruce still sounded ultra-polite as if addressing a business colleague. He was never going to change. She didn't want him to really. It was reassuring, comforting. At least he showed her respect.

'Yes, I said yes, if the offer is still there?'

'Of course it is. God I love you. Thank you, you've made me so happy. I've been dreading the answer if it was a no.' Bruce pulled her up to standing and kissed her deeply. Opening the tiny velvet box he had clasped in his other hand, he took out the gleaming diamond and ruby ring carefully hued to catch the light at every angle. Gently, Bruce guided it over her knuckle to sit proudly on her finger.

Walking back down towards the main party, Doug and his guests stood in awe. A bottle of best Cristal Champagne held aloft was ready in Doug's hand to be opened with a nod and a wink.

'Well, what is it Champagne or Prozac my buddy?'

'Champagne of course, I never doubted it.' yelled Bruce. Doug raised an eyebrow.

'Of course you didn't, of course you didn't.'

Chapter 24

THE FINAL RECKONING

Zara looked out over the hazy sunset, the soft amber merging into the ocean creating a shifting mirage. Deciding to venture out from their villa for some private 'me' time, her mind felt in desperate need of a reprieve from being constantly in someone's presence. Having her life change overnight from being able to pursue any direction on a whim had taken her by surprise in how scary it could be to adapt. Now she had another full-on partner to contemplate in her plans. Although she was in no doubt Bruce was special, she couldn't help feel a little sad she'd left part of her individual life behind. To the last hour she'd clung onto that independence, relishing her moments alone to reflect.

The sea breeze of the Perth coast ruffled her hair. She could feel the saltiness on her lips now, as she ran her tongue gently over them. Zara found the ocean calming. It was always a time of contemplation for her, where she could run over ideas and endlessly throw her thoughts backwards and forwards, asking the wide blue expanse of sea for an answer to her dilemma.

Trailing her toes through the sand, Zara sat on the sidewalk, feeling the warm stone beneath her legs. Now that the cast had been removed not long ago, her thigh felt sensitive to touch and temperature changes. It was a weird sensation in comparison to her undamaged side. Shuddering at the memory of how her plans may have been so easily destroyed she scanned the horizon. Tiny figures moved around, accompanied by laughter and shouting in the far distance. It appeared to be a group of lads playing, a very competitive volleyball match, by the shrill pitch of voices shifting on the breeze. Memories came roaring back of her school days, of early morning clubs she'd protested so much in joining. One, the thought of rolling out of bed so early to be at school and the second, the thought of exercise at such an ungodly hour; now she'd become a bit more accustomed to this format. It still wasn't one she totally relished with full on enthusiasm though Clare's, one of her past school buddies, words ricocheted around her head.

'It'll do you the power of good, besides we can impress the key sixth form boys into the bargain, who just happen to hang out at that time of the morning.' Zara had stared incredibly at her, suspecting there were just a few white lies going on in the persuasion tactics. 'At least it will show them we exist on the sports circuit too.' Clare happened to be the perfect athlete, excelling in most areas of exertion. Zara, on the other hand was average, a plain Jane. Neither Olympic material nor left at the start line to struggle home last. All Zara could remember was the stinging sensation on the base of her wrists as she pounded the ball up over the net. Clare had the ability of effortlessly hurling it high to her opponent, just at the right angle to make them lunge

376

forward and give victory to her side. Zara had enough trouble even getting it over the net, let alone having a tactic on where to plant the ball.

The rough pebbly exterior started to leave indentations in her thighs, her fingers traced the knobbles and bumps that covered every inch of the structure. The restlessness wasn't disappearing. It felt strange to feel so despondent. Why wasn't she exhilarated at her new future? The wedding was great, no major hiccups, bar the odd punch up at the bar over the bridesmaid snogging the best man. Well hey, normal practice at any English wedding, it wasn't so in the USA. It was nice to know her relatives could cause a commotion just at the vital moment. That certainly brought a smile to her face providing a bit more spice to any future Loxley events.

The hot sand trickled through her toes, soothing and hypnotic she watched it grain by grain fall back onto the beach, merging once more from many individual grains to one single shifting mass.

Suddenly, Zara was aware of someone sitting down nearby. It was one of the players from the team. His heavy breathing was noticeable as he slowly recovered from his exertion. She tried hard not to make it obvious she was looking as she glanced sideways pretending to brush her hair from her eyes. His side profile looked strangely familiar as if she'd seen him before somewhere, a personal resemblance imprinted on the memory cells.

It was hard to recognize clients with their clothes on. Many a time she'd bump into a past patient, they'd greet and banter with her, but she remained in the dark, trying hard to fathom where they'd met or how to answer any questions thrown at her, without dropping herself in a decidedly big pit on occasions. They probably thought she was distant and rude.

Zara rubbed her eyes and looked back at the sunset. She was probably tired and the jetlag hadn't disappeared yet. Besides, she would hardly know someone on the other side of the world. It may be a small world as the saying goes but she was pretty damn sure it wasn't that tiny. As long as it wasn't Mr. Glenshaw or Ms. Lintel she would be happy. Though knowing her luck it was more than likely she may bump into one or the other. She shivered at the thought of it.

The lad had become aware of her sitting there and turned to look across. Zara hesitated and thought it rude not to speak, so deciding to offer neutral territory, commented upon the game. Not that she could remember much about the rules. He laughed; she clearly had said something ludicrous but couldn't make out what it was. The light from the setting sun dazzled Zara's eyes, his form appeared only lit in silhouette.

A shout directed across the beach towards the stranger, beckoning him to return sharpish and join the game. He turned to reply to Zara, his tone of voice causing her stomach to clench in shock and excitement at the same time. His accent sent waves through every cell of her body. The lad smiled and waved to his friends shouting he wouldn't be a moment, totally unaware of the reaction he was causing until he too turned towards Zara. Instantly recognizing her, a smile slowly crept across his face. They locked eyes both shocked as each other.

'What in hell's name are you doing here? Of all the places to bump into you,' Zara found herself abruptly asking. The shock had completely made her forget her manners and rudeness prevailed. 'I thought you'd returned to the UK ages ago?'

'I had for a while but you know, the old wanderlust kicked in again, then a short term job offer came about. I applied for a few when I was out here just in case a position came up. So here I am, back in Oz again.' He appeared to hesitate and looked faintly embarrassed, trying not to look too directly in her eyes. Needing to explain a little more he added, 'I tried several times to get in contact with you but your number never connected. I wasn't on the family Christmas card list so my trail to track you down came to a dead end. I umm…..' He hesitated unsure how to put what he wanted to say into actual words, 'I wouldn't have contemplated coming back to Oz if I'd managed to touch base with you. I didn't want it to end that way at all.'

Her mind raced back to the last time they'd actually chatted. Since Bruce she had really lost touch, assuming it had been Brett's decision. God if only she'd known. Her relationship with Bruce may have changed direction more dramatically than she thought. It was too late now; her life had moved on. A crushing blow settled in the pit of her stomach which was churning pretty violently all of a sudden.

Zara had so many questions. She wanted to blurt them all out at once, but the one most pressing on her tongue was not one she should have been asking. Her voice became hoarse and tongue tied.

'Still single or now an honest man?' She really didn't want to know the answer. Neither one would make her any happier. Now married, she shouldn't be enjoying even this chance conversation, it all seemed so unfaithful and deceitful. Especially since her internal sexual radar was leaping sky high.

'Oh, I was engaged nearly, got the confetti in the hair but it just didn't feel right so decided to run in the opposite direction. Gut instinct I think.' He glanced at Zara, noticing the pain appear in her eyes at this comment, 'No I'm kidding, still young, free and single. Not sure who would want me with my gadding around the globe. I even let you slip through my fingers didn't I?' He paused for a response but none came. 'What about you?'

Zara felt his eyes focus properly on her. Fully aware of what he was thinking, and wanting to know. For once in her life she wished she could lie, but the words came out too quickly.

'Sort of the same, but I didn't follow my instinct, unlike you.' Clearly wishing she had, as those wedding nerves may have been more sixth sense than harmless fears, but if she hadn't been married she sure as hell wouldn't have been here. Australia wasn't her first choice of travel destination. Being halfway there via America compared with living in Britain, it was definitely a closer long haul place to visit for their special honeymoon.

Yes, Brett had crossed her mind when the choice of destination came up. But it was fleeting. It seemed a lifetime ago when they'd last seen each other, just a fond memory that never formulated a conclusion. Zara had never expected this the first day she arrived. Australia was huge; this was one blast from the past that was blowing her mind. He stared thoughtfully into her eyes. The mischievous spark was still there. She could see the same glint, the same excitement when she met him the first time.

For what seemed an eternity, Zara focused on this human being who had entered her life so many times, both never getting the right combination correct. Why? Why had it never worked? It was always the wrong timing. She tried hard to drink in every drop of his presence to remember him; it was as if this was the final part of the journey unable to go any further.

Brett leant forward fumbling in his pocket he pulled a piece of crumpled paper out and placed it in her hand. Pressing her fingers over it he hung on for a few seconds longer than a casual friend would.

'Here take this, it's where I'll be staying back home in a couple of months. Our paths might cross again; never say never.' He leant forward and kissed her gently on the lips and winked.

'Well, you did follow me to the other side of the world. I must be pretty good. I better get back to the game otherwise there might be a riot.' Laughing, though his feelings felt hollow, he stepped forward to embrace and pull her in close. It was fleeting lest he cause her any grief with her new partner, uncertain where he may be at that precise moment. What he really wanted to do was linger, hug her deeply, kiss her passionately to rekindle and ignite what they'd lost. Now there was a wall of unspoken words. He had little choice but to walk away, although this made him feel sick inside.

'Take care and call me.' His words floated on the breeze as he backed away. Zara was sure she noticed a tinge of regret in Brett's eyes, but she may have imagined it. She watched him as he slowly headed back to the game, turning several times to wave.

Brett immediately cursed as he walked, for not trying harder. It was clearly too late; Zara had moved on in a pretty permanent way. He should never have assumed she'd be patiently waiting in the wings for him to fulfill his dreams. Why, a girl like her was bound to be snapped up! He'd been flippant and foolish. She hadn't been that far away; he should have took leave and visited and found the cash somehow. His bloody ego had got in the way.

Sighing deeply, Zara felt any energy she had drain out of her like a spiraling eddy. Her heart sunk and she tried not to let the tears flow, as once they did she knew it would be too hard to stop them. To hide her feelings in front of Bruce, hysterical crying on your first day of honeymoon wasn't something you could defend or make excuses for; Bruce didn't deserve that.

As she watched Brett's retreating figure grow slightly hazy as the distance between them lengthened, it felt as if he'd been a mirage, a dream, something she'd conjured up out of the crashing waves. Sitting back, she tried hard to relax and take stock of her sudden reaction at seeing him so abruptly in the flesh. No, she couldn't fake the sensations. They'd been immediate.

Strangely, she felt comfort that he'd stepped back in her life even only momentarily. Her stomach tingled with butterflies at the anticipation of what might be in the future. Maybe your soul mate didn't have to be on the same path in life, just meet you at the crossroads, both of you taking the same turning at times, moving and flowing back together. Zara had a feeling Brett would probably always be there for her, where ever in the world he happened to be. It just wasn't going to be now. She'd have to get used to it.

A voice called her name and Zara was yanked back to the reality of life now. Her new husband walked slowly towards her. For whatever reason she was to enjoy his company at this time, however much the appearance of Brett had shaken her up. Zara composed herself.

'Hi, I was just getting some air and enjoying the scenery; I hope you didn't worry too much?'

'No, just wondered why you were so long. I was missing you. Come on, let's go for a sunset walk together and maybe have a drink at that bar we saw when we first arrived. Tonight would be the perfect moment to indulge.'

Zara tried hard to show some sincere enthusiasm but her mind was somewhat distracted. Clasping his hand and turning slightly, she glanced over her shoulder at the game in the distance just faintly making out the figure of Brett. Deep inside a voice whispered in her head to him….. 'Wait for me, please wait,' With a confused and bewildered heart she walked away from the game towards the sunset, hand in hand with her life as it should be for now.

SEQUEL TO REKINDLING CONNECTIONS

Available 2015

'Are you ready? The taxi's here. We're going to be late at this rate.'

'Yes, just checking I've everything. Bonny Scotland is not so bonny at this time of year, believe me. I've been there. When was the last time you touched the sacred soil?'

'Some time ago I must admit; probably when I was a young brat of a thing.'

'Bruce, I can't imagine you as a brat at any age. Frederick your brother maybe, but you never.'

Bruce leant over to give his wife Zara a kiss delicately on the lips. He lingered long enough to show he loved her to bits, tenderly stroking her hair.

'You say the sweetest of things. I can't wait to show you off to the rest of the clan.' He breathed heavily and panted a little as he lugged the suitcases out to the cab driver that was impatiently waiting. Once packed to the rafters it glided onto the LA Boulevard, speeding up as it merged onto the main freeway.

Zara was secretly quite excited at the prospect of returning to the UK. It had been well over a year since their wedding in the Hamptons. She had a fair few plans to catch up with the many relatives and friends whilst overseas. Her agenda was packed. Besides, meeting Bruce's distant family would be a bonus.

Not many had travelled over on the big day so this would be their first meeting.

The many tales of his Scottish ancestors were intriguing. She was half expecting Robert the Bruce to be on the wall. Having travelled half way round the world to meet the love of her life, who originated from a country practically on the doorstep, (well nearly, Britain was small compared with America, and good old Brighton was only eight hours away from Bruce's homeland on a good run) seemed absolutely crazy.

Of course her LA lifestyle was not without its charm. It was the main reason why she had embraced the offer of a full time position as assisting sports therapist. Who wouldn't have when you're young, free and sadly, still blatantly single at the time. The new horizon seemed the ideal way forward. Now a few weeks of damp, cold weather would be good for the soul. This trip would bring her back to the reality of the UK. The contrast might hit Bruce somewhat. He'd been so used to heat every day of the year bar their odd jaunt to New York in the winter months. It might well come as a nasty surprise to him. Longjohns would be the order of the day if he had any sense.

~ ~ ~

Touchdown was in heavy fog that cleared slightly by the time they made it through customs and were heading to the main exit. Beaming from behind a large notice bearing their surname was Max.

'Hello, how was the journey? Some time since you've been over here, eh boy? You might see a few changes.' Uncle Max slapped his nephew heartily on the back and winked at his new wife. 'Glad he's brought the family. I understand you know our fair country a little.' Max beamed at Zara and lifted her luggage as if it was a feather into the rear of the car. After much shuffling around of the paraphernalia stored in there, he rammed the cases in the back of the Land Rover which had seen better days, beckoning her and Bruce to jump in.

The journey to where they were staying at Uncle Max's was a ride in itself. Suspension of the old jeep was not much to be desired. Zara found herself hanging on for dear life as Uncle Max swung round the country lanes fearlessly. She'd forgotten how travel sick you could become on the quaint UK roads, unlike the wide cruise control network abroad.

'How's my old brother doing? Still being a male cougar in that brassy country of the Americas?'

'Yes, dad's not changed. Freddie is a definite by-product of the Loxley side of things.'

'Good, he wouldn't be the same if he lost that flirting spark. You should have seen him in his heyday. Not one lassie able to resist him. I have to admire Vivian for taming him, one strong woman she is.' Bruce grimaced privately, knowing full well what Uncle Max meant where his mother was concerned. When she was organising or in charge nobody, not even his father, got away with anything. Her disdainful look could kill the moment in seconds. His father was frequently on the receiving end of it.

'Mum hasn't got him completely under control. She does her best but at times Dad is a law unto himself.'

Uncle Max roared with laughter, a strong throaty chuckle, so much so he nearly took out the side mirror on an overhanging bush. 'Oh yes, he's not one to control himself. This small town was never going to be big enough for him. I knew he would be escaping to pastures new before long.'

Zara watched as the countryside spread out for miles around now rather barren, with brief glimpses of orange bracken offset with pale heather. Both helped to break up the landscape's harshness. Imagining having a breakdown out here was not a favourable idea. Glancing into the rear of the vehicle she noticed Max had quite a few survival articles. There was a long trussed up thick rope, blankets and what appeared to be a billy can and gas stove. At least they could make a cuppa and keep reasonably warm if they did get stranded.

As the Land Rover leaped about sending them both tumbling around the rear of the vehicle, Zara held tightly onto Bruce's hand.

'Well Bruce, what's been happening in La, La land? Hope you've been keeping your nose clean. What's the new partner like? Been a couple of years since you mentioned the news in your last letter and your kind invite to the wedding. As I said before the old ticker couldn't have taken the journey. I look a beast of a man Zara, though sadly my internal cogs aren't working as well as I'd like.'

'It could be too much haggis Uncle Max.' A loud laugh echoed around the jeep as Uncle Max was beside himself in hysterics again. He certainly liked to enjoy himself thought Zara. 'Business isn't bad, Uncle Max. Been a little tough at times, but we're keeping everything afloat. Can't say the new branch has been as easy in New York, what with the wedding last year and the financial market so up and down. Steve always seems to have a solution up his sleeve.'

Zara was aware of Bruce's grip hardening and a faint twinge of the muscles trembling. Her sensitive touch when working could pick up most things in the nervous system. Pain, relaxation, anxiousness; Bruce was not a happy bunny one little bit answering this question. Even his tone of voice had altered. It hadn't been the first time he'd reacted differently when Steve's name came up in conversation. Since Zara's accident prior to the wedding she was now becoming extremely suspicious of Bruce's business. It certainly was not as 'hunky dory' as he liked to make out. Without doubt her intuition on meeting the compelling Stephen was to not trust him one iota. His brash, arrogant attitude towards everything, gave a first impression he could be most unpredictable in business if it didn't go his way. Bruce could well be the scapegoat Steve might need if he wasn't careful.

'You've gone a bit silent lassie, he hasn't got you working for him yet then? The Loxley work ethic is a hard one. My brother was always ambitious. Bruce has probably inherited that powerful trait. Where I'm concerned, I've always liked my home ground. I'm hoping you'll see why I stayed on home soil and wasn't tempted by those artificial lights, not to mention the

American bullshit.' Uncle Max, amused by his own sense of humour, started chuckling again.

'No, no, I'm not sure I could work in the highly stressed world of finance. I prefer the more relaxed world I dwell in,' replied Zara.

'Good point, not to say many Scots indulge in a rubdown up here. Can't remember any time I've had a female lay her hands on me for money.' A crescendo of a deep gruff started again. Zara had a feeling too much mirth was probably causing the old ticker to weaken more than old age. Her lips curled and before she could avoid it she was joining in. 'Too darn cold up here to take your clothes off most of the time probably.'

Bruce looked perplexed at them both. In the rear view mirror Uncle Max curled an eyebrow, smiling warmly at Zara, 'Your old Man hasn't changed much since he was a nipper. Never could get a joke.'

Bruce's hearing pricked up. 'What, of course I can. The jokes were always in the gutter most of the time.'

'It's what makes the world go round son, what makes the world go round…Hopefully this fair maiden you've been privileged to marry has loosened you up. It comes from your mother's side, all that primness. Our clan are more rough and ready for action. It's in the blood generally.'

Looking back at Freddie, Bruce's younger brother, she could well see he took after that side of the family. No conversation ever stayed on track, before Freddie had put his penny's worth into corrupting it.

Bruce shifted uncomfortably in the seat as Uncle Max probed deeper about his business affairs. Although he was genial and making polite conversation, Bruce's

389

tense demeanour stayed. With a slight hesitation in answering and a general glossing over details, it was clear to Zara something wasn't right. Turning her attention to the house they were approaching, it was obvious Uncle Max definitely hadn't had to indulge in a quick fix loan.

'Wow,' thought Zara. Although a little ramshackled it was one pretty big pile of an estate he owned. The gravel road arched round next to a huge expanse of rough grass dotted with heather and rocks. The rosy hue was shimmering in the frosty air. Scotland was indeed looking pretty cold outside and acclimatising may take them awhile. When she visited her home city of Brighton it was normally a gentler climate, at least two to four degrees higher. She could never understand how Gina tolerated the northern weather conditions long term. But now she was obviously well and truly in love and pretty settled.

Edinburgh would be one destination on her to do list whilst in the local vicinity. Gina, having finished at University, had now moved on from her godforsaken internship. (Vivid memories of some Christmas parties she'd gallantly endured to keep her friend company sprang to mind.) Now shacked up and comfortably co-habiting, Tilly was a perfect match to Gina's zany personality. She was ideal for her other half, if you happened to swing that way. Gina seemed very happy and settled last time they'd spoke.

'How far is it to Edinburgh from here, Uncle Max?'

'Oh, not far. Around an hour on the train. A bit of a stopper, but lovely journey. Are you missing the shops already?'

'No, not at all. I just have a friend from the past that resides there. I'd like to catch up with her some time.'

'Good on you girl. Make the most of your stay. Got young Margaret's lad coming over for dinner this week, Bruce's cousin. Thought you might like to catch up. Been a fair few years since you were both at the old house.'

Bruce nodded, relaxing a little and lessening his grip on Zara's hand as the conversation moved off his work. 'Probably way back in our teenage years is the last time we saw each other. Be nice to meet up with him again.'

'Splendid, we'll get you settled in once Freddie has arrived. I'll show you around the estate tomorrow. It's changed a little over the decade.'

'Yes please, what I can see now looks fantastic.' Zara's face lit up.

'You might not think that of the house. In need of a little tender care but the costs are high maintaining a place like this nowadays. My housekeeper and game keeper keep the wolves from the door. But it does need a fair bit of money spent on it. Maybe I might need your services in the future Bruce.'

'I wouldn't,' joked Zara, 'They're all sharks in Bruce's trade. Her husband caught her eye and tried hard to smile but it was very half-hearted.

Once the bags had been eased from the rear of the Land Rover, Max led them through the impressive oak door into the main entrance hall. Zara stood enthralled at the height of the ceiling. The history seemed to seep out of every nook and rough injury of the old oak panelling. The knocks of life.

'I bet this place has some stories to tell over the years. When was the mansion built originally?' enquired Zara, keen to learn its secrets.

'Oh, I think it dates back to the seventeenth century. It's been in the Loxley family since it was built. Must have the deeds some place, detailing how much it cost to build originally. Doubt you'd get the front porch built nowadays for that princely sum.'

'This could be a pretty interesting stay; never studied history in great detail but do love a story behind a dwelling. The walls must absorb so much over the years.'

'Certainly done that. There's been some wicked parties in the mansion; Highland fling and hunt balls. Those were the days. It's been a long time since we had one of them.'

'Shame you can't resurrect one again. I'm sure the boys would help out. The setting would be just perfect.'

'Oh, maybe they could. Have to think about it at the next shoot. I'll show you some of the customs we have here in the country. I'm sure you will like it.'

'Really?' Zara flinched a little not sure shooting live game was on her first choice for a wish list. She better not be rude as Uncle Max was trying hard to make her feel so welcome. She smiled sweetly and followed him up the wide staircase with Bruce in a world of his own.

Once unpacked, Zara noticed Bruce was still very quiet. He sat in the armchair that looked out over the hills and moors in the distance. He seemed hypnotised with the view and not really taking anything in as she chatted in the background.

'Bruce…. Bruce! Are you just jetlagged or is something wrong? You seem so distant. Especially since Uncle Max probed about your work. Is everything ok? We didn't have to come over if you needed to be sorting problems out. If there is a problem, that is.' Pausing from sorting her belongings, Zara came over and sat down in front of him. Grasping his hand she focused on his face trying hard to achieve some eye contact. Not that lie detection was her forte. Something to do with the eye movement to the left or was it the right? By the time she's remembered, the suspect would have been onto some other subject. 'You can talk to me, you know. I may not know a lot about finance and the loan business but at least a problem shared can be less of a burden.'

Bruce looked deep into her eyes for once focusing on her completely. He still seemed hesitant but forced a smile. It was clearly a way to reassure her things were fine. 'I'm ok, just probably a little tired from the journey. The business will run without me for a while. This is our time. In fact since the wedding I think we need to have a little fun again. The local area has some great walks. Maybe not quite the best bars and restaurants we are privileged to have back home, but if I remember, they do know how to have a pretty good time. Especially when they start on the grog or whatever they like to call it in the British Isles.'

Zara grinned. Bruce was so old fashioned at times. Reassured for the moment and keen not to probe too deeply, as tiredness was certainly underlying the mood, she pulled him up to standing. Leaning in, she pressed her lips gently to his and hugged him close.

Whispering in his ear softly, 'Let's have some fun then as soon as we wake first thing.'

You can purchase this novel or future novels by the author Nicky Abell-Francis via your local bookshop or direct from the publisher www.feedaread.com. Available on Amazon in Kindle format too.

Please visit www.nickyabellfrancis.co.uk to learn more about the writer, leave reviews or follow on social media

Twitter: @nabellfrancis
Facebook: N Abell-Francis Author

Lightning Source UK Ltd.
Milton Keynes UK
UKOW02f2302070317
296047UK00001B/2/P